THE SHAAR PRESS

THE JUDAICA IMPRINT FOR THOUGHTFUL PEOPLE

by
Chaim Eliav

translated by
Libby Lazewnik

A
SHAAR
PRESS
PUBLICATION

PERSECUTION

Intrigue and suspense
and a city
entangled in danger

Published by **SHAAR PRESS**
Distributed by MESORAH PUBLICATIONS, LTD.
4401 Second Avenue / Brooklyn, New York 11232 / (718) 921-9000

Distributed in Israel by SIFRIATI / A. GITLER BOOKS
10 Hashomer Street / Bnei Brak 51361

Distributed in Europe by J. LEHMANN HEBREW BOOKSELLERS
20 Cambridge Terrace / Gateshead, Tyne and Wear / England NE8 1RP

Distributed in Australia and New Zealand by GOLDS BOOK & GIFT SHOP
36 William Street / Balaclava 3183, Vic., Australia

Distributed in South Africa by KOLLEL BOOKSHOP
22 Muller Street / Yeoville 2198 / Johannesburg, South Africa

ISBN: 0-89906-668-2 Hard Cover
ISBN: 0-89906-669-0 Paperback

Printed in the United States of America by Noble Book Press Corp.
Custom bound by Sefercraft, Inc. / 4401 Second Avenue / Brooklyn, N.Y. 11232

1

On the stroke of midnight, Don Carlos Carneiro got out of bed and doused the oil lamp. Pitch darkness reigned in his tiny cabin in the ship's stern.

He padded to the door, pressing his ear to it. No sound reached him from the other side. The silence was so complete that he was able to make out the slap of the waves in Amsterdam harbor against the sides of the vessel.

Don Carlos quickly divested himself of the uniform he wore — the uniform of admiral of the Portuguese fleet. In its place he donned a simple sailor's suit which he had taken care to prepare earlier in the day. Very quietly and with extreme caution, he opened the cabin door a crack and peered into the dark corridor. He stood there a moment, straining to pick up the sound of voices.

There was only silence. The entire crew of the flagship *Vera Cruz* slept the sleep of the just. This was their first night's rest in a long time. The date was April 4, 1641, and that morning the flagship had weighed anchor in the port of Amsterdam after a difficult, storm-tossed voyage.

Don Carlos left his cabin and stealthily made his way to the stairs. He climbed them rapidly to the upper deck. To his great good fortune, he found the guards asleep.

Under different circumstances he would have had them up before a tribunal; today, he gazed on them with sympathy.

"They're exhausted," he thought. The voyage had drained them, and they'd been up since the crack of dawn scrubbing, scraping, and painting the ship in honor of the state visit soon to be paid by heads of the Dutch regime to him, Don Carlos, the king of Portugal's personal emissary.

Yes, this was one time when Don Carlos found no cause to complain of his guards' negligence. There were no witnesses to see him slip away from the ship and lose himself in the shadows of the winding harbor streets.

...Just seconds later, a black-garbed figure descended from the ship and hurried off in Don Carlos' wake...

⤳〇⤝

Don Carlos didn't walk — he ran through Amsterdam's sleeping streets. He knew the place well: This was not the Portuguese admiral's first visit to Holland's capital. Even on this moonless night he passed unerringly through the dark alleys and narrow lanes. He reached his destination with no time lost: a house surrounded by a stone wall, tall and broad, with a massive iron gate fixed in the center.

Don Carlos paused near the gate. For safety's sake he turned around as his eyes probed the night on every side to determine whether he had been followed. At last, satisfied, he approached the gate and rapped three times. After a moment he knocked three more times, and then added four more knocks: the prearranged signal.

He heard footsteps approach from inside the house. At the prospect of the meeting ahead, a piercing joy suffused him. The gate swung open and a beam of light shot out to illuminate the inky blackness.

...At the corner of the narrow street stood a shadowy figure: the man who had

been following Don Carlos. He counted the houses from the corner. The light, he saw, came from the fourth house. That was important to remember...

⋙⋘

Don Carlos drew a deep breath. "In spite of everything," he thought gratefully, "I've made it here!" Only two weeks earlier, he would never have believed he'd step over the threshold of this house again.

The youth who had opened the gate led him to a sitting room. Awaiting Don Carlos was the owner of the house. He sprang to his feet, making no attempt to conceal his emotion.

"*Bem vindo* (Welcome), Don Carlos," he cried, running to embrace his visitor. "How are you? Welcome in G-d's Name, my dear Don Carlos!"

"Yes, here I am, Reb Menashe." He was in the home of Amsterdam's Chief Rabbi... Amsterdam, where Jews were permitted to live as they wanted, to observe the Torah and its commandments freely and openly. "In this house, I am not Don Carlos, admiral of the Portuguese fleet and the king's intimate friend. No, Reb Menashe — here I'm a simple Jew, a Jew by the name of Yitzchak ben Yisrael."

That was the name his father, the Catholic professor Fernando Elviras, had whispered in his ear on his deathbed. The name, he said, was bestowed on Don Carlos during a secret *bris milah* ceremony held for him when he was a baby. As such, Don Carlos held it sacred.

Emotionally, Don Carlos ended, "So please, Reb Menashe, though I still live in Lisbon, in this house call me Yitzchak — Yitzchak ben Yisrael Carneiro."

"It shall be as you say," Reb Menashe agreed, smiling. The rabbi was visibly moved at the sight of his old friend. The knowledge that Don Carlos ran a grave risk every time he visited Amsterdam made the moment all the more poignant. "How wonderful to see you. It's been so long!"

"My joy is double yours, Reb Menashe." Don Carlos sighed. "My exile is growing more difficult and more bitter with each passing day. What wouldn't I give to be able to uproot myself and come live here in Amsterdam — a city that knows no suffering, no persecution — a place where it's possible to observe the commandments openly and unafraid! Can you possibly know how much I long to be able to dedicate my remaining years to the study of the Torah of which I know so little?"

"Yitzchak," Reb Menashe replied warmly, "your time will come. 'Hashem guides a man's steps.' Heaven will lead you along the right path." His tone changed. "But, my friend, why have you stayed away for two years? You have no idea how much I worry about you! I wonder constantly whether or not our activities in Portugal are successful. I've had no news about our men operating there in secret. When you didn't arrive half a year ago, immediately after Succos, I was afraid that the accursed Inquisition had managed to penetrate your secret and uncover your true identity, and had perhaps already sentenced you, Heaven forbid, to death by fire — as they wish to do to all Jews who practice their faith secretly." He spread his arms fervently. "But here you are, standing in my house, alive and well. *Baruch Hashem!*"

"Indeed, Reb Menashe — *baruch Hashem!* The G-d of Avraham, Yitzchak, and Yaakov, in His great kindness, has helped me implement our plan. No one in Portugal suspects that the Rabbi of Amsterdam, a former Marrano, is the man behind our whole operation. Not even the Marranos themselves have been told from where the teachers and *mohalim* came. And they don't ask. They know it's dangerous. Thank G-d, the underground network of secret Jews is flourishing! Our people are active not only in Lisbon, Portugal's capital, but also in Oporto, Coimbra, and Eldorado."

The sitting-room door suddenly swung open. In the doorway stood the boy who had opened the gate for Don Carlos earlier.

"Yes? What is it?" asked Reb Menashe.

The boy seemed nervous. "I heard a knocking at the gate, Rabbi — exactly the same number of knocks as our honored guest here made. Thinking that perhaps the Rabbi was expecting another guest, I opened the gate."

"Yes? Who was it?"

"A man stood there, dressed in black, with only his eyes showing above the scarf that covered his face. I asked him: 'What do you want?' In a thick, muffled voice, he said, 'Who lives here?' When I answered, 'Rabbi Menashe ben Israel,' the man didn't react at all. He just melted back into the darkness."

Reb Menashe and Don Carlos exchanged an anxious glance.

"Did anyone see you enter my house?" Reb Menashe asked fearfully.

"No! No one saw me. I took all possible precautions." Don Carlos shook his head. "Impossible! It's probably just a false alarm. Perhaps some drunkard thought it would be fun to fool around at this hour of the night."

The rabbi slowly relaxed. "All right, then. We'll continue our discussion. I know you want to hurry back to your ship."

"Yes," said Don Carlos. He paused somberly. "I have to tell you that all is not well with our community of Marranos in Lisbon."

Reb Menashe's face blanched. "This is bad news, Yitzchak!"

Don Carlos made no answer.

"What happened?" Reb Menashe asked in growing alarm. "Tell me!"

"Arnaldo... Arnaldo Rodriguez was captured..."

Reb Menashe froze in his seat at this bitter news. He made no outward sign of his feelings; he only stared straight ahead, speechless.

Don Carlos had known that the information would grieve the rabbi. Arnaldo Rodriguez was a close personal friend. His home was in Amsterdam and he'd grown up there. He and Reb Menashe had been partners for years in the study of Talmud and *halachah*. And it had been Reb Menashe himself who had asked Rodriguez to return to Portugal — to sacrifice his full, free Jewish life in Amsterdam and to live in Lisbon as a Marrano. In other words, to live publicly as a Catholic and secretly as a Jew. It was a way of life that had the danger of death, should Arnaldo's mask be stripped away, perpetually hanging over it like a brooding shadow.

Reb Menashe had asked him to do this because he believed Arnaldo Rodriguez the only man worthy of serving as rabbi to the community of Marranos in Lisbon. Reb Menashe had believed that Rodriguez, with his forceful and charismatic personality, would succeed in guiding the other Marranos to greater Torah observance despite the difficult circumstances under which they labored. Arnaldo was a courageous man, a man who didn't know what fear was — except the fear of Heaven. He was a Torah scholar and a pious, enthusiastic Jew who had happily dedicated his life to the good of his people.

And now — he'd been captured...

After a lengthy silence, Reb Menashe whispered brokenly, "Tell me. Tell me how it happened..."

Don Carlos sighed. "It happened on Purim. They discovered, those evil ones, that a certain basement in the university was used as a meeting place for prayers. For three years we succeeded in keeping the existence of this *minyan* secret. Approximately 40 men came there to *daven* each day. Most of them were part of the university itself: professors, researchers, students, and administrators. All of them Jews trying to observe the *mitzvos* of the Torah as best as they possibly could.

"This *minyan* was discovered on Purim as they read the Megillah. We don't know exactly how the evil Inquisition agents learned our secret, but at the moment they burst into the room there were nearly 60 men present. Do you know what that means? A thriving *minyan* — and a catastrophic tragedy!"

Soberly, Don Carlos continued his story.

"Among the congregants were two high officials who worked for the Ministry of Finance, a number of respected businessmen, a guest from far-off Brazil, and some simple folk. The accursed Inquisitors questioned and tortured these men for a full year. The prisoners suffered unimaginable horrors. In the end, all of them 'confessed' to their 'sins.' They admitted that they had kept the Shabbos to the best of their ability. They admitted that they had fasted on Yom Kippur. They confessed that they did not eat bread on Pesach and had never tasted pork."

Tears coursed down Yitzchak's — Don Carlos' — cheeks as he added, "They suffered hellish agonies. And in the end, the more prominent among them were sentenced to the fires of the *auto-da-fé*."

"Have they gone to the stake yet?" asked Reb Menashe.

"Not yet. But their fate is hastening toward them. The king has already granted his approval to the decree."

Reb Menashe didn't answer. He sat sunk in thought, his spirit wandering to the prison of the cruel Inquisition in Portugal. With every fiber of his soul he felt the pain of that gallant band of Jews, now shattered and broken, awaiting their deaths... And among them his dear friend, Arnaldo Rodriguez, whose Hebrew name is Raphael Chaim.

Arnaldo, his good friend. Together they had grown up in Amsterdam, both members of a congregation of forced converts who had returned to Judaism. Together they had attended the Talmud Torah affiliated with the Portuguese community in Amsterdam, the Bais Yaakov; together they had learned Torah from their great leader, Rabbi Yitzchak Uziel. Arnaldo had eventually gone into business, where he had done very well for himself, particularly in trade with Dutch emigres living abroad. Reb Menashe continued in the study of Torah, authoring books on Judaism for the benefit of the Marranos whose knowledge of the Torah was so pathetically scant.

But neither man had been able to rest comfortably while tales of their brothers' suffering in Spain and Portugal circulated. The few Marranos who succeeded in escaping that hell told hair-raising stories of the terrible hardships that afflicted the secret Jews, of their terror-filled lives and their never-ending pain and distress.

"We must do something! We must do something!" These were the words that kept repeating themselves whenever the two friends heard the refugees' stories.

"We cannot sit with our hands folded," Arnaldo would declare forcefully. "It's impossible for us to watch from a distance while so many of our Jewish brothers are born for all intents and purposes Christian, with never an idea that they are really Jews. We, who've been fortunate enough to live in freer lands, are responsible for our brothers who are suffering, imprisoned, and besieged in other countries. And especially so in Portugal, where we two were born, Menashe!" Thus spoke Raphael Chaim (Arnaldo) Rodriguez. "Do you hear me, Menashe, my friend? We must do something!"

Reb Menashe agreed wholeheartedly. "But what can we do, my dear friend?"

"Perhaps we should travel there? Maybe we can send them books to study, *mohalim* to circumcise their newborn babies, Torah scholars to teach them secretly?"

"Are you really prepared to go there, Arnaldo? Are you willing to place your life in danger for your brothers' sake?"

Arnaldo, the prosperous and respected businessman, had been taken aback at the directness of the question and didn't respond. The conversation had ended there. Reb Menashe remembered well how the two of them sat for several more hours in the Bais Yaakov synagogue, studying the Torah portion that dealt with the sacrifice of Yitzchak.

Early the next morning, Arnaldo had come to Reb Menashe's house. "Something must be done," he said with quiet intensity. "And I am prepared to do it." A spasm of pain crossed his face as he added, "If... if I don't return, please look after my wife Cecelia and our three children. See that they continue to grow up as Jews. And... tell them who their father was..."

In this way, the Jewish underground in Portugal was born.

Now the entire mission was in grave danger. Arnaldo had been captured.

Reb Menashe roused himself from his bleak thoughts.

"Tell me, Yitzchak, is it possible to do something? Is there any way to save those Jews, including my friend, the *tzaddik*, Arnaldo? Is there any chance that the king will commute their sentence to life imprisonment?"

Don Carlos did not reply. His silence spoke more eloquently than any words could have done. The room was filled with a weighty sorrow.

A moment later Don Carlos stood up, saying, "Reb Menashe, I must hurry back to my ship. As a G-d-fearing Jew who believes in Hashem and in His holy Torah, I know only one thing: We must go on. In two days from now, several of my sailors — faithful Marranos — will arrive at Alfonso Migal's warehouse to purchase a large quantity of fine fabrics, my gift to the ladies of Lisbon's royal court. I hope that among the bolts of cloth the *chumashim* we ordered will be hidden, and also your important work, "Consiliador" ("The Conciliator"). You have no idea how many people in Portugal you've saved from heresy and apostasy through that book." His voice was low but ringing as he finished, "We must go on, Reb Menashe, and Hashem will help us."

Don Carlos left the house and hurried through the sleeping streets of Amsterdam, back to his flagship, his cabin, and the burdens of his rank.

...And the shadow, dressed in black, took note. For four hours the admiral of the Portuguese fleet, Don Carlos Carneiro, professed Catholic, had sat in the home of the Rabbi of Amsterdam, who was known to be engaged in the fiercest of battles against Christianity...

2

Paulo de Henrique, secretary of the "Holy Office" in Lisbon, prepared to leave his house. As he opened the door, a thin scroll of paper — thrust into the narrow space between lintel and doorpost — fell to the floor. He bent, retrieved the scroll, and stared at it in astonishment.

Slowly and carefully, he removed the red ribbon that bound the paper, unrolled it, and read its contents. De Henrique, a respected priest who numbered among the leaders of the Holy Inquisition in Portugal, felt the blood drain from his face. He stood in the street close by his home and let the cool morning breeze fan his cheeks. It was Sunday, the Christians' day of rest, and churchbells filled the air of Lisbon, capital city of Portugal, with their heavy, resonant tolling.

With trembling hands Paulo de Henrique slowly folded the paper with its vital and disturbing information, and hid it deep in the folds of his brown monk's robe. Rapidly he directed his steps toward the home of the man who headed the "Holy Office," the leader of his order, *Padre* João Manuel.

"*Padre*," said de Henrique, as he approached the dread leader of the Inquisition, "read this note!"

João Manuel accepted the paper from his secretary with his habitual expression: a mixture of severity and arrogance. He was a man who never smiled, who never betrayed any emotion whatsoever.

But this time, as he perused the contents of the note, his face registered shocked dismay. Momentarily forgetting his self-importance, he demanded, "How did this reach you?"

"I found it tucked into the door of my house," the secretary replied. "I don't know who put it there."

"When did this happen?"

"Now — literally, right now — when I left my house on the way to church for Sunday Mass. Instead, I hurried directly here to you, *Padre*."

After a long moment of silent deliberation, Father João Manuel said:

"Let us go to the Office and search through the Inquisition files. I don't believe — I simply cannot believe — what I have just read!"

The two priests strode through Lisbon's streets in silence, each absorbed in his thoughts. The city was still wrapped in its Sunday morning sleep. The priests' steps resounded clearly in the hush, superimposed on the intermittent tolling of the churchbells. It was a short walk to the large stone building that served as Inquisition headquarters.

This was a building whose very appearance struck fear in the hearts of Lisbon's residents. From within the tall walls that surrounded it they could hear clearly, from time to time, agonized screams from the throats of Jews who'd been forced to convert and were subsequently unmasked as secretly loyal to their faith.

The citizens of Lisbon did their best not to pass that particular street, and especially that particular building.

João Manuel himself opened the heavy iron gate that led into the courtyard. The two priests hastened up the broad stone staircase in the building. The long corridor was dim and gloomy at this hour of the morning, but the pair strode confidently to the archives room, where the Inquisition's records were stored. This room was adjacent to the interrogation and torture chamber.

"Let us see what is written in the 'Amsterdam' report." From a metal cabinet João Manuel removed a heavy parchment scroll inscribed with the single word "Amsterdam."

"What a city of sinners," he remarked, spreading open the scroll which contained all the information available to them on Amsterdam. A considerable amount of that information, assiduously collected by Inquisition agents, dealt with Marranos who had fled to that city to live the lives of free Jews and to practice the tenets of their faith openly and without fear.

"I don't understand," remarked de Henrique, as his companion scanned the parchment spread before them on the table. "Why does His Majesty continue to maintain such close ties with the government of that city? Why doesn't he demand that Amsterdam hand over those heretics who fled the justice of our holy faith — those traitors who dared return openly to the religion of their fathers?"

"You're right. But I believe — if what was written in that note is indeed true — things will soon begin to change... Here! I found it." *Padre* João Manuel planted an eager finger on a certain point on the parchment. "Here's the name, 'Menashe ben Israel,' that appears in your note! Let's see what our agents from Amsterdam have to tell us." He pored over the parchment. "Listen to what it says:

> *...in addition, the witness testified to the fact that, some eight or nine years ago in a Jewish synagogue in the city of Amsterdam, he saw a 'new Christian' wearing the white prayer shawl that Jews wear in their houses of worship. When the witness engaged this Portuguese Jew in conversation, the Jew told him that his name was Manuel Diaz Suero and that he had been born on the island of Madeira.*
>
> *The witness later learned from other sources that this new Christian had indeed been known by that name and had been born on that island. But in Amsterdam he was called by the Hebrew name, Menashe ben Israel — and he held the position of chief rabbi and teacher of the faith of Moses.*
>
> *This man told our witness that he had recently shipped two crates of books that he himself had written. One was sent to Spain and the other to Brazil. The name of the Jewish book is Commentaries on the Holy Writings. The witness has a copy of this volume, which he is prepared to present before the court..."*

João Manuel moved on to another document. "Listen to what is written here:

> ...in addition, he testified that at that time (that is, in the year 1635) he, the witness, was in Amsterdam on some unspecified date in the company of two Jews. One of them called himself Menashe ben Israel and was rabbi of the Jewish community there. The second Jew's name eludes his memory. Among other things, these two Jews complained of the pressures they had endured in Spain and Portugal to abandon their faith. As they continued to converse, the man Menashe declared to the witness, with great fervor, that nothing Spain could do to the Jews would prevent them from remaining Jews, and that all the 'new Christians' in Spain and Portugal are actually only forced converts. And he went on to say that each year Jews from Holland travel to Madrid, capital of Spain, to Lisbon, and to other cities in those two countries, to circumcise the children of these 'new Christians.'
>
> When the second Jew heard this, he seized Menashe's hand and whispered that it was foolish to tell such things to the witness, who was liable to repeat them on his return to Spain, with dangerous consequences for the Jews living there. After this warning Menashe began to speak in a joking manner, claiming that everything he'd said up till then had not been meant seriously. The witness pretended to believe him. And the subject was dropped..."

Padre João Manuel put down the "Amsterdam" parchment and looked at his secretary.

"Interesting reading, eh?"

"Most assuredly," returned de Henrique.

"So that is Menashe ben Israel," mused the *padre*.

"And it was his home that the great Don Carlos visited — our illustrious admiral and personal friend of the king!" Paulo de Henrique was outraged.

After a moment, João Manuel said softly, "If the information in the note is really true."

"And why, *Padre*, should you suspect that it is less than the truth?"

"I didn't say that. All I meant to imply was that the matter bears investigation. We must be very, very careful before we accuse Don Carlos of being a secret Jew. Do you understand? Don Carlos has many enemies in the royal court. It is possible that one of them wrote the note to induce us to arrest the admiral and force a confession from him. You know as well as I do that he will confess in the end, they all do..." The priest chuckled. "And if it should turn out that we were mistaken, I need not describe what will happen to us. The king will have us removed from our exalted positions and thrown into prison."

The flow of the *padre's* speech halted suddenly. An evil glint came into his eyes. He gave his secretary a penetrating glance and seized de Henrique's shoulders in a forceful grip. With soft, slow emphasis, he said, "Hear me well, Paulo. If we investigate this matter thoroughly, watching all Don Carlos' movements, and learn that he really did meet with the heretic Menashe ben Israel... Then Lisbon will witness a faith trial the like of which she has not seen for years. We will tie him to the stake in the very heart of the city! Not even the king himself will succeed in taking him out of our hands alive." He smiled his sinister smile. "What do you say to that, de Henrique? A story like this doesn't happen every day, eh?"

"*Padre*," said de Henrique, "the witness related that the heretic Menashe ben Israel sends agents and books into Spain and Portugal. That means that there are men here who receive them. Am I right in assuming that an underground may exist here?"

"You're right. It is certainly possible. And it is also possible that Don Carlos is the leader of this secret organization!" João Manuel's voice grew thoughtful. "An underground Jewish network inside Catholic Portugal, led by an intimate of the king's? In truth, a heartwarming tale!" He shook his head. "No, it seems too farfetched to be true..."

"*Padre*," de Henrique said urgently, "we must begin a speedy investigation. It is out of the question that a man who is even suspected of crimes of such magnitude be permitted free access to the royalty and the army. I will appoint some of our most talented investigators to the job. They'll spy on Don Carlos day and night, until we catch him!"

"The first thing I want you to do is discover who put the note in your door. This is important. You have a big job ahead of you now, Paulo. We must be careful... extremely careful."

De Henrique smiled. "I intend to succeed, *Padre*. We will see Don Carlos mount the burning stake, in the name of the love and mercy of our holy faith!"

The two gripped each other's hands in a strong handshake, wished each other luck, and passed from the archives room.

When de Henrique left Inquisition headquarters, deep in thought, the churchbells were still tolling and the streets of Lisbon still slept.

3

magnificent carriage, to which two black horses were harnessed, came to a halt late one night outside one of Lisbon's most stately homes. Don Carlos, splendid in his white admiral's uniform adorned with gold epaulets, descended from the carriage. The soldier guarding the door stood at attention as Don Carlos entered his spacious house. He had just returned from the king's palace, where he tendered a detailed report on his successful excursion to Amsterdam.

Don Carlos' mood was elated. He had managed to persuade the Dutch government to sign a seafaring treaty with Portugal, and the king had been fulsome in his praise of the admiral's efforts on his behalf. Don Carlos now enjoyed even greater favor in the royal court than before.

He had scarcely begun to rest from the day's labors when a rhythmic pounding at the outer gate reached his ears. This was a signal he'd been expecting. He jumped up with alacrity and went himself to open the gate for his late-night guests, a pair of Marrano sailors who served on Don Carlos' flagship, the *Vera Cruz*. It was their job to make sure the holy books that Reb Menashe ben Israel provided in Amsterdam arrived safely at Don Carlos' home in Lisbon. Disguised as a couple of humble porters, they dragged a heavy crate into the house. The books were concealed inside. Without a word, they followed Don Carlos into an inner room and deposited the crate precisely where he indicated. Then, just as silently, they left.

Don Carlos sighed with relief: This part of the operation had gone smoothly, thank G-d! Locking the door securely behind him, he approached the case. He must complete the second part of the operation this very night. There were still long hours of travel ahead of him, while the darkness lasted.

He had just lifted the lid when a discreet knock at the door roused him. Hurriedly he replaced it and went to open the door. His houseboy stood there.

"*Senhor*," he said, "*Senhor* Pedro Alvares has arrived. Shall I let him in?"

Don Carlos concealed his chagrin. "Yes, yes, certainly, Antonio. Show him into my study and tell him I'll be right with him."

Pedro Alvares served as an officer on the admiral's flagship. He was also Don Carlos' personal secretary. Don Carlos had specifically chosen him for the job. This promising young officer, who clung fervently to Catholicism, was in actuality a Jew. He was the son of Roberto da Silva, a university lecturer in Lisbon who had been burned at the stake when Pedro was still an infant. Da Silva had been caught participating in a Pesach *seder* and was sentenced to death along with his wife. The Dominican was monks had seized the baby Pedro, then only six months old, and raised him, taking care to conceal his Jewish origins from him.

But Don Carlos knew who Pedro was. Pedro's father, the professor, had been Don Carlos' brother.

For these many years, Don Carlos had interested himself discreetly in young Pedro's welfare. And when Pedro was old enough, Don Carlos managed to manipulate events so that Pedro came to serve in Portugal's fleet. In this way, Don Carlos hoped to keep him close, and perhaps — with Hashem's help — to one day reveal the secret of the young man's true identity: son of a holy martyr who had died *al kiddush Hashem*, for the sanctification of G-d's Name.

He was usually happy when Pedro Alvares came to see him. There was always the hope in the back of his mind that an opportunity might arise to draw the youth closer to the faith of his fathers. Tonight, however, Don Carlos would have preferred to dispense with the visit.

"If only I could take him into this room and show him what the crate contains," he thought wistfully. But even as he entertained the thought, he knew that the time was not yet ripe.

He left the room with its precious secret and made his way to the study, where Pedro Alvares waited.

"Good evening, *Senhor*," Pedro greeted his admiral. "I knew you would not be angry about receiving me so late at night. I am very curious — what did the king say to you? Does he appreciate your efforts in Amsterdam, and is he satisfied with the treaty you signed there?"

"Yes, Pedro," Don Carlos replied affably. "The king praised my efforts to the skies! He sees this treaty as an opening for our fleet to begin trading with new lands across the sea. He was especially pleased with the way we've dealt with the threat of pirate attacks: His Majesty believes that Holland will stand by her promise to deny haven to these pirates, who generally seek refuge in the port of Amsterdam. And this is important, very important."

Young Pedro listened eagerly, admiration stamped on every feature. *When is he going to leave? Don Carlos thought impatiently. How can I drop a hint that this is not a good time for me to entertain visitors?*

"And did His Majesty," Pedro said, "ask you about all the heretics from the ranks of new Catholics who have fled to Amsterdam? I mean the apostates who've escaped from Lisbon and returned openly to their Jewish faith. How infuriating it is!"

Mastering his emotions, Don Carlos said quietly, as though the matter was one of complete indifference to him, "No. The king chooses to leave that to the Holy Inquisition. They are certainly doing a fine job, eh, Pedro? I have no doubt it will manage in time to lay its hand on those sinners who have fled our borders."

"I don't know. I think it's His Majesty's duty to help the faithful in their important work. I think that if we begin trading with Holland, we must also demand that they take action against those evil creatures!"

Don Carlos forced himself to reply equably, "Of course." His heart felt leaden at this vitriolic outpouring from his fellow Jew. He patted back a polite yawn. "However, my dear Pedro, I'm exhausted from our voyage, which ended only yesterday, and from the long hours I spent at the palace today. Let us continue this discussion tomorrow. Good night!"

Don Carlos escorted his young guest to the outer courtyard and warmly took leave of him. As he closed the gate, he was seized with a sudden urgency. He ran back into the house, never stopping until he was once again in the small room where the crate stood. He must hurry. The time appointed for the rendezvous had already passed. Who knew if they were still waiting for him?

Rapidly he exchanged his uniform for civilian clothes. Opening the lid, he removed a stack of securely tied books from the crate. With these under his arm he strode across the room to a spacious wardrobe that stood against the far wall, opened the door, and entered. He closed the door firmly behind him. Then, with a sure grip, he turned the knob of another door facing him inside the wardrobe. The inner door opened to admit him. Slowly and cautiously, Don Carlos began to climb down a flight of stairs, invisible in the impenetrable darkness.

The stairs led him into a wide cavern. If not for the fact that Don Carlos knew every nook and cranny there, he would surely have foundered in the dark. He arrived presently at a second set of stairs. He climbed them quickly, opened a door, and was once again inside a large closet. When he stepped out, he was standing in an empty house on one of Lisbon's quiet side streets.

Don Carlos left the house soundlessly. It was already after 1 a.m. A short distance away stood a carriage to which a pair of horses were harnessed. He approached cautiously. Darting glances right and left, he saw no one in the still street to disturb his peace of mind. One leap took him into the carriage.

"What happened? Why are you late?" an anxious voice asked in the darkness.

"Thank G-d, I've arrived. There were unexpected delays. Now let's be on our way. And let's hope they're still waiting for us."

Slowly at first, and then with greater speed, the carriage started forward on the road leading north.

$$4$$

Pablo de Henrique admitted two young monks into his office in the Inquisition building. They were the pair he had dispatched to shadow Don Carlos.

The two sat facing de Henrique's desk. They appeared shame-faced.

"Well?" de Henrique said impatiently. "Report!"

"He's disappeared," one of them whispered.

De Henrique roared, "What do you mean, disappeared?"

"We don't know. He hasn't been seen leaving his house for two days now."

"But who says he's gone? Perhaps he's ill."

"We checked that," the second monk offered. "As you ordered, we've spent the past two days watching outside his home. When we saw that he wasn't leaving it, we sent one of our men, Miguel, to find out why. Miguel dressed himself as a high-ranking officer and came riding up to Don Carlos' house on horseback. He hammered on the outer gate. The maid appeared and said, '*Senhor*, Don Carlos is not at home.'

"Our 'officer' persisted. 'I was invited here by Don Carlos. It is imperative that we discuss urgent military matters. I must enter!'

"But the maid just shook her head and repeated, '*Senhor* is not at home. *Senhor* has gone on a long journey.' And then she closed the gate."

The monks fell silent. Fearfully, they watched de Henrique's face redden with rage. They well knew how dangerous he could be when angry. Hastily, they added, "Your Grace, be assured that we watched the house extremely well. We stood guard day and night, alert at all times. No one could suspect us of doing otherwise. And we can state with complete confidence that nobody left through the front gate, Your Grace, in those two days."

"Are you certain? Certain in every sense of the word?"

"Yes, *Padre*. We are certain."

De Henrique began pacing agitatedly up and down the room. His hands were clasped behind his back and his head moved with ferocious nervous energy as he walked. The young monks watched him in growing alarm.

Without warning, de Henrique wheeled around. He approached the desk where his henchmen sat. Slamming his fist on the desk, he screamed, "*Where could Don Carlos have disappeared to?*"

The monks hung their heads.

"We don't know, *Padre*," they answered timidly. "We followed your orders exactly. Since noon on the day before yesterday we've had his house under surveillance — and without arousing the slightest suspicion. We disguised ourselves as a couple of drunken laborers and followed every movement around Don Carlos' house.

"He returned home on that first night, very late. Shortly afterwards, two porters knocked at his gate. When the gate was opened, they took a heavy crate from their wagon and carried it into the house. Then, half an hour later, a young officer showed up — we couldn't get a good look at his face — and despite the late hour was admitted into the house. Since then, two days have passed without any sign of Don Carlos."

"A young officer?" de Henrique thought aloud. "A young officer visiting the fleet admiral in the middle of the night? Strange. Very strange..."

De Henrique locked his gaze on the monks and asked forcefully, "Who was the young officer? At least tell me that! Bring me his name!"

Trembling, the monks repeated, "We don't know, *Padre*."

"But we must find out! He may be the key to what is going on in Don Carlos' house!" De Henrique moved in closer, his expression threatening. The monks' trembling grew more pronounced. With eyes that spat fire, de Henrique hissed, "You have until tomorrow night, do you hear? By tomorrow night we must know the identity of that young officer. Understand?"

Dumbly, the monks nodded.

"It's highly suspicious! Young officers don't visit their superiors at that hour of the night."

"Yes, Your Grace," the monks whispered.

De Henrique's tone became musing. "A heavy crate, you said?"

"Yes, Your Grace. They seemed hardly able to lift it, those two porters."

De Henrique sank into his seat. He turned over in his mind the facts they'd gleaned from the "Amsterdam" file in the Inquisition's archives the other day. It had said there that, from time to time, Rabbi Menashe ben Israel sent shipments of holy books to the secret Jews in Spain and Portugal. Was this one of those boxes? Was Father João Manuel right in suspecting that a secret Jewish underground was active in Portugal — and that Don Carlos was its leader?

What to do now?

A thick silence filled the room. De Henrique rose and began pacing again, thinking furiously. The young monks sat utterly still, watching him.

Suddenly, the silence was shattered. Into the room burst the figure of another youthful monk. It was Roberto Nunes, who had been dispatched by de Henrique in an attempt to learn the identity of the person who'd left the note in de Henrique's door.

"Your Grace," Roberto said breathlessly before he'd taken more than two paces into the room, "I found him!"

"Who?" For a moment, torn from his thoughts, the priest was nonplused.

"The man who hid the note at your house! The story is true! Don Carlos, admiral of the fleet and personal friend of His Majesty, the king, visited Rabbi Menashe ben Israel's home in Amsterdam. I've spoken to the man who followed him there!"

"Really?" The cry burst simultaneously from every throat in the room. Excitement dissipated the tension that had reigned there only a moment before.

De Henrique leaned forward eagerly. "So quickly? Who is he? What's his name?"

Roberto smiled. "It's not so simple. I promised the man I wouldn't reveal his name. Only on that condition was he willing to share the story with me — to tell me how he trailed Don Carlos through the streets of Amsterdam that night. I have his consent to give his name only to de Henrique, secretary of the Holy Office. He is afraid of having others know.

"In Amsterdam, my informant tells me, he learned that there are forced converts — secret Jews — serving the Inquisition in Portugal, who regularly pass on warnings to individuals suspected by our Holy Office. In this way, these suspects, these betrayers of our true faith, are able to flee the country with their lives and escape the just wrath due to them."

Young Nunes stopped speaking. Abruptly, he advanced to where de Henrique stood, leaned closer, and whispered a few words in his ear. De Henrique looked astounded. Then, with a broad spreading smile, he exclaimed, "Unbelievable! You have succeeded beyond all expectation, my son."

He turned on the other two priests. "You see? *This* is called success! *This* is called a holy service for our faith!"

The hapless pair squirmed with envy at Roberto's good fortune, an envy mixed with grudging admiration.

Roberto Nunes, with all eyes upon him, spoke piously. "Yes, only in the merit of our holy faith did I succeed in unraveling the mystery of the note as quickly as I did. I put on a sailor's outfit and went down to the harbor. Each evening I'd visit a different tavern, mingling with the sailors there and pretending to be drunk. And a drunkard, you understand, says things a sober man never would!

"On the first night, I smashed my glass against the wall to attract everyone's attention and bellowed in my 'intoxication': 'May our savior send you all into the flames of purgatory! Not one of you even cares that Don Carlos is a Jew! Your own admiral — a Jew! Ha, ha, ha... *I know!* In the morning I'll be going around to the royal palace to tell His Majesty. I'll shout it as loud as I can: *A Jew!* A Jew at the head of the fleet! Ha, ha, ha... A Jew!

"On the first night, nothing happened. At first, the sailors just laughed at me. After a while, when I wouldn't stop screaming, they simply picked me up and threw me out into the street. The same thing happened on the second night."

Roberto looked around, enjoying his place in the limelight. He was well aware that he had his audience's complete and unwavering attention. He cleared his throat and continued his story.

"On the third day I decided to try again. I went into a different tavern hard by the docks, ordered a drink, and after a quarter of an hour's time began shouting the same thing as on the previous two nights. This time they began to beat me, because many of the sailors there served on the flagship *Vera Cruz* under the direct leadership of Don Carlos. Suddenly..."

"Yes?" gasped de Henrique.

"What happened?" the two young monks asked breathlessly.

"I'll tell you. Suddenly, a very distinguished personage came over to me. No, no, I won't say his name. I promised him... He chased away the sailors who were beating me, lifted me from the floor, and carried me to a dark corner of the tavern. There he sat me down at a table. I, naturally, continued playing the drunkard.

"'Why do you claim that Don Carlos is a Jew?' he asked in a hard voice.

"'Because I want to,' I answered, laughing. 'I know that he's a Jew. What concern is it of yours how I know? I know, and that's that. And tomorrow I'm going to tell what I know to the king.' And I laughed some more.

"He stared at me searchingly. I could sense that he wanted to tell me something, but was afraid to. So I continued my charade: 'What, isn't he a Jew? Ha, ha, ha...'

"The man grabbed my shoulders and began shaking me with all his might. 'Tell me!' he screamed into my ear. 'How do you know that he's a Jew? Do you realize what a serious thing you're saying?'

"I pretended to sober up. 'I heard them talking about it.'

"'Heard who talking?' he asked impatiently.

"'What do you mean, who? Them!'

"Again, he seized my shoulders. 'Tell me — *who*?'

"'The priests.'

"'Which priests?'

"'The Inquisition priests.'

"'And what did they say?'

"'They said they'd received a note that said he's a Jew. But they don't believe what the note said. They think it's a false accusation.'

" '*What*?' screamed the man. 'They don't believe?'

" 'No — but *I* believe,' I told him innocently. 'So why are you squeezing my shoulders like that? It hurts!'

"The man didn't let go. I could see that he was so overwrought, he hadn't even heard what I said. I knew I'd found the man I'd been looking for.

"'Listen,' he said emotionally, 'Do you know the priests of the Holy Office? Do you know them?'

'Yes,' I said. 'De Henrique, Secretary of the Holy Office, is my uncle. But what's wrong? Why are you so upset?'

"'I will explain,' he said, more quietly now. 'I'm the one who put the note in the door, and I'm the man who followed Don Carlos in Amsterdam. And it's true! He's a secret Jew! He poses a danger to our nation and to our faith. Tell your uncle it's true!'

"That's all," Roberto finished. "That's my story."

De Henrique was the first to speak.

"Tell me, my dear Roberto — is this man willing to continue being of service to us? Will he continue spying on Don Carlos?"

"No," answered Roberto. "In his opinion, his job was done the moment he brought his news to your attention. But he *is* prepared to testify, if it comes to that."

De Henrique sighed. "That could be a long time off. The Inquisition has fallen indeed from the glory of its former days. Today, it's impossible for us to imprison a person without clear proof that he is really a secretly practicing Jew. First we have to uncover the fact, then find evidence to prove it, and only then can we clap our hands on him."

The secretary of the Holy Office strode over to the two monks who had failed in their task.

"There is a great deal of work ahead of us. Holy work. I want it done. And quickly."

"Yes, yes, *Padre*," the monks said, cowed. "We promise."

5

The screams and groans finally subsided as the prisoners languishing in the Inquisition dungeons fell into an exhausted sleep. At this hour, 3 in the morning, fatigue finally overcame the pain and suffering of the day's long interrogation and torture. Utter silence descended on the fearsome building, in which every window seemed like the entrance to a unlit tunnel. It was a building that inspired dread in the hearts of Lisbon's residents.

Alfonso Alvares, in the guardroom beside the dungeon gates, stood up. He wore a long, woolen monk's robe. He had relieved the guard at midnight and still felt alert and wide awake. Picking up a flaming taper, he closed his book and went to a small cabinet beside the wall. Noiselessly he removed a set of keys. Then he extinguished the taper: What he had to do now was better done in the dark.

Just as soundlessly, he approached the gate that led to the prison cells, selected a key from the ring, and carefully unlocked it. He passed through the gate and locked it again behind him. Down he went, into the bowels of the earth, to the prisoners' quarters.

He knew the way well. As a guard he had traversed this route hundreds, if not thousands, of times before. Sometimes he brought prisoners up for interrogation; other times he returned them. He brought them food and went down to silence them when the screams grew too tumultuous: *"I'm innocent!" "I'm no Jew!" "What do they want from me?" "Oh, the pain... My bones, they're broken..."*

But this occasion, he knew, was different. And dangerous. This was the first time he was descending these stairs at Don Carlos' behest.

Alfonso walked through the pitch-black corridor. He passed cell after cell. His footsteps aroused no one. He stopped in front of one cell, quickly unlocked it, and passed inside. "If anyone sees me," he thought, "I can always say that one of the prisoners had become unruly and I came to quiet him."

As his eyes grew accustomed to the dark, Alfonso was able to make out the figure of a man asleep on the floor. The prisoner's clothes were torn and tattered; he was rail-thin, with sores covering his legs, arms, and face. Alfonso stepped closer and gently shook him.

The prisoner didn't budge. Alfonso nudged him harder: no reaction.

"Perhaps he's dead?" he wondered apprehensively. This prisoner had undergone severe tortures that day. Had he been unable to withstand them?

"No," he whispered. "It's not possible!" Turning the broken prisoner over onto his back, he began speaking to him in low, urgent tones.

"Arnaldo. Arnaldo Rodriguez, wake up! I have news for you!"

Still no response. With renewed tension, Alfonso began shaking the prisoner with force. "Arnaldo! Arnaldo... *Raphael Chaim!*"

Arnaldo Rodriguez's eyes flew open in shock. "Who's that?" he shouted. "What do you want from me?"

"Ssh... Ssh..." Alfonso placed a finger over Arnaldo's lips. "Don't shout. Be quiet. I am a friend!"

Arnaldo was no calmer, but he hadn't the strength to put up a fight. As the stranger continued to grip him firmly, Arnaldo thought vaguely that perhaps this was yet another interrogation. Who knew what tortures were yet in store for him until they finally tied him to the stake?

"Arnaldo," Alfonso whispered in the prisoner's ear, once he'd succeeded in pulling him into a sitting position against the dungeon wall,

"Arnaldo, Reb Menashe ben Israel knows of your plight. Don Carlos asked me to tell you that many prayers are being said on your behalf in Amsterdam. They're fasting, giving charity in your name... Arnaldo, are you listening?"

The news didn't appear to interest the prisoner much. His head lolled on his shoulder, as though recent events had sapped his will to live. Alfonso persisted.

"Arnaldo, listen to me. When he returned from Amsterdam, Don Carlos decided to do everything in his power to rescue you. Arnaldo — *yeshuas Hashem k'heref ayin* — Hashem's salvation can come in the blink of an eye. A plan has already been set in place. Don Carlos is planning to set sail to Brazil in a few days, and you will be aboard his ship."

Arnaldo opened his eyes and gazed sadly at Alfonso. His breathing was labored and the words emerged in staccato spurts:

"Leave me alone, you spy! I don't believe you. I don't know who Don Carlos is, or this rabbi in Amsterdam. Do you want me to denounce somebody? Well, you've come to the wrong person! Tell those who sent you here that I, it's true, am a Jew and will not abandon the faith of my fathers — not even when they tie me to the stake. But I don't know any Don Carlos or any rabbi in Amsterdam."

Voices sounded in the corridor. Alfonso froze. Who could it be? As the voices came closer, he shrank against the wall, scarcely daring to breath.

Judging from the footsteps, there were at least two people there. They spoke quietly.

"I wonder why Alfonso left his post."

"Something must have happened. He is loyal and devoted. There have never been any complaints against him."

"True. Well, this will have to be investigated in the morning, *Padre*. We cannot simply leave our `treasures' unguarded here in their cells, can we?"

Both men laughed. The footsteps grew fainter and the voices faded away.

Alfonso breathed again. He hurried over to Arnaldo, clutched his shoulders, and said urgently, "Arnaldo Rodriguez, known by the Hebrew name Raphael Chaim — please believe me! I, Alfonso Alvares, am a Jew like you, despite this monk's robe. I come from Don Carlos, who asks after your health and sends his encouragement. Please hold fast to the belief that Hashem will help you, and hope that the plan we're weaving will succeed..."

Alfonso looked deep into the eyes of this broken man, who only a few months earlier had been the leader of the community of Marranos in Portugal. He looked deep, and prayed inwardly that Arnaldo would survive until the rescue plan could be set in motion. Then, silent as a shadow, Alfonso left the cell.

He closed the door after him and began padding quietly toward the staircase leading up to the gate.

There, on the steps beside the table, waited his closed book, the extinguished taper — and the head of the Holy Office, *Padre* João Manuel, accompanied by his secretary, Paulo de Henrique.

Alfonso climbed slowly, trying with all his strength to retain a cool, composed manner. Inside, his heart pounded frantically.

"So, my young friend," said Father João Manuel, "why did you abandon your post? And what have you been doing down in the dungeons with the prisoners?"

"Oh, Your Grace, as I was reading St. Augustine's work, I heard wild screams from one of the cells. I hurried to see what was happening there. I wanted to quiet him."

Paulo de Henrique and João Manuel exchanged a quick glance.

"Don't you know that you acted against orders? It's against the rules to enter the dungeons during the night hours."

"But..."

"No buts, my young friend. It's not your job to calm a hysterical heretic, who is tasting in this world the hell that awaits him in the next."

Alfonso looked properly abashed. "I understand, Your Grace."

"Besides," continued the *Padre*, "we passed through all the corridors on the lower level. We didn't see you there. Where were you?"

Before Alfonso could reply, de Henrique's evil tones came to his ears:

"Perhaps you will be so kind as to step into our `workroom' for further discussion of this matter?"

Alfonso knew that his fate was sealed. As he followed the two Inquisition heads, he suddenly became aware of two young monks treading softly in his wake...

6

The carriage bore Don Carlos northward at great speed: He must reach Oporto by dawn. Beside him sat Rodriguez de Oliveiro, leader of the secret community of Marranos in Oporto and its environs. In his public persona de Oliveiro was a lawyer, famous across northern Portugal for dedicating his time and money to helping the poor who had become entangled with the law. The two sat silent throughout the long journey, although the coachman, too, was one of their own. Sheer tension prevented them from conversing normally.

The carriage reached the outskirts of the city just before daybreak, but didn't enter it. Instead, the driver veered into a side road leading to the fields and the forests beyond. The coachman whipped his horses mercilessly, urging them to greater speed. It was imperative that they reach the cover of the forest before the first farmers were astir in the fields. No one must witness the carriage's progress as it snaked through the meadows instead of the king's high road. Faithful Catholics to a man, those farmers were all too likely to ask dangerous and unwanted questions. All through Portugal, the hunt for "new Christians" was on — or, more accurately, for those "Christians" who continued to practice their Judaism in secret. Don Carlos was afraid...

At last, the carriage came to a halt at the entrance to an orchard. Don Carlos and de Oliveiro exited hurriedly and were quickly swallowed up by the trees. After a few moments the coachman stood up, looked around to make sure no one saw him, and opened the carriage door to remove a heavy stack of books. He covered these with his wide cloak and ran into the orchard.

Weaving his way through the abundant fruit trees, he reached a hut hidden deep in their midst. There he found Don Carlos and his host, de Oliveiro, deep in conversation. The coachman deposited the books with a farewell salute, received the men's thanks with a silent incline of his head, and then disappeared the way he had come. The carriage had to be concealed.

De Oliveiro glanced up at the sky. "The sun will rise soon," he told Don Carlos with a smile, "and then I can provide you with the means of performing the *mitzvah* of *tefillin*."

Don Carlos' face lit up. Ever since Arnaldo Rodriguez, along with a large group of Marranos, had been captured, *tefillin* were no longer to be found in Lisbon. The two pairs being used in the makeshift *shul* on that ill-fated morning were seized by the evil Inquisition agents. Don Carlos looked at de Oliveiro in wonder, his eyes framing a question without words. How had a precious pair of *tefillin* come into his possession?

"You won't believe it," his friend said, divining his thoughts. "The way I obtained these *tefillin* was nothing short of a miracle — an open miracle from Heaven!

"As you know, out of fear of the Inquisition we hid our sole pair of *tefillin* here in this orchard, beneath that stone... About a year ago, they vanished. One morning a number of our people slipped into the orchard to put on the *tefillin,* and found it gone. You can imagine our reaction. We were terrified that somehow the hiding place had been discovered. For many months no one visited this spot, for fear that Inquisition spies were watching."

"In that case, why have you brought me here?" Don Carlos asked, a furrow of apprehension appearing on his brow.

"It's all right. For months our men circulated in the fields without arousing any suspicion. They could not find a single farmer or local priest who seemed especially interested in this orchard. We never saw the Inquisition searching this place or paying any attention to it whatsoever."

"Well, you must have wondered — how did the *tefillin* disappear?"

"A cat, maybe," de Oliveiro shrugged. "Or some yokel who didn't know what it was he had found, or else forgot to notify the authorities. Perhaps a Marrano, unknown to us, found and took them. I don't know. The important thing is, today we have *tefillin* again — and they came to us straight from Heaven!"

"Yes, that's the important thing. But what do you mean, 'from Heaven'?"

"From Heaven, meaning, with Heaven's help. Two weeks ago, a tragedy occurred in the city's center. We had several days of very stormy weather — something this part of the country hadn't seen in years. It was frankly dangerous to walk outside. The high winds practically lifted people off their feet! The air was full of flying objects, moving at tremendous velocity and capable of inflicting severe injury on anyone they struck.

"On one of those nights, while the storm was still raging, we heard a tremendous crash. People woke up terrified, wondering if pirates were shooting at us from offshore, as they had in the past. I went out into the street; as a city councilman I felt it my responsibility to find out what had happened. In the center of the city, I found a huge crowd gathered together. They were standing silently around a fallen church spire that the powerful wind had toppled.

"Believe me, Don Carlos," de Oliveiro continued, "it was a miracle that that steeple fell at night and not during the day. In the daylight hours, it would most likely have crushed tens, if not hundreds, of passers-by on that busy street.

"As I stood there with the others, I glimpsed in the darkness — among the piles of stones and rubble — some straps. They looked like *tefillin* straps! In amazement, I moved closer to the spot, and the crowd made way for me respectfully. As though I was merely curious, I bent and picked up the small bundle. They were indeed *tefillin* — hidden, apparently, by a 'faithful' Christian, probably one of the priests associated with this very church. He had hidden it in the most secure place in town — the church spire!

"I managed to disguise my excitement. Stooping again, I picked up one of the small bells that had been detached from the big steeple bell at the top of the tower, and also some pieces of wood, as if I had nothing more in mind than collecting a few personal souvenirs. In the dark, no one in the crowd saw anything strange in what I was doing. And now," da Oliveiro ended with a broad smile, "our small community at Oporto has a pair of *tefillin!*"

⟨⟩

De Henrique entered *Padre* João Manuel's office. He was worried. Don Carlos' disappearance from his home had disturbed his peace from the moment he'd heard about it. What did it mean? Where could he be? De Henrique had decided to share his worries with the leader of the Inquisition.

He found João Manuel at his desk writing a letter.

"*Padre*," said de Henrique without preamble, "I'm afraid that serious things have been occurring right under our very noses. It's clear to me now that, beyond any doubt, Don Carlos is a secret Jew. We found the man who placed the note in my door. At the moment, however, we would still be hard put to prove it.

"We also know that Don Carlos has not left his house for two days, and yet he is not at home! The maid told one of our agents, sent to investigate the matter, that her master had gone on a journey. What do you think of all this, *Padre*?"

João Manuel did not answer immediately. He set aside his pen and pondered a while. Finally, he said, "I don't know, de Henrique. I don't know what to say. It's your job to investigate the matter thoroughly. It's possible that, although with G-d's help we've managed to capture Arnaldo Rodriguez and the band of sinners who cowered in his shadow, we may not yet have laid hands on all the heretics in our city. And if I'm correct, we must act quickly." He peered at his secretary. "Any suggestions?"

"I don't know, *Padre*," de Henrique answered helplessly. "Don Carlos is a very important person. He is both admiral of the Portuguese fleet and a personal friend of the king's. We can't fight him; his influence at court is significant. If we were to imprison him pending further investigation, chances are that we, too, would end up in the dungeons. We must act shrewdly, deviously, and with faith that we are performing the will of our Savior!"

"It seems to me," the Inquisition leader said, "that we must also act with courage. We have to organize a search of Don Carlos' house, in order to determine exactly where he is."

"But, *Padre*, how can we?" de Henrique asked fearfully. "The king will be furious!"

João Manuel rose decisively to his feet. "We're going to the king, you and I," he declared. "We will go to the palace immediately and request an audience. He won't put me off — I, who stand at the head of the Inquisition — if I tell him I regard this matter as urgent."

De Henrique was about to reply when João Manuel came around the side of his desk, placed a hand on his secretary's shoulder, and said, "Come, let's go. This is no time for talk; we must act. Let us place our suspicions before the king. It is my hope that he will allow us to proceed as we see fit."

7

As dawn illuminated the skyline of Oporto, the sun's first rays penetrated the secret orchard where Don Carlos Carneiro and Rodriguez de Oliveiro sat talking.

A sound of snapping twigs stopped the flow of words as though by magic. Somebody was coming. Don Carlos and Rodriguez moved with lightning reflexes. Together, they lifted an iron lid that was fixed in the center of the orchard. Seizing the ropes they found inside, they manipulated themselves into the depths of the hole below, replacing the lid after them. Their hearts pounded fiercely as they awaited developments.

Seconds later, a sound reached them — a rhythmic tapping on the metal lid. They relaxed. The newcomer was one of their own, a fellow Marrano.

By dint of long practice and by bracing themselves on the sides of the hole, they clambered up and pushed open the lid. A hand reached out to help them.

"My dear, dear brother!" The newcomer, João Batista, hugged Don Carlos. The words poured from him in an emotional torrent. "How wonderful to find you here! It seems like we haven't seen each other for years. What's the news from the capital? And what of Arnaldo? Isn't there any way to save him from those wicked ones? You have no idea how we've been praying for him, pleading with Hashem to end our suffering and free our rabbi and leader from the accursed Inquisition. Tell me, Don Carlos — is there any chance the king will commute his sentence?"

Don Carlos heaved a deep sigh.

"You must understand, João Batista, that I have to be extremely careful in broaching the subject to the king. He's a fanatical Catholic, as you know, and quite evil besides. Apart from that, the Inquisition leaders have him firmly under their thumb."

He sighed again.

"The situation is very complicated. If the king begins to sense that I have any compassion for the 'enemies of G-d,' I'll lose favor in his eyes as well. Then I would not be in a position to help anyone at all. I have not yet found the right words to say to the king, words that might have some chance of swaying him." He threw up his hands in a gesture of despair. "I don't know what to do. But my friends are working on a plan now to free Arnaldo from prison and help him out of the country. Part of the fleet will be sailing to Brazil in a few days, to our sovereign settlements in the north of that country. Arnaldo will escape in one of the ships. The plan is still secret, though. I don't really want to talk about it..."

Rodriguez broke in to tell the two brothers, "Gentlemen, it's time to daven *shacharis.*" He went to a nearby tree, carefully removed a piece of wood from the trunk, and pulled out a pair of *tefillin.*

"These are the *tefillin* I managed to save from the compassionate hand of the Church that night. With your permission, João Batista, shall we let our honored guest from Lisbon put them on first?"

Don Carlos' face was suffused with feeling. It had been a long time — much too long — since he had been able to wear *tefillin.*

He remembered the last occasion well. It had been two years before, at the University at Coimbra, where he had delivered a talk on Portugal's naval power. Afterwards, a number of professors had invited him to a festive meal. At the very end of the meal, just moments before sunset, they brought him a pair of *tefillin.* He still had no idea how, with no spoken word from him, they had divined that he was, like them, a secret Jew.

As he took the *tefillin* from Rodriguez, he recalled with anguish that the entire group of professors had been arrested months later and, after torture, burned at the stake *al kiddush Hashem...*

Trembling slightly with the emotion of the moment, Don Carlos rolled up his left sleeve, placed the *tefillin* straps around his arm, and with great concentration recited the blessing: "Blessed art Thou, Hashem, our G-d, King of the universe, Who has sanctified us with His commandments and has commanded us to put on *tefillin.*" Then he placed the other *tefillin* on his head and again, slowly and with deep feeling, recited the *berachah.*

Rodriguez and João Batista answered with a fervent "Amen." It seemed to them that the trees, too, added their own silent "Amen." When Don Carlos had finished reciting the *Shema Yisrael,* he removed the *tefillin* and handed them to Rodriguez.

Both Rodriguez and João Batista noticed that the admiral's eyes were brimming with tears.

⁓)⁓

Four splendid horses, pulling a luxurious coach, came to a halt outside the royal palace. The coachman leaped down with alacrity. Bowing almost to the ground, he opened the door. The first to emerge was Paulo de Henrique, Secretary of the Holy Office. He was followed by the head of the Inquisition, *Padre* João Manuel. Three more monks stepped out after them, and the entire entourage approached the palace gates.

The royal guards permitted these honored visitors immediate access to the palace. The priests walked with a gravity and an air of self-importance that reflected the opinion they held of their own worth. Every servant in the broad courtyard bowed humbly as they passed, wondering what brought such eminent religious figures to the palace at this hour.

At the entrance to the palace, de Henrique presented a letter to one of the guards, requesting an urgent audience with the king. It was an unconventional request, but one that the priests knew the king would not refuse. Even the king could not disregard the awesome power of the Inquisition.

In due course, accordingly, they found themselves standing before the king. João Manuel executed a deep bow and raised the large cross he carried. The king inclined his head, indicating that the priest might speak.

"Your Majesty, the king," the *padre* began in pompous tones, "shield and protector of our holy faith in our beautiful land, ruler of the seas and most benevolent monarch! The purity of our faith stands in grave danger. It is this danger that has brought me to beg an immediate audience with His Majesty, the king." He paused, waiting for a sign.

The king uttered but a single word: "Continue!"

"Your Majesty undoubtedly knows and appreciates the devoted work we do in eradicating the heretics in our midst. This is exceedingly difficult work, Your Majesty! It demands a great deal of us. Unfortunately, each time we believe that we have finally rooted out the enemies of our Savior, we find that the devil still taunts us. We are constantly discovering fresh enemies of the true faith, particularly here in Lisbon... Until, at times, it begins to seem to us that all of her citizens are secret Jews!"

The *padre* lapsed into silence once again. He was well aware of the impact of his final sentence. The king's face remained impassive. Once more, he commanded, "Continue!"

"And now, Your most exalted Majesty, just a few days ago, our Holy Office was terribly shaken up. We received awful tidings, tidings we are still trying to absorb. We knew it was imperative that we lay these facts before the king, so that he might guide us in his wisdom and show us how we may come to the truth of this matter in the pleasant and compassionate manner consistent with our holy faith."

This spate of words apparently angered the king, already put out by the unexpected demand for an audience. In his impatience he shouted, "Well? What's on your mind, then!"

João Manuel inhaled deeply. He glanced at his companions for moral support. "Your Majesty, Don Carlos Carneiro..."

The king shot to his feet and opened his mouth as though to speak. Then, thinking the better of it, he slowly resumed his seat on the throne and said, very quietly and with deadly emphasis:

"Does the head of the Holy Inquisition mean to tell me that Don Carlos Carneiro, my trusted advisor and admiral of my fleet, is not true to our faith?! Are you trying to hint that *he* is a secret Jew — that he is a traitor to the king who has elevated him and shown him favor?"

"No, no, Your Majesty," João Manuel hastened to reply. "All I wish to say is that a suspicion has been raised against him. We have heard something, and are desirous of investigating the matter further. We are not sure — and we wish to be very sure. No one will be happier than we if this accusation turns out to be a lie, a dastardly attempt to besmirch the name of an upstanding citizen. But we must do our job."

The priest broke off. On his throne, the king closed his eyes and pondered. The hall was plunged into a state of suddenly heightened tension. Not a muscle quivered as the monks stood stock still, eyes fixed unwaveringly on the inscrutable figure of their monarch.

After long moments of thought, the king opened his eyes.

"What have you heard?"

Padre João Manuel said, "Don Carlos returned from Amsterdam this week. He was seen entering the home of that city's rabbi, the heretic Menashe ben Israel — that is, Manuel Diaz Suero, whose family returned to the practice of Judaism upon reaching Amsterdam."

"How has this come to be known?"

"A member of the ship's crew followed him. It happened in the dead of night. Don Carlos was not dressed in his uniform. The follower has told us his story."

The king was quiet again. This time, the silence stretched even longer than before. At last, he asked, "And what do you want now?"

"Your Majesty, we wish to speak with Don Carlos, but he has disappeared."

The king stirred.

"Disappeared? What do you mean, disappeared? Where could he have disappeared?"

"We don't know, Your Majesty. For two days now, we have posted guards at the entrance of his home, and he hasn't left it. Yet when we sent someone to request a meeting with him, a maid provided the information that her master was gone — on a journey, she said. We don't know how he could have traveled, when he has certainly not left his house through the front door."

Padre João Manuel paused, then added, "We would like to request permission from His Majesty, the king, to search his house."

The king did not reply.

"I, personally, wish to enter his house to see what is happening there," the priest continued persuasively. "If I find everything in order, why then, I've merely paid a polite visit to an honored friend. And if I do not..."

Impatiently, the king cut him off. "Permission granted."

Rising from his throne, the king made an imperious gesture: The audience was ended.

With deep, reverent bows, the monks took their leave of the royal presence. No word was exchanged until the assemblage had returned to their coach. Then João Manuel told his secretary, "We must make haste to organize the search of Don Carlos' house. I am not sure of the king; he may send messengers of his own to forewarn Don Carlos. We must hurry."

The horses seemed to sense the *padre's* urgency. Kicking up their heels, they galloped at headlong speed in the direction of Inquisition headquarters.

8

"*P*adre, do you think the king believed us?" de Henrique asked.

They were seated in João Manuel's office in the wake of their visit to the palace. The mood was euphoric.

João Manuel did not reply at once. His distant expression betrayed the fact that his thoughts had wandered. In his inner eye he was already visualizing Don Carlos bound to the stake, the dread *auto-da-fé*. All of Lisbon would laud him, João Manuel, for his magnificent triumph in running to earth a traitor in the very court of the king!

"*Padre*," de Henrique tried again, "do you think the king believed us?" The question had been troubling him since their audience. The king's manner had been cold — cold enough to arouse de Henrique's suspicions.

João Manuel folded his arms and fixed his eyes on the ceiling. After a moment, he leaned closer to de Henrique, as though about to impart a secret. De Henrique waited with bated breath.

"I don't know," João Manuel said. "I just don't know."

De Henrique stared at him in dismay.

"And because I don't know," the superior priest continued, "I am still delaying my visit to Don Carlos' house."

Octavio Azevedo, a high-ranking priest who had been part of the recent delegation to the palace, was seated with them. He was a reticent man, by habit so miserly with his speech that the nickname given him behind his back was "the fish." But when he finally did deign to speak, everyone listened. The others listened to him now.

"My esteemed friend," Octavio said in slow, sonorous tones, "you are right. The matter is not at all simple. I am very much afraid His Majesty has granted permission for us to investigate the matter only because he is certain that we will find nothing. This will give Don Carlos an opportunity to fight us with all the means at his disposal. And he will succeed in hurting us, despite all our strength. He is very powerful. I believe that His Majesty would like to see our influence lessened. After all, is not even the king himself afraid of us?"

Octavio's pronouncement punctured the bubble of self-importance with which the priests encased themselves. Clearly agitated, de Henrique rose to his feet. He went to the room's single window and moved aside the heavy curtain, letting in the last of the daylight. Then he left the room, mumbling something about fetching drinks.

When the secretary had gone, Octavio hitched his chair closer to João Manuel's. "Between the two of us," he whispered in the other's ear, "I'm not sure of de Henrique. I don't know if he's trustworthy and reliable."

João Manuel roused himself. For the first time since the meeting had begun, he displayed a sign of life.

"Do you harbor a suspicion? Do you have any proof?! We all know that the Inquisition is crawling with monks and priests who are actually secret Jews. It is difficult to point to any one individual, but we can definitely sense the effects of this betrayal beneath the surface. Why, just yesterday we detained a young monk for questioning. We found him wandering around among the prison cells without any justifiable reason."

"Who was it?" Octavio demanded.

Padre João Manuel smiled evilly. "My dear Octavio, do you want me to begin suspecting you, too, of being a secret Jew? Why this sudden interest in the name of the man we arrested?"

Octavio blanched. He knew that the merest whisper of a suspicion was enough to prompt the Inquisition to horrific tortures, aimed at eliciting "confessions" for sins never committed. He himself had participated in many such cruel torture sessions. Did João Manuel really suspect *him*? His heart quailed.

De Henrique returned, bearing a tray of cool, refreshing drinks. He distributed two of the glasses and kept one for himself. "Well?" he asked, glancing from one man to the other, "did you decide anything while I was gone?"

Neither man answered. Each was wrapped in his own thoughts and dark, churning suspicions.

De Henrique, oblivious, continued, "Octavio is right. We must proceed with caution. We cannot present ourselves at Don Carlos' house as Inquisition investigators. Rather, we must arrive in such a way that, if nothing comes to light, may be interpreted as a simple, friendly visit — as we told the king. That way we protect ourselves." Again he glanced from one to the other. "Well? What do you think?"

"As you do," both answered with one voice.

"In that case, *Padre*, we must act quickly. You yourself said so when we left the palace. Let's move! Nightfall is not far off. It is not more than a half-hour on foot to Don Carlos' house. Shall we walk?"

João Manuel lifted his hand in a gesture of restraint.

"Slowly, slowly, my friend. To rush into action without thinking each step through is also a form of laziness — mental laziness, hiding behind a flurry of physical activity. It is not enough merely to present ourselves at Don Carlos' house, asking to speak with him. We must also consider what we will speak about! It must be a topic that will not arouse his suspicions, and yet allow us to learn everything we need to know." He paused. "Any suggestions?"

Octavio ventured, "I think we should speak about Amsterdam."

"Amsterdam!" exclaimed de Henrique.

"Yes, yes — Amsterdam! Don Carlos has visited that city a number of times. We can tell him we wish to learn more about the Marranos who fled there and have returned to Judaism."

João Manuel burst into laughter.

"A good idea. Even a brilliant one! If he, Don Carlos, is connected to those heretics in Amsterdam, as the note accused him of being, he will be placed in a quandary — and we will sense it. And if not — if he is innocent, a faithful Catholic — then he will be happy to supply us with the information we seek. It will be a meeting of friends, all working together for the good of our people, our country, and our holy faith. A splendid idea, Octavio!"

"In that case," de Henrique pleaded, "let's be off at once. The situation is liable to change at any moment if we don't hurry."

"No." João Manuel shook his head decidedly. "I am already fatigued by all that has transpired today. I want to be refreshed and alert for this meeting."

His eyes met those of the other two, and a slow smile overspread his features.

"Tomorrow morning, gentlemen. Tomorrow morning, with the grace of our Lord and Savior, we will pay Don Carlos a visit."

It was dinner hour at the prison.

Alfonso Nunes, the young monk charged with distributing the meal to the prisoners, was in no hurry. As the anguished voices rose from the dungeon level, groaning for the meager rations allotted to them, Alfonso Nunes remained upstairs, pretending to busy himself with the preparation of food that had long since been standing ready.

Again and again, Alfonso's eyes strayed to the window looking out on the courtyard. His attention was riveted to another window across the way — that of *Padre* João Manuel's office. When he saw the curtains drawn, he grew tense with expectation. Minutes passed before he heard what he was waiting for: footsteps. He knew to whom they belonged. Rapidly, Alfonso loaded an enormous tray with many portions of food. At the moment when he judged the newcomer to be standing outside the kitchen door, he pushed it wide open.

He nearly collided with his illustrious visitor. De Henrique stepped back, startled.

"Oh!" Alfonso blurted. "I'm so sorry! I beg your pardon, Your Grace — I didn't know you were standing there."

De Henrique placed a soothing hand on the young monk's shoulder. "What you did not know, you can not be held accountable for. No apology is necessary. Go about your work, young man."

Alfonso began moving toward the stairs. Before he reached them, he wheeled around abruptly, as though remembering something he'd been meaning to ask.

"Excuse me, *Padre*, but can you tell me — who is supposed to be relieving me at midnight?"

De Henrique frowned. "I don't understand. Isn't there a roster of night guard duty?"

"Yes, yes, of course there is. But... But Enrico Caraval was taken sick today, and I don't know who will be replacing him."

De Henrique began to mentally review the list of available monks who might be recruited to do guard duty in Enrico's place that night. Alfonso broke into his thoughts.

"I am ready to remain on duty all night," he said eagerly, "so that I may have leave to visit my mother in her village tomorrow. I am not at all tired, *Padre*. I can do the job. Trust me!"

De Henrique smiled. Inclining his head, he gave his consent. "Let us try it and see. Now, do you remember? After you give out the dinners, and for the rest of the night, there is no need to go down into the dungeons. And naturally, conversing with the prisoners is absolutely forbidden. Is that understood?"

"Yes, sir. I am grateful to you, sir."

De Henrique departed for home. Alfonso made haste to distribute the food to the languishing prisoners, so pathetically broken in body and spirit. Then, once again, he prepared to wait.

Approximately one half-hour before midnight, Enrico Caraval appeared for duty.

"You can go back to bed, Enrico," Alfonso told him. "De Henrique asked me to tell you that you're exempt from guard duty tonight. I'm taking your place. Sweet dreams!"

Enrico was astonished.

"B-but — but why? What happened?"

"Nothing special. It's just that I'm doing double duty tonight so that I'll have a chance to visit my sick mother tomorrow. She lives alone in a village. So good night, Enrico."

Enrico hesitated. He sensed Alfonso's urgency to see him go. Why?

But he was not inclined to delve too deeply into the matter. The prospect of a good night's sleep in his own bed tipped the scales heavily against further investigation. If Alfonso wanted to do double duty, let him!

"Well, good night, Alfonso. Watch them well. Don't let any of them escape their little holes..." Chuckling, Enrico passed into the night.

Alfonso was left alone. In another hour or so, he would return to the dungeons. He had received instructions to speak with the prisoner Arnaldo Rodriguez tonight — that is, Raphael Chaim of Amsterdam — to prepare him for what lay ahead.

The orchard came slowly to life. As the morning sky lightened and Don Carlos, Rodriguez, and João Batista put on *tefillin*, the valley began to fill with farmers from the environs of Oporto. Slowly, one by one, individuals began trickling into the orchard.

They spaced their arrival at wide intervals so as to avoid arousing suspicion. Dr. Roberto Mochado, son of Oporto's mayor, Jaime Mochado, had decided to run the risk of bringing his infant son — already three months old — into the covenant of Abraham. The circumcision was scheduled for this very morning. The *mohel* was Don Carlos, newly arrived from Lisbon for this special occasion.

In due course the baby made his appearance, well wrapped in a small bundle of hay, such as might be found in any field. The good women of the community had provided wine and cakes as well. Rejoicing filled the orchard — but it was a quiet rejoicing, clothed in secrecy and shadowed with fear.

Neither Don Carlos nor the guests were inclined to linger. As soon as the baby arrived, the *bris milah* ceremony began. Roberto Mochado, the father, was much moved. He was keenly aware that discovery would result directly in a painful death at the stake. And yet, precisely because of the great danger, his heart was joyous. He had merited the fulfilling of this *mitzvah* not in peace and calm, as other Jewish communities did, but in fear and dread. In his eyes, this made the *mitzvah* doubly precious — and also, he fervently hoped, in the Eyes of Hashem.

He was already mentally planning his and his family's escape to Amsterdam. Once he was safely established there, he could permit himself even greater pride in his infant son, who'd been circumcised with such devotion and sacrifice. Yes, he thought — Oporto could find itself another doctor, the city was not dependent on him.

The celebrants crowded around the proud father with cries of "*Comprimentos! Comprimentos!* (Mazel tov! Mazel tov!)"

"I envy him," one guest murmured, as though to himself.

"Why do you envy him?" another, overhearing, asked.

The first guest turned. "I envy his courage! I envy his invincible faith. And I envy his spirit of self-sacrifice..."

"You're right," the other said soberly.

Roberto's father, mayor of the city, was not present in the orchard. He was a devout Catholic, with no idea in the world that his son had reverted secretly to the practice of Judaism. Roberto had discovered an old document in his father's house one day, describing the family's history. Emotionally, he'd read about previous generations, and of his father's grandfather, who had been forced into a Christian conversion. The revelation stirred him profoundly, and eventually led to his own return to Judaism. He had found his way to Rodriguez de Oliveiro, leader of the Marranos in Oporto. And now, here he stood at his own son's *bris milah*.

Don Carlos, too, was deeply moved. A great many things had occurred in the course of the past few days: his meeting with Reb Menashe ben Israel in Amsterdam; putting on *tefillin,* after all this time, in this secret orchard hidden deep in the hills; circumcising a Jewish child, and bringing *chumashim* and other holy books in Portuguese translation to the Marranos of Oporto...

Those guests who lived in the city were first to leave. They dispersed slowly, in ones and twos, gradually mingling with the field hands. Others returned to the city by more devious routes.

As for Don Carlos, he would await nightfall, and the carriage that would take him home to Lisbon.

9

lack night descended on the city of Oporto. As the fields emptied of farmers heading home to enjoy their well-earned rest, Don Carlos prepared to leave the secret orchard and embark on his return journey to Lisbon.

He was satisfied with his accomplishments. The holy books he had brought with him had reached their destination safely. He had been privileged, beyond all expectation, to put on *tefillin*. And he had circumcised a Jewish baby and brought him into the covenant of Abraham. If only he could have told Reb Menashe ben Israel about it! How the Amsterdam rabbi would have rejoiced at the news... But who knew when he would be able to visit Amsterdam again?

These thoughts accompanied Don Carlos as he approached the dense line of trees that marked the orchard's perimeter. Impatiently, he waited for the first faint noise from the fields beyond that would tell him his carriage was arriving. Many miles stretched ahead of him and he was anxious to return home, if possible, before daybreak. Two days away from home was long enough. What was happening at his house — in his city — with his fleet — at the royal palace? And most of all, how were the plans for Arnaldo Rodriguez's escape progressing?

His heart beat faster at the thought of the young Marranos in Lisbon who were his co-conspirators in the daring plot for Arnaldo's rescue. Witnessing Reb Menashe's anguish at the news of Arnaldo's imprisonment and death sentence, Don Carlos had made up his mind to save Arnaldo, come what may. And now, here he was in Oporto, many miles from the place where his young friends were weaving their plot under the very nose of the Inquisition. Was all proceeding according to plan? Had his friends succeeded in making contact with the secret Jews among the band of monks who served the Inquisition itself? Two days was a long time. He longed for home.

From afar, he caught the pounding of horses' hooves. Was it his carriage? Or... someone else? Hadn't Rodriguez told him that the enemy had already succeeded in finding this place once before?

He waited tensely. The noise of galloping hooves and turning wheels was louder now, and much closer. A moment later, Rodriguez himself burst into the orchard and signaled urgently for Don Carlos to follow him. They climbed into the coach, which instantly turned back into the fields. Making its way without benefit of a road, the carriage speedily bore them a good distance away from the city. Only then did it regain the high road leading south, for Lisbon.

Midnight had come and gone. Alfonso Nunes sat in the Inquisition guardroom and was afraid. According to his instructions, he was supposed to have gone down into the dungeon to give his message to Arnaldo Rodriguez. But he was afraid. He remembered what had happened only the night before to his friend Alfonso Alvares.

No. Before he went, he must find a way to protect himself from a sudden visit by de Henrique, Secretary of the Holy Office.

As he brooded in the deep silence of the Inquisition building, the germ of a cunning idea arose in Alfonso's brain. He stood, picked up the burning taper that stood on the table, and used it to light his way to the small kitchen that was used to prepare the prisoners' meager rations. Among the stores that lined the shelves, he found what he was seeking without difficulty: a flask of oil. This he took with him to the broad stairs that led out to the heavy iron gate fixed in the tall wall surrounding the building. If de

Henrique took it into his head to pay another nocturnal visit to the prison, it would be a little difficult for him to climb those steps, Alfonso Nunes thought, as he poured the contents of the bottle over the stairs.

He felt confident now. Should de Henrique arrive, he would surely slip on the oily stairs. He would cry out for help. And the only one capable of hearing or of helping would be himself, Alfonso Nunes. That helping hand might even earn him a promotion and a bonus! Alfonso smiled in the dark.

Moving quickly, he was soon standing on the lower level, outside Rodriguez's cell.

"Raphael Chaim," he whispered. "Raphael Chaim, do you hear me?"

Raphael Chaim was sound asleep.

Alfonso cast a hasty glance at the adjoining cells and at the stairs. The silence was total. He felt himself beginning to panic. More than anything, he wanted to complete his mission and return to the regions above.

"Raphael Chaim!" he called again, more urgently. "Wake up! I have a message for you. A message of hope! Tomorrow night we're getting you out of here. Raphael Chaim, do you hear me?"

Raphael Chaim didn't hear. "Maybe he's dead," Alfonso thought in alarm. It was not at all uncommon for prisoners to die in their cells of the injuries inflicted on them in the grisly torture sessions. Often their bodies were discovered only a day or two after the fact...

There was no choice. Alfonso quickly opened the cell door and slipped inside. Stooping over the recumbent form, he seized Rodriguez and began shaking him violently. The prisoner awoke in terror.

"Who are you? What do you want from me? Haven't you tortured me enough? Leave me alone!"

Alfonso placed a hand firmly over Rodriguez's mouth to stifle his cries. The prisoner lacked the strength to oppose him. He lay still.

"Ssh," he whispered. "I am a friend. One of Don Carlos' men. Tomorrow, Raphael Chaim, we are taking you out of here. The flagship *Vera Cruz* is waiting to set sail for Brazil. She will take you to Pernambuco, to Rav Yitzchak Abuhav, who is no doubt familiar to you from Amsterdam. He is the rabbi of Rispa now. Yes, yes, Rispa is under Dutch control, but our king has signed a treaty with Holland. Our ships can dock there now. Who knows, perhaps Heaven brought about the treaty so that we can get you there. Do you hear me?"

Rodriguez didn't react. But his eyes were wide open.

"Yes, Don Carlos himself will sail that ship. So wake up! They've sent me to prepare you for the trip, for your escape from prison. Try to sleep during the day tomorrow, so that you'll have strength for the night. Do you hear me?"

This time, Rodriguez nodded weakly. Alfonso continued whispering in his ear: "You must be strong. You will need all your strength tomorrow night, to walk at least until the front gate."

Alfonso reached into the folds of his brown monk's robe and removed a small flask. It had a pungent and not unpleasant aroma.

"Here, take this. It is a special mixture for strengthening the limbs. Drink a few drops every few hours. Let's hope that, with Hashem's help, you'll be strong enough by tomorrow night."

Arnaldo Rodriguez did not answer. He only extended a frail hand and took the flask. Alfonso was satisfied. Arnaldo — that is, Raphael Chaim — would cooperate tomorrow night. He would let them remove him from his cell.

He must hurry and leave now. But first, he turned to Arnaldo and whispered, "Be of good hope, Arnaldo. Pray to Hashem that our plans succeed. Trust in Him. May the part I play in helping snatch your life from the Inquisition's cruel grip atone for my sins — for the fact that, though I've returned to Judaism with all my heart, I still continue to live in the shadow of the false cross, and to serve the Inquisition."

Alfonso rose quickly from the floor, locked the cell door behind him, and climbed the steep narrow steps to the guardroom he had been instructed not to leave all night.

There was no one there, thank G-d. He had succeeded in giving Arnaldo Rodriguez the message entrusted to him, and no one had come along to discover what he was doing.

But, moving over to the table, his heart stood still. A Latin prayerbook and a lit taper had been there when he left. Now they were both gone.

10

Don Carlos didn't feel very well. The fast-moving coach tossed him to and fro, especially when passing through the bumpy, boulder-strewn fields on its way to the high road. He and Rodriguez were scarcely able to exchange a word as they clung to the sides of the swaying carriage and to the window frames.

Suddenly, without the slightest warning, the carriage stopped. It remained where it was, leaning precariously to the left. With considerable effort, the two passengers managed to get the door open and leap to the ground.

They found the agitated coachman attempting to calm his horses.

"What happened?" they demanded.

"The left wheel fell off, and the axle's broken. We're in trouble."

Rodriguez pursed his lips. "What do we do?"

The coachman's response was to jerk a thumb heavenward, as though to say, "It's all in His hands."

"But I must reach Lisbon as soon as possible!" Don Carlos said impatiently.

The coachman spread his hands. "There's nothing I can do, *Senhor*. We'll have to wait for daylight. Maybe a passing carriage will help us then."

"No! Impossible! I *must* get to Lisbon, come what may!"

Both the driver and Rodriguez stood silent. Don Carlos cried, "I'll ride the horse. Unharness him from the carriage!"

"Alone?" Rodriguez exclaimed. "Don Carlos, do you realize how dangerous that is? And what if anyone meets you on the way? What if you are recognized?" He lowered his voice. "Don Carlos, don't endanger us all to no purpose. You are too important to us to be allowed to fall into the Inquisition's hands. It's enough that Arnaldo Rodriguez has been captured."

Don Carlos hesitated. Then he heaved a deep sigh.

"I understand," he said quietly. "But what are we going to do?"

Alfonso Nunes was terrified. Who could have visited the guardroom in his absence? Who had taken the taper and his prayerbook? Was he under suspicion? Had anyone been following him? And what would become now of the daring plot to rescue Arnaldo Rodriguez?

He left the building. Full night blanketed the courtyard, the stairs, and the iron gate fixed in the center of the wall. Had someone managed to climb the steps without slipping on the oil?

He didn't know what to think. The matter remained a mystery — a frightening and unfathomable mystery.

Returning to the guardroom, he passed through to the kitchen, found another taper, and lit it. A second inspection of the small quarters showed no trace of any visitor. His fear intensified. What to do now? What to answer if difficult questions were put to him?

Shakily, Alfonso sat down and began mouthing a silent prayer to the Creator of the world. In his heart of hearts, he was already prepared for the worst...

The sky over the main road between Oporto and Lisbon began to grow light. A purple band colored the edges of the horizon, slowly pushing back the night. As Don Carlos examined the sky, he prayed for a miracle — a reverse of the miracle from the one wrought for Joshua at Givon. He wanted the night to last another few hours, to give him a chance to figure out a way to reach Lisbon before daybreak. They had been standing at the side of the road for two full hours, completely at a loss.

"*Rabbos machshavos b'lev ish,*" Don Carlos murmured aloud as he fought off a wave of despair, "*v'atzas Hashem hi sakum.*" *Man may entertain many notions, but only Hashem's plans endure.* He had hoped that this morning would find him aboard his flagship, supervising the preparations for the long voyage to Brazil. Instead here he stood, rooted to this spot at the side of the high road, utterly helpless.

"*Teshuas Hashem k'heref ayin!*" Rodriguez countered softly. "Hashem's salvation can come in the blink of an eye. We must stand up to our challenges. These are tests sent to strengthen us. They show us whether or not we truly love Hashem. This is a *nisayon*, Don Carlos — a test! Everything in the world is a test for us, in order to benefit us in the end. A test, Don Carlos!"

Don Carlos remained quiet for a considerable amount of time before finally replying, on a note of supplication, "I know."

Suddenly, out of the darkness that still held the road in its grip, came the clatter of hoof beats drawing an ornate carriage. It was approaching from the north, headed apparently for Lisbon.

"Need any help, *Senhors*?" called a voice from inside the coach.

"Yes!" Don Carlos replied quickly. "We have urgent business in Lisbon, and our axle's broken."

"One of you," the voice continued, "can climb up and sit beside the coachman. Another may sit inside."

"We are three, sir."

"Ah. Well, then, another may sit up beside the coachman."

"*Muito obrigado* (Thank you very much)!" Don Carlos cried.

Rodriguez tugged at Don Carlos's sleeve and whispered, "You sit inside the carriage. When full daylight comes you may be recognized if you are up front."

Accordingly, Don Carlos hastened to open the carriage door. He fairly flew up the two steps at its foot, and disappeared inside.

Three gentlemen were there, seated on the plush cushions. Don Carlos reeled and nearly fainted. With a monumental effort, he controlled himself.

One of his fellow passengers was the Archbishop of Lisbon, Ministro Rocha Azevedo. He and Don Carlos had been friends for years.

⇒⌒⇐

De Henrique was up before daybreak. He dressed in his long cassock and dropped a silver cross on a chain around his neck —a birthday present from Don Carlos some years before. Kneeling, he prayed that their mission to Don Carlos' house this morning be crowned with success.

He tasted a morsel of breakfast, then made his way to João Manuel's house. For all he knew, the Inquisition leader might have changed his mind overnight about the projected visit to Don Carlos' house. De Henrique was determined that the visit take place.

Lisbon lay wrapped in sleep. A pleasant breeze wafted at de Henrique as he strode through the quiet streets, and the early morning birdsong sounded sweetly in his ears. He felt fine. Don Carlos would be theirs soon. He just knew it.

⇒⌒⇐

Don Carlos shoved his hat well over his eyes and pretended to sleep. He was seated on the floor of the carriage, at the archbishop's feet. Had the archbishop recognized him? He fervently hoped not. Why should it enter the archbishop's head that this stranger to whom he had offered use of his coach, clad in the clothes of a simple farmer, was admiral of the Portuguese fleet? It would take a truly vivid imagination to come up with such a suspicion.

Still, Don Carlos was uneasy. He had spoken with the archbishop in explaining their plight on the road. Suppose the archbishop had recognized his voice? They were good friends, after all, and had enjoyed many conversations together!

The carriage rolled on toward Lisbon. The archbishop didn't take any notice of the guest at his feet. This worried Don Carlos: Why didn't the archbishop take a greater interest in the stranger he'd picked up on the way? Was it because he harbored suspicions about that stranger?

Or was it possible that the archbishop had simply dozed off? Don Carlos dared not tilt up his hat to take a peek and reassure himself. Anyway, that wasn't the important thing right now. His mind whirled with half-formed plans for leaving the coach without arousing suspicion. Even through his hat brim he could tell that the sun had fully risen on a new day. They were already very close to the capital. What to do?

As the carriage approached the city, Don Carlos stirred restlessly on the floor. There was no reaction from the seated passengers. His body doubled up, as though wracked by severe spasms. As the spasms grew in strength, he began to writhe and moan. The groans soon turned into screams of pain. The archbishop and the others sat up. "What is the matter, *Senhor*?" they asked in alarm.

They attempted to calm him, but the slightest touch brought on another cry of pain. The archbishop stuck his head out the window and ordered the coachman to halt the horses. "And tell this man's friends to come attend to him. *Senhores*, come quickly. Your friend is ill!"

Rodriguez jumped down from his lofty seat and quickly opened the carriage door. His eyes widened in astonishment and dismay at the sight of Don Carlos writhing on the floor.

"What's the matter? It is I, Rodriguez! What's wrong with you?"

Rodriguez reached down to lift the hat that covered Don Carlos' eyes, but Don Carlos recoiled, shrieking, "The light! The light!"

Rodriguez was bewildered. He glanced at the archbishop, who was no less dumbfounded.

"Perhaps," one of the other passengers ventured, "the daylight hurts his eyes."

The groans did not stop. Don Carlos began muttering incomprehensibly, as though in a feverish delirium. Rodriguez crouched beside him, his ear to Don Carlos' mouth.

"Tell me, what's the matter? What's wrong?"

"I... want... home. Take... me... home! Don't... you... understand... what... I'm... saying?"

Don Carlos seized Rodriguez's collar spasmodically and yanked his head close. Rodriguez heard him whisper, "Get me out of here. I'll explain later."

Rodriguez lifted his head and looked at the archbishop.

"Honored sir, my good friend here is apparently ill. I remember him suffering a similar attack some two years ago. He was very sick then. I'm worried."

The archbishop inclined his head compassionately. "I shall be happy to drive him home. Is his house far from here?"

"I thank you, sir. It was truly a miracle that brought you to our aid on the road. What would we have done if this attack had occurred with no help in sight?"

As he spoke, Rodriguez attempted to help Don Carlos to his feet.

"His house is right here," he continued, supporting Don Carlos down the steps to the street. "There, the second house from the corner... Thank you again, Your Grace, in my friend's name. All the best to you."

Rodriguez didn't wait for an answer. He closed the carriage door behind him and, together with the driver who'd accompanied them from Oporto, helped a still groaning Don Carlos walk toward the second house from the corner — which was definitely *not* his home...

The archbishop and his fellow travelers cast a curious glance at the trio as they staggered down the street.

"Do you have any explanation for what just happened?" one of the travelers asked presently.

"No," answered the archbishop, following a short pause. "No, I don't have an explanation. But all the same, there's something suspicious in the strange scene we just witnessed." He shook his head. "A very strange scene..."

11

appy and confident, de Henrique rapped on Father João Manuel's door. At the back of his mind was the uneasy awareness that he was being rather presumptuous in presenting himself at his superior's private residence, but his burning desire to act against Don Carlos outweighed his scruples.

Although the sun had hardly risen, João Manuel himself opened the door. *So, the lazybones woke early today,* de Henrique thought sardonically.

De Henrique bore no great respect for the Inquisition leader. In his opinion, the *padre's* investigations were never conducted as thoroughly as they ought to have been. He rarely displayed the necessary ardor in bringing to the stake those "new Christians" who were found to be secret Jews. It had occurred to de Henrique more than once that possibly — just possibly — João Manuel himself was a secret Jew! After all, hadn't they all seen how difficult it was to distinguish a devout Catholic from an imposter? Look at the finger of suspicion pointing now at Don Carlos, no less a personage than admiral of the entire Portuguese fleet!

"*Bom dia!* ("Good morning!")," João Manuel greeted him, smiling broadly.

"Bom dia, Senhor," replied de Henrique, skeptical of that smile. Where was João Manuel's customary impassivity this morning? Such a smile, particularly when offered to someone disturbing him this early in the day, was very strange.

"Come in, my friend." The head of the Inquisition invited the Secretary of the Holy Office into his home with a gracious gesture. De Henrique passed through the door. This startling display of friendliness disconcerted him. What lay behind those smiling eyes?

As they walked into a generously proportioned sitting room, João Manuel asked, "So, today we visit Don Carlos?"

His voice held a note that alerted every nerve de Henrique owned. Nervously he returned, "Of course. Is there any question?"

Padre João Manuel did not answer at once. He took a seat and motioned for his secretary to do the same. Finally, he said, "Perhaps it is better to postpone our visit. In the final analysis, we don't really have enough evidence to support the suspicion against him."

Hah! thought de Henrique angrily. The two sat facing each other across a small table. A young serving boy placed a heaping bowl of choice fruits in the center of the table, bowed reverently, and slipped away. De Henrique was rapidly losing patience.

"What do you mean, not enough evidence? We have the note, don't we? Besides, our own people have talked to the man who placed the note in my door!"

João Manuel smiled tiredly.

"Yes, I know. Still, it is not enough."

To cover his agitation, de Henrique took a fruit and began peeling it. He was furiously disappointed. Was his hope, the delicious anticipation he'd been harboring all morning, to be blown away like a puff of smoke? Throwing Don Carlos into prison would shake the regime at Lisbon to its very foundations. It would be the topic on everyone's lips and would enormously increase his, de Henrique's, stature in the city. Everyone knew that he was more active in his pursuit of heretics than was João Manuel. And most importantly, the Inquisition's prestige would increase. It would return to the glory of its former days... Why couldn't his lazy superior see that?

"Padre," said de Henrique slowly, weighing every word, "has something happened to change your mind? After all, the king is with us. What is there to be afraid of?"

Padre João Manuel deliberated for a moment before choosing a fruit from the basket. He chewed silently, staring at the basket all the while.

"No, no, no," he said at length. "Nothing has happened. What makes you think so?"

"It's just a feeling I have. I think it's a great pity, *Padre.* I've already prepared the delegation that is to accompany us — three respected priests and ten of the king's honor guard, along with an officer. Who knows? We may have to enter his house by force! And we may have to arrest him on the spot."

João Manuel glanced sharply at his secretary. "I don't understand."

"What is there not to understand? It's quite simple. I haven't wasted any time. I've prepared everything we'll need to make our investigation complete. If it should come to light that Don Carlos is, indeed, a secret Jew, we will arrest him immediately." He paused, then added thoughtfully, "That is, if we find him at home..."

Two emotions passed, fleeting but obvious, over João Manuel's features. The first was worry, and the second — fear.

"They came last night," he said softly, "and asked me to drop the investigation against Don Carlos."

De Henrique sat up in amazement. "Who came?"

"That I cannot tell you. But the request came from someone high up in the king's court."

"I don't understand! I spoke to the king's son, His Royal Highness Prince Alfonso, only this morning, when I asked him for a contingent of guards. *He* is certainly acting according to the king's wishes, isn't he?" When João Manuel did not reply, he persisted, "Don't you think so, *Padre?*"

João Manuel was in a quandary. His nocturnal visitor had been none other than Prince Alfonso himself, asking him to halt the investigation at once. Here was a strange situation. What was happening at the king's residence? When, he wondered, had the prince truly been acting at the king's behest — when he'd helped de Henrique, or when he brought his warning to him, João Manuel, last night?

What devious plots were unfolding in the royal court?

De Henrique pushed back his chair and began pacing through the wide room. His host watched him with a mixture of curiosity and apprehension. João Manuel harbored a definite — if unacknowledged — fear of his secretary...

Suddenly, de Henrique came to a full stop. Stepping closer to João Manuel, he said quietly but distinctly, "*Padre*, I don't know what you'll decide. As for me, in one hour's time I intend to gather my men and proceed as planned — to Don Carlos' house."

He moved again, until he was very close to João Manuel indeed. The other, meanwhile, had risen to his feet and stood facing him. De Henrique ended, "Whether or not you accompany us, *Padre*."

Lifting the hem of his robe, he walked rapidly to the door and opened it. Just before he left, he turned his head and said over his shoulder, "That young monk we caught wandering around the dungeons near the prisoners' cells has not yet confessed. He underwent a series of excruciating torture sessions yesterday, but is still not talking. But he will. Oh, yes, he will! He is hiding something, *Padre*. Both of us know full well that he will talk..." Laughing evilly, de Henrique added, "Just as Don Carlos will talk. We will break him until he confesses to his link with the Jews in Amsterdam. He will live to rue his betrayal of the one true faith, and of the king's trust. Our king's, and our people's!"

He turned back to the door.

"De Henrique. My friend." João Manuel spoke the words even as he began to move forward. "I am coming with you."

De Henrique bestowed a smile on his superior as he waited for him to catch up. A smug elation arose in him. He had brought the head of the Inquisition to his knees.

12

Before daybreak, Alfonso Nunes made haste to clean the oil from the stairs. He filled a bucket with sand, which he poured all over the slick steps. When the oil had been absorbed, he filled another bucket with water and washed the sand away. He hoped that the stairs would completely dry before morning, along with every trace of what he'd done in the night. He hurried back to the guard-room and pushed open the door.

His heart shriveled with terror.

Two people awaited him inside. One was a middle-aged priest, severe of countenance, with a bald pate that gleamed in the sun's first rays. The other was much younger, a monk with a youthful face.

Alfonso Nunes recognized them both, although he did not know them by name. Though he had never spoken to either man, he had glimpsed them often, walking the Inquisition corridors. He had no idea what positions they held. The older man had Alfonso's Latin prayerbook; the youth held the ta-per. It took every ounce of willpower to keep his panic from showing.

The newcomers did not say a word. They merely gazed at him — as though, Alfonso thought with rising hysteria, they were looking for a crack, a single sign of fear in his face...

Still without a word, the older priest extended the prayerbook. Alfonso hesitated, then took it from him. The youth placed the taper on the table — in exactly the same spot, Alfonso noted, that it had occupied when Alfonso had left the room to descend to the dungeons.

The older man gestured roughly for Alfonso to be seated. He and his companion remained on their feet, both watching his every move with penetrating stares. Alfonso read open threat in their eyes.

"Yes, my young friend," the older priest spoke at last. "Now you know who took your prayerbook when you decided to go for a stroll to sniff the fresh air of the dungeons!"

He lapsed into an ominous silence. With growing trepidation, Alfonso waited.

He didn't have to wait long. The priest continued, "You were not careful enough, my young friend. You thought that de Henrique was moved by your willingness to serve guard duty all through the night. It would be well worth your while to act more circumspectly when dealing with a man of the world such as de Henrique. Do you understand?!"

Alfonso bobbed his head in a single jerky acquiescence. His first mistake, he thought in dismay.

"Your request seemed very odd to de Henrique," the priest continued. "In a word, he grew suspicious, though he had no idea exactly what to suspect. But remember —" his tone grew silky with overt menace — "that just last night, another Alfonso was arrested here. Isn't that so, *Alfonso*? He also had an unaccountable yearning to take a stroll among the prisoners' cells, just when they need their rest in order to face another round of 'pleasures' next morning — in the torture room. That will explain why de Henrique was troubled by your request, and why he asked us to stay behind this night to keep an eye on you."

Alfonso knew when he was beaten. He had already made his peace with his bitter fate. He would be no different from the many other human sacrifices exacted by the accursed Inquisition. It occurred to him suddenly how very young he was — only 25. Too young to die...

"Really," said the younger monk, "your idea of spilling oil on the stairs was brilliant. Still, no matter how clever a person is, it's impossible to predict everything that might happen. It never occurred to you, did it, that in one of the rooms overlooking the courtyard were two of de Henrique's watchdogs? A valuable lesson, my friend — a lesson to last a lifetime!"

Alfonso Nunes nodded numbly. The fear had left his eyes, replaced by resignation. He had no need for lessons "to last a lifetime." At a loss as to what to do, he sat mute.

The older monk took up the ball again. "What were you looking for down there, my dear Alfonso?"

His voice was soft and pleasant. Even through the fog that enclosed him, Alfonso found the other's hypocrisy unbearable. Though he knew himself doomed — his fate sealed — he was determined not to disclose his secret. He would die without revealing the reason for his trip to the dungeon. In that way, perhaps his death would serve as atonement for his sins, and especially for the fact that he did not flee to Amsterdam when he'd had the chance.

They were patient, those two Inquisitors. Outside, it was already broad daylight. From the depths arose the first anguish-filled cries of the awakening prisoners. Some pleaded for water to drink, while others cursed the new day, a day that would bring nothing but new tortures and fresh suffering.

"*Tell me what you were looking for!*" thundered the priest.

Alfonso muttered, "Nothing. I just went down there."

Both priests burst into derisive laughter. "No one 'just' goes down into the dungeons. Just to feast your eyes on those miserable human beings who profane our Savior's name?" The priest paused. "Well, Alfonso? What took you down there?"

Slowly, with infinite menace, the monks advanced on Alfonso. The older one laid heavy hands on Alfonso's shoulders. The hands were inches away from his throat. Had this priest, Alfonso wondered fearfully, ever throttled an unfortunate prisoner in the course of an interrogation? The mere thought made it difficult for him to breathe.

"I repeat, Your Grace, I just went down. A foolish thing to do, I know — but people often do foolish things. "

The older priest gazed at Alfonso intently. *Don't be afraid,* Alfonso told himself. *Don't be afraid.* He concentrated on returning the priest's look, stare for stare. *You are a Jew!* cried a small voice within. *Show him that a Jew*

— *even a Jew who has been captured and is on his way to die — is stronger than the enemy that acts against him.*

"And I'm telling you," the priest continued, "that you went down to the dungeon to obey some instructions you were given. We would very much like to know what those instructions were, and who sent you!"

The thick hands began to increase their pressure on Alfonso's shoulders.

The thought of the torture and pain in wait for him were more frightening than the pain itself. At that moment Alfonso was afraid. Terribly afraid.

He roused himself to respond forcefully, with confidence. He felt a sudden surge of new strength.

"That is not true, Your Grace. There were no such instructions. I have never betrayed the church. Have compassion, honored sir."

The two priests exchanged a meaningful glance. The older one dropped his hands from Alfonso's shoulders, straightened up, and said, "You are lucky, my friend. When de Henrique ordered me to watch your movements through the night, he permitted me to choose my partner. As you can see, I chose my young friend here, Faria Lima."

Alfonso's eyes were drawn to those of the young monk, who inclined his head slightly in his direction. Alfonso sensed that the other was laughing inwardly. He was bewildered by this strange session, with this pair of interrogators who told him tales and offered words of advice.

"You wanted to outsmart us by pouring oil on the stairs. But de Henrique outsmarted you and left us behind here in the building, to dog your steps..."

The priest breathed deeply. When he spoke next, there was a new note of tension in his voice.

"And we — that is, I, Alvarez Cabral and my young friend, Faria Lima — have outsmarted de Henrique... Be calm, Alfonso. We are your brothers. We, too, secretly keep the laws of the Torah. We are faithful to what we have learned from our teacher, Arnaldo Rodriguez — that is, Raphael Chaim! It was him you went to see down there, wasn't it?"

Alfonso didn't answer. The older man extended a hand and a warm smile. But Alfonso didn't shake that hand. He was afraid of a trap. It was possible that the Inquisition had uncovered some details of the plan to squirrel away Rodriguez and were attempting by every means to learn the rest. If they could not learn it through fear and torture, they would try cajoling and trickery.

"Alfonso — beware!" whispered the small voice inside.

The priests sensed that Alfonso did not believe them. The fear and the tension one could see in his eyes. Stooping, the younger monk said softly in Alfonso's ear, "*Shema Yisrael, Hashem Elokenu, Hashem Echad.*"

Alfonso did not move a muscle. It was true that this verse served as an identifying signal for Marranos. True, the monk had pronounced Hashem's Name the way the Marranos did in their prayers. Walking through the streets of Lisbon, or crowded into the city square with a cheering throng watching a "heretic" being tied to the stake because he had admitted to observing the Sabbath or fasting on Yom Kippur, one might hear his neighbor whisper those words to himself, "*Shema Yisrael,*" and know that he was a Marrano, that he was a brother, that he longed for someone of his own kind to be close to at this difficult moment. Secret Jews from every walk of life used this signal: writers, artists, government officials, military officers, even monks in their monasteries.

The average Catholic naturally attached no significance to the phrase. It never occurred to him that there was any meaning behind those whispered words; and so, he did not react to them. But a Jew who practiced his faith in secret was moved to his core by that whisper, and would withdraw to a quiet corner to converse with his fellow sufferer, to exchange news and pursue friendship, so vital in the lonely and difficult world of the secret Jews in Lisbon.

But Alfonso did not react. Who knew whether these two were laying a snare for him? The Inquisition's agents were known not only for their outstanding cruelty, but also for their cunning. He steeled himself and pretended not to understand.

The morning sun thrust its golden light into the room. Stirrings of life were beginning to sound in the corridors. More than one of those who passed the guardroom glanced inside, curious, at the trio and their strange interrogation.

The older monk decided to conclude matters.

"A pity. A great pity, Alfonso, that you do not believe us. We did not reveal ourselves to you at once because we wanted to see how strong you are under interrogation. Don't worry, we will leave you alone now. Of course, we will not reveal a thing to de Henrique. We will tell him that all went routinely last night, and that you stood guard faithfully all through your watch."

The elder priest clapped Alfonso's shoulder with seeming affection. Again, Alfonso did not react.

But when the pair had left the room, his shoulders began to heave with silent sobs.

13

Emerging from his house on de Henrique's heels, *Padre* João Manuel was surprised to find three carriages lined up at the curb. They were harnessed to splendid horses with gleaming manes and coats. In the last two carriages sat aristocratic monks, three to a coach.

The delegation de Henrique had prepared was ready and waiting.

João Manuel did not always relish his secretary's efficiency. De Henrique's burning zeal, especially in his pursuit of "new Christians" (as the Marranos were popularly known), had been the cause of unpleasantness in the past. "What does he hope to prove by all this?" he fumed inwardly. "That he is more loyal than I to the church, to our faith, to the king and the pope?"

However, he was astute enough to know that he had no choice but to follow de Henrique's lead now. To hold back, to counsel caution and less speed, would arouse suspicion about his own motives. Why, he — João Manuel himself! — might even be accused of being... He shook his head firmly. That possibility didn't bear thinking about.

De Henrique's confident voice reached him, in the tone of a command: "*Padre*, we must get in now." He nodded at the first carriage.

João Manuel acquiesced without a word. Gathering the skirts of his cassock, he climbed into the waiting carriage. Just as he seated himself, a troop of soldiers of the Royal Guard came marching down the street in their direction. João Manuel threw a questioning glance at his secretary.

"It's nothing, *Padre*," de Henrique assured him. "The king has sent us an escort, as I requested. If our entrance to Don Carlos' house is barred, we may need these men to force an entry. I'm sure you'll agree that it would be unseemly for men of the church to take such an action, publicly at any rate. That is the army's job. So here they are."

De Henrique climbed into the carriage, closed the door after him, and waved at the coachman. Cracking his whip over the horses' backs, the coachman set out. He did not inquire about their destination; apparently, he already knew. The horses trotted sure-footedly along, apparently also in the know...

The Inquisition leader and his secretary sat shoulder to shoulder, but there was a coolness between them. João Manuel was tense with expectation. Where would this adventure lead him? The memory of Prince Alfonso as he'd appeared in his late-night visit rose up in the priest's mind:

"*Padre*," the prince had said, "I must order you to drop the investigation into Don Carlos immediately."

"Why?"

"The purity of our holy faith is very, very important to the royal family, and to my revered father, His Majesty, the king. In fact, it is just as important to us as it is to you, men of the church and the Holy Inquisition. We respect and esteem the work you perform so selflessly, to cleanse our camp of heretics and free it of danger to all devout Catholics." Here the prince had paused before adding, with heavy emphasis, "But we very much require the services of Don Carlos."

João Manuel's face had been lit with aristocratic piety as he replied, "Neither a government nor a nation stands on the shoulders of a single individual. Everyone has his replacement. But not our holy faith!"

The prince was undeterred. "I understand, *Padre*. But His Majesty, the king, needs this particular man at this time. He is a military leader without peer. Under his command our fleet has managed to free our country's merchant vessels from the threat of pirates. Don't you know the terrible damage those pirates have wrought on our economy? The treaty Don Carlos signed with Holland has put the port of Amsterdam off-limits to them as a refuge."

"Yes," answered João Manuel. "I do understand. I both understand and appreciate this important achievement. But Don Carlos did other 'important" things in Amsterdam as well. Things that may prove harmful to our regime. Doesn't His Highness, the prince, realize that any harm to our Catholic faith and its dominion over the people injures the royal family as well? I am speaking here of injury that has nothing to do with sea pirates.

"Your Highness knows that the shadow of suspicion has fallen on Don Carlos. It seems that he has been aiding and abetting secret Jews. Lisbon is full of them!" He peered at the prince. "Doesn't it bother His Royal Highness to know that the admiral of the fleet and the king's trusted adviser may be operating on instructions from the heretics' rabbi in Amsterdam, Menashe ben Israel?"

By the light of the flickering taper João Manuel read anger in the other's face. The prince maintained his composure with difficulty.

"It is possible," Prince Alfonso said after a prolonged silence. "It is definitely possible that Don Carlos did do what you suspect him of doing. But you must admit, *Padre* — it is still only suspicion. You are not sure. Has it not crossed your mind that Don Carlos' enemies at court may have laid a trap for him? Is this not a reasonable assumption? He has many enemies who resent his friendship with my father, the king. Will you lightly instigate an action that may harm the king himself? Think well, *Padre!*"

João Manuel sensed the implied threat in the prince's last words. It frightened him. The Inquisition's strength was dependent on the goodwill of the king and his court. He was loath to diminish that strength.

And yet, he answered sharply, "Is a flesh-and-blood monarchy more important in the king's eyes, and in yours, Your Highness, than the purity and sanctity of our faith?"

As he uttered this impassioned query, João Manuel grasped and raised the silver cross he wore on a chain around his neck. The eyes of the two powerful men locked in fiery, silent combat.

Presently, in a calmer tone, João Manuel remarked, "All we wish to do is to ask Don Carlos a few questions. We will be the first to rejoice if he emerges innocent of the charges against him."

Prince Alfonso rose abruptly. He threw a cold glance at João Manuel — still peacefully seated — and snapped, "I strongly advise the Holy Office to desist from this investigation. You do not know where it might lead you, *Padre*. You have no idea what a difficult situation de Henrique is urging upon you."

With that, the prince strode briskly to the door and opened it. But before he passed through, he added the chilling postscript: "His Majesty, the king, himself sent me here tonight."

The door slammed shut behind him. *Padre* João Manuel heard the snorting and pawing of the prince's horse as he sprang aboard, and then the receding sound of hooves galloping into the distance. In seconds, the sound was swallowed by the night that covered Lisbon.

The carriages were nearing Don Carlos' house. There was, João Manuel realized, no other option open to him now. The visit would take place. The investigation would continue. He must prepare himself for any outcome, for all consequences that might accrue to him from the king and his son.

But one sentence echoed in his mind and gave him no peace. Again and again he heard Prince Alfonso voice: *"You have no idea what a difficult situation de Henrique is urging upon you."*

What had the prince meant by that?

In truth, João Manuel knew very well what he had meant. But there was no time to think of that now. The carriages had pulled up in front of Don Carlos' house.

De Henrique was first to leap to the ground, with the energy of a young boy. He helped his superior descend and then arranged the rest of the entourage to suit him. João Manuel gazed upon the graceful facade behind the tall gate. He had visited this stately home many times: He and Don Carlos were friends. This fact made the present situation even more difficult for him.

De Henrique rang the bell that hung above the gate.

No one answered. The gate remained firmly closed.

He waited a moment, then rang again. Still no reaction from inside the house. He rang the bell longer this time. It seemed to him that someone lifted the curtain at the window a fraction, peeked out for an instant, then dropped it again.

"Did you see that?" de Henrique cried triumphantly. "Someone *is* home!"

"No, we didn't notice anything," answered two of the accompanying monks.

De Henrique cut them off impatiently. "There, on the left — didn't you see someone lift the curtain and then drop it?"

"Maybe..." the monks acknowledged reluctantly. Disagreeing with the powerful de Henrique was unhealthy. De Henrique seized the rope and yanked it again and again. A series of long, loud peals erupted from the bell. From under lowered lids the monks watched this display of undignified behavior on the part of the Holy Office's secretary.

The prolonged pealing had its effect. A door opened and a young maid appeared in the doorway. She was wide eyed and shaken.

"What do the honored gentlemen want?"

De Henrique was about to answer, when he suddenly recalled the presence of his superior. Stepping back ungracefully, he passed the privilege of speaking to João Manuel, who said, "We have come on behalf of the Inquisition. We would like to speak urgently with *Senhor* Don Carlos Carneiro."

"He is not home!" blurted the maid, and closed the door in one lightning swift motion.

14

That was too much. De Henrique shook with fury. The gall of that maid, slamming the door in the faces of such a delegation! Without bothering to consult Father João Manuel, he turned to the soldiers waiting a short distance away.

"Men of the king's guard!" he cried. "Your hour has come! I have here an order from His Majesty, ordering you to obey the Holy Inquisition. And the Inquisition commands you now to break down this door! We must not allow such a slight to our faith and our church to pass unanswered!"

What happened next was totally unexpected. João Manuel strode forward and placed himself between de Henrique and the soldiers. Trembling with rage, he declared in ringing tones, "*I* am the head of the Inquisition! I am the one who decides! You have not received the command from *me* to break into this house, home of Don Carlos Carneiro, admiral of the fleet!"

Casting upon his secretary a glance of withering contempt, João Manuel added bitingly, "Not every wild and undisciplined action will be sanctioned here. Do you understand?"

De Henrique was thunderstruck. This side of João Manuel was new to him. The rest of the delegation stood stiffly, averting their eyes from the spectacle of their superiors squabbling in the middle of a Lisbon street — and in front of a troop of royal soldiers.

The secretary clenched his fists. This was no time to engage in battle with the head of the Inquisition. The day would come when he would exact his vengeance for this insult! But not yet. Not yet. This was not the moment.

He stepped back and said, "I beg Your Grace's pardon. You are right. Please, you resume command of this operation to uncover the truth about Don Carlos." He bowed slightly. "*Padre.*"

João Manuel recognized the disrespect behind de Henrique's facade. "Yes, my friend," he snapped. "Many things would look different in our Inquisition today were I permitted to deal with them. Many things... including a number of innocent unfortunates whose deaths might have been averted. You know full well what I'm referring to, don't you, friend secretary?"

De Henrique burst out, "But *Padre*, this is not —"

Before he could complete the sentence, a pair of monks interposed between them: "Please, Your Graces! We are undermining our mission — and our position. Tomorrow we will be the laughingstock of Lisbon. Right now we must investigate Don Carlos' house, not distract ourselves with other matters. Please, sirs, a little Christian patience and cooperation..."

Neither João Manuel nor de Henrique were calmed by this plea. Reluctantly, João Manuel grasped the bell rope and yanked it hard. The bell clanged, harsh in the morning stillness.

As before, no one answered its summons. The door remained firmly closed. No face peeked through the window curtains. The house was wrapped in utter silence.

Father João Manuel beckoned to the officer in charge of the king's guard. "Please make the following announcement. If the door is not opened to us within a very short time, it will be broken down!"

The officer nodded once, then approached the gate and shouted at the top of his lungs: "Hear this, household of Don Carlos Carneiro! Hear the king's order and the order of the Holy Inquisition. You are to open the door immediately to the exalted delegation that desires to enter!"

There was no answer forthcoming from the house.

"Why aren't they answering?" one of the delegation asked with some agitation.

De Henrique, in better control of himself now, answered with quiet confidence, "You heard what the maid said — he's not home. Our own spies received the same information two days ago. And yet, we know that he has not left the house through this gate. Does the house have another exit that we don't know about? This must be investigated! Or perhaps he is at home, but for some reason is reluctant to see anyone? We don't know, but one thing is certain. There is something mysterious here. Something very suspicious..."

João Manuel waited a few moments. Then he turned and signaled to the soldiers. The mounted troops leaped off their horses and three of them approached the door with battering equipment.

"Slowly," cautioned João Manuel. "Bang on the door a few times and then stop. Perhaps those inside will see that we mean business and will stop being so strangely obstinate."

The soldiers advanced to their task. The noise of their pounding reverberated in the street. Monks and soldiers alike waited to see the result.

The blows elicited a reaction. The front door swung open to reveal Dona Beatriz, Don Carlos' wife. She was ashen and shaken.

"Haven't you been told that Don Carlos is away from home? Please come back tomorrow or the next day. He will be back then, and will receive you with the courtesy you deserve. But now leave us, please!"

Even those standing at a distance could see the tears in the lady's eyes, and all could hear the distress in her voice.

"Yes, *Senhora*," João Manuel said. "However, even if your husband is not at home, please allow us to enter. We would like to ask you a few questions. For example, where is Don Carlos now? What business engages him apart from his fleet duties?" He paused. "May we?"

"No, no, it is better not," Dona Beatriz answered with a visible agitation that deepened the delegation's suspicions. "*Padre*, I'd expect more patience and consideration from a man of the church like yourself. Come back tomorrow. He will be back then!"

"Where did he go?"

Dona Beatriz shrugged. "He went off in his coach..."

De Henrique broke in impatiently. "But we must enter the house. We have authority to do this — if not with your consent, then by force!"

"But why?" she pleaded. "What have we done?"

Smiling wickedly, de Henrique said, "That is exactly what the church wishes to find out."

He didn't wait for an answer. There was no holding him back at this point. He waved at the guardsmen, who fell furiously upon the gate. In minutes, they had uprooted it.

Dona Beatriz shrieked once, then hurriedly closed the door. The honored delegation ran up to the door just as it slammed shut.

"Dona Beatriz! Dona Beatriz!" João Manuel called. "We are already at the door. Don't force us to break it down!"

Suddenly, the door was flung wide open. Dona Beatriz stood in the doorway, trembling with rage. Pride and scorn flashed from her eyes in place of her former fear.

"Shame on you!" she cried. "Shame on what you have done! You have profaned your calling and stained the church you profess to represent. What is this supposed to mean, *Padre*? The king is my husband's friend!"

"Please," João Manuel said placatingly, "Let us come in and I'll explain everything."

The delegation thrust itself through the door, ignoring Dona Beatriz's angry expostulations. "This is not right! My husband is not at home. This is a private residence!"

"*Bom dia*," called a new voice — a familiar one — from the house's interior. Everyone, including Dona Beatriz, turned to the figure standing at the other end of the long room.

Don Carlos stood there, facing them.

He was wearing his dress whites and looked every inch the admiral he was. With measured steps he approached the group.

"Beatriz," he said, "What is all this noise at the door? Let my friend come in." To the delegation he spread his hands and said, "What an exalted group of visitors! How have I earned this honor? If my friend, *Padre* João Manuel, has paid me a visit at the head of such a delegation, there must be grave matters to be discussed. And I see my friend Paulo de Henrique, too. How are you? Is it in my honor that you wear the silver cross I gave you on Saint Christopher's Day?"

Don Carlos led his flustered guests to an arrangement of sofas in a corner of the room. Drawing the curtains to let in the warm Portuguese sun, he gestured for his guests to be seated.

Dona Beatriz was in shock. She stood as if paralyzed in the doorway. It was a miracle, a miracle from Heaven, her husband appearing at that moment. But panic gripped her: What would the Inquisition men think? She had just been telling them that Don Carlos was not home. Would they grow more suspicious than ever? Everyone seemed to be under suspicion in Lisbon these days. Everyone was afraid of his neighbor, on the lookout for secret Jews. She stood motionless, at a loss as to how to proceed.

Don Carlos took note of her distress. He told her lovingly, "Please bring some fruit and sweetmeats for our guests, Beatriz."

The delegation watched her go. Something, they thought, was not right here. Why had Dona Beatriz insisted that her husband was not home? Why had she resisted their entrance so forcefully? What was she afraid of? What was she hiding? What were *they* hiding?

De Henrique gritted his teeth. "I'll be back," he vowed silently. "Yes, I'll be back! I must learn what is really happening here. I will uncover Don Carlos' secret and publicly shame him — Don Carlos, who may be a friend of mine, but has a much closer relationship with *Padre* João Manuel."

"Well, *Padre*, my friend?" Don Carlos said, facing the delegation's leader. "What brings you to my house at such an hour?"

"Weren't you home, Don Carlos?" João Manuel asked silkily.

"Why do you ask?"

"Your wife, Dona Beatriz, insisted that you weren't home — that you'd traveled away and would be back tomorrow."

Don Carlos threw back his head and laughed. In the course of his life as a Marrano he had schooled himself to dominate his emotions and never let them reveal what was in his heart.

"That's what she said? Interesting. A good woman, my wife. And a loyal one. I asked her to see that I wasn't disturbed for a few days while I rested up after my voyage to Amsterdam and before the one to Brazil. I wanted absolute peace and quiet. That's why she decided to tell all visitors that I wasn't home." He shook his head, smiling. "Yes, a good woman."

De Henrique didn't believe him. João Manuel, also, was not certain that he was hearing the whole truth.

"But what brings you to my house this morning, gentlemen?" Don Carlos asked.

João Manuel cleared his throat. "You've just returned from Amsterdam, Don Carlos."

"True."

"Well, we've been following the heretical activities of one Menashe ben Israel for some time now. We know that he tries to influence Lisbon's 'new Christians' to return to Judaism, and we wished to consult with you. We want to hear your views on this rabbi, and on Amsterdam. Is it true that that city is filled with Portuguese citizens who've fled the mercy of our Holy Inquisition?" He leaned forward. "Don Carlos, do you know that man?"

Leaning back again, he added with casual cunning, "Perhaps you have even met him. We hear that he's close to government leaders there. They have a great respect for him. Is it true?"

"True," Don Carlos answered dryly. "He's a special favorite of Amsterdam's intellectual elite. And not only in Amsterdam. The rabbi is also admired in Denmark, Sweden, France, and Italy."

"But he is a heretic — a destroyer of our faith!" de Henrique exploded.

"True," Don Carlos said again. "And yet, those countries respect him. What can we do? Not everybody is as sensitive to our faith as you are."

De Henrique subsided into silence, nursing dreams of vengeance.

"Don Carlos," resumed João Manuel, "perhaps you can advise us as to the best way to combat this man and his influence on the 'new Christians.'

Have you by any chance heard of individuals from Lisbon who come to Amsterdam to meet him or his messengers? These details are very important to us, Don Carlos."

His host smiled broadly, despite his unease. It was not difficult to sense the heavy suspicion in the air. Who could tell what they might know about him or his friends?

"Certainly, I'll be glad to help," he said enthusiastically. "What's more, I was planning to do it even before you asked, *Padre*. On my return from Amsterdam, I resolved to do everything I can to fight the fugitives from Portugal who've embrace their old faith. I deplore the desecration this brings to our church. While it's not my job — I'm a military man — as a devout Christian I must do what I can to promote our holy faith.

"I decided to write down everything I know about Amsterdam. Details about Menashe ben Israel, names of people who escaped our country for Amsterdam, along with ideas for stemming the tide of fugitives. But *Padre*, the project will demand a great deal of my time. I promise you faithfully that I'll use the days of our voyage to Brazil and back to write it all down. Is that all right, *Padre*?" He smiled. "For this kind of request, such a large delegation was really unnecessary!"

Don Carlos was afraid to stop speaking, lest he be bombarded with unwanted questions. There was a smell of danger in the room. Something had happened, but he couldn't guess what it was.

Before João Manuel could speak, Don Carlos glanced at the door and called, "Oh, *bem vindo* (welcome), Pedro!"

Every head turned. At the door stood a young officer. He bowed deeply to the churchmen.

"This is Pedro Alvares," Don Carlos introduced, "my personal secretary, who accompanied me to Amsterdam. He will also be able to tell you what Menashe ben Israel has been up to."

Pedro Alvares smiled happily. The smile pierced Don Carlos' heart. "Pedro, my brother's son," he thought in anguish. "When will I be able to make known to you who you really are?"

Abruptly, he rose to his feet as a sign that the meeting was over. "Pedro Alvares has come to escort me to the harbor. There is still a great deal of work to be done to prepare the ships for our voyage to Brazil. I must hurry away now, *Padre*, forgive me. I guarantee that I will do what you've requested."

The delegation rose to its feet. De Henrique ground his teeth in frustration, but there was not much he could do now. His only hope had lain in the fact that Don Carlos was away from home.

João Manuel was aware of being insulted. He permitted Don Carlos to escort him to the door, where his host said, "Once again, I beg your forgiveness, *Padre*. But my work is waiting for me. His Majesty, the king, has high hopes for this trip to Brazil..."

Outside, near the uprooted gate, João Manuel turned on de Henrique. "Your unruliness today has tarnished our Inquisition's good name!"

Without another word, João Manuel climbed into one of the waiting carriages and motioned to the driver to depart. It was clear that he had no wish to ride back to Inquisition headquarters in de Henrique's company.

15

on Carlos closed the front door and returned to Pedro Alvares. Though inwardly in a turmoil, his face wore a mask of impassivity. He was very much afraid of his young aide, a devout Catholic. Pedro mustn't guess how he felt.

"We are in the final stages of preparation for the journey, sir," Pedro told his admiral. "In approximately one hour, as you instructed, officers from all ships will be meeting on the *Vera Cruz* to report on their state of readiness."

"Yes, of course," Don Carlos replied absently. His mind was on his recent guests. What had João Manuel and de Henrique actually wanted from him this morning?

Dona Beatriz entered the room.

"Carlos," she called urgently, "please come into the kitchen for a moment."

He didn't like the look on her face. "Has something happened?"

"Nothing in particular. But I want to show you something." She turned to Pedro Alvares. "Will you excuse us, Pedro?"

Pedro smiled politely and inclined his head. Don Carlos followed his wife out of the room and down a passage to the kitchen. Dona Beatriz closed the door, whirled around to face her husband, and said trembling and without preamble, "Carlos, I'm afraid. Let's get out of here!"

Don Carlos attempted to calm her. "There's nothing to be afraid of, my wife. My standing with the king is strong. He needs me."

"There is no one stronger than those accursed churchmen," she replied with quiet intensity. "They have the power to bend anyone to their will — even the king. You know it's true, Carlos!"

"Yes, but still —"

"You didn't see their faces when they asked me to let them into the house. If you did, you'd share my fear now. I tell you with my woman's intuition — they know something about you. I don't know what it is, but they have some suspicious information against you."

Carlos sighed deeply. He struggled to maintain his equilibrium. When he spoke to his wife, his tone was even and patient. "I will visit the king today to discuss this matter with him. Perhaps I'll also pay a call on João Manuel and ask for an explanation." He shook his head grimly. "I didn't like the look of de Henrique this morning."

"Carlos, listen to me. They know you were away from home these past two days. They're suspicious."

"But I explained to them that I was resting up from the voyage."

"And I'm telling you that they didn't believe you!" She clasped her hands. "Their spies are everywhere. Could someone have seen you in Amsterdam, going into Rav Menashe ben Israel's house?" When her husband didn't answer, she cried softly, "Carlos, I'm afraid! Let's escape — now! Leave your position and your honor behind, all the false glory the king has heaped on you! Let's run to Amsterdam and live openly as Jews as long as we're granted life. That will be true glory, and all the honor we really need."

Don Carlos stood as one petrified. His wife's suggestion that he'd been shadowed in Amsterdam came with all the force of a thunderbolt. He suddenly recalled the stranger who had rapped on the rabbi's gate while he was in the house. He had paid the incident little heed at the time, but it seemed sinister now. The stranger had used the arranged number of knocks — the signal he'd agreed upon with Rav Menashe. Had that been nothing but coincidence?

Rav Menashe's serving boy, he remembered, had mentioned that the stranger asked about his, Don Carlos', identity — in Portuguese. Another coincidence? Or the long arm of the Inquisition?

Terror seeped through his bones to lodge at last in his heart. Had his double identity been exposed?!

"You may be right, Beatriz," he said slowly. "Perhaps we should escape. But today I'm conducting a meeting of Marranos here in Lisbon. Since Raphael Chaim's arrest, I'm carrying a heavier load of responsibility."

"But I'm afraid!"

Don Carlos' tone suddenly hardened. "I am a sea captain of many years' experience. I am admiral of the Portuguese fleet! You know that the captain is always the last one to abandon ship. Whatever happens, our fate is in Hashem's hands. In His wisdom, He will have mercy on us. Besides..."

Don Carlos stopped, moved closer, and whispered, "Besides, I must rescue Raphael Chaim from death at the Inquisition's hands. I will not give de Henrique the satisfaction of seeing him burned at the stake! Our plan calls for Raphael Chaim to escape from prison this very night. We plan to hide him aboard one of the vessels sailing for Brazil — may Hashem help us."

"Yes, you are sailing away tomorrow for many months, far away from the Inquisition and the troubles they bring. But what about me and the children?"

Don Carlos was at a loss. "Maybe," he answered hesitantly, "you could go live at our house in Eldorado. It's quieter there, and there are fewer suspicious eyes around."

"I don't know." She bit her lip, then burst out impetuously, "Let's flee, Carlos. Let's run now! My heart is warning me..."

Don Carlos spoke gravely and with emphasis.

"Hashem's salvation comes in the blink of an eye. It is He Who guides a person's steps. I must do what I have undertaken to do, Beatriz. If Hashem grants me success in rescuing Raphael Chaim from the accursed Inquisition, then perhaps we can find our way to a safe city where we can live as Jews. I don't think Amsterdam is the right place for us. I am well known there, and Amsterdam is crawling with Catholic spies. Maybe Antwerp, or Venice. Or we could even go to *Eretz Yisrael*... But for now, be calm. Put your trust in Hashem. Strengthen yourself to believe that this is all a test. He wants to see if we cling with all our hearts in the faith of our fathers, despite the troubles we encounter along the way. Be calm, Beatriz."

Dona Beatriz buried her face in her hands and wept.

Don Carlos watched her a moment, then sadly and silently left the kitchen. Together with his aide, he left the house and made for the harbor, and his waiting ship.

～）～

Slowly de Henrique climbed the broad staircase to Inquisition head-quarters. Humiliation and fury raged in his breast. He was alone; *Padre* João Manuel had driven directly home. The rift between them was an open affair now. De Henrique did not believe it would ever be healed.

He worried that João Manuel would attempt to have him removed from his position as secretary of the Holy Office.

"If only I could prove that João Manuel is a secret Jew," he thought wistfully. "I would inherit João Manuel's position. Head of the Inquisition!" Then Lisbon would be truly cleansed of Jewish heretics. Absolutely cleansed, once and for all! Everyone would praise de Henrique then. They would see what he was truly capable of. *Then* they would know!

He made his way along the corridor to his office. Monks fell silent at his approach, nodding in greeting. But de Henrique, seething with pride and anger, hardly saw them. His entire being was bound up in his hatred of Don Carlos. That snake had succeeded in overturning his whole plan! Because of Don Carlos, he, de Henrique — the man all of Lisbon feared — had been made into a mockery before his fellow monks.

Still, the visit had not been totally in vain. It had served to strengthen suspicion against Don Carlos. Dona Beatriz, the wife, had behaved in a very bizarre fashion. It was clear that she had something to hide. De Henrique was still unable to decide whether or not Don Carlos had been at home all along. If not, where had he been? And how did he leave, if not through the front gate?

He entered his office. First he partially drew aside the heavy curtains at the tall windows, then seated himself in his armchair and leaned back heavily. Closing his eyes, he gave himself up to his thoughts.

Before long, a surge of new life filled him with fresh purpose. No one would steal his prey — his victim — Don Carlos! He *was* a Jew! Yes, a secret Jew — of that de Henrique was certain. If *Padre* João Manuel was afraid to continue the investigation, he, de Henrique, was not. He would pursue it to the bitter end! Don Carlos Carneiro's family was trying to hide something, and de Henrique was determined to find out what it was. Could his house be sheltering a cell in the Jewish underground? A synagogue, perhaps, where the Jews congregated in secret to pray and engage in other forbidden rituals... Eight such cells had already been broken up during the past three years in Lisbon alone. It pained de Henrique to think of so many seemingly good Catholics leading a two-faced existence, attending Mass on Sundays and secret synagogues on Saturday. How many of them were walking the streets of his city?

He opened his eyes. His decision was made. He would smash Don Carlos utterly and completely. Energetically, he seized a small bell that sat on his desk and rang it three times. His office door opened and a young monk asked politely, "What does His Grace wish?"

"Call Luis. Tell him I want to see him at once."

Luis would do what needed to be done.

16

De Henrique was impatient. It seemed to him that eons had passed since he'd summoned Luis. Rising restlessly, he went to the window and pushed aside the curtain to its full extent. He was afforded a view of the wide courtyard surrounding the Inquisition building. It was all but deserted. Here and there on the cobblestones monks strode slowly, alone or in pairs, the hems of their long brown cassocks sweeping the ground. De Henrique knew why the place was so empty. This was the hour of the day when prisoners were escorted from the dungeons to the interrogation and torture rooms. His people were busy with their holy work. Very busy indeed.

But Luis was not involved in that work today. Where was he? De Henrique couldn't spot him among those strolling in the courtyard.

He returned to his armchair. If anything, his tension had increased. Despite his determination, something whispered that his prey might escape his clutches after all. Why was João Manuel being so obstinate about breaking off the investigation? What was he afraid of?

He had lost count of the number of times he'd studied Don Carlos' dossier. He opened it again now and flipped through its pages, searching for the thread, the single fact that would consolidate the suspicions against the admiral. If he could only find that, the rest would follow. Under the friendly persuasion of the torture room, Don Carlos would confess to his sins. De Henrique had seen mighty men broken in the dungeons of the Holy Office.

But the file contained nothing new. Only the same dry facts. Don Carlos Carneiro, born and raised in Oporto. His parents? Nobody special — not enough information about them. At a young age, after two years in a monastery, he'd been drafted into the army. Numerous applications for transfer to the navy had been favored at last, and through persistence, diligence, and loyalty he had risen to his present high position. It had been five years ago, after a battle off the coast of Morocco, that the king appointed Don Carlos commander of the Portuguese fleet. Since then, the flagship *Vera Cruz* had docked into the port of Amsterdam five times.

Here it was, thought de Henrique — one of the keys to the puzzle. Why had he sailed for Amsterdam so often? Even the new alliance with Holland had been forced on the royal family against the clergy's wishes: The church had no desire to sign treaties with heretics. Don Carlos doubtless desired closer ties with that country in order to facilitate his links with the Jewish community in Amsterdam, and its rabbi.

De Henrique's eyes narrowed as he thought of that rabbi, who was systematically poisoning the minds of so many new Portuguese converts to Christianity. The Inquisition knew of his activities but had been helpless until now to do anything about them. (Perhaps, while he was at it, it was worthwhile dispatching Luis to take care of the rabbi, too?)

"But how?" de Henrique asked the empty room. "How can I prove it?"

How to uncover the link between the new treaty with Holland and Don Carlos' possible visits to Menashe ben Israel — like the one he'd read about in the mysterious note?

According to the file, Don Carlos' behavior had been unexceptional. Upon his promotion to admiral, the Inquisition had had him followed for some months in a routine testing of his loyalty to the church. Nothing untoward had emerged. No one had seen him change into a clean white shirt on the seventh day, the day the Jews called their

Sabbath. Don Carlos attended Sunday Mass regularly. No, his record was clean.

What to do?

Disappointed, de Henrique closed the file. He raised his eyes to the door, as though hoping it would open to bring him salvation. Where was Luis?

Then he remembered: Beatriz. Dona Beatriz! Eagerly, he re-opened the folder. Perhaps in the details of her life — that woman who had treated him and his fellows so disrespectfully that morning — lay the clue he'd been seeking. The clue to the family's Jewish identity...

Dona Beatriz was the daughter of Faria Lima Albuquerque, an eminent treasury official. And her grandfather — ("Now here's something interesting!" exulted de Henrique) — had been accused of being a Jew. He'd been caught observing the Shabbos. Bursting into his home one Friday night, Inquisition agents had found, after an exhaustive search, a pair of candles on an inner windowsill. The candles had been warm, clear proof that they'd been extinguished only recently.

On the following page was a detailed summary of the grandfather's trial. He had confessed in the end to his sins. After a public atonement in Lisbon's central square, he had been granted a pardon.

De Henrique was skeptical of such "repenters." He knew from experience that these atonements were for public consumption only. The moment the danger had passed and the eye of the Inquisition was focused elsewhere, the penitents found their way back to their secret Jewish practices. Surely this grandfather — Delfim Neto Oliveira was his name — had passed his heretical ideas on to his descendants. Dona Beatriz's blood was tainted with the Jewish poison that had come to her — from him!

Yes, yes, thought de Henrique in rising frustration — but how do I prove it?

It all depended on Luis. *Where was he?*

⁓⌒⁓

A pair of white stallions stepped briskly through the city streets in the direction of the harbor. They carried Don Carlos and his aide, Pedro Alvares.

In his dress whites, gold epaulets winking at his shoulders and the tall blue admiral's hat with its streaming red ribbon, Don Carlos cut a figure that drew every eye. Pedro Alvares, riding along beside him, was accorded some small measure of honor by virtue of his proximity to the great and much-admired admiral, about to set off on a historic voyage to the newest Portuguese conquest — Brazil.

Sailors, glimpsing the admiral's approach, stopped what they were doing and stood at attention. Don Carlos rode among them at a slow, steady gait, back straight and eyes forward. A respectful silence greeted the man who enjoyed the king's high favor. When they reached the gangway leading to the flagship, Pedro leaped from his horse and seized one of the reins of Don Carlos' spirited steed. In a flash, Don Carlos dismounted.

A large contingent of ships' officers awaited him at the foot of the gangway, saluting smartly. Don Carlos climbed up to the deck, paused a moment to survey the still furled sails, and passed into the inner recesses of the ship. The officers followed in a body.

They took seats in a large, well-appointed conference room. The ship's chaplain raised his cross and said a short prayer for the success of the upcoming voyage. Those present genuflected and murmured, "Amen."

Don Carlos took the floor.

"Gentlemen, you have been privileged to serve as officers in the king's fleet. As you know, this is our final meeting before we set sail tomorrow for Brazil. This will not be an easy voyage by any means. Those of you who have already traveled this particular route will know what I mean. We will sail for many months, trusting in G-d's good will, in our brave crewmen, and in our own resources as sea captains.

"Five vessels will set sail tomorrow. Our purpose: to strengthen the ties between the new territory and Lisbon, our beautiful capital. Departing with us will be *Senhor* Julio Crispineiro, who will take up his post as governor of Brazil. His job will be to represent His Majesty the king, across the sea, to tend to the king's concerns and see to the security of our settlements there." He paused, his tone growing subtly harder as he added, "It's very possible that we will also be called upon to rid these seas of pirates who threaten our merchant vessels coming from Brazil."

Don Carlos sent an appraising glance around the vast table. "Now, gentlemen, are you ready? Is our crew well prepared? Have the ships been inspected from bow to stern? Have the timbers and chains been reinforced? Are the masts and sails in top condition?"

The officers met his eyes without replying. After a minute the admiral resumed, "The great ocean is known for its storms. Should we encounter one, it will be each ship for herself. It is imperative that we be completely prepared for any eventuality. If there is anything that I, personally, can help with, please let me hear it."

An officer from one of the ships ventured, "I'm not sure we have enough provisions on board for such a long voyage."

Don Carlos nodded, then glanced at another officer as though to encourage him to air his own concerns.

"I'm not certain of my crew's morale," the second officer said slowly. "Or a part of the crew, at any rate. A good number of them joined us only yesterday, and they're unfamiliar to me."

"Which ship do you serve on?" Don Carlos asked.

"The *Santa Lucia*."

Don Carlos' breath caught in his throat. He hoped no one noticed his agitation. Feigning calm, he asked, "What exactly worries you?"

"I don't know where they're from. They don't look like any fleet sailors I've ever seen — sailors you can count on in a crisis."

Fear gripped Don Carlos. He had to distract attention from what was happening on this officer's ship, and transfer him to another ship immediately. But who to put in command of the *Santa Lucia* in his place? He'd have to go there right after this meeting to see for himself how matters stood.

At that moment, a young crewman entered. He saluted the admiral and handed him a folded note. The officers watched in mild curiosity as Don Carlos scanned its contents. With growing interest, they noted the way the blood rushed from his face, leaving him deathly pale.

"Excuse me, gentlemen," Don Carlos said, rising. "I must leave you for a few minutes."

Without another word he departed the conference room. Outside, in the passage, he turned left and walked on until he reached steps leading down to the lower deck. He opened the first door on the right, entered, and closed it firmly behind him.

There was one man in the room. He began speaking at once.

"I'm afraid, Don Carlos, that someone has disrupted our plan. De Henrique has summoned Luis."

Don Carlos whitened further. "How do you know this?"

"I know."

"How did you get aboard this ship?"

A shrug. "I managed."

Don Carlos' thoughts veered to de Henrique. What was that foul priest plotting against him? There had not yet been time for an audience with the king; Don Carlos had been planning to attend to that right after the officers' meeting. He was beset now by a sense of urgency. Perhaps his wife was right. Perhaps the danger was far greater than he had thought...

He turned back to the bearer of the worrying news. "What do you think de Henrique wants with Luis?"

"I don't know."

"Have you heard anything?"

"Nothing."

"And what are we to do now?"

"Wait. Maybe we'll have more details later on."

Without waiting for an answer, the man crawled nimbly through one of the portholes and vanished. Don Carlos hurried back to the passage.

Suddenly, he stopped short. He was certain — almost certain — he'd heard stealthy footsteps behind him. Following him? Or was he imagining the whole thing?

Was Dona Beatriz's panic infecting him, too?

In any case, Don Carlos knew one thing. The situation had changed. Things were no longer as they had been yesterday or the day before. He must be wary. Very wary...

He returned to the conference room where, in short order, he adjourned the meeting. Don Carlos entrusted all the final details of the preparation schedule to Pedro Alvares' capable hands. Then he called for his stallion and galloped, unattended, toward the king's palace.

He had gone no more than half the distance when a coach and four horses swept abruptly into his path, blocking it completely.

17

At the very last moment, Don Carlos managed to halt his galloping horse. He was furious at this unlooked-for obstacle in his way. With a practiced hand he yanked at the reins; his horse, still jittery, reared up on its hind legs and waved its front hooves wildly in the air. As if in response, the horses harnessed to the obstructing coach pawed the ground nervously. Don Carlos dismounted, his face suffused with anger.

The anger was mingled with apprehension. It felt as though his life was beginning to slip out of his control. Events seemed to be piling up with ominous intent all morning, ever since he'd returned home to find his parlor full of Inquisition men. The sudden appearance of this strange carriage did not please him at all. It straddled the road before him like a warning.

But he would not succumb to his fears! He was still an important figure in this city, and not to be manipulated like a schoolboy. With a firm, unhurried step he approached the carriage. Its owner — whoever it might be — was about to discover who Don Carlos was. He would pay for his rash act.

Still, his stomach clenched in trepidation, as it always did when he sensed himself in the presence of danger. Passersby threw him curious glances as he went.

"*Pai* (Father)!" shrilled a young boy, "that's Admiral Carneiro!" The cry shattered the silence that had fallen over the other witnesses to the scene.

"Quiet!" the father hissed, tugging unmercifully at his eagerly straining son.

Don Carlos attracted attention wherever he went. Even when he stood beside the king himself at official functions it was impossible not to notice him. He radiated presence. The tall, erect bearing, the well-built physique, the features that were pleasant yet strong combined with his admiral's uniform to imbue him with a glamorous aura. All eyes followed him now as he stepped up to the carriage.

He was standing at the very door, when it abruptly opened. When he caught sight of the person seated within, Don Carlos' heart quailed. Smiling at him from the interior of the carriage was Father João Manuel, head of the Inquisition in Portugal. The taste of that morning's visit was still bitter in Don Carlos' mouth.

"Oh my, what a surprise," João Manuel greeted him. "I'm glad we've met this way."

"Truly, the pleasure is all mine," Don Carlos answered automatically, his expression belying the polite words. He accompanied them with an exaggerated bow, almost a mockery.

João Manuel's expression hardened. "But Don Carlos, I really did want to meet you! Since we parted this morning I've been searching for a way we can talk without being overheard by my secretary, de Henrique."

Don Carlos picked up the note of scorn as the priest referred to his secretary. His thoughts began galloping like race horses. Obviously, an investigation had indeed been instituted against him in the dark recesses of Inquisition headquarters. Equally obvious was the animosity that had sprung up between the two priests. His wife, Beatriz, was right — perhaps more so than she knew. It was Don Carlos' hope that the squabble between João Manuel and his secretary might be turned to his own advantage. Perhaps he could weave a path between the two powerful figures — a path that would afford him an escape from the investigation itself.

His anger rapidly dissipating, he waited.

"Can we speak now, Don Carlos?" João Manuel asked.

If João Manuel was anxious to have a talk, so was Don Carlos. He expected to learn a great deal from such a conversation. For one thing, it might clarify for him what sort of accusation was being leveled at him by the Inquisition. He already knew that the primary suspicion against him centered around his visit to Amsterdam, and Rabbi Menashe ben Israel. But there was still a good deal that was shrouded in fog. What did the Inquisition know — and what didn't it know?

Don Carlos let none of these thoughts reveal themselves on his face. He stood by the carriage door, calmly indifferent.

"Excuse me, *Padre*," he drawled, "but must it take place this minute?" He was the picture of a man with important affairs on his mind, a man in a hurry.

João Manuel shifted on his cushioned seat. A dark gleam sprang into his eyes. His smile was sinister as he drawled in his turn, "It doesn't have to take place at all, *Senhor*. Not now, and not later. It all depends on how much you value your life, Don Carlos."

Don Carlos turned thoughtful. He understood the priest very well. There was no question in his mind now: He was in grave danger. Still, he affected an expression of surprise on his features, and spoke as one who is greatly interested in what is being said to him, though at the same time slightly bewildered. "What danger are you talking about, *Padre*? I don't understand!"

"One who desires to understand, my dear friend, must lend an ear. He does not learn by talking, but by listening! Is that not so, Admiral Don Carlos?"

"I'm listening," Don Carlos said simply.

"No, not that way. Come into my carriage. The coachman will tie your horse to the rear and we'll drive to one of the city parks. There, under the shade of the trees, you will understand far better." He gave Don Carlos a meaningful glance and added, "Far from prying eyes and ears..."

Don Carlos pretended to hesitate. The priest leaned forward, studying Don Carlos' face for a clue to his intentions. "I meant, my friend, far from de Henrique's ears, and even further from his keen eye." He paused before adding a final inducement, "Aren't you even curious to know what I wish to talk about? Or perhaps you already know, and are only pretending not to?" He laughed heartily.

Don Carlos remained impassive. He would not fall into the priest's trap. His face would not give away what was in his heart. Many years' experience as a Jew in hiding had sharpened his sense of self-preservation and given him an almost absolute self-control. At moments such as this, he could understand the verse, "And those whose hope lies in Hashem will find new strength." It was talking about inner strength, the kind that leads to self-control, which in turn protects a man in times of danger.

"Well, Don Carlos?" urged João Manuel.

"A man of faith is always in the right, *Padre*." It seemed as though Don Carlos had decided to do him a favor. "I accept your invitation. I only hope our talk will not take too long. We sail for Brazil tomorrow, you know."

"That remains to be seen, *Senhor*."

And João Manuel's tone — and even more, his smile —implied: "There is much you don't know, Don Carlos..."

The door opened. A shaven head and alert eyes appeared in the gap. "Your Grace wanted me?"

De Henrique raised his eyes. When he saw the speaker, a smile split his heavy-jowled face. "Certainly! Come in, Luis *querida* (my dear)."

Luis was disgusted. This show of affection, from a man who was constitutionally incapable of loving anyone but himself, sickened him. De Henrique was about to entrust him with one of his dirty jobs.

Luis entered the room and approached the desk, which was laden with the files of Inquisition victims. Among the heaps of files he glimpsed an inkwell, a quill sticking out at a slant. There was a whip lying there, too: On occasion, de Henrique enjoyed personally beating his victims. Though not in the line of his official duties, such extra exertion made him feel buoyant and powerful.

The false smile was still plastered over the secretary's face as he asked, "What took you so long, Luis?"

"I've only just returned from town. As Your Grace knows, not every commission goes smoothly."

"Yes, yes, I know." De Henrique bit his lip.

Luis knew how difficult it was for de Henrique to refrain from venting his rage when his orders were not promptly executed. The blackguard wanted something from him — something out of the ordinary. That was clearly the reason behind his remarkable restraint now.

"What's going on, Your Grace?" Luis asked politely.

De Henrique did not answer at once. As he considered his reply, he absently lifted the whip and dangled it from his hand. Luis watched with interest. He had never seen de Henrique in such a mood before. There was something interesting in store for him, that much was certain.

"Luis, I'm sure you're aware of how much we appreciate what you do for us, strengthening the faith and bringing heretics to justice. You've accomplished quite a lot to date!"

"Thanks to Your Grace," murmured Luis, bowing.

He knew what sort of job de Henrique had in mind for him. As an Inquisition spy, he was sent from time to time to break into suspects' homes to seek out evidence of Jewish practice. No house in Lisbon was safe from Luis and his colleagues. They'd become expert as cat burglars by now. In the course of their activities they'd managed to uncover proof of Jewishness in the most surprising places — in the homes of seemingly devout Christians. Numbered among these were Christians who engaged in persecuting Jews. Why, once the mask had been stripped from one of the Inquisition's cruelest interrogators! It had been a shock to discover that the very man who was instrumental in burning other Jews at the stake was himself a Jew. He had denied the accusation forcefully, but Luis's proofs were irrefutable...

"So we're certain you won't let us down this time, either," de Henrique continued.

"I am certain of that, too. But what task are we speaking of, *Senhor*?"

De Henrique leveled a penetrating glance at Luis and answered softly, "Don Carlos."

Luis evinced surprise. It was suddenly difficult to breathe. De Henrique watched his reactions closely; he enjoyed making an impression. Luis decided to let him enjoy himself to the fullest. In a voice that was clearly much moved, he asked, "What happened?"

"Suspicions. Serious suspicions. We suspect him of being a 'Marrano' who practices Judaism in secret. And more than that —that he's the leader of a Jewish underground in Lisbon, a hotbed of heretics. The trail has led to Amsterdam, to the home of the heretic Menashe ben Israel."

"Unbelievable! Does the king know?"

De Henrique inhaled deeply through his nose. "The king knows. But there's a problem."

"What's that?"

"We don't have proof. I mean clear proof." De Henrique replaced the whip on his desk.

Luis ventured, "Could the accusation possibly be false?"

"Possibly. But I, personally, am convinced that it's true. As an experienced hunter of heretics, I feel in my bones that Don Carlos is linked to the Marranos."

Luis was disturbed, and he made no attempt to hide his feelings from de Henrique. It was his hope that his agitation would lead the priest to further revelations.

"Such an elevated position! Lisbon will reel from the shock!"

"Yes," replied de Henrique. "And because of that, we must make sure that every detail is in place before the investigation is completed. Before we can approach the king for his royal stamp of approval."

Luis was quiet. The news upset him greatly. Lisbon would not be the same if Don Carlos was exposed as a Jew. Through his turmoil, he heard de Henrique say, "And you, Luis, can be a great help! *You* can get us the proof we need!"

"I don't see how, *Senhor*."

De Henrique rose from his seat and went over to one of the locked cabinets that stood in the corner. From the folds of his monk's habit he pulled a heavy key ring. Selecting a key, he unlocked the cabinet. Though Luis strained to see through the gloom, it was impossible to make out what de Henrique pulled from one of the shelves.

De Henrique came closer and handed Luis a sealed package. "Open it," he ordered.

Luis did as he was told.

"Familiar?" de Henrique asked.

"Yes!"

It was a pair of *tefillin*. No doubt it had been removed from the home of a Marrano who'd been wearing it at the moment of his capture. De Henrique apparently hoarded such artifacts in that locked cupboard. But what did this have to do with Don Carlos?

De Henrique left him little time for speculation.

"Luis, I want you to find the evidence we need against Don Carlos! Search his house tonight — a thorough search. See if he doesn't have some sort of hidden cellar, such as we've found in the homes of other Marranos in Lisbon. Seek out any scrap of proof of his being Jewish. You know what I'm talking about: candles, *tefillin*, Hebrew prayerbooks, *tzitzis* fringes, and the like." De Henrique peered at him with fierce intensity. "Luis, everything depends on you! And it must take place this very night — tomorrow, Don Carlos sails for Brazil. I must lay my hands on him before he sails. *I must!* Understand?"

Luis saw the fierce determination in the secretary's eyes. It was no use hesitating or protesting. He inclined his head. "I will do the best I can, *Senhor*. But what need have I for these *tefillin*?"

This was a difficult moment for de Henrique. This was when he must expose an innocent young monk to the seamier side of the Inquisition's methods. His face hardened and he said sharply, "If you don't find any evidence to support our suspicions, you are to hide those *tefillin* in his house. Tomorrow, in our official search, we will find them. Understand?"

Luis could not believe what he was hearing. His expression was one of immense shock. In his eyes were the beginnings of resistance, which quickly withered under the force of de Henrique's threatening glare.

"Of course, *Senhor*," Luis answered almost inaudibly. Without another word, he bowed and left the room.

18

F ar from any seeing eye, at a certain point along the coast road leading north to Oporto, *Padre* João Manuel called a halt to the coachman. Don Carlos descended from the carriage first. As the priest followed, Don Carlos wondered apprehensively whether he'd made a terrible mistake in agreeing to join João Manuel here. By driving off in the *padre's* carriage, Don Carlos had placed himself squarely in the Inquisition's hands. He should have insisted on an audience with the king first.

But there was no turning back now. What was done was done. He tried to guess what was in the priest's mind as they strolled side by side along the seashore, a pleasant sea breeze tickling their faces and playing with their hair.

João Manuel began innocently enough. "Don Carlos, how many years have we been friends?"

Surprised, Don Carlos answered cautiously, "If I said 30 years, I don't think I'd be exaggerating."

João Manuel appeared to be caught up in thoughts of his own. Presently he said, "And I'd say it was longer. That is, if you count the two years we studied together at the Dominican monastery, with Father Benedictus 'the White.' We called him that because of his extremely pale skin, remember?"

"Of course I remember. He taught us Latin, and the writings of Hieronymous." *What a waste of time,* Don Carlos thought impatiently. *Was it for this that he dragged me all this distance?*

"Yes," said João Manuel meditatively. "Yes, those were interesting lessons."

A silence fell upon the two men — a tension-filled silence. They continued walking. João Manuel bent and scooped up a clod of earth, which he proceeded to slowly crumble in his fingers, letting the gentle breeze scatter the dust. In another minute, Don Carlos thought angrily, he'd explode — and hang the consequences!

He drew a deep, quivering breath. *"Padre?* What is the purpose of this talk?"

The priest stopped abruptly in his tracks and turned to Don Carlos'. Their eyes met. Don Carlos tried to read in the other's gaze the answers he sought. He found it impossible. *Padre* João Manuel's glance was veiled. And yet, Don Carlos was able to discern a hidden gleam of wickedness — and a malicious delight.

When João Manuel spoke, all his earlier warmth had disappeared. "Don Carlos," he said sternly, "if you don't know it yet, I am telling you now — you have been accused of being a Jew! Moreover, you are accused of associating with an enemy of Christianity, one of the greatest enemies we have today, one Menashe ben Israel. He is originally from Madeira; his parents left Portugal for Amsterdam, where they resumed their Jewish practice. It is not enough for him that he is personally a heretic; he spends a great deal of time and energy waging war against Christianity. We know that he is in constant contact with the Jews of Spain and Portugal, and that he helps them secretly. We have already uncovered a number of these Jews. And now a reasonable suspicion has been leveled against you. You are accused of standing behind the hidden underground of Jews in Lisbon, and — who knows? — also in other cities and towns throughout the kingdom, perhaps." He peered intently at Don Carlos. "Now do you know why I wished to speak with you?"

"No," Don Carlos replied, in a tone as firm as that of João Manuel.

The priest was surprised. This was the last reaction he'd expected.

"Now I'm the one who doesn't understand," he said slowly. "Perhaps I didn't make myself clear enough?"

Don Carlos was a soldier. He knew that, in order to succeed, it was vital to strike back at the enemy without mercy. Otherwise, all was lost.

"*Padre*, if you'd been truly suspicious of me, I wouldn't be walking beside you now. I'd be languishing in one of the Inquisition's dungeons. I've known you too many years — and your friend, de Henrique, too — not to know how you'd behave if you honestly suspected me. I —"

"Don't call de Henrique my friend!" João Manuel broke in, his face darkening. "He's no friend of mine."

"Forgive me. But you must realize that I can't take your words seriously. I understand that my dear 'friends' at the royal court are trying to harm me. And how better to attempt that than by leveling this sort of low accusation against the admiral of the fleet and a close confidant of his Majesty, the king — to accuse him of being a Jew! They know well enough that the ignorant masses will rejoice at the chance to drink my blood." His voice sharpened. "Have you any proof, *Padre*?"

"Proof? Of course we have proof!"

Don Carlos breathed deeply. "I am certain, *Padre*," he said softly, "that you have proof. It's no difficult thing to arrange all the proofs in the world. My question is, how do you know that the proofs are genuine, and not the fruit of some underhanded plot? How can you be sure that my enemies have not fabricated this whole thing against me?"

João Manuel didn't answer. He was well aware that this was precisely the weak point in the Inquisition's case. All they really had to rest their suspicions on was the note de Henrique had brought him — and even now, João Manuel was not totally convinced that de Henrique himself hadn't been behind that. Uneasily, he recalled his midnight conversation with the prince, who'd ordered him to drop the investigation because the king had need of Don Carlos.

He turned gravely to his companion. "Don Carlos, you are mistaken. Whether or not the proofs are genuine is beside the point. The important thing is what we do with them. De Henrique is determined to see you burned at the stake."

Don Carlos threw the Inquisition head a sharp glance. He had gleaned the hint in the priest's words. Quickly, he asked, "And you? You are not determined to see that?"

João Manuel smiled wearily. "Not now," he replied frankly.

"And yesterday?"

"Yesterday doesn't matter. It is today that counts. Today I am interested in teaching de Henrique a lesson, even at the price of saving your neck. That's all I have to say."

"I understand. I won't ask any more."

Don Carlos really did not have any desire to question the priest further. He knew all he needed to now. He knew that his wife, Dona Beatriz, had been right. He understood that he'd been unmasked, and would not be able to masquerade as a Christian much longer. Perhaps it was a good idea to bring his family aboard ship tomorrow and take them along to Brazil? Or maybe — maybe he'd do something extremely daring, and sail instead to Amsterdam? There he and his family could abandon ship and lose themselves in the Bais Yaakov community... But even as he toyed with these ideas, Don Carlos knew that they were futile. He must find out exactly what João Manuel wanted from him.

He heard the priest's voice as if from a distance. "Don Carlos — will you help me save your life?"

Strangely, there was a plea in João Manuel's voice. Don Carlos felt subtly strengthened.

"What do you mean?" he demanded. "How can I help you save my life?"

"I will explain. Do you recall the writer, Julio Guimarães?"

"Yes, certainly."

Don Carlos remembered him well. He was one of Portugal's foremost authors. He was also a member of the secret Marrano community in Lisbon — until he was captured one day, and sentenced to death. But he had escaped from prison, aided by the Jewish underground, who had spirited him out of the country.

"And do you remember Pedro Oliveiro?"

"Why shouldn't I remember? He was one of our best officers!"

Deep in thought, Don Carlos frowned. What was the connection between those two names? The most glaring link was the fact that Oliveiro, too, had been accused of being a Jew, had been sentenced to death by fire, and had been daringly rescued from his fate by the Jewish underground. Oliviero had been actually en route to the *auto-da-fé* when a group of Marranos, disguised as drunken soldiers, started a brawl in the street. In the fracas, the prisoner had been whisked away. He, too, had found his way out of the country.

Why had João Manuel suddenly chosen to bring up those two men — and precisely here, at the seashore? Could he possibly, Heaven forbid, know something of the plans to rescue Raphael Chaim from prison this very night?

"Don Carlos," the priest asked, "do you remember that both those men managed to escape the just decree imposed upon them?"

"That's right."

"And afterwards, both of them vanished."

"I remember that, too," Don Carlos answered carefully.

"And perhaps you know who was behind their escape?" João Manuel continued.

Don Carlos' palms were damp and his heart thumped irregularly. Without realizing it, he'd fallen right into an Inquisition interrogation. They knew something! He must flee, as quickly as possible. He would bring Beatriz and the children on board his ship tomorrow. He must hope that the king would grant his authorization for such a move. There was no other choice.

"Why, no," he answered with studied casualness, as he tried to force the moist sea air into his lungs. "How would I know?"

"Don Carlos, if you help me, we can find out who rescued them and helped them escape from justice."

João Manuel wheeled around and returned to the carriage. A moment later he returned, a small packet in his hand. He extracted a folded page from this and handed it to Don Carlos.

Don Carlos stood immobile, the paper in his hand. "Open it," João Manuel ordered. "Open and read it."

Don Carlos did as he was told. Slowly he unfolded the paper. It was, he saw, a piece of official naval stationery, with the king's seal embossed on top, the identical seal found on the fleet's sails. How had this paper come into the Inquisition's hands? he wondered. Those devils were everywhere!

He focused on the writing:

> *To His Excellency, protector of the faith against all incursions by the faithless, Senhor Padre João Manuel, leader of the glorious and holy Inquisition:*
>
> *I feel compelled to let you know, immediately upon my return from Amsterdam, what I chanced to learn at one of the gala feasts held in our honor by the government there. Although well aware of our antipathy to enemies of our faith, and especially to those Christians who have fled to that city and returned to their own religion, they did not refrain from inviting many of those heretical figures to their parties. The Jews there, as you know, enjoy complete freedom and hold positions of responsibility in the city. Their influence increases yearly, due in particular to their business affairs, which are spread throughout the world. They reach India both by land and by sea, and their ties to Brazil are also very strong.*
>
> *At one of these official functions, a certain Jew came over to me and introduced himself as Julio Morteiro. He, as Your Grace doubtless recalls, was one of those sentenced by the Holy Office to be burned at the stake, and who vanished from prison one day. He was slightly drunk, which loosened his tongue from its customary restraint. In short, he revealed the name of the man who was behind his rescue from the sentence he deserved, and no doubt deserves today. The name he mentioned was Paulo de Henrique, Your Grace's secretary.*
>
> *Ever since that conversation I have known no rest. It is hard for me to believe what I heard. On the other hand, it would be irresponsible to utterly deny the man's testimony. On the following day he visited the flagship Vera Cruz and begged me to forget what he'd said the night before. He claimed he'd said those things while drunk and therefore was not to be held accountable for what had come out of his mouth. His ef-*

forts to make me forget what I'd heard only redoubled my doubts. Don't we both know that, when a person has drunk too much wine, it is then that the truth emerges?

My dear Padre, old friend, I don't know what to think. I am performing my duty in passing these incidents on to you, exactly as they occurred. If necessary, I stand willing to testify to them.

Don Carlos sent a testing glance at João Manuel. Where was this plot leading? "Who wrote this?" he demanded.

The answer was brief and pointed. "You did!"

"I? What makes you think that, sir?"

Instead of replying, João Manuel commanded, "Sign it!"

"No!"

"Sign it, if you value your life. Why do you refuse to understand? The suspicion that will cling to de Henrique when this is made known will dissolve the case against you."

"Is this how you conduct your affairs at the Holy Office? Aren't you supposed to stand for truth and Christian humility? You're supposed to represent all that is good and true. How can we now trust the Inquisition's justice?"

Father João Manuel smiled evilly. His left hand played spasmodically with the cross that hung around his neck. It had not occurred to him, when devising this false note, that Don Carlos would refuse to cooperate. Unfortunately, the admiral still did not seem to realize how shaky his own position was.

"Innocence," João Manuel said slowly, as though weighing every word, "is a good trait, certainly. I commend you. However, if one refuses to keep an eye on what is going on around him, in this crooked and complex world of ours, he will find himself unable to take his place in human society. Don Carlos! Don't matters conduct themselves similarly in the royal court? Plots and intrigues and power struggles? And doesn't your military fare the same way?"

Don Carlos was in a quandary. He knew full well what went on around him. Still, he had never knowingly engaged in a false accusation against another person. On the other hand, de Henrique certainly deserved to die;

he had personally caused the death of more than one Marrano. He was cruel and wicked and an avowed enemy of the Jewish people. What to do?

This is your chance, Don Carlos, a voice whispered eagerly inside him.

What would his teacher, Rav Menashe ben Israel, have advised? What was the Torah view on the choice he faced?

He was not yet certain where this plot was leading. He did not entirely trust the head of the Inquisition. He had by no means ruled out the possibility that João Manuel was laying a trap for him. However, it was clear that there was no love lost between him and de Henrique. What to do?

He stood alone at the seashore, alone with one of the most powerful men in the kingdom — a man who could have him destroyed if he didn't obey. Was it best to accede to his request and embroil himself in an internal Inquisition struggle? What would the king say to this sort of intervention by the military in affairs of faith? And if de Henrique bested João Manuel in the fight — certainly a possibility — then he, Don Carlos, would find himself in an exceedingly difficult spot.

What to do? Where to turn for help?

"Still and all, my friend," Don Carlos said finally, "I can't do it. I have never lied before, and I cannot begin now. I am persuaded that my life is not in mortal danger, and that I will succeed in proving that this was all a villainous plot laid against me by my enemies..."

"A great pity, Don Carlos," snapped João Manuel, snatching the letter from the other's hand. "You have just made the mistake of a lifetime!"

Padre João Manuel wheeled around. With rapid steps he returned to his carriage. Brusquely motioning for Don Carlos' horse to be untied from the rear, he climbed inside and rode off toward the city.

Don Carlos and his horse stood alone at the edge of the sea.

19

Don Carlos stood immobile beside his faithful horse. The slam of the carriage door still rang in his ears, and the thudding of the hooves that bore João Manuel away sounded to his overwrought imagination like an alarm presaging some imminent danger. What would the Holy Office's next step be? He had no inkling. But there was one thing he did know, with chilling certainty: His refusal to play João Manuel's game had transformed the priest into a sworn and deadly enemy. It seemed to Don Carlos that there were very few choices left open to him...

The sky darkened until the sea was submerged in the gathering dusk. The setting sun briefly painted the horizon purple and orange and then disappeared, leaving behind a deepening indigo skyline. Even his white horse took on the mantle of night. Don Carlos patted its mane absently, soothingly.

"Yes, my loyal one," he whispered. "Today, it seems, I ride you for the last time. We've come a long way together, you and I. You've been faithful to the end. You've never given away my secrets, though many a time you've witnessed my meetings with Jews like myself. Jews who are forced to practice in secret the faith of their fathers, Avraham, Yitzchak, and Yaakov... No, you never gave me away. Human beings don't know how to keep a secret; human beings look for ways to harm their fellow man. You're not like those who handed my secret over to those accursed ones, those sons of Satan."

He heaved a deep sigh, still stroking the thick mane while the horse stood stolidly by. "This is the end, my dear horse. Tomorrow I leave Portugal — forever. My job here is ended. The king will no doubt take care of my fleet. He'll appoint someone to replace me. But I have one last task still left to do here. Tonight I must take care of our small community of Marranos in Lisbon. Let's return to town. Let me involve you one last time in a great *mitzvah* — the *mitzvah* of helping my tiny, beleaguered people... my fellow Jews."

It seemed to him that the horse understood every word. If not, why were his large, gentle eyes so sad?

A short time later, Don Carlos was at the harbor.

Though night had fallen over Lisbon, the port was still a hive of activity. Every hand was busy with preparations for the next day's voyage to Brazil. Sailors on deck worked by torchlight. Through their shouts, curses, and snatches of song came the officers' staccato orders. Don Carlos, listening, felt a pang: He loved this scene, and the current of life that ran through it. The last time...

He turned to the flagship *Vera Cruz*, where he hoped to find his aide, Pedro Alvares. He needed Pedro urgently.

How beautiful the ship looked by the light of the many flickering torches, even with sails furled and masts bare. Tomorrow she would be revealed in her true glory. Her sails and pennants would fly proudly in the freshening wind. Real pain pierced Don Carlos' heart. The moment of parting from shore was never easy. Tonight, he had the additional anguish of knowing that the end of his admiralship was drawing near.

But he had the satisfaction of knowing that he was about to sacrifice his great love for the sea on the altar of his love for the Torah, *mitzvos*, and his small but gallant band of Marranos. And also — he'd forgotten — for Raphael Chaim's rescue from the Inquisition's dungeons, and his return to the bosom of his family in Amsterdam. Amazing as it seemed, in the rush of events that had occurred that day, the rescue plot had slipped his mind — the plot that, at this very moment, must be reaching its pinnacle. If the plan succeeded and Raphael Chaim was freed, he hardly cared what became of him personally. He would have fulfilled his mission.

He spotted Pedro Alvares the moment he stepped on deck. His aide was deep in conversation with a small group of officers.

"Pedro!" he called. Startled, Pedro spun around, forgetting to stand at attention.

"*Sim, Senhor?*"

"Pedro, I need you now."

Without a moment's delay, Pedro left the other officers and hurried over to Don Carlos. Pedro was the only one on whom Don Carlos could fully rely. He had always served his captain faithfully. Apart from that, Pedro was his own brother's son. Perhaps on this, their final voyage together, he would at last be able to reveal the secret of Pedro's origins and persuade him to flee with him to Amsterdam....

"Pedro, I've decided to take Dona Beatriz and the children on this voyage."

"Why? What is it?" Pedro asked anxiously. "And did the king grant permission?"

"Leave the king to me. I'm sure he'll give his consent after I explain my reasons to him. I need your help to bear a certain load to the ship. Please hire a coach and join me at first light."

"*Sim, Senhor.*"

"Thank you, Pedro."

Pedro searched his admiral's face curiously. That 'thank you' was out of character from a man accustomed to having his orders obeyed unquestioningly and as a matter of course. It seemed exceedingly strange. Clearly, something was troubling Don Carlos. But there was no time to go into it now. The admiral had already turned and left the flagship.

Don Carlos made his way to the *Santa Lucia* — the vessel that would, if all went according to plan, bear away the prisoner Raphael Chaim.

From the officer's remarks at their meeting, it was apparent that something was brewing among the crew, something to do with the group of unfamiliar sailors that had come aboard for the trip to Brazil. It was up to him to see to things personally, to prevent any undesirable and harmful consequences...

Stepping aboard the *Santa Lucia,* he was struck by the absence of sailors on deck. Tools were tossed about haphazardly, as though abandoned in the middle of work. A mysterious silence brooded over the ship. With quickening steps, Don Carlos descended the stairs to the ship's belly, where the crew and officers' quarters were located. There was no sign of life. The corridors were deserted. A sharp apprehension twisted in Don Carlos. Where was everybody? What had happened here? They were due to sail tomorrow!

The admiral paced through the passages with mounting anxiety, throwing open the doors of cabin after cabin. All were empty. Had everyone decided to visit the dockside taverns — tonight, when they were under orders to prepare for the voyage? He could envision the harsh punishments that would follow such a rash act. Don Carlos had hoped that all would be quiet aboard ship by midnight, with all the sailors securely inside their cabins. That way, no one who did not have business knowing about it would have any idea of Raphael Chaim's secret embarkation. ("*If* the plan succeeds," an inner voice amended warningly.)

He was on the point of returning to the upper deck when a sound reached his ears, gathering gradually in volume. He followed the noise to the end of a passage and arrived at the *Santa Lucia*'s mess hall. It was filled with sailors. Shouts, curses, and even blows flew about the room. It seemed to the astounded Don Carlos that neither the ship's captain nor its other officers were making any attempt to halt the fracas...

His sudden appearance in the doorway plunged the room into swift silence. It was the lull that comes after a storm. In growing fear and trepidation, every man present stared at their fleet admiral, Don Carlos.

Luis got out of bed at nightfall, refreshed by a long sleep. De Henrique and his foul plots had shaken his equilibrium. Tonight, Luis knew, would be decisive. Not only his own fate, but those of others — perhaps many others — hung on his success. His talk with de Henrique might have complicated the plan, however. Luis frowned in deep concentration, trying to devise a scheme that would throw the wool over that wily fox's eyes — the fox who sat so complacently in his Holy Office. Holy? Luis laughed inwardly. How holy could it be if it boasted a creature like de Henrique? How he despised that man!

Luis left his room and the Inquisition building. An hour's walk through the night brought him to an isolated house, situated on one of Lisbon's quieter side streets. He knocked on the door several times in rapid succession, then waited impatiently for it to open. When it did, he made haste to disappear inside.

The others, seven in all, awaited him in the large, well-lit room. They were all young monks, garbed in brown wool cassocks that swept the floor. Luis strode to the center of the room and began without preamble: "I had a talk with de Henrique today."

The others watched and waited expectantly. All seven of them were faithful members of the Inquisition corps charged with tracking down suspected heretics. They had all served previously in His Majesty's army and taken part in battles against Portugal's enemies. Every one of them had displayed courage and daring on many occasions. It was for these reasons that Luis had chosen them for this special work. Their secret and sometimes dangerous job had taught them the virtues of silence.

"He ordered me," Luis continued, "to fabricate proof to implicate Don Carlos Carneiro of being a Jew. What have you to say to that?"

"Interesting," one of the monks said dryly, almost indifferently. He was the oldest of the group. The others maintained their silence.

"Naturally, he praised me — actually, us — and our past success in bringing suspects to justice. People whom no one would have dreamed of being disloyal to Christianity."

Luis eyed his small audience and added, "And what do you say to this praise?"

Now a smile rose to some of the monks' lips.

Luis proceeded, "He's certain that we can bring about Don Carlo's indictment as well. He gave me a pair of *tefillin*, our dear secretary, with instructions to hide them in Don Carlos' house if I don't find any other evidence that he is of the Jewish faith. Nice, eh?"

"Interesting," the oldest monk intoned once again.

"And he would like our visit to Don Carlos' home to take place this very night. Tomorrow, the fleet sails to Brazil. His Grace, secretary of the Holy Office, would dearly love to clap hands on Don Carlos before he sails out of reach. He has a hearty appetite for blood, that one!"

Silence.

"But you know well enough that that's the last thing on our minds tonight. Tonight we must prepare our little surprise for de Henrique..."

His words acted like a magic wand, propelling the small group into a flurry of activity. Luis covered his bald pate with a hairpiece, retaining his monk's robe. His only other change was switching the cross on his breast to a larger one — a silver cross, such as those worn by high-ranking priests. Three of his companions donned the uniforms of high government officials. The remaining four men put on army uniforms under their voluminous robes.

Luis inspected his cadre carefully. Then he took a bundle of forged documents from a small casket and distributed them. Though they knew their upcoming roles by heart, he nevertheless briefed his men again.

"Tonight, with Hashem's help, we are going to free Raphael Chaim from prison. We will bring him aboard the ship *Santa Lucia* the way we've planned. People will be waiting there to hide him and take care of his needs until we reach Brazil." He paused. "I say 'we' because we, too, will be going aboard and leaving Portugal."

The surprise was total. He had never revealed this portion of the plan to them. Quickly, Luis explained: "Yes, this is a change in the plan. But there's no choice. From what de Henrique told me, I believe there's strong suspicion against Don Carlos. De Henrique is pinning all his hopes on the job he gave me. The fool hasn't realized that, in all these years, we've never handed him a single Marrano. All our victims have been loyal Catholics.

"Naturally, we'd never have thrown them to the wolves unless we knew that they were rabid Jew-haters. We treated them the way they treated us. They accused our brothers of being secret Jews and caused many to die, so we told tales about them and made sure to find the evidence we needed to 'prove' the allegations... that they were Jews. This was the easiest way to avenge ourselves on our enemies, who are also Hashem's enemies: to hand them over to the Inquisition."

Luis stopped. The others gazed at him with profound interest. Breathing deeply, he continued, "That's all. At dawn tomorrow a careful search will probably be made of Don Carlos' house. If the *tefillin* I was supposed to plant there are not found, our true identities will become known. We have no choice but to vanish. Our job here is finished. All we can do is hope and pray that our Creator will allow us to begin again in another place on the face of the earth — openly, as Jews. Perhaps the merit we've earned from rescuing our brothers from the enemy's claws will stand us in good stead, and, with His help, we will succeed."

The others seemed to grasp suddenly the danger into which they had fallen. If only they could say good-bye to their parents, their families... but that, apparently, was impossible.

"What will happen to Don Carlos?" someone asked.

Luis sighed. He lifted his hands in a gesture of despair. "I don't know. I really don't know. If we manage to sail away tomorrow and he isn't stopped, we'll find some way to let him know that he's been caught in de Henrique's web. It's hard for me to believe that he doesn't sense it already. But anything can happen. Honestly, I don't know." He perked an ear. "It seems to me that our carriage has arrived."

Luis extinguished the flaming taper. One by one his men left, spacing their departure by intervals. When everyone was inside and the carriage wheels had already begun to turn, Luis leaped suddenly down and ran back to the house. He had forgotten to bring along the tools he needed for the break-in...

20

S lowly, Don Carlos entered the mess hall. In the dead silence even the hiss of the waves were clearly audible. Every sailor stood at attention, rigid as statues. Every eye in the room was hard at work avoiding the admiral's glance.

Don Carlos strode straight into the heart of the crowd, the men stepping back to make way for him. He walked with erect bearing and measured tread until he reached the ship's officers. They looked utterly miserable.

Without removing his eyes from the officers, Don Carlos lifted and then dropped his hand. Instantly, with a noise like a rustling breeze, everybody sat. The movement eased the tension slightly.

The admiral's voice sliced through the room: "May I know what caused this uproar?"

No one answered.

"Where is the ship's captain?" he demanded. "Why is he not present?"

One of the officers stepped forward, saluted, and said, "He went ashore, *Senhor*. To take leave of his family."

Don Carlos cleared his throat. "Then maybe you can explain what this disgraceful scene is all about."

The officer was abject. Nervously he half-turned toward the throng of sailors watching him.

"A group of some 40 sailors were brought aboard, *Senhor*. They don't belong to our regular crew. I don't know who gave the order to bring them here, but —"

"I did!" Don Carlos snapped.

The officer's abjection grew. It was only at the admiral's direct command — "Continue!" — that he found his tongue again.

"The regular crewmen didn't like it. They don't know the new men and aren't used to them. And the new men don't look like seasoned sailors." Uncertain how his words were being received, the officer subsided.

"And then what happened?" Don Carlos prompted impatiently.

"And then — the fights began. At first it was only words and curses. In the end, blows were exchanged. It doesn't take long, as *Senhor* knows, for sailors to come to violence. We were just trying to end it..."

Don Carlos frowned. He knew very well who the new men were. They were a group of Marranos who urgently needed to leave the country. The Inquisition was snapping at their heels. They'd gathered here from every corner of Portugal and had been in hiding in basements and cellars throughout Lisbon for the past two weeks. It would be these men, too, who would see to Raphael Chaim when he was brought aboard — which, if all went according to plan, should take place in just a few hours. He thought of Luis, responsible for springing the prisoner from his denk trap in the Inquisition dungeons.

He cast a forbidding glance on the sailors, trying to distinguish the Marranos from the regular crew. He found it impossible to tell the difference — and that was all to the good. The more his Jewish brothers resembled old seamen, the less suspicion would be directed against them. The Inquisition doubtless infiltrated the fleet, too, with its iniquitous spies. Even on the wide sea it was necessary to be vigilant.

Still watching the sailors, he pondered his next move. He must find just the right words to calm this upheaval, or it would be impossible for

Luis to bring Raphael Chaim aboard later. His gaze softened. Let the men relax a bit, he thought. When he spoke, his tone was pleasant:

"I especially chose the *Santa Lucia* for these men. It is imperative that they learn how to be excellent sailors immediat ly. Of all the ships, I knew that you would receive them the most effeciently. Yours is the most proficient of all the crews sailing with us tomorrow. And the most dedicated. These things have not escaped my notice. Therefore, I believed these new men would find a welcome reception among you."

He paused. A glimmer of a smile appeared on his face. Leaning slightly toward the packed room, he said very softly, in a voice filled with deep disappointment, "Was I mistaken? Has the Christian generosity we cultivate throughout our fleet abandoned this splendid ship?" He paused. "And what of the respect due to His Majesty's orders?"

Leaving these words to echo behind him, he turned and left the room.

He climbed up to the deck alone and then descended ashore. He must hurry home. There was still a great deal of work to do, to prepare his own personal escape from Portugal on the morrow.

≈)≈

The carriage rattled and swayed along Lisbon's dark streets. Of the passengers crowded within, Luis was the only one who didn't sit quietly. He spent the duration of the ride sticking a beard onto his clean-shaven chin. The small auburn goatee added color and a measure of dignity to his face. He hoped that the wig and the goatee would be sufficient to disguise his identity at the Inquisition gates, where he planned to request a night's lodging for himself and his companions. He had no such qualms about the others being recognized: Their presence at that fearsome building was not frequent at all.

The carriage pulled to a stop in front of the locked iron gate. The coachman climbed down and rapped on it smartly. A small window, set in the gate, opened to reveal a pair of suspicious eyes. An otherwise invisible sentry barked, "Who is there?"

Luis descended from the coach with a mustered air of self-importance, as befit a high-ranking church figure. He thrust an official-looking document in front of the soldier's nose.

"*Boa noite* (Good evening), young man," he addressed the guard. "My name is Antonio Cabral, a bishop of the northern hills. We have travelled many leagues today. To our dismay, we did not succeed in reaching Lisbon before nightfall, where we had hoped to spend the night as guests of His Grace, João Manuel, or his friend and esteemed colleague, Paulo de Henrique. I hope that the guest house beside the chapel in the courtyard is not full of visitors tonight, so that my men and I may shelter and rest there till the morning. We are continuing south tomorrow." He lowered his voice confidentially. "You see, my good man, we are in hot pursuit of a young monk who murdered the head of one of our local monasteries. According to reports, he's fled southward. Will you open the gate for us?"

The eyes in the window stared at him in open skepticism. The soldier hesitated, torn by doubt. His orders were clear: to open the gate to no one unless he recognized him. On the other hand, the stranger had shown him a document in which, by the light of the wavering taper, he was identified as one of the senior churchmen in the north. Should he open the gates, de Henrique would doubtless go on the rampage. Should he deny the visitors entry, de Henrique would probably scream at him for his imbecility in not letting them into the guest house. In either case, de Henrique seemed likely to be angry.

Shrugging, the guard opened the gate and allowed the carriage into the dark courtyard. The passengers alit. As he turned to relock the gate, a mighty blow caught him on the back of the head. There was no time for even the slightest scream to escape before he slumped unconscious to the ground.

Two of Luis' men lifted the sentry and carried him quickly to a dim corner of the courtyard. There they bound him and gagged his mouth with a rag that had been well saturated with chloroform. He would not awaken till morning, which should give them ample time for their purposes. One of the men removed his cassock to reveal the military uniform beneath. In seconds, a new "soldier" was standing guard at the gate.

The rest, led by Luis, ran toward the main building. They caught the guard there by surprise and overpowered him. In short order they gagged him and tied his arms and legs. Leaving another uniformed "sentry" in his place, the remaining men dragged the overcome guard with them down the steps to the dungeons. They would make use of their prisoner in good time.

Even in the dense blackness below, Luis knew his way around the dungeon passages. In a shorter time than one would have believed possible, they were standing outside the cell they wanted. Raphael Chaim slept soundly inside.

Luis opened the leather bag he carried and extracted a metal saw. At once he began sawing rapidly through the chain that held the cell door fast. The sound roused the occupants of the adjoining cells.

"Silencio (Quiet!)" someone shouted.

"Ssh," one of Luis' men admonished. "We're trying to save one of the Inquisition's victims from the flames. Do you want to interfere?"

An immediate hush fell over the dungeon. Luis' men sensed the presence of prisoners standing at their cell doors up and down the passage, grasping the bars with their last remaining strength and watching the startling scene unfold before them. Even in the gloom it was possible to see the gleam of their eyes. They were eyes filled with wonder, pain, curiosity, and pleading...

Suddenly, from the top of the stairs came the "sentry's" booming voice:

"Here you are, *Senhores* — take this torch to light your way down to the dungeon."

Luis stopped sawing and lifted his head in sudden panic. His man was attempting to warn him in time — they had visitors! The prisoners who had stood up to watch threw themselves onto the floors of their cells and closed their eyes as if in deep sleep.

Luis' men stared at him fearfully. Their breathing all but stopped as they listened to the sound of the newcomers' slowly descending footsteps.

21

uis was the first to recover. Quickly gathering his tools into the leather bag, he handed it to one of his men and motioned for him to conceal himself in the heavy gloom further along the passage. Then he had others drag the unconscious guard to a distant turning in the dungeon, out of sight. At the other end of the passage, by the stairs, he could already see the dust raised by the pair of priestly inspectors.

The men looked to Luis for a way out of this predicament. He was a master at extricating himself from difficult situations. Luis' eyes were narrowed in anticipation of the upcoming battle of wits. Abruptly, he gestured for two of his men to come closer. Grasping them by the hair, he pulled their heads close enough for them to hear him whisper:

"Pay attention. In a few minutes the inspectors will find us. They'll be surprised, and it will take them a second or two to recover. The danger is that they may run straight back to the stairs to call for help. We must prevent that at all cost. Understand?"

The men nodded to signify their comprehension. In the deathly stillness, the noise of their ragged breaths was overloud.

"Now," Luis continued, "I want you to go that way as quickly as you can." He pointed to the left. "After you've passed about 20 cells, you'll find that the passage bends to the right. Turn with the bend and follow it until you arrive at a point behind our visitors' backs, not far from the stairs. That way, in any event, you can prevent their running for reinforcements. With G-d's help and if we all cooperate, we'll overcome them. All right?"

The two didn't even take the time to answer. They darted to the right and ran off madly into the darkness, which soon swallowed them completely. Luis motioned for his remaining companions to move back into the shadows. He himself was the last to do so, keeping a wary eye on the approaching torchlight, which played over the cell bars and the prone figures crumpled within. Possibly, by this ploy, they could prevent a confrontation with the monks.

They were young, he saw, and totally unsuspecting. The two chatted loudly as they made their rounds, apparently not caring a whit that they might be disturbing the prisoners' much-needed sleep.

"A cold night," the one holding the torch remarked. Luis recognized him: one of the newest inductees to the Inquisition ranks. His home was in the south, though Luis wasn't sure exactly where.

"Cold, but pleasant," the second replied.

"So what do you think? Will the quarrel ever end?"

"Which quarrel?"

"What do you mean, which? The quarrel between *Padre* João Manuel and de Henrique, of course! Or haven't you noticed that they're not speaking to each other?"

"Certainly I noticed! One keeps interfering in the other's investigations. It's not the first time it's happened, and it won't be the last."

"Hearsay has it that they've involved the king and his son in this fight of theirs. If the royal court decides to look into the way things are run here, most of us are likely to end our days in this dungeon!"

"I think it's time to send them both home. A peaceful retirement in one of our small southern villages wouldn't do either of them any harm! There, they could continue quarreling to their hearts' content — or wile away the time dreaming of the good old days when all of Lisbon trembled at the sound of their names. Do you have any idea how much power those two wield?"

"You're right! They've already done their service for the faith. You can't take their accomplishments away from them. Today, thanks to them, Lisbon is free of those Jewish pigs. They've run the pigs down everywhere — in the military, in the government, in the university. But now they're ruining the atmosphere around this place. We're all gradually being sucked into their ugly quarrel."

They strolled and chatted as if they had all the time in the world. Though the torch flashed intermittently into the cells, the inspectors paid scant attention to the condition of the inmates. As the monks neared Raphael Chaim's cell, Luis and his companions shrank back as far as they could into the shadows. Half the chain on the cell door had already been sawn in two. Luis was clutched by a sudden, paralyzing fear: Would they notice? Would they suspect what was happening here tonight? He and his men stood immobile, hardly even breathing. The monks had reached the cell.

Why were they stopping? Why did they shine the torch over the slumbering prisoner?

"He's asleep, the dog — the head dog."

"What are they waiting for? Why don't they burn him in the *auto-da-fé* already? It's been two years since the last 'act of the faith.' The people want something to stir them up, something to put a little scare into these 'new converts.' They've been just outrageous lately!"

The inspectors gazed dispassionately at the prisoner. In the shadows, Luis and his friends prayed silently. Thus far, the priests had noticed nothing untoward.

"Who knows if they've managed to track down everyone who followed this heretic? He certainly seems to have had an influence on a good many people. Looks like they're still hoping to get more information out of him. It was de Henrique who managed his capture."

"Not true," retorted the other. "This success was João Manuel's."

The first monk glared angrily. He opened his mouth as if to say something, then thought the better of it. Best to finish the tour of inspection in peace. Instead, all he said was: "I think they suspect someone new."

"So I've heard. Who is it?"

"It's hard to believe, but I've heard it's Don Carlos himself. De Henrique wants to arrest him before they sail to Brazil."

"And *Padre* João Manuel? What does he want?"

"I don't know. But it seems they've been fighting about that, too..."

He broke off suddenly. "Look!" he screamed. He pointed at the ground some short distance away. His companion followed the line of his frightened gaze. The young monks clutched each other. Out of the shadows protruded a foot...

Luis gave them no opportunity to collect their wits. He lunged out of his place of concealment with all his strength, crashing squarely into the monks. They had no chance to emit so much as a syllable. One of the inspectors fell in the collision, while the other — the one holding the torch — turned and attempted to flee. He was too late. Luis, lying winded on the ground, managed to grab his ankle as he flew past. The noise the monk made as he crashed to the stone floor was not pretty. One of Luis' men darted forward and extinguished the torch. In seconds, after a small tussle, the monks' hands were securely bound behind their backs and the sashes of their cassocks stuffed into their mouths.

Even as his men dealt with the two additional prisoners, Luis was already back at work on the stubborn chain. He sawed with all his might, biting his lips in desperation. At last, it yielded. The men burst into the cell. Two of them picked Raphael Chaim up and bore him to the stairs. Two others trundled the monks and the still unconscious guard into the cell the prisoner had just vacated.

"It'll be a pleasure to see them spend the rest of the night in here," one of them hissed.

The other answered grimly, "It will serve them right to have a taste of what they dish out to these prisoners."

A fresh chain was pulled out of Luis' leather bag. It was used to re-lock the cell door. Then the whole group ran up the stairs to the ground floor, where their "sentry" waited impatiently.

"Did you meet the inspectors?" he asked in agitation.

"Yes," one of his companions answered. "And how!" They made their way out of the building to the waiting carriage.

"And where are they now?"

Luis answered with satisfaction, "They're prisoners of the Inquisition. All three of them are crowded into Raphael Chaim's luxurious quarters. May it be an atonement for our sins! And now," he continued, businesslike, "let's go. We lost too much time in there. Let's leave this place behind — forever."

In the carriage, they tenderly removed Raphael Chaim's prison garb and substituted farmer's clothing characteristic of northern Portugal. Raphael Chaim slept throughout.

"He's weak. Very weak. Will he stand up to the long sea voyage?"

"Who knows? May Hashem grant him strength!"

The carriage swept into the streets of Lisbon. The "sentry" at the gate leaped aboard, leaving the gate unguarded. On they lumbered, quick as could be, toward the harbor...

At the mouth of the harbor, the horses were halted. Without exchanging a word, the men placed the pitifully weak Raphael Chaim into a large cargo crate they'd prepared for him. Until the last possible moment they left the lid open, so that the erstwhile prisoner — should he awaken — might breathe fresh air for the first time in months. At the harbor gates, however, they closed the lid and draped a bale of old clothes across the top. They hoped the holes they'd bored in the sides of the crate some hours earlier would suffice to let Raphael Chaim breathe.

The carriage continued slowly until it was beside the berth of the *Santa Lucia.* A profound silence enveloped the ship: Its crew was sound asleep after the day's labors. As it rolled up to the foot of the gangway, not a muscle quivered inside the coach. Every pair of eyes was raised to the deck. They had reached the most difficult portion of their plan. Were the two sailors patrolling the deck their own men — or not?

Luis stepped out of the carriage and lifted his head to see the deck and its patrolling guards. He raised and dipped the glowing taper in his hand three times — the arranged signal. There was no response from the deck.

Again he performed his maneuver with the taper. And again, no reaction. Luis returned to his companions.

"They're not answering."

"What do we do?" someone asked from the darkened interior.

"I don't know."

"There's no going back now!"

"I know. But what will you have us do — board the ship by force?"

Without waiting for an answer, he returned to the ship. His mind churned with half-formed plans for reaching the deck without arousing suspicion. One last time he raised the taper, praying for the life of Raphael Chaim, the man who had chosen to exchange his comfortable life in Amsterdam for an underground exile in Lisbon.

A sailor peered over the railing on the deck and shouted at Luis, "Hey — you there! What do you think you're doing? Don't you know it's forbidden to come near a fleet vessel?"

Luis quaked. "Where are our men?" he wondered. "What's happened to them?" Drawing a deep breath, he shouted back, "We're sailing with you tomorrow. We've got an authorization here, signed by the admiral, Don Carlos Carneiro." As he spoke he pulled a bundle of documents from a pocket sewn into the folds of his cassock. "Where's Martinez?"

"Who's Martinez?" the sailor bellowed back angrily.

Luis was at a loss. Martinez was leader of the group of Marranos who had boarded the ship a few days before. What now?

"So can I board?" he asked.

"I don't know. Wait till morning." The sailor vanished.

Luis returned to the carriage. "The situation is tricky. I'm not sure how best to proceed. But one thing is very clear: We can't wait for morning. We'll be discovered if we do. De Henrique will surely break into Don Carlos' house to find the *tefillin* he wanted me to plant there, and he won't find them. Then he'll come looking for us. Maybe he'll even link us to Raphael Chaim's escape. We must disappear in a hurry!"

"How long before they find out what happened in the Inquisition dungeons tonight?" one of his men asked.

"I don't know." Luis countered. "But probably not long. We have no choice: We must leave this place now. We'll go to Rodriguez Cavaliero's house. His basement has tunnels leading to many hidden places. After that, with Hashem's help, we'll figure out what our next step should be." With that, he jumped into the carriage.

The coachman started the horses at a slow walk, trying to attract the least possible attention to their progress through the harbor. Luis' head sank into his hands; it was a difficult moment for him. Suddenly, one of his companions uttered a muffled shout.

"Look! Luis, look — up on deck!"

There on the deck, clear for anyone to see, a flaming taper rose and fell three times...

Luis flew out of the still-moving carriage and ran headlong back to the ship, brandishing his own taper. He motioned urgently for the carriage to return to the foot of the gangway. Four sailors descended to meet them.

"Everything all right?" Luis asked anxiously.

"Yes, thank G-d."

On both sides of the carriage doors opened and men poured out. Without speaking, they passed the laden crate into the sailors' waiting arms. The crewmen carefully lifted the precious cargo onto their shoulders and began their climb back to the upper deck. They knew that it was their own leader they bore on their shoulders. Luis and his men followed them. Behind, the carriage rumbled slowly away to lose itself in the sprawling streets of Lisbon.

On deck, a young officer awaited them. He held a finger to his lips to signal the need for absolute silence. Then he led the way to a passage leading down into the ship's belly. The others trailed him on tiptoe, fearful of making the slightest noise. Even the sailors, weighted with their burden, did their best to muffle their labored breaths. They must reach their destination with no time lost.

Then, on the steps, it happened.

One of the sailors slipped, and the crate nearly slid off the others' shoulders. A crisis loomed as they desperately snatched at the box before it should tumble down the stairs with a noise that would wake the entire crew. With a monumental effort they managed to pin the crate against the wall — but not without a certain amount of unavoidable racket. Everyone froze, waiting to see whether they had woken anyone. Three full minutes passed before they permitted themselves to breathe normally once more. The crisis, it seemed, had been successfully averted. They continued their descent into the ship's depths.

But at the very bottom of the steps they came face to face with no less than the ship's captain, furiously trying by the light of a flickering taper to identify the men who had disturbed his sleep. Beside him stood two officers, right hands crossed over to grasp the sword hilts dangling to their left...

22

"**B**eatriz," called Don Carlos the moment he opened his front door. "Beatriz! Where are you?"

There was no reply. The house was dark: not even a single glowing taper to illuminate the gloom. Don Carlos' nerves were already stretched to the screaming point. His anxiety made him tremble. Where could she be?

"Beatriz? Beatriz!"

Had de Henrique and his henchmen been back? It couldn't be!

He groped along the walls until he found a taper. He lit it. Grasping it in his hand, he proceeded from room to room. To his relief, there were no signs of a search, no evidence of unwanted visitors or a hasty retreat. *Then where was Beatriz?*

"BEATRIZ!" he shouted with all his might.

"Ye-e-es," came a voice from a distance.

He waited impatiently. After a few moments his wife appeared in the salon. All his fear and anxiety turned to anger.

"Where were you?"

She gazed at him and said simply, "In the cellar."

Don Carlos knew which cellar she referred to. For years they had conducted clandestine Pesach *seders* there for members of their tiny hidden community — sometimes several days in advance of the true date, to confuse the Inquisition agents who were watching for the disappearance of suspected Marranos on the night of the fifteenth of Nissan. In that cellar, more than once, prayer services had been held when the other secret places became too dangerous. Christians who were unmasked as Jews often hid there, out of sight, until the wrathful eye of the Inquisition was turned elsewhere. From that cellar, too, ran a secret tunnel that led to a house at the edge of the city from which it was possible to step into the city's streets without being followed.

"What were you doing there?" Don Carlos demanded.

Dona Beatriz sighed, but didn't answer.

"What are the sighs for?" he pressed.

"Carlos," she replied in the tone of one resigned to her fate, "I'm frightened. Very frightened. Ever since those people from the Holy Office came here this morning, I've had no peace."

"And now," Don Carlos said soberly, "I've caught your fear."

Beatriz paled. Her handkerchief dropped from her nervous fingers, but she didn't bother to pick it up. "What happened?" she cried. "Has something happened in the city? In the royal court? Aboard ship?"

"First, tell me why you were in the cellar."

She reached for the nearest chair and sank into it, burying her face in her hands so that he might not see the streaming tears. Her shoulders shook. Don Carlos watched her, then asked again, sharply, "Why did you go down to the cellar? Tell me!"

"It doesn't matter now," came the answer, muffled through the fingers that still covered her face. "Not now, after what happened in the city today."

"But I haven't told you anything yet. Answer me, Beatriz!"

The crying stopped. She removed the hands from her face and lifted red eyes to her husband. "My heart — my woman's heart — has been telling me since this morning that we're in great danger. So I decided to go down to the cellar and remove all traces of Jewish activity. Don't be angry... I buried the *siddurim* and the *tallis* deep in the ground. I know exactly where. If Hashem has pity on us and this terrible time passes, I'll be able to find them again. But now — I'm afraid, Don Carlos. If those accursed ones return, I don't want them to find a single thing to hang their suspicions on. I was in the midst of this work when you called. I'm sorry."

Don Carlos sat down too. He knew how justified his wife was in what she'd done. She had behaved wisely and well. But it had taken her action to drive home the reality of his new situation. His house — the house that had hosted numerous members of the royalty in its time, as well as leading clergymen and Inquisition figures — was no longer safe!

He raised his hands in surrender, as though to say, "What can we do?" Then, very gently, he said, "Go on, Beatriz. Finish the job you've started. But it's not really so important anymore. Beatriz, we're leaving. To my sorrow, we must flee Portugal."

Beatriz was startled but not displeased. "I'm ready," she said promptly. "I hardly even care any longer. But — where are we going?"

"I don't know. We sail to Brazil tomorrow. Prepare our clothes, and the children's. Take as little as possible, so that no one will suspect our intention. We'll leave everything behind, all the gold and silver. They'll think we plan to return from this voyage. Pedro Alvares, my trusted aide, is coming at dawn to help transport what we need to the *Vera Cruz*. He's the only one who knows that you're joining us." He paused somberly. "He's the only one in this city I can still trust."

"And what of Raphael Chaim?"

Don Carlos shrugged. "How can I know? I hope Hashem has been with us, and that Luis has been able to accomplish his task. I pray Hashem will blind our enemies' eyes so that Raphael Chaim can escape. By now he should be aboard ship — *if* all went well. I want with all my heart to return him safely to his home in Amsterdam."

He rose. "And now, Beatriz, I'm going to say good-bye to a few friends... Those who will have to carry on the sacred work in my place."

He went into one of the inner rooms and entered the closet that led to the cellar. There he exchanged his naval uniform for civilian clothes and disguised his features with a false beard. Once again he traversed the hidden tunnel that led to the safe house at the edge of town, and stepped from there into the dark street.

⁊⸞

It was a star-studded night. Seeing it, Don Carlos felt a pang of homesickness. He knew he would never see Lisbon again.

Avraham, too, he remembered — our first father — had gazed upon the stars as Hashem promised: "Thus will be your children." Once, in Amsterdam, Rav Menashe ben Israel had explained the meaning of these words to him: Just as mankind does not wield power over the stars, so, too, the nations of the world will not have power over the Jewish people.

Don Carlos smiled bitterly. How ironic to recall that heartening prophecy tonight! A more appropriate verse might have been, "And your children will be as the dust of the earth." The Jews of the world *he* knew — and not only in Portugal — were for the most part downtrodden... oppressed almost to the very dust! Here he was, walking about his own city in disguise, to avoid recognition. His own beloved city, which he must flee like a dishonored thief.

He stopped and raised his eyes to the sky again. He loved the black canopy spread above him, sprinkled with stars like jewels — stars without number, winking at him out of the blackness. What secret were they trying to whisper to him?

In the wonderful silence streaming at him from the stars, he heard the answer:

"You are mistaken, honored sir, admiral of the Portuguese fleet! Your very escape is a lesson in how little the nations of the world control our people. One hundred and fifty years after the majority of these Jews converted, to all appearances, to Christianity, a portion of them have still managed to transmit the faith of their fathers to their children after them. Haven't you noticed how little control the gentiles have over their religious lives? Isn't it marvelous how many of our own people are so ready — despite their Catholic upbringing — to persevere in the observance of Torah and *mitzvos*?"

Now, as he paced the streets of night-time Lisbon, he remembered the moment when his father Fernando Elviras had revealed the monumental secret that he, Don Carlos, was a Jew. His father had taken him out of the city, up into the hills to a lonely spot where there was no one to overhear their fateful conversation. Don Carlos recalled how agitated and even frightened his father had been, not knowing how his son — young officer and devout Catholic — would take the news. Would he be angry? Would he accept the father's revelation or reject it in favor of continuing his present comfortable lifestyle? He might even choose to react in the most dangerous way of all, and inform the Inquisition that his father was a heretic! It had happened, after all, in other families.

Don Carlos remembered how shaken he'd been, and how he'd retreated to a monastery for a few days to be alone with himself. The notion that his father was a Jew, and he a Jew's son, had pierced him to the core. He'd felt mortally wounded. Eventually, after much anguished thought, he decided to accept the yoke of Torah so suddenly revealed to him. And he, Don Carlos, was not the only young man in Lisbon to make this decision. That very fact was proof that even when the Jewish nation was comparable to dust, the world had no power over it. The stars — the stars of Lisbon — were right!

He became aware of the intense cold and turned up the collar of his overcoat. He continued walking slowly, seemingly at his ease. The streets were deserted at this hour of the night. Only the occasional howl of an unseen dog disturbed the peace. As he passed one house he heard the strains of a violin, slow and sad. Tears sprang into his eyes...

At last he reached his destination. He paused by the door, looked around, and knocked the prescribed number of times. Silvia de Lima himself threw open the door and said with shining eyes, "*Boa noite* (Good evening)! What is the illustrious admiral doing at my humble home at such an hour?" His smile stretched from ear to ear as he opened his arms to embrace his guest.

But Don Carlos didn't smile.

De Lima's arms fell to his sides. His keen intuition told him that something had happened — something serious. Don Carlos tried to thaw his frozen attitude with a small smile, saying, "And why shouldn't I want to enjoy a discussion with the eminent judge, Fernando Jorge Silvia de Lima?"

The judge cast a penetrating glance at his visitor, whose forced smile didn't fool him for a minute. With one hand on Don Carlos' shoulder, he led him silently into a spacious parlor. Still without speaking, he poured his guest a glassful of fine wine. The two sat beside the glowing fireplace, and a small dog came to nestle at Don Carlos' feet. Presently, it changed its mind and leaped up into its owner's lap.

De Lima waited for Don Carlos to speak first. Don Carlos sipped his wine, then raised the glass to his host and said with another unconvincing smile, "Well, that's that, my friend."

De Lima didn't ask what he meant. As a Marrano living in the heart of Lisbon, he knew well enough.

"Who?" he whispered.

"De Henrique."

"De Henrique?" The words shot out of de Lima in surprise and anger.

"Yes!"

Judge de Lima knew de Henrique well — knew him as one of the city's slyest and most dangerous men. As a civil judge, he had come up against him more than once. Many of de Henrique's victims, freed from prison after proof had been brought forward of their being true and pious Christians, had sought legal redress before the judge. Had de Lima wished, he might have had de Henrique arrested and indicted as a common felon. De Henrique particularly enjoyed bringing accusations against rich citizens, so that the church might impound all their wealth — of which he, personally, made sure to get his commission. The men at the Holy Office, well aware of this practice, chose to remain silent.

De Lima remembered a financial scandal that had rocked the Holy Office some five years earlier — a scandal in which de Henrique was involved. With great exertion, the clergy had managed to hush up that ugly affair.

De Henrique liked money. But why persecute Don Carlos? The admiral was not a particularly wealthy man. The dossier on that other scandal was available to the judge, easily accessible through the court archives.

One might, de Lima thought, make use of it now, in order to stop de Henrique from hounding Don Carlos.

"What do you plan to do?" he asked.

Don Carlos lifted his head and looked squarely at de Lima. "I'm leaving tomorrow. I'm taking Beatriz and the children with me."

"Without fighting back? Without involving the king?!"

Don Carlos searched for words. "They know something," he said slowly. "They know that I visited Rabbi Menashe ben Israel in Amsterdam."

De Lima's hand shook as he replaced his glass on the table. With an abrupt motion he pushed the dog off his lap. The dog gaped at him with startled eyes and emitted one small yelp. Leaning toward Don Carlos, de Lima asked, "How do they know?" His voice held fear.

Don Carlos sighed and took another sip of wine. "I wish I knew."

"Who told you about it?"

Don Carlos knew that the answer would surprise his friend. "*Padre* João Manuel."

"João Manuel?" De Lima was clearly astonished. "Even before any official investigation is launched, he told *you* of their suspicions?"

Don Carlos nodded.

De Lima's thoughts galloped like war-horses in the thick of battle. He was fully cognizant of Lisbon's complex internal life. He knew the rivalries and factions that existed among the various institutions there. Like a burst of lightning on a gloomy night, understanding burst forth: "What, have they quarreled again?"

"Seemingly," Don Carlos answered, his wry smile mirroring his friend's.

De Lima rose from his seat and began pacing the room, deep in thought. His steps were muffled by the thick rug that covered the center of the room. Abruptly he turned and exclaimed, "See here, Don Carlos — this won't do! You must stay here, keep your position, and fight that devil! Our community needs you. Tomorrow morning I'll rouse all of de Henrique's enemies. Perhaps we'll manage to bring him to justice before he has a chance to begin his investigation against you."

Don Carlos' smile was brief and weary. "I think it's too late now. In any case, suddenly I feel weary. This life of tension is so difficult — a life that calls for caution at every step. Perhaps, if I hadn't decided yet, I might have taken up your offer. I might have recruited my friends at the royal court, and even in the corridors of the Inquisition itself, to fight that devil once and for all time." He paused sadly. "But I've decided. I am no longer in Lisbon. My heart is already in Amsterdam — or Hamburg — or Turkey. In my heart, I am no longer Don Carlos Carneiro, the admiral, but Yitzchak ben Yisrael, living in a free city where I can be a Jew openly, observing the Torah and its *mitzvos*. Maybe I'll manage to earn a living as captain of some ship in my new country — because I love the sea!" He gave de Lima a sorrowful look. "Leave it, my friend. It is Hashem's will."

De Lima was outraged. "Impossible! We cannot go on without you! Captain Don Carlos should be the last to leave the ship — he certainly doesn't sink it as long as it can still stay afloat! Do you want to destroy our small community of Marranos? Without you, it will disintegrate, Don Carlos!"

Pain pierced Don Carlos' heart. Communal *seders* they'd shared paraded before his eyes; hours of prayer, and fewer precious hours of study — the *Chumash*, or else Rav Menashe's book, *Consiliador*. At those times, he and his people had encouraged one another in strengthening their faith and their ability to withstand the Inquisition's terrors. He saw celebrations, secret *chuppahs* where young couples were bound to one another as Jews. From time to time they'd managed to persuade other young people to join them, to remember who their fathers were and to carry on their traditions. No, it wouldn't be easy to leave it all behind! Everything he'd overseen, in the fleet and in his community. Everything he'd managed to build together with Arnaldo Rodriguez — Raphael Chaim — who might, at this very hour, have succeeded in escaping the death sentence imposed on him...

And yet, despite it all, he shook his head in disagreement.

"It's too late, my friend! I can't go back on my decision. With Hashem's help, I hope to leave this country tomorrow without those accursed ones laying their hands on me."

Don Carlos handed his host a large envelope.

"In this envelope, my dear de Lima, are the names of our people throughout Portugal. Guard it well. Keep it well hidden from those who would rejoice in its capture."

He stood up to his full height. Gripping de Lima's hand, he shook it strongly. A celebratory note crept into his voice as he cried, "From this moment, you are leader of the Jewish community in Lisbon and all of Portugal. I wish you good *mazel!*"

With damp eyes he regarded his friend for a last, long moment, before turning and leaving the house.

23

The shock was total.

Luis' men stared in dismay at the captain. Nobody moved. The casket containing Raphael Chaim weighed heavily on the four sailors' backs, but they, too, stood immobile, not daring to set it on the ground.

Luis was aware of acute danger. Just minutes before the completion of their mission, this officer was capable of ruining everything. Without warning, he leaped up the steps until he stood face-to-face with the irate captain, whose eyes glowed like a pair of torches in the dark.

Luis had decided to bluff his way through this sticky situation with a nonstop stream of words.

"*Senhor*, I'm very sorry we disturbed you. It was an accident. One of the sailors slipped, and the cargo crate nearly fell. We beg your forgiveness, *Senhor*. You must be very tired after your preparations for the voyage. We understand how important every hour of sleep must be right now, knowing that you set sail tomorrow. So I very much hope you understand that the noise was made by mistake, not intentionally. We tried with all our might to walk quietly, so as not to disturb anyone — believe me, Your Excellency..."

The captain opened his mouth as though to try to stem the tide of Luis' speech. But Luis didn't give him the chance. On he rushed, without pause:

"Your Excellency must understand that we have made a long journey from the north, rushing to arrive before nightfall. However, we were not successful. We are merchants for the most part, but some of us, as you see, are clergymen. Here are the authorizations we received from the admiral of this armada, His Excellency Don Carlos Carneiro. Your Excellency will understand that we've had an arduous trip. We hoped with all our hearts to arrive at the harbor before nightfall, but we ran into obstacles on the road. One of our horses died unexpectedly and precious hours were lost before we could find a replacement. We were afraid we'd lose our chance — that we'd have to wait months before the fleet next sails for Brazil. However, praise the Lord, we managed at any rate to come in time. What we need now is a few good hours of sleep. May we, with your permission, proceed to our cabins, Your Excellency?"

Without waiting for an answer, Luis signaled for his men to proceed. The captain and the two officers accompanying him stepped back and drew their swords. The men stopped in their tracks. Luis' bluff hadn't worked.

The captain bellowed, "WHO ARE YOU?"

Luis sighed. Assuming a timid air, he smiled ingratiatingly. "Ah, I understand. Your Excellency wants to know our names? Please — of course! My name is Alfonso Neves, and I am a priest, officiating at Coimbra. My intention is to sail to Rio de Janeiro, in Brazil. I will help one of my brothers in the church in his holy work, and in organizing Inquisition activities there. After all, many of our 'new Christians' have emigrated to that country. Who knows whether or not they've thrown off the yoke of the church and resumed their fathers' heretical practices? We must strengthen our supervision over them. Am I not right, *Senhor*? And perhaps we shall even succeed in bringing the cross to those heathen wild men, the native Brazilians themselves! Here, Your Excellency, are our papers, all in order. They will show that I've come on church business. And here" — Luis pulled another document from his cassock —"is the authorization from the admiral's staff."

Luis thrust the papers at the captain, who pushed them roughly aside without vouchsafing them so much as a glance. Luis thought fast. The captain was obviously well aware that the stranger on his ship was trying with a flood of words to confuse and distract him. On the other hand, he was tired and longing for his warm bed. He might seize on any excuse to bring this stupid conversation to an end.

The captain advanced until the tip of his sword rested against Luis' throat. There was hardly a hand's-breadth of space between the two men. Luis could hear the captain's tense breathing and he could see the cold, cruel eyes. *"Don't be the first to look away,"* he told himself. Mustering all his courage, he stood his ground, trying to relax despite the feel of cold steel against the tender flesh of his throat. Not a muscle quivered in Luis' face as he returned the captain's gaze openly and steadily, as though to say, "You don't scare me a bit."

To Luis' men, the moment seemed to stretch for an eternity. Their eyes were riveted to their leader, fighting desperately for their mission. The sailors bearing the crate also watched Luis in fearful silence. Nobody could help him now.

The captain moved his furious face even closer to Luis'.

"I'm not interested in hearing any more of your stories," he said in a low, threatening hiss. There was hatred in every syllable. "Tomorrow at dawn, before we sail, we'll chat again. Right now, you are all under arrest. And if I grow too suspicious, I won't hesitate to send you all back ashore! Even His Excellency, Admiral Don Carlos Carneiro himself, won't be able to save you then. Do you hear? Or maybe, to entertain my loyal sailors, I'll simply throw you overboard as a present to the hungry sharks that patrol these waters. Your bundle of papers doesn't interest me a a bit!"

He considered a moment, then added, "But there is one thing I'd like to know right now!" He removed the sword-tip from Luis' throat and placed it on the wooden crate. *"What are you hiding in that box?"*

Luis' men stopped breathing. Their eyes narrowed in panic. All was lost. Their daring plan had failed utterly. In another moment Raphael Chaim would be revealed to the ship's officer. They could already see themselves transported to the flames of the *auto-da-fé* in the central square of Lisbon before a shouting, jubilant crowd. Perhaps their burning would be such a festive occasion that even the King and his courtiers would come to witness the spectacle. It was an honor they would be happy to do without...

But Luis hadn't given up. He looked affronted.

"What are you asking, sir? That crate contains our personal belongings! Traveling together all this distance, we decided to pack all our things together. That's much simpler than each man carrying his own pack. Does His Excellency wish me to open the box? Please!

"Yes — and at once!"

Luis turned to the waiting men and motioned for the sailors to place the crate on the floor."Who has the key?" he asked.

The crate had no lock — or key. His men knew that, and they knew that Luis knew it. Their brows wrinkled as they tried to guess why he was asking for something that did not exist.

Then one of them figured it out. He stepped forward and bowed low. "The key was in my pocket, sir. But I can't find it now. It seems to be lost."

There had been no time to think. He didn't know if he'd said the right thing, or the very worst. Luis gazed at him in astonishment.

"Lost? Then how will we get our things out? If we're forced to break the crate, it won't be worth a thing!"

The man hung his head.

"Search your pockets again," Luis ordered. "Carefully this time." He peeked at the captain out of the corner of his eye.

The man executed a thorough search. Presently he lifted his hands in a gesture of despair: "Not there!"

"Can't you remember where you put it?"

"I'm sorry, sir. I do remember, though, that when we came up on deck I still had it."

One of the sailors ventured to add his voice to this bizarre interchange. "Could it be that it fell when we slipped on the stairs?"

"It's certainly possible," Luis answered quickly."I'll go up and look." He turned humbly to the captain."*Senhor*, can you loan me your taper for a moment? I want to run up on deck to search for the lost key. It would be a great pity if we had to break open the crate."

The captain gave him a look that combined scorn with doubt. "Something here doesn't smell right. Open that box immediately!"

Luis allowed his face to become suffused with anger, then pretended to make a mighty effort to control his rage and treat the captain respectfully. "That's exactly what we're trying to do! Didn't Your Excellency hear that the key was lost? If you'd be willing to lend me your taper, I'll run upstairs to quickly search for it. Why are you treating us like criminals?"

Luis extended a hand. The captain hesitated. His glance swept the group standing motionless at the side, watching. Without quite being able to explain why, he found these men frightening. Luis' hand was still outstretched.

The captain yielded. He handed Luis the flaming taper.

"I hope you realize that this is an uncommon courtesy on my part," he said gruffly.

"And I," Luis said with a great show of humility, "thank you for it from the bottom of my heart!"

"I'm giving you a short time to search for that key — do you hear me, sir? Meanwhile, no one else is to leave this spot. Don't force me to rouse the guards. I tell you frankly, I don't believe a word you've been telling me."

"I understand, *Senhor*," Luis answered, already on his way to the stairs. His men silently made way for him to pass. Their leader's intentions were a closed book to them. What was he up to?

As Luis climbed up on deck, one of the men also slipped away. It was Sariamento, the new ship's officer who had greeted the newcomers tonight. In the dark, nobody noticed his disappearance. He climbed up on deck in Luis' wake.

"What do we do?" Luis muttered, as he stooped in a searching position near the floor of the deck. "I'm worried."

Sariamento was also worried. "Why did you ask permission to come out here?"

Luis lifted his head. "I hardly know. I just wanted to gain some time, to be alone for a few minutes. To think about what to do. And also — to pray!"

"You're right. I think that's the only thing that can help us now. *Senhor* Sacramento, the captain, is still angry at Don Carlos for forcing him to take us aboard. He wasn't about to accept your group as well." He paused. "But why are you joining us at all?"

"We're in a serious predicament. By tomorrow morning de Henrique is going to discover my true identity. He's after Don Carlos' head, and wanted me to help him. Naturally, I deviated from orders. You know that Arnaldo Rodriguez is lying below. Right now, he's still asleep. But what happens if he wakes up before we find a way to hide him?"

Sariamento gasped,"You did it? You rescued him? *Baruch Hashem*! His cabin is all ready. It was hard work preparing a hiding place for him."

"Yes, but how do we get him safely to the cabin? Sariamento, my friend, think of something!"

The deck was deserted. The sails had been hung on the masts, though not yet unfurled to display their full glory. The wind whistled through the riggings before continuing on to blow over slumbering Lisbon. Sariamento put the city at his back and gazed out over the dark sea, symbol of their hope for a new life.

"So what do we do?" Luis pressed."I must go down already."

Sariamento was still silent. He had been on board ship all of one day so far and knew hardly anything about the crew or the ins and outs of life on the *Santa Lucia*. Yesterday, during the outbreak of fighting between the old hands and the new, when the veteran sailors had tried to have the newcomers ousted from the ship, Sariamento had noted the way the first officer had taken their side. The officer had done his best to calm frayed tempers and to protect the new men's rights. The regular crewmen had defied him, and one of the other officers had shouted that Captain Sacramento didn't want them on his ship. Still the first officer had stood his ground. If Don Carlos hadn't suddenly appeared as he did, there was no telling what the outcome might have been.

During the hours that followed, the officer — Alvaro Gomez by name — had tried to engage the new crewmen in conversation. He had asked them many questions, eliciting detailed information about each of their lives. Despite his suspicions, Sariamento had tried to answer civilly. As they spoke together, Gomez had murmured — almost incidentally — the words, *Shema Yisrael*, and then continued talking of other things. Sariamento, standing now on the deck beside Luis, still couldn't make up his mind: Was Gomez a Marrano who had been trying to discover whether they were the same? Or a spy, laying a trap for them?

"Sariamento," Luis' voice broke into his thoughts,"what will be? We've been 'searching' for the lost key for a long time now. Who knows what that angry captain is doing down below?"

"Luis, I'm going to wake up the first officer, Alvaro Gomez."

"Do you know him? And what can he do for us?"

"I'm not sure I know him... But it's time for us to trust in Hashem. At this point, there's not much left to lose. You go back down to your men and that pleasant captain of yours, and try to buy us some time. I hope to be back immediately."

Sariamento vanished in the darkness, making his way down by another exit. With a heart filled with trepidation, Luis went back to the group at the foot of the stairs.

"I'm so sorry, Captain. I searched in the dark but didn't manage to lay hands on that key. Maybe we'll have more luck in daylight."

The captain didn't answer. In fact, it seemed to Luis that he'd hardly attended to a word he'd just said. His men, too, no longer stood exactly as he'd left them. What had occurred while he was gone?

The men were standing in a semicircle in front of the casket, as thought guarding it. What was going on? Had the captain, spurred by impatience and his own suspicions, attempted to break it open by force? There was no way for Luis to know. He peered into his men's grim faces, and the captain's, trying to divine from their expressions what had occurred in his absence.

"Your men," the captain said in a tight voice,"have defied orders, *Senhor*, ah —"

"Alfonso Neves," Luis supplied helpfully.

The captain exploded. Brandishing his sword menacingly close to Luis' head, he screamed, "I don't need your help! Are these men imbeciles? Have they forgotten that *I* am captain of the *Santa Lucia*, and not them? A sailor who defies my orders — dies! That is the law of the sea! It is unfortunate that you men are private citizens, so I cannot bring you all to swift justice. But disobeying orders is still disobeying orders — *is that understood?*"

"Yes, yes, we understand," Luis replied humbly.

"And now, I order you and your men to leave my ship!"

Luis did not hasten to comply. He prepared for a last stand. Waving a fist, he cried,"*Senhor*, you are right. You are captain of the ship! But you are not the commander of this armada! You are not admiral of this fleet! We came aboard by the authority of Don Carlos Carneiro. Don't you think we will apply to him through church channels, to tell him about your conduct to us tonight? To us — loyal Portuguese citizens, sailing to Brazil on behalf of our country! The law is the law, and defying the law is defying the law. However, *Senhor*, right at this moment you, too, are disobeying orders! And all because we unintentionally woke you up. Do you think Don Carlos will accept *that* as an excuse?"

Luis was shaking. He advanced on the captain, ready to strike. The fact that they had not yet succeeded in hiding Raphael Chaim tormented him. Time was passing; dawn would break soon. In just a few hours de Henrique would be creating a furor. Who knew what would happen if, by that time, he and his men were not securely concealed in the depths of this big ship?

The captain was taken aback. Luis' straight talk had unnerved him. He had no way of knowing this clergyman's exact standing in the church hierarchy. One did not pick fights with the church!

Luis saw with satisfaction that he'd succeeded in raising doubts in the captain's mind. He turned to his men and called to them past the captain's shoulder,"Well, you've heard who we'll have to live with for the next few months! I suggest that we leave the ship and send a delegation to the admiral in the morning.

"Pick up the crate!" he ordered the sailors."We're leaving!"

The men began to climb. Behind them, the four sailors — with some assistance from Luis and two of his men — hoisted the crate to their shoulders and followed the others to the stairs...

24

Though the captain clearly itched to react, he hesitated. In silence he watched Luis and his men make their way slowly toward the stairs, tentatively returning his sword to its scabbard. His two young companions did the same.

Suddenly, a loud call was heard from behind.

"What's going on here?"

The captain stiffened in surprise. He turned his head to see who had spoken. It was Alvaro Gomez, his first officer, seemingly materialized out of nowhere.

"Nothing," the captain said tersely. "We were being boarded by a group of strangers — civilians. Luckily, I woke up and caught them."

Gomez looked interested. "Who are they?"

"They told me some story, but I don't believe a word their leader said. I think he said his name's Alfonso Neves."

"What? They simply wanted to board the ship — without authorization? Impossible!"

The captain was not quick to reply. He focused on the stairs, where the last of the strangers were still climbing. When the final leg was no longer visible in the light of his taper, he yawned and said, "They showed me some sort of document, with Don Carlos' order to take them aboard. I didn't even read it!"

Gomez was astounded. "*Senhor*," he said sharply, "Aren't you afraid we'll get in trouble again? Wasn't what happened here yesterday enough — that new group of crewmen joining us without our knowledge?"

The captain yawned again. Exhaustion had him in its grip. "Maybe. Maybe you're right. This might involve us in further trouble. We'll decide what to do tomorrow. Right now, I'm going back to bed. *Boa noite*."

The captain threw his first officer a smile that was closer to a sneer. Gomez followed him silently. Lack of sleep, he thought worriedly, was clouding the captain's mind. He didn't fully appreciate the possible outcome of his action.

"Captain!" he called anxiously. "Captain!"

The captain slowed and finally stopped. Reluctantly, he turned. "Yes?"

"Perhaps the captain will permit me to handle this matter as I see fit? I think it's vital that we avoid another clash with the admiral, sir — and on the very day we set sail!"

The captain narrowed his eyes. Hastily, Gomez added, "Sir, I'm not doubting your judgment! But I'd like at all costs to avoid additional strife. Don't you trust my loyalty, after five years as your first officer?"

The captain's face was nearly split asunder by yet another enormous yawn. When he finished, he snarled, "Do what you want! I'll be happy if you can get them all off my ship. But make certain not to allow them to stay on board without a thorough investigation. You must find out who they are and why they want to come with us — and especially what they've got in that accursed box of theirs! I'm going to ask you for every detail tomorrow."

"*Sim, Senhor*," Gomez answered briefly.

The captain opened the door of his cabin. With his hand on the knob, he turned once more and said, "But Gomez, see that I'm not disturbed too early. I heravy appoint you captain of this ship until I wake."

Gomez waited until the captain had vanished inside his cabin and the two younger officers had walked away. Then, galvanized into sudden action, he ran up the stairs to the upper deck. He met Luis and his companions there, surrounding Martinez and hanging on his every word.

"But Gomez promised to help us," he heard Martinez say desperately. "Any minute now..."

"Quickly, friends!" Gomez whispered. "It's time to disperse to the cabins Martinez's men have prepared for you. Don't be afraid of me! I, too, know what 'Shema Yisrael' is, and Hashem's Name.* Martinez will lead the way and show you where you'll be spending the duration of the voyage." He glanced at Luis with a glimmer of a smile. "Alfonso Neves will stay here, to help me prepare the results of the 'investigation' I must submit in the morning to Senhor Silvia Caitano Sacramento, captain of this ship."

The men followed Martinez unquestioningly. He led them by a different route into the depths of the ship — one that circumvented the captain's and officers' quarters. The four sailors were especially careful with their crate, and the others helped them navigate the steps in the darkness. Only when they reached the lower passage did Martinez pick up the pace. There was a dim light here, which allowed the men to follow him without too much difficulty. At the farthest end of the passage he took a large key from his pocket and opened the door to a narrow cabin.

"Let the sailors enter first, with the crate," he whispered.

The sailors set down their burden and breathed easier. Martinez gestured for them to leave quickly, each man to his own berth. Even as he carefully shut the door behind them, Luis' men had fallen on the crate and were opening it. They removed the old clothes they had used as additional concealment and looked upon their leader, who lay cramped and unmoving. There was no sign of life on his sleeping visage.

"Quickly!" they urged each other. "Quickly!"

They lifted Raphael Chaim out of the crate and laid him on the bed that stood against one wall. Three men set to work vigorously massaging his limbs, neck, and chest. Raphael Chaim began to stir. The men sighed in relief.

Raphael Chaim's breathing was shallow and uneven. Someone brought him a cup of water. "Drink a little, Raphael Chaim. Don't worry, you're in good hands."

It was hard to gauge his reaction in the gloom. All too soon, however, it became clear that he was refusing the drink. He tried to push away both the hand and the proffered glass, but lacked the strength. In a weak, rasping voice he asked, "What happened to me? Where am I? Who are you?"

The men thanked Hashem in their hearts: Their leader was talking!

The man holding the glass said, "Raphael Chaim! Let us all thank Hashem — you're free! You're out of prison! We are Luis' men. Do you remember Luis? We rescued you from the filthy hands of *Padre* João Manuel and de Henrique!"

Raphael Chaim lay back. His breathing was still heavy and restless.

"You're aboard a ship that's sailing to Brazil in a few hours. Cheer up, Raphael Chaim! From there, it will be easier for you to get home to Amsterdam. But you must first grow strong. Hold on! Trust in Hashem, and be strong!"

The others gazed on the stricken man on the bed. Had he been able to grasp what they had said to him? As they watched, Raphael Chaim's breathing grew easier and more even. Seemingly, he believed them. They smiled gratefully.

"Now," said Martinez, "I'll show you where to hide him during the voyage. He mustn't stay here, understand?"

Martinez crouched down and ran his hands over the floorboards. After a moment he pried up a loose board. A deep hole appeared.

"Here," said Martinez. "There's a ladder leading down to a secret room below. We spent hours yesterday, preparing this place. Raphael Chaim must stay hidden there during the day, lest someone stumble upon him by accident. Two of you will live up here. You'll bring him up at night for a breath of fresh air. Tomorrow night a doctor — one of our own people — will come to examine him. He'll also dress his wounds and administer necessary medicines. The rest of you come with me now. Every pair will be assigned to a separate cabin. Try to stay out of sight as much as possible during the trip."

The men nodded and followed Martinez from the cabin.

The two who stayed behind prepared for a short night's sleep. Fatigue sapped their energy — the kind of bone-deep weariness that comes in the wake of terrible tension, of uncertainty, of a sudden plunge into grave danger. One of them spread clothes on the floor while the other collapsed onto the room's second bed, his eyes closing of their own accord.

Not many seconds had passed before his friend roused him: "Roberto, get up! Raphael Chaim is calling, but I can't understand what he's saying! He seems to be afraid. Get up, Roberto! I'm worried. He's sweating terribly."

The two went over to Arnaldo Rodriguez's bed. He was thrashing about and crying aloud. He must be silenced at all cost! Roberto dipped a rag into a water jug that stood in the corner and moistened Raphael Chaim's lips.

"Pedro," he called, "you're right — he *is* sweating! Bring the water here so I can wash his face."

Pedro hurried to do as he was asked. The two bent over the bed, sponging Raphael Chaim's face and forehead and speaking soothingly to him. Raphael Chaim never stopped groaning and calling. Something was troubling him. There was something he wanted to say...

At last, he succeeded in lifting a hand. He touched Roberto's head and lightly grasped his hair. Roberto allowed himself to be gently pulled until his ear was nearly touching Raphael Chaim's lips. He heard him whisper, "You are Luis' men?"

Roberto nodded.

"Why — have — you — brought — me — here?"

"Master," Roberto answered emotionally, "we rescued you! You're on your way to freedom! You are leaving Portugal!"

Raphael Chaim's face grew pinched with anger.

"I — don't — want! Return — me — to — the — death — pit!"

Staggered, Roberto burst out, "B-but why, Raphael Chaim? The Torah says, 'And you shall choose life!' "

Raphael Chaim didn't answer at once. Even whispering was a hardship for him. Soon he tugged at Roberto's hair again. In a suddenly stronger voice, he asked, "Why have you brought me here? Why not the others who were captured with me?"

Roberto bowed his head. With his two hands he grasped Raphael Chaim's emaciated one. "But master, we couldn't save everyone! Don Carlos gave orders to rescue you, because you were our leader! You came to us and sacrificed your own freedom to be with us! We are in your debt. Raphael Chaim, we are in exile and cannot act exactly as we please. Rescuing you was a dangerous and tricky operation — and we're still not certain we've succeeded! At daybreak, when this matter comes to light, there will be an uproar in the city. The king will doubtless order the army to help the Inquisition hunt you down."

The shadow of a smile touched Raphael Chaim's lips. He gave a barely perceptible shake of the head.

"I refuse!" he managed to utter, almost inaudibly. "I want you to return me to prison. I won't be able to live in peace knowing that my brothers, alongside whom I have suffered these past two years, are still in that dungeon. I am a Jew! And a Jew doesn't behave that way. You say that I'm your leader — then obey me now!"

Lifting his head slightly, he raised his voice and asked, "Where is Luis? *Where is Luis?* I want to speak to him!"

He dropped back, exhausted. His eyes flickered open and shut. Roberto and Pedro gazed at him with compassion, at a loss for what to do next.

Suddenly, there came a sharp rap at the door. For an instant the two men froze in their places. Then, seizing Raphael Chaim by his arms and legs, they pleaded in anguished whispers, "Please try not to make a sound, Raphael Chaim! We have to hide you." Quickly they thrust him under the bed.

Roberto positioned himself in a prone position on the bed while Pedro went to open the door.

No one was there. There was the sound of retreating footsteps down the darkened passage.

Pedro shut the door and leaned against it, pale and drained. Shakily, he told Roberto, "I think we're facing difficult days aboard this ship."

"I think so, too, Pedro. We must be very alert — especially for Raphael Chaim's sake. Should we leave him where he is for the present?"

"It's not a very secure hiding place."

"I know. At daybreak we'll bring him down to the hidden room below and do everything we can to make sure he's safe."

Gently they drew Raphael Chaim out from under the bed. To their relief, he had fallen into a deep and blessedly peaceful sleep.

⁓⁓

Luis and Gomez stood on the starlit deck and gripped each other's hands in a strong clasp. They had completed their plan for the appeasement of Captain Silvia Caitano Sacramento. Luis would approach the captain to beg his forgiveness. In addition, Gomez had decided to exact a hefty fine from Luis' group, to be spent on a lavish wine party for the ship's officers on their successful arrival in Brazil. The money would remain in the captain's keeping for the duration of the voyage.

Thinking of this last detail, they smiled. It was a smile that bespoke their profound knowledge of human nature. Captain Sacramento would doubtless squirrel away a neat portion of the fine into his own personal coffers.

Martinez appeared on deck. He spotted Luis. "All your men are in their cabins. You've got to do the same, and stay there until we're safely at sea. Follow me!"

25

The thud on the door was powerful. In its wake came the noise of galloping hooves, retreating into the distance. De Henrique woke with a start. His room was pitch dark. Had he really heard what he thought he'd heard? He lay unmoving in bed, afraid to budge. In the silence he could distinctly hear the pounding of his heart. What had caused the mighty thud? Was someone trying to issue a warning? And who could it be?

His first suspicion rested on *Padre* João Manuel. Yes, it was entirely possible that his superior, the "glorious" head of the Inquisition, was behind this episode. He was trying to take his revenge for what had happened between them yesterday. And... could Don Carlos also be involved? He must have realized that the Inquisition was on his heels. A smart man, Don Carlos — and a powerful one. The priest's visit to his home must have made him aware that there were people in Lisbon who knew too much. Could he be the one behind the bang on his door tonight?

On the other hand, it was entirely possible that neither João Manuel nor Don Carlos was behind it, but a relative of one of his victims — one of the many men he'd had imprisoned, tortured, and from whom he'd ex-

tracted a confession of being Jewish before burning them at the stake —
seeking vengeance.

Through his fear he felt a certain satisfaction in the knowledge that the
Inquisition's enemies understood who their real enemy was; that de
Henrique was the potent figure at the Inquisition, and not *Padre* João
Manuel... It was even possible, he thought wildly, that they had *all* joined
forces against him! Perhaps Don Carlos was using a disgruntled relative
to do his dirty work, with João Manuel providing his support and protection... The thought was like a pile of stones settling on his chest.

What concerned him most urgently at the moment, though, was the
question of whether or not someone awaited him near the door — someone with evil intent against him. Were the thud on the door and the
galloping hooves only a ploy to distract him from the real danger? De
Henrique didn't know what to think.

In the end, he rose slowly from his bed. Cautiously moving the curtain
aside a fraction, he peered out into the deserted street. Although the first
intimations of light were already apparent at the very edges of the sky, it
was still too dark for de Henrique to tell whether a human figure stood
beside his house. He let the curtain drop back into place. "I must be careful," he told himself. For a moment he toyed with the notion of
abandoning his plan to have Don Carlos arrested — especially if all these
forces were aligned against him.

Suddenly, he remembered Luis. Where *was* Luis? He had promised to
report to de Henrique, even in the middle of the night, on the results of
his search of Don Carlos' home and whether he had managed to hide the
tefillin somewhere inside. Could Luis have been captured by Don Carlos'
men? Might he have revealed the nature of de Henrique's instructions? It
would be terribly humiliating for the priest if his underhanded methods
became public knowledge. A powerful fear seized hold of him.

Presently he shook off these troubling speculations. He tightened his
lips and clenched his left fist, which he pounded into his right hand. A renewed self-confidence surged through him. No! He would persist to the
end! Don Carlos *would* go to prison, come what may!

And *Padre* João Manuel — what of him? De Henrique gave a frus-
trated sigh.

He dressed quickly and waited for daylight. It would be a simpler matter then to see if an ambush awaited him outside. He lit the taper that stood ready by his bed and began prowling the room restlessly. At one point he knelt, and prayed for success in bringing down Don Carlos. Rising to his feet once more, he crossed to the window and peeked out again. The courtyard was clearly visible now; as far as he could tell, it was empty. Dared he risk opening the door?

He went into his kitchen and found a sharp knife. With slow, even steps he walked to the front door. He stood behind it and began, with great care, to push it open. One foot remained lodged at the foot of the door so that he might, if the necessity arose, prevent someone outside from forcing his way in. Through the crack he'd opened he permitted himself a quick peek out.

There was no one there. He opened the door a little wider. That was when he caught sight, at some little distance from the door, of the rock that had been thrown at it. There was a string attached to the rock. It seemed to him, peering out in the uncertain light, that there was a paper attached to the far end of the string.

He breathed easier, reproaching himself for his cowardly fears and fancies. No stranger stood there waiting for him. Quickly he went to the rock. There was indeed a note tied to it. He picked it up gingerly, opened and read it.

A broad smile split his face. With a much lighter step, he re-entered his house.

"That's it!" he crowed. "I've done it! Thank you, my Lord. Don Carlos is in my hands now!"

Despite the early hour, de Henrique hurried to the royal palace. It was imperative that he obtain the royal stamp that would permit him to arrest Don Carlos without delay. He now had the proof he needed. The man who had left him the first note had now handed him a second vital message. But why do it in such a way as to frighten de Henrique out of his wits? And why leave the scene in such a hurry? Probably, he thought, it was dangerous for the man to be seen near the home of an Inquisition officer.

De Henrique smiled with satisfaction. This would be one of his greatest triumphs. All Lisbon would hail him today! And maybe — just maybe

— he would succeed in putting an end to *Padre* João Manuel, too, once and for all!

⥈⥇

Don Carlos was tense. He stood uneasily in the center of the spacious room, an arm resting on one of the packing crates they'd prepared to take with them to Brazil. Beatriz, his wife, watched him anxiously. Their three small children ran and played among the crates.

"I don't understand why he hasn't come yet," Don Carlos fretted aloud.

"Who?"

"Pedro Alvares! He was supposed be here at daybreak. That's what we agreed on yesterday. That's why I pressed you to work through the night to pack everything we can take with us. I don't understand why he hasn't arrived by now! He's always been extremely punctual in carrying out my orders."

"This is the darkest hour, Carlos. This is when we must say good-bye to everything we've had here. It's bound to be difficult. Try to stay calm, my dear. We can pray to Hashem and hope that all will go well — that he will show up soon."

"Yes, I hope so. I want to hope so. It was my intention to leave the city before it awakes. I don't want to be seen leaving on the flagship together with my family."

They fell silent. Beatriz rose from time to time and opened the door to see whether anyone was coming. Every breath of wind sounded like horses' hooves and raps on the door.

"Carlos!" Her voice was quiet but pleading. Don Carlos turned to his wife. "Yes?"

Beatriz only sighed and wrung her hands. Don Carlos prompted, "What did you want?"

"Carlos, will we ever see Lisbon again?"

"No!" At this tension-filled moment, he had no patience for sentimentality. "Wasn't it you who wanted to leave the city as quickly as possible?"

Beatriz wiped away a tear: "Yes, you're right. But will we really ever see her again?"

"No."

A silence fell between them. Beatriz lifted her head and looked at the majestic chandelier that hung in the center of the room. She was leaving it behind to whomever would take over their home. Every Shabbos, long, beautiful candles had glowed there. The chandelier had been a house-warming gift from the queen. The queen herself had attended the gala affair Don Carlos and his wife had hosted on that occasion. The wine, Beatriz remembered, had flowed like water that evening. Paulo de Henrique had been one of the honored guests. He'd certainly been far friendlier at that party than he'd been during his terrible visit this morning. Anger and fear at the memory made her tremble.

At that moment, they caught the sound of horses and a slowing carriage. Don Carlos roused himself. "He's come! Hurry and open the door, Beatriz."

But the door opened before Beatriz could move.

"*Bom dia querida, amigo* (Good morning, my dear friend)," said a familiar, much-dreaded voice. De Henrique stood in the doorway, laughing horribly. Behind him stood three grave-faced Inquisition monks and a number of royal guardsmen.

Don Carlos did not return the priest's greeting. He merely directed a look of scorn and loathing on de Henrique.

"Does the admiral permit me to enter his home?" de Henrique asked with mock humility.

"With no great pleasure," Don Carlos answered crisply. "However, my home is always open to visitors."

"*Bom dia, Senhora* (Good morning, madame)," de Henrique said to Dona Beatriz with a deep bow. Beatriz did not deign to so much as look at the intruder. She stared unwinking at the great chandelier and did not reply.

De Henrique pointed languidly at the crates piled high throughout the room. "I see your preparations for the family's journey are complete."

Don Carlos said nothing.

"In other words," de Henrique purred, "I've come just in time."

The smile disappeared from his face and was replaced by a wicked gleam. He advanced on Don Carlos with a consciousness of his own authority. At his signal, a nearby monk handed him a parchment scroll.

"I require you and Dona Beatriz to stand," de Henrique commanded. "I have an order from His Majesty, the king!"

Don Carlos' blood froze. His strange meeting with *Padre* João Manuel at the seaside yesterday had prevented him from seeking an audience with the king. He had hoped to visit His Majesty this morning instead, to bid him farewell before the fleet's departure. At the same time, he'd planned to complain about the spurious and unfair accusations being leveled against him. But de Henrique had outsmarted him. He had made his move first.

Beatriz rose slowly and came to stand beside her husband.

De Henrique unrolled the scroll and read in a ringing voice:

"His Majesty, king of Portugal and its colonies abroad, presented with clearcut proofs implicating one of Portugal's foremost sons with secret heresy and betrayal of our church — to wit, Don Carlos Carneiro, admiral of the fleet — has decided to remove him from his position of authority and to take away his royal protection, so that the Holy Office may pursue its investigation to its completion. This is being done to exorcise the evil from our midst. The glorious Portuguese fleet will sail to Brazil as planned, under the leadership of Vice-Admiral Roberto Machado de Lima. Should the allegations against Don Carlos Carneiro be proven groundless, the king will judge the matter anew and will decide at that time whether to return the accused to his former post."

De Henrique lifted his eyes from the scroll and studied Don Carlos to gauge his reaction. But there was none. Don Carlos remained impassive, eyes glued to a spot in the center of the open door. Dona Beatriz made no effort to check the tears that coursed down her cheeks. The children, forgotten, abandoned their play and inched toward their parents as though they sensed impending danger.

"So, Don Carlos," de Henrique boomed. "The farce is ended. Your mask is stripped away. Now you and Dona Beatriz will come with us. The Inquisition has a great many questions it wishes to put to you."

"Are you telling me I'm under arrest?" Don Carlos asked in amazement.

"You're intelligent enough to understand that that was His Majesty's intention!"

"You're making a very big mistake. I don't know who is weaving this web of lies around me, but I do know one thing: You have no proof at all that these hideous accusations have any truth to them! There is no shred of evidence against my wife or me. And you know that full well, de Henrique. We were friends long enough..."

De Henrique cut him off impatiently. "That has no bearing on the matter, Don Carlos. There are accusations and there are proofs. Telling proofs, Don Carlos. Otherwise, the king would not have hastened to place you in my hands. You were a favorite of his!"

Don Carlos heard the glee in the priest's voice as he crowed over his triumph. There was no point in answering him right now. After a moment, de Henrique continued, "Well, shall we go? The *Senhora* will accompany us, of course."

Dona Beatriz suddenly absorbed the enormity of the tragedy being enacted. She knew of the horrible tortures awaiting her at the hands of these evil men. She glanced at her husband's face, which seemed carved of granite. A single anguished cry erupted from her:

"The children! What will happen to the children?"

De Henrique smiled his cruel smile and said soothingly, "Don't worry, *Senhora*. The children will be in very good hands from now on. They will be placed in one of the monasteries on the outskirts of Lisbon, where kind nuns will care for them. Have you any preference as to which monastery in particular? I assure you, your opinion will carry weight with me, *Senhora*!"

Dona Beatriz stood absolutely silent, caressing her two sons' heads as they clutched at her skirts on either side.

26

One thought kept running over and over through his mind: Have the ships set sail? Is Raphael Chaim safely aboard the *Santa Lucia*? Did they manage to rescue him from the Inquisition's clutches in the end?

Don Carlos was seated on the cold stone floor of a tiny, dark cell. His hands were bound behind him, his bones still ached from the force of his fall when his jailers had flung him inside. He was still dressed in his admiral's uniform.

With an effort, he held his head erect: De Henrique might appear at any moment, and Don Carlos would not give him the satisfaction of seeing him downtrodden. He had no idea what they had done with Dona Beatriz — or the children. The pain in his heart was almost unendurable. He bit his lip, willing himself to muster every reserve of inner strength. And that strength, he knew, came from his faith in the G-d of Avraham, Who had been with him in the fiery furnace. Now it was Don Carlos' turn to be tested. And hadn't he been preparing for this moment every day since his acceptance of his heritage?

It was the fate of every Jew, and particularly of the present generation's Jewish Marranos in Portugal and Spain. This was the price one paid for being exiled. *"And because of our sins we were exiled from our land"* — he recalled the words of the *tefillah* he had recited in the Bais Yaakov synagogue on the single Shabbos he had been privileged to spend in Amsterdam, four years before. Had the Inquisition begun to shadow him even then?

His eyes gradually grew accustomed to the dark. The sole illumination came from a small window fixed in the iron door. A single ray of light entered that way, very faint, as though ashamed of facing Don Carlos in his imprisonment. The silence was profound.

No one had approached his cell in the hours since he'd been hurled inside — not to talk with him, not to interrogate him, not to bring him something to eat. He was very hungry. From time to time he heard footsteps in the corridor, doors opening and slamming shut, heartrending groans. Then the silence would return, depressing and filled with fear.

His thoughts turned to Amsterdam. How would Rav Menashe receive the news of his imprisonment? Don Carlos stirred restlessly. If only he knew that Raphael Chaim was safe, he could face his fate more calmly. At least then, he would know that he'd accomplished something in his life, before the decree had been passed that he join the long chain of Jewish suffering.

Footsteps in the corridor again. He lifted his head and listened. The steps came closer, and then there was the sound of a key scraping in the keyhole of the metal door. Don Carlos stiffened his resolve: He would maintain his dignity and his pride. Those dogs would not subdue him easily. The binding of his hands, intended to break his spirit in advance of his interrogation — and possible torture — had failed of its purpose. "Even if I walk in the valley of the shadow of death I will fear no evil because You are with me." King David's haunting words echoed over and over in Don Carlos' mind. These were his thoughts as Don Carlos was being transported to the Inquisition building in de Henrique's coach.

The door opened. Don Carlos did not vouchsafe those who entered so much as a glance. His eyes were focused on some indeterminate point in the darkness. The two young monks stared at him in astonishment, not untouched by a certain fearful respect:

"*Senhor* Carlos Carneiro, we have come to take you to *Padre* Paulo de Henrique's office for interrogation. We will help you stand."

The monk's voice was soft and quiet, like that of a theological student addressing his superior at the monastery. Apparently, the news of the eminent Don Carlos' arrest was difficult for them to digest. The monks came closer and helped the prisoner to his feet. The binding on his hands remained. He was escorted in silence to de Henrique's office.

De Henrique was leaning back in his comfortable armchair, his round face wreathed with joy. The small eyes, encased in their folds of fat, blinked continuously, as though performing an ecstatic dance. Don Carlos took note of the blinking as he entered. He knew de Henrique well, and knew that the action of those eyes did not portend a sense of peace. "He is uncertain," Don Carlos thought with a quick rise of hope in his chest. The inquisitor was not as sure of his ground as he would have liked his prisoner to believe.

"*Bem vindo, Senhor* (Welcome, sir!)" The secretary of the Holy Office broke into a broad smile.

Don Carlos' only answer was a look of pride mingled with open contempt. De Henrique cleared his throat and said, "Don Carlos, it's up to you now. I will be very happy to be shown that we have erred — that you are no secret Jew, as the evidence in our hands would indicate. You cannot imagine our pain and distress at learning that the suspicion of heresy rests on you."

Don Carlos remained silent. He was revulsed by the other's hypocrisy. If only he could spit in de Henrique's face! The secretary seemed to have completely put from his mind the memory of all the help Don Carlos had rendered him in his climb up the Inquisition's ladder. Don Carlos bitterly regretted now all the times he had spoken for de Henrique to the king.

"Don Carlos, you know full well that there is no power in all of Lisbon that can stand up against an interrogation by the Holy Office. Every person who falls into our hands ends by answering every question that we put to him — sooner or later. It all depends on how much he is willing to suffer. My advice to you is: Avoid unnecessary suffering, both for yourself and for your wife, Don Carlos!"

There was a note almost of pleading in the cruel voice. Don Carlos liked that. De Henrique, holding as he did the upper hand, was begging him not to spoil the script. Don Carlos said coldly, "I wish to be questioned by the head of the Inquisition, *Padre* João Manuel. You are merely the secretary. Secondly, order your minions to untie my hands. Unless you do, I will say nothing at all to you."

De Henrique swallowed the insult. His eyes resumed their incessant blinking. The mention of *Padre* João Manuel's name suffused him with rage, mixed with uncertainty. He had no idea where João Manuel would stand in this matter, or what relations existed between him and Don Carlos. Another thing he did not know was the role being played by members of the royal court and the military, who were interested in preventing this interrogation at all cost. It was de Henrique's wish to obtain Don Carlos' confession with all possible speed — before João Manuel entered the picture to twist matters to suit his own ends... or before anyone else might take it into his head to try and save the admiral from the just and compassionate judgment of the Inquisition.

De Henrique rose from his armchair and softly pounded on his desk, dislodging two or three documents which slipped to the floor. With slow, measured steps he approached the prisoner. His hands were clasped behind his back and his whole body seemed to shake with nervous tremors and an uncontrollable anger. The light of victory had vanished from his eyes as they stared deep into Don Carlos'. The hatred between them was palpable.

"Don Carlos!"

De Henrique pronounced each syllable slowly, as though sifting them in his mouth before letting them out. Don Carlos could see the way the priest was struggling mightily to suppress the volcanic emotions that raged in his breast. De Henrique's right hand flashed out and gripped the lapel of Don Carlos' coat. The hand clenched in a fist, pressed hard against the exalted prisoner's chest.

"Don Carlos, I know how hard it is for you to adjust to this new situation — to the sudden change in your status. But the scorn and the arrogance in your eyes are worthless now. You are a prisoner of the Holy Office! You are in an Inquisition jail, whether you like it or not!

Understand? You've seen this morning that the king is no longer prepared to stand behind you. He is no longer susceptible to the words that fall from your honeyed tongue!"

De Henrique was standing very close to Don Carlos now. When Don Carlos tried to take a step or two back, the priest yanked him back and forced him to return his gaze, stare for stare. Even before the interrogation and torture began, de Henrique wished to squash Don Carlos' spirit and make him forget that just yesterday he had been one of the most influential men in the city.

His clenched fist pressed painfully on Don Carlos' chest. It was becoming difficult for the prisoner to breathe. Still, Don Carlos kept hold of his wits. He must not give in — whatever the cost, he must not give in! Words emerged jerkily from his mouth:

"It is... still not clear... de Henrique... I am still not... sure whether... the order you read in the... king's name... was not falsified. You people... are expert at... things like that." He labored for breath. "Besides... Besides... even if it is the king's writing... it's only a temporary... victory for you. I don't know... what lies you have told him or how... you persuaded him to believe you!... You've made a big mistake... My friends won't keep silent..."

De Henrique laughed heartily, as though this speech had amused him. "The mistake is yours, Don Carlos. Faced with the evidence we provided, His Majesty had no choice but to grant me the right to investigate the matter." His fist continued to press Don Carlos.

"You arranged... to search my house. And what did you find?... Nothing!... Nothing to prove... that I am a secret Jew, G-d forbid... So what proof are you talking about?... The malicious lies... of my enemies!"

Uneasily, de Henrique remembered that he hadn't found the *tefillin* he'd ordered Luis to plant in the admiral's house. And where had Luis disappeared to, for that matter? Perhaps Don Carlos had caught him in the act and hurt him somehow. The words burst from the priest before he could stop them: "Don Carlos, where is Luis?"

Don Carlos was surprised. How did this question connect to the difficult conversation they'd been having? Were they trying to link him to Raphael Chaim's rescue?

"Who is Luis?" he asked with every sign of astonishment. A shiver of fear ran through him. Had the rescue attempt failed and Luis fled? Uncertainty pierced him like an arrow.

De Henrique didn't answer. He had nearly revealed one of the dirty cards in his deck. His fist opened slowly and Don Carlos could breathe again. With a heavy tread de Henrique returned to his armchair. Don Carlos watched his every move, puzzled. "Something is troubling him," he thought. "But how is it connected to Luis?"

De Henrique roused himself quickly from his thoughts.

"There were no lies, Don Carlos. No malicious plots against you. I'm speaking about facts, my dear former admiral of the glorious Portuguese fleet. From eye witnesses!"

And then, with no prior warning, he shot out a direct question: "At midnight on the fourth of April 1641, Admiral Don Carlos Carneiro visited the home of Rabbi Menashe ben Israel in Amsterdam. True or false?"

The final words were roared at Don Carlos. The two monks standing at the end of the room flinched and drew themselves in as though to avoid being noticed.

Don Carlos felt as if he, too, were losing his self-control. "Lies!" he screamed. "Wicked lies — and also stupid ones, because I am far too well known to do something as foolhardy as that. Can't you see that yourself, de Henrique? *Me*, in a rabbi's home? I am known throughout Amsterdam, de Henrique. The entire city knows me! Don't you think that my ship's officers and all the sailors under my command would not know in a minute if I did something as stupid as that? Am I so witless in your eyes that you could believe me capable of endangering my position by visiting a rabbi's house — especially a renegade New Christian who has betrayed his faith? Apart from which, what possible business could I have with such a fellow?"

De Henrique listened closely to this outburst. He felt like a fisherman watching the thrashing of the fish already caught in his net.

"And do you, Don Carlos," he asked, "think that I am so stupid? Do you know me as someone who listens to old wives' tales or marketplace gossip? Do you hold me, and the rest of us at the Inquisition, as utter fools? We have proof about your movements that night, Don Carlos — an eyewitness to the precise route you took through Amsterdam's streets to reach that heretic's house. We even know the precise pattern of knocks you used to gain entrance, a number that had obviously been pre-arranged by the two of you, before you disappeared into his house for four full hours!"

De Henrique peered into his prisoner's face to gauge the effect of his words. He tried to find a crack in Don Carlos' steely armor — a crack of fear, of despair, of pleading... especially of pleading. But the only sign that Don Carlos had even heard him was a tiny, nearly invisible smile. He kept his face rigidly impassive, though he knew in his heart that the evil had indeed come upon him. He recalled that ill-fated night in Rav Menashe's parlor, when the servant boy had told of a black-garbed stranger who had used the prescribed number of knocks. That told him, beyond the need of any further evidence, that the Inquisition had been on his heels even then. Who knew what else they had learned about him?

"Well?" de Henrique sneered. "What have you to say for yourself, my dear admiral — the celebrated gentleman who only this morning was the pet and favorite of His Majesty, the king?"

"Nothing, my dear friend so celebrated for his cruelty, *Padre* Paulo de Henrique, right hand man of *Padre* João Manuel, the Inquisition's best man. Nothing, except a firm denial of all this as a tissue of lies — not the first of its kind to be heard inside these walls, I'm sure. And you know, de Henrique, that I am well versed in the sort of lies that circulate in this place. Isn't that true, my dear secretary of the Holy Office?"

This was a direct challenge. Don Carlos had inflected the word "Holy" to hold a world of contempt. The two young monks tensely watching the debate felt distinctly uncomfortable. But they said nothing.

De Henrique shot up from his chair, the layers of fat on his body quivering like waves on a stormy sea. He would have liked to murder Don Carlos on the spot... But no. He had a better idea. He would prolong this prisoner's life with special tortures and exquisite suffering, to punish Don Carlos for trying to humiliate him. Once again he made a fist and pressed it against Don Carlos' windpipe. Don Carlos felt as if he were choking.

"Fear for yourself, Don Carlos..."

"Fear," Don Carlos gasped, "resides only... in black souls... sinners before G-d and man... Not in in the hearts... of honest men... my dear... friend..."

"Don't call me your dear friend — foul Jew that you are!"

Suddenly, de Henrique drew his fist back and hurled it at Don Carlos' nose. Blood began to spurt from it, but Don Carlos could do nothing to stanch it with his hands still bound securely behind his back.

De Henrique intended to follow up this first blow with others, but before he could act on his intention the door of his office opened and four young monks burst in.

"*Padre!* *Padre*, come quickly! They've broken into the prison! They took Arnaldo Rodriguez! The guards were stunned with blows — we found them tied up in Rodriguez's cell! The adjoining prisoners claim they neither saw nor heard a thing! Come quickly!"

De Henrique and the two monks who had escorted Don Carlos to the room left the room at a run. Don Carlos, left alone, was jubilant. "*Gracias a D-eus!* Raphael Chaim has been rescued! May the mighty Name of the G-d of the Jews be blessed now and forever."

27

De Henrique's office was suddenly empty. Only Don Carlos remained, frozen in the center of the room. He was still reeling from the shock of learning how much his wicked enemies knew of his activities, and in what precise detail. Beyond the eerie silence that reigned in the room, Don Carlos heard echoes of de Henrique's sneering, triumphant laughter. All at once he began to tremble. The cruel blow he'd received at the Inquisitor's hands made itself felt with a vengeance. And this, he knew, was only the beginning — the sinister prelude to the tortures that awaited him in this accursed place.

Blood continued to pour unabated from his nose but, with his hands still bound behind his back, he had no way of stopping it. If only he could free them, he would use this extraordinary opportunity to make his escape. If he could only flee this horrible building without being apprehended, he believed that maybe — maybe — his luck would change.

His first move would be to head directly for the royal palace. He was hopeful that the king would listen to his story. It was difficult to believe that his enemies had succeeded in completely poisoning His Majesty's mind against him. Don Carlos would plead his own case with all the urgency and eloquence at his disposal, claiming that his enemies had fabricated the entire case against him. And the king would listen. After all, he owed Don Carlos a tremendous debt of gratitude for all the victories at sea the admiral had won for Portugal. His Majesty's glory and strength derived in great measure from those victories. Today, no one dared attack a ship that bore the Portuguese flag.

His fantasies did not end there. They tumbled about in his overstimulated imagination, weaving ever more fantastic possibilities. Perhaps he would even succeed in exacting his rightful revenge of de Henrique! Now, as prisoner of the Inquisition, Don Carlos regretted his rejection of *Padre* João Manuel's offer the previous day: to sign a letter denouncing de Henrique as a traitor and heretic. In the evil world in which he found himself, it was not always possible, or desirable, to remain the sole bastion of righteousness.

He shook his head in frustration. These were futile musings, nothing more than the fantasies of a desperate and despairing man. Every effort to free his hands led only to greater pain, and the pain brought him sharply back to an awareness of his situation. He was de Henrique's prisoner.

Don Carlos listened attentively, but did not hear voices through the open door. The others were still busy searching for clues to Raphael Chaim's whereabouts. All their attention was riveted on locating and recapturing the escaped prisoner. Despite all, this represented a unique chance for Don Carlos to try to win his freedom. What did he have to lose? At all cost, he must try. But how?

He shook his head. Even if he ran outside with his hands tied, surely some kind soul would untie them for him. He would do it. He began walking slowly toward the door.

But he had not anticipated the pain. Every step was an exquisite agony, as the cruel ropes cut deeper into the flesh of his wrists. His skin felt as though it was being singed by flames. A few seconds were enough. There was no way he could make his way out of the building and into the street in this condition. Don Carlos gave up.

Even more slowly than before, he returned, in utter despair, to his former place in the center of the room.

The Inquisition building was still quiet. Don Carlos glanced at the desk, piled high with reports. Each one, he guessed, contained testimony to condemn yet another of the Holy Office's victims. Perhaps the testimony against *him* was also hidden in one of those documents. He was consumed with a sudden desire to see the evidence that had been so painstakingly compiled against him — and especially the names of those who had shadowed him in Amsterdam. Don Carlos was standing near the desk. Clenching his jaw and adjuring his mind to ignore the pain, he advanced the last few steps.

Desperately, with the fury of a savage beast, he began sorting through the papers with his teeth. However, when he tried to open one in that manner, he found the job beyond him. He tried once more, and failed again. His anger grew, and his impatience. One last time he seized a document between his teeth and attempted to pry it open. That effort met with the same lack of success as the ones before. In the attempt, some of the documents were loosened from their places and slipped to the floor. That was when he caught sight of the dagger.

The sun's rays through the window caught the dagger's golden hilt and made it shine. Don Carlos rooted frantically through the records with his chin until he reached the dagger. He took the hilt in his teeth. "A pretty dagger," he thought. "And prettier still if it were buried in de Henrique's heart!"

Slowly he straightened, the dagger still held between his clenched teeth. Bracing himself against the waves of pain from his wrists, he began the tedious journey to the wood cabinet that stood in a corner of the room. The agonizing trip took an eternity. He could not remember a time when he had ever needed such courage, such stamina, merely to move from place to place. Just as he reached the cabinet, he caught the sound of voices approaching along the corridor.

He sprang into action. If only his enemies did not return before his job was finished! To his ear, the voices sounded agitated in the extreme. A trio of young monks flew past de Henrique's open door without so much as glancing inside. Was all this activity connected with Raphael Chaim's disappearance?

With rapid motions of his head, he thrust the dagger's blade repeatedly into the cabinet's wooden door. At last, to his satisfaction, the blade stuck.

He straightened painfully, watching the way the dagger — nose firmly embedded in the wood — still vibrated gently. With a quick glance at the open door, he set to work.

A careful turn of his back and bending of the knees brought his hands and wrists into contact with the blade. Gently, with a slow up-and-down motion, he began sawing through the ropes that bound his hands. He could sense the dagger gradually slicing through the rope, strand by slender strand. Every ounce of his concentration was focused on the task. Just a little more effort, and he would be free. He decided that, before he ran, he would find his file and carry it to the king. Would the benevolent G-d help him?

He held his breath as the sharp blade neared his wrists. He must fully cut through the bonds without piercing his skin. The muscles of his tautly extended arms began to ache. He willed himself to a last bit of patience — and was rewarded. The final strand fell away, and his hands were free.

One hand grasped the other and tried to massage away the agony of the previous hours. When he had the use of his fingers again, Don Carlos pulled the dagger from the cabinet. Gathering the sawn-through ropes from the floor, he hurried over to the desk. He placed the dagger in its case and hid it inside his shirt. He might yet find use for it again! He threw the torn rope out the window into the courtyard.

Hurriedly he rummaged through the records on the desk. Time was running out for him. He must discover who had testified against him — who the secret enemies were who had hauled him down from his position of honor and security and exposed his Jewish identity. The names would be useful when he saw the king. And even if he was captured and imprisoned again, the information would help him in his dealings with de Henrique and the other interrogators. He was very familiar with the law of the Inquisition, which permitted the accusers to withhold from the accused the names of those who bore witness against him. In this way, many innocent people — devout Christians among them — had been condemned to death as secret Jews... and all because someone wanted to take revenge against them or to plunder their wealth, be it a house in town or a choice vineyard in the field.

His breath caught in his throat. He'd found it! He held his own dossier in his hands at last. Without waiting an instant, he opened it and began riffling eagerly through the pages...

⤙⤚

A stunning blow on the back of his neck returned Don Carlos to the reality of his surroundings. He turned cautiously — to find an enraged de Henrique standing behind him, brandishing his whip.

"Jewish pig! *Who freed your hands?*"

De Henrique's eyes bulged and the vessels of his face stood out, bold and crimson. He was poised at the very edge of madness. Don Carlos did not answer.

De Henrique raised the whip threateningly. Don Carlos shot out a hand and seized the priest's wrist. When he spoke, his voice was low and silky.

"De Henrique, don't be too sure of yourself. Don't think that all the power in this house resides with you alone! The fact that my hands are free proves that I have friends here."

De Henrique's look was incredulous — and worried. In Don Carlos' eyes he read confidence and a knowledge of impending success. The priest opened and shut his mouth, uncertain how to proceed.

Don Carlos pressed his advantage. "I understand that someone has escaped from the dungeon. From the way you all reacted, it's apparently somebody important."

"What business is that of yours, Don Carlos? You are nothing but a prisoner yourself. You have no rights in this place."

Don Carlos smiled. "You're right — it's no business of mine. But it only goes to prove that he, too, has friends in the Holy Office. It's worthwhile being more careful when dealing out violence, torture, and trickery to innocent men..."

"*Silence!*" de Henrique bellowed. His face grew impossibly redder, and the veins stood out on both sides of his neck. He strode over to the door and shut it forcefully. With slow, menacing steps, he advanced on Don

Carlos. Don Carlos moved back, his body tense and expectant. He did not remove his eyes from the Inquisitor's for a moment. The priest, he knew, might attack suddenly and insanely, with no thought to his calling or his position. Raphael Chaim's disappearance had dealt a severe blow to his inflated ego and his empty pride. And the suspicion —aroused by Don Carlos — that there were secret enemies plotting against him within his own organization was driving him insane. In this state he was liable to do almost anything.

"De Henrique," he said softly, soothingly, "take care. The king is alive and well, the courts of justice are functioning, and you could easily find yourself behind bars if you do anything rash."

De Henrique paid no heed. The pupils of his eyes rolled wildly. He continued to advance on Don Carlos, holding the whip with its leather skin intertwined with metal strands. His hatred for Don Carlos was almost a palpable thing. Don Carlos was afraid he might be forced to defend himself with the dagger. The prospect did not make him happy.

His back was already pressed against the wall of the cabinet. His enemy was only two steps away. Don Carlos braced himself for the unavoidable blow...

Suddenly, a ringing voice spoke out.

"What is the meaning of this behavior? De Henrique, have you taken leave of your senses? Have you forgotten that you are in a consecrated building? What am I to make of this, Paulo de Henrique?"

De Henrique whirled around. In the doorway stood *Padre* João Manuel, furious.

But behind the fury, Don Carlos could see the joy that radiated from the Inquisition leader's face.

28

adre João Manuel was clearly enjoying de Henrique's discomfiture. The scene that had met his eyes as he entered the room gave him immense pleasure. He had never seen his secretary behaving so wildly, almost like a beast out of a primeval forest. It pleased him to see his adversary in a degraded position. Now it was up to him to make the most of the situation.

He walked slowly into the room, drawing out the process in order to lengthen de Henrique's humiliation. Don Carlos he ignored completely.

João Manuel halted beside de Henrique, who hadn't budged.

"Tell me," the head priest asked, almost conversationally. "Do you like yourself at this moment?"

De Henrique did not reply. He stood as if paralyzed, still crouched in the position he'd assumed for the attack. Only his eyes moved, searching João Manuel's anxiously and then sliding away again.

"Will you stand up straight, de Henrique?" João Manuel suddenly thundered. His tone quieted and was filled with mockery. "Don't you agree, most esteemed secretary of the Holy Office, that you have succeeded in disgracing your position, the church, and the holy cross by this outrageous behavior?" He raised his hands to Heaven in a supplicating gesture. "The good Lord has done us a favor by bringing me here just in time to avert a disaster. How all of Lisbon would jeer if they could know how you've behaved this day. To attack a prisoner— a suspect! Have you forgotten that you are a representative of the true faith, de Henrique, and not the leader of a band of street hoodlums? Eh?"

From his corner, Don Carlos observed the pleasure the *padre* was deriving from the encounter. The sight afforded him enjoyment, too. "The cat is baiting the mouse", he thought. Cats will often play with their victims, delighting in the vision of their increasing discomfort and desperation. De Henrique, it was clear, was experiencing both those feelings to a marked degree. "How can I turn this to my advantage?" Don Carlos mused.

Padre João Manuel thrust a forefinger beneath de Henrique's chin and tilted it upward, forcing the secretary to look directly into his eyes. It was a move calculated to add to de Henrique's humiliation.

"You have injured us gravely," João Manuel continued, pouring salt on the wound. "I honestly do not know if I'll be able to defend you before a council of bishops. In all truthfulness, I will be forced to describe to them the degrading scene I've just witnessed. I'll do my best of course"— he shook his head as though the cause was already lost— "but it is highly doubtful whether they'll permit you to continue in your role of Jew-hunter in Lisbon." He leaned closer. "Now do you understand what you've done to yourself?"

"What hypocrisy!" Don Carlos thought.

"A pity," João Manuel purred, "to end such an illustrious career in this way."

Don Carlos decided to add fuel to the flames. "*Padre*?"

João Manuel threw him a cold, withering glance. "An accused man has no right to open his mouth! I shall be the one to grant permission to speak!"

The priest turned his head away from Don Carlos. The exchange, however, had afforded de Henrique a tiny respite. He straightened his shoulders, smoothed his cassock and adjusted the brown skullcap perched on his large head. He knew that he'd been caught in a compromising act, but still refused to leave the arena completely to his opponent.

"*Padre*," he said in a small, respectful voice, "are you aware that they've spirited away the prisoner Arnaldo Rodriguez?"

João Manuel had already heard the devastating news. His first reaction had been to wonder how he might arrange to have the blame fall squarely on de Henrique's shoulders.

"I know," he said curtly. "But what has that to do with your demeaning behavior just now? The circumstances of the heretic Rodriguez's escape will have to be looked into very carefully. Apparently, there is some flaw in the security procedure. I believe, de Henrique, that this falls under your domain!"

It was an additional arrow hurled at de Henrique's heart. In his capacity as secretary of the Holy Office, de Henrique was indeed directly responsible for organizing guard duty in and around the dungeons. But de Henrique persevered:

"I understand you, *Padre*. But do you know that the suspect standing here had his hands securely bound when he was brought into this room? They're untied now! It happened, *Padre*, while I was absent from the room... While I was down below, where I was summoned on the heels of Rodriguez's disappearance." He paused. "Now do you understand what connection the escape has with what just occurred here?"

João Manuel studied his enemy's face, trying to read his intentions. He must beware, lest the wily snake prepare a trap for him. At length he answered, ""No. I do not see any connection."

De Henrique's confidence and courage were rapidly returning. "The connection is there, *Padre*— and it's a serious one. There are traitors in this building! The same hands that untied the accused also participated in Rodriguez's escape. That is my conclusion!" He paused, then added softly, "And that, Your Grace, falls into your domain."

João Manuel was uncomfortable. He had long known that a number of Inquisition interrogators and guards were actually Jewish spies, merely acting the part of loyal Christians. However, he had never done much to change the situation. So long as the interrogations proceeded more or less as they ought to, with the proper number of suspects condemned to death or to long prison sentences, he could justify the Holy Office's continued existence. Even the Roman pope was satisfied with their work. On the occasions when one of the prisoners vanished, every effort was made to conceal the bitter fact from the public. Why shake the foundations of the Holy Office and cause men to be suspicious of one another?

But this time, João Manuel understood, de Henrique would not let the matter lie. He would demand an investigation— and who knew whether he himself, *Padre* João Manuel, head of the Inquisition, might not fall victim to de Henrique, as so many others had before him? It was a difficult dilemma. What to do?

"How do you arrive at that conclusion?" he asked coolly. "It seems to me, de Henrique, that your excessive zeal in hunting down heretics, in any place and at any price, has developed this satanic imagination of yours. Besides, you wish to gain personally from arousing suspicion within this very building. Am I not right, de Henrique?"

Mocking laughter poured from de Henrique's lips. Now it was his turn to play.

"You are mistaken, *Padre*! Is it so hard for you to believe that there is one man in this place who intends to seriously protect the stature of our faith in Lisbon? You ask how I arrive at my conclusion? Ask him, *Padre*!" The secretary pointed dramatically at Don Carlos in his corner. "Ask him who freed his hands!"

João Manuel transferred his gaze to Don Carlos. His eyes were cold and cruel, devoid of the smallest trace of their former friendship. Don Carlos knew that the priest was furious with him for not going along with his plan to topple de Henrique once and for all by signing the forged document. And perhaps his refusal had been stupid. This scene today would have played itself out very differently had Don Carlos agreed to sign the paper at the seaside yesterday!

But what was done was done. Was there a chance that he could convince João Manuel that he was prepared to do everything in his power to destroy de Henrique?

At any rate, he must try.

He heard the *Padre* ask, "What do you have to say about all this?"

"Nothing!"

"What do you mean, nothing? Who untied your hands?"

"De Henrique knows," Don Carlos said simply.

De Henrique lunged forward, until arrested by João Manuel's outstretched arm. Ignoring him, the *padre* asked, "What are you trying to say?"

Don Carlos breathed deeply, then exhaled and said, "*Padre* João Manuel, you know that I am willing to tell you everything— though not, naturally, in the presence of your secretary. But I will not answer a single question until the terrible suspicion is lifted against me!"

"Suspicion?" bellowed de Henrique. "Is it nothing more than suspicion? We have explicit testimony against you! Testimony that gives undeniable evidence of your guilt— to the fact that you are a Jew!" De Henrique was deadly afraid of a conspiracy between João Manuel and Don Carlos, which could end by destroying him.

"If there are witnesses," Don Carlos returned, "I demand that you present them to me!"

De Henrique hastened to answer before his superior could. "You know our rules very well. We are not permitted to bring the accusers before the accused. You must rely on the purity of our intentions, and trust that we would not condone the bearing of false witness."

"I have no such trust— and you know very well why!"

With a quick glance at João Manuel, Don Carlos continued, "*Padre*, you asked me a question. I will not answer it willingly until I can stand face to face with my accusers. It will be interesting to see whether they will have the courage then to smear me with such baseless lies."

"If you will not answer willingly," de Henrique said roughly, "the torture room awaits. It will help you to speak!" He was still determined to prevent João Manuel from coming to an understanding with Don Carlos. The *padre* made an imperious gesture, demanding silence.

"I think," he told de Henrique, "that in this case we will accede to the suspect's request. After all, the law does not actually forbid it. It merely states that we are not required to present the accused with the witnesses against him. If we choose to do so, we may."

He was prepared, this time, to disregard a longstanding Inquisition practice, in order to hear Don Carlos' explanation of his intriguing words, "De Henrique knows who freed my hands." It was important that he learn what had been meant. Don Carlos knew full well what the *padre's* intentions were toward his secretary.

"B-but," sputtered de Henrique, "But it's impossi—"

"Silence!" João Manuel found de Henrique's strenuous objection to bringing forward the witnesses all the more reason to hasten their arrival. He went over to the desk, where he found a small bell. He proceeded to ring this vigorously. A few moments later two young monks appeared in the doorway, ready for whatever job their leader would hand them.

"In here," said João Manuel, handing the monks a bulging dossier, "you will find the witnesses' names and addresses. I want you to bring them here at once, to provide further testimony to the Holy Office tribunal. And hurry— the matter is very urgent. Understand?"

"*Sim, senhor!*" The pair vanished in the blink of an eye.

An air of tense expectancy held the room after they'd gone. *Padre* João Manuel appeared outwardly calm, paying no attention to anything de Henrique tried to tell him, until the secretary too fell silent. Don Carlos had no idea what awaited him in the upcoming confrontation with his accusers. He must gather all his wits now, and all his strength, in order to deny their allegations and destroy their credibility. That was his only chance to extricate himself from this dire situation.

Meanwhile, the three were quiet.

Half an hour had crawled past when the door opened again. The pair of young monks entered, flanking a third individual whom they presented to *Padre* João Manuel.

"You," João Manuel said abruptly, pointing at the newcomer. "Are you the witness who is prepared to testify that Admiral Don Carlos Carneiro, standing here in this room, is a Jew?"

There was a brief silence, and then the briefer reply: "Yes!"

Don Carlos felt as though he were being ripped apart. Had his flagship been foundering in a torrential storm he could not have been more wounded. Dizziness assailed him, blackening his vision. The blood pounded frenziedly through his veins and his heart thumped painfully. The entire room began swaying like a drunkard.

Don Carlos swayed too, then sank onto the cold stone floor in a dead faint.

29

No one rushed to lift Don Carlos from the floor, where he lay prone and unmoving. All attention was focused on João Manuel. Every person in the room breathlessly awaited his instructions. Even de Henrique uncharactistically held his tongue.

But João Manuel did not say a word. He merely stared at Don Carlos, huddled unconscious on the floor. There was no pity in his glance, only a profound curiosity. He wanted very much to know why the sight of the witness had upset Don Carlos so much. Having been his friend for many years, he was fully aware of admiral's well-earned reputation for unflinching courage and nerves of steel. So what had happened here? What lay behind this mysterious behavior?

Thoughtfully, he gestured at the young monks. "Bring a bucket of cold water and rouse him."

The water was brought and Don Carlos duly doused. It caught him full in the face and ran in rivulets down to the stone flagging. Don Carlos stirred but did not open his eyes. The monks were happy to provide a few ringing slaps on the face to help him along. His eyes flew open and he gaped up at the figures standing over him.

Immediately, the monks seized his arms, lifted him to his feet, and hustled him over to a chair by de Henrique's desk. João Manuel, de Henrique, and the witness remained glued to their places, watching.

Padre João Manuel observed Don Carlos closely. The man who sat before him now bore little resemblance to the proud, confident admiral who had fainted moments before. That other Don Carlos had not known the meaning of fear. This one sat trembling in his chair, eyes wide and anxious. What had happened to wreak this transformation? The mystery gnawed at the priest, though he made no outward sign of his burning curiosity. In a distant, almost uninterested voice, he asked, "Does the suspect recognize the witness?"

Don Carlos slumped in his chair, shoulders sagging and eyes downcast. The Inquisition leader raised his voice slightly: "The suspect will answer every question that he is asked here — promptly!"

Don Carlos' answer came at once, weak and defeated: "Yes, I recognize him."

"Good!" *Padre* João Manuel turned to the witness. "Although the official investigation has not yet begun and you will be called upon to return and testify before the formal Inquisition tribunal, it will be very helpful to our interrogation if you will provide us with the details of your testimony here today. Please!"

The *padre* seated himself in de Henrique's chair behind the desk. As he did so, his eyes met his secretary's for a fleeting instant. He read anger there, and was pleased. Here was another opportunity for him to demonstrate to his would-be usurper that even in de Henrique's own office it was he, João Manuel, who ruled.

But this was not the time for such musings. João Manuel turned in his seat and gave the witness his undivided attention.

The witness related his story.

"It happened suddenly. I was standing by one of the doors leading into the belly of the flagship, the *Vera Cruz*. It was midnight. The night was very quiet, with only the sound of the wind blowing gently through the sails. I couldn't sleep, and decided to go up on deck for some fresh air. And suddenly — I saw him."

The witness breathed deeply. He was obviously finding it difficult to tell his story in his admiral's presence.

"I saw him. He was wearing a disguise, but I recognized him at once. It was he, no question about it. I noticed that he was looking around carefully in all directions, to make sure no one had spotted him. When he was sure he was alone on deck, he hurried to the gangway and ran down to the quay.

"I don't know why, but a tremendous curiosity took hold of me. I ran after him to see where he was going at such an hour, and in such a disguise. By chance, a black cloth curtain was lying nearby, and I draped it over myself so that no one would recognize me. I ran after him. It was hard staying on his trail in the darkness of the Amsterdam streets, but the noise of his hurrying footsteps helped me. So I was not far away when he stopped at a certain house in the city. He knocked a few times, in a specific order, and then disappeared through a gate that was opened to him and then quickly closed again.

"I was stunned. Why was the fleet admiral of Portugal visiting a private home in Amsterdam at midnight? And who was it that he was visiting in this mysterious manner?

"I couldn't resist. Creeping closer to the gate, I knocked in the same way I'd heard him knock. As I'd hoped, a servant opened the gate. When I asked him whose house it was, he answered, 'This is the home of the chief rabbi of Amsterdam, Rabbi Menashe ben Israel.'

"The gate closed again, and again I stood in the dark — in total shock. The image I'd cherished had shattered in an instant into tiny fragments. It was very hard for me to absorb the fact that the celebrated admiral of the Portuguese fleet had secret dealings with a Jewish rabbi, a heretic famous for his hatred of the church. Upon our return to Lisbon I felt a great need to pass on what I'd seen to the Holy Office, which would do as it saw fit with the information."

The witness fell silent. Each word had been like a physical blow in Don Carlos' face. Every pair of eyes in the room was riveted to the suspect, waiting to see how he would react. Don Carlos neither moved nor spoke. His own eyes were fixed on a remote corner of the stone floor.

João Manuel did not let him enjoy the luxury of silence for long.

"What have you to say, suspect?"

Very slowly, Don Carlos lifted his head. He bent a long gaze on the witness, a deeply pain-filled look. Still no syllable passed his lips. Only when the witness cast down his eyes did Don Carlos look away from him.

"Well?" Father João Manuel prompted harshly.

"If I wanted," Don Carlos began quietly, almost inaudibly, "I could deny the whole story. I could try to prove to a court of justice how a tissue of lies was fabricated. I personally have seen many such false tales circulated in Lisbon, tales that bore innocent men to prison or their deaths. But..."

He broke off. The others witnessed the inner struggle that revealed itself so clearly on his haggard features. Some powerful emotion was choking the stream of his words, making it impossible for him to speak.

"Continue!" João Manuel barked without compassion.

"But... since the story is told by Pedro... Alvares, my trusted aide... my personal secretary... for whom I have done so much... I will not deny his tale..."

The air in the room seemed to quiver with tension. No one uttered a sound. It seemed to them that even their breathing had ceased in the face of this storm of emotion. Don Carlos ended simply, "It is true. I was in the rabbi of Amsterdam's home that night — Rabbi Menashe ben Israel."

He felt lighter now that the words were spoken. His head lifted higher and the crumbs of his old confidence reassembled themselves. In his eyes a new spark glimmered — a spark shadowed with the sadness of one who had made peace with his destiny. De Henrique could not restrain the crow of triumph that erupted from his throat — until João Manuel's icy stare froze the secretary's victorious laughter and brought the blood rushing to his face.

"Does the witness have anything to add?" The *padre* maintained his official tone, distant and aloof.

"Yes." Pedro Alvares avoided Don Carlos' eyes as he spoke.

De Henrique burst out impatiently, "Well? What is it?"

The outburst enraged João Manuel. He whirled on the secretary and said, in exactly the same intonation, "*Well?*" The two young monks blanched, and exchanged a quick, frightened glance.

Pedro Alvares cleared his throat. "As you will remember, I arrived at Don Carlos' house at the same time that you, the heads of the Inquisition, were there. After you left I remained behind to discuss with the admiral details of the fleet's upcoming voyage to Brazil. Suddenly, his wife called him to her from the kitchen. Knowing his secret, I couldn't resist eavesdropping on their conversation."

Pedro Alvares noted the spasm that crossed Don Carlos' face at this revelation.

"I'm sorry. But I must fulfill my duty to my faith, so that my conscience may rest easily and not torture me... Well, Don Carlos and his wife spoke openly together about their secret Jewishness, and their desire to flee Portugal before they were exposed. I can deliver the exact details of their conversation to the tribunal."

Pedro fell silent. Though he was trying hard to maintain his composure, he found it difficult to believe that he, a young officer, must testify against his own captain. He gathered strength by reminding himself that he was performing his duty to the church, to his king, to his nation, and to the army. It was difficult, very difficult, but he had no choice.

Without warning, Don Carlos rose from his chair and drew himself up to his full height. Standing there, tall and regal, honor and integrity seemed to radiate from him as it had at all the military ceremonies he'd attended at the king's side. Father João Manuel made no attempt to stop him. There was an almost superstitious awe in his dealings with Don Carlos. Though a prisoner and an acknowledged Jew, João Manuel found himself, against his will, according the man a reluctant respect.

"Pedro Alvares," Don Carlos cried, "stand at attention and look at me!"

Years of military training had done their work well. Pedro leaped to his feet. His shoulders were back, his spine straight, and his bearing taut.

"Now," Don Carlos continued, "listen!"

Pedro's body stiffened even further.

"Eighteen years ago, Pedro," Don Carlos announced, as though conducting a military parade, "the well-known professor of philosophy, Roberto da Silva, was arrested here in Lisbon. Do you know what his awful crime was? Being a Jew! The Inquisition surprised him and his family, along with some ten other Marranos, conducting a Pesach *seder* in the cellar of their home. Have you heard this before, Pedro?"

Pedro shook his head in the negative.

"Well, Pedro, there's something you must know now. Professor Roberto da Silva was your father!"

The words detonated with all the thunder of a ship's cannon during a battle at sea. Pedro Alvares felt the skin of his face burning as though being lashed mercilessly by the cruelest of whips. His eyes began blinking involuntarily and darting around the room. They traveled first to João Manuel, then to de Henrique. An uncontrollable panic seized him. What would they think of him now? What would happen to him? But through the overwhelming fear and doubt, his posture did not waver. He maintained his military bearing, as his captain had ordered.

Don Carlos continued, "And that's not all, Pedro. Professor Roberto da Silva was... my brother!"

Pedro's legs began to quiver. All his limbs were plagued by a sudden strange weakness. *Only let me not fall. Let me not faint!* was his inward prayer. The thought of being the son of a Jew, of a heretic, filled him with self-loathing. His head pounded fiercely.

"In other words, Pedro, I am your uncle. Yes, yes — *your uncle!*"

But the torture was not yet over. Don Carlos was still speaking. "You, Pedro, were just a small boy when your parents were arrested. And just as my own children were torn from me yesterday and handed over to the 'good' monks, so you, too, were sent to a monastery. Y-you were only three years old..."

Don Carlos collapsed in his seat and buried his face in his hands. The memories, and the knowledge that he'd come to the bitter end of his struggles, tore down the wall he'd erected around his heart. His body shook with the force of his sobs.

A moment later, he lifted his tear-stained face and said brokenly, "Above all, Pedro, your sainted father asked me to watch over you. He asked me to make sure you received a good education — and most of all, that I'd help bring you back to the faith of our holy fathers and mothers. I have done everything I could for you, Pedro, except for this last thing. I have not succeeded in penetrating the gates of your heart. I have failed to open it up to the truth of our forefathers, Avraham, Yitzchak, and Yaakov.

"I failed, Pedro. And so, instead, it was you who betrayed me to the enemy! Soon I will taste the same fate that my brother — your father — tasted. Your father, who was tortured in this very building... and who was burned at the stake two years later in the public square of this city you love so much."

Don Carlos glanced quickly at de Henrique. "You won, de Henrique! My congratulations! Yes, I am a Jew — a Jew who is proud of the faith of my fathers. But I have never betrayed my king or my country, although I did not believe in the faith you forced upon my grandfather's grandfather. I served the king faithfully as a loyal citizen should, and as my Torah orders me to do."

Don Carlos stood again. On trembling legs he approached Pedro, standing sightlessly in the same rigid position. He placed his hand lovingly on the younger man's shoulder and said softly, as a father would, "My dear Pedro, what I longed to tell you for so many years and could not manage to say, I will tell you now. Return to the faith of your holy fathers. Return, and let your return atone for the death that is to come to me by your hands!"

Don Carlos leaned forward to kiss his nephew on the forehead, but was stopped by a mighty roar that shook the room.

"ENOUGH!"

The word had burst from de Henrique's throat. He found the spectacle unendurable. Don Carlos' attempt to win his nephew away from Christianity ripped his composure to shreds. Disregarding João Manuel's presence, he screamed at the two monks, "Take him out at once!"

The pair fell on Don Carlos, tore him away from Pedro, grasped his arms, and dragged him from the room. Don Carlos put up no resistance.

Pedro Alvares continued to stand at attention, eyes closed to everything that was happening around him.

30

It was a moonless night. Total darkness reigned, but he did not lose his way. After traversing a number of streets he stopped beside a tall iron gate. Glancing right and left to make certain he was unobserved, he rapped three times on the gate. A brief pause, and he added four more sharp raps.

He moved back from the gate and melted into the darkness. In the deep silence of the Amsterdam street he could hear his heart beating excitedly. He willed the gate to open — and yet he dreaded its opening. Fear of the upcoming interview paralyzed him. How would he explain what had happened?

A sudden shaft of light pierced the dark street. It came from the house's open doorway. A youth came striding down the narrow path leading to the gate. The gate slowly swung open.

It's the boy who opened the gate that other time. The thought came and went like the flight of a shooting star. He emerged from the darkness. The boy peered at him with open suspicion.

"*Boa noite* ("Good evening")," he said, bowing politely. He had opened his speech in Portuguese deliberately, although Dutch was the language of the city. He knew that the language spoken at the rabbi's house — like that of all the Jewish refugees from Portugal — was the tongue of their native land.

The youth did not reply. Instead he retreated slightly and positioned himself behind the gate, holding it with one hand to facilitate its quick closing if necessary. The boy was clearly alert to the possibility of danger to Amsterdam's chief rabbi because of his open war with Christianity, particularly from the Inquisition that was imposing its horrors on the Jews of Portugal and Spain.

Noting this, the visitor made sure to imbue his own voice with calm and confidence. "May I see the rabbi?" He prayed that the boy would see no sign of the inward turmoil he was trying so hard to conceal.

Instead of responding to the query, the boy asked brusquely in Dutch, "Who are you?"

The man breathed deeply. He had no desire to reveal his identity at this moment. After a brief silence, he said, "I have an important message for the Rabbi. A message from Don Carlos Carneiro, admiral of the Portuguese fleet."

The boy would still not yield. "He sent you? I don't believe the rabbi knows him."

The man was startled. This youngster was displaying an experience and canniness beyond his years. Were all Jewish children this clever? He had heard stories enough about their deviltry — but what about their wisdom?

At first he did not know how to answer. Finally, he burst out candidly, "No! But I am here on his behalf anyway."

The boy took the stranger's measure. The man was not dressed after the manner of Amsterdam's citizens, and he spoke a fluent Portuguese. He had heard that particular accent many times on the lips of those who visited the rabbi's home, particularly those who came secretly, at midnight or in the hours before dawn. The stranger's answer piqued his curiosity, but also rang alarm bells. Why wouldn't he identify himself? The boy began slowly easing the gate closed.

The man hurled himself forward, gripped the bars with both hands, and thrust his leg in front of the gate to prevent it from fully closing. Supplication was in his voice as he cried, "I beg you, let me see the rabbi!

I have important news for him! Believe me, please. You have nothing to fear from me, I promise you!"

The youth pushed with all his might on the gate, but the stranger would not let it shut.

"Who are you?" the boy demanded again.

"They — call me —" the man gasped, straining to keep the gate open, "Pedro — Alvares. I am Admiral Carneiro's — aide — and personal secretary. And I — request permission to speak with the rabbi."

"Are you Jew? A Marrano?"

"I... don't know."

The answer, so indicative of the speaker's confusion and bewilderment, did not allay the boy's distrust. On the other hand, he sensed that the stranger was speaking honestly. It seemed to him that the man was near despair.

"I'll ask the rabbi if he'll see you," he said finally. "But first let me close the gate. I promise to bring you an answer."

Pedro eased his grip on the bars, and the gate slammed shut.

After that things began moving quickly. He had hardly recovered from the battle of the gate when it swung open again. The youth, calm now and smiling, invited him inside. "The rabbi says he's prepared to speak with you, even though he does not know the man whose name you mentioned."

Just moments later, he was standing in the rabbi's study. Pedro looked curiously around the notorious heretic's room, the room of a man whose very name made the Inquisition in Portugal gnash its teeth in frustration. The man who stood before him was short and plump. His beard was long and his eyes wore the unmistakable stamp of a scholar. There was a good deal of sadness in those eyes, too. Even as the rabbi looked him over from head to foot, it was obvious that his thoughts were elsewhere — somewhere far, far from Amsterdam.

The rabbi pointed at a chair that stood beside the large desk. Pedro took his seat. His eyes swept the walls, which were lined with bookcases filled with row upon row of books, marching shoulder to shoulder like soldiers on parade. A lone taper was the room's sole illumination.

Pedro waited for the rabbi to speak first. He was uncertain how to behave here. Only two months ago, it would never have entered his mind that he might ever be seated in this room, facing this man. All his life he'd held an aversion for Jews, and especially for those who professed to Christianity while secretly practicing their Judaism. And now — the wheel had turned.

The rabbi did not speak. With a motion of his head he indicated that he wished to hear what his visitor had to say.

"My name is Pedro Alvares. I was military aide to Admiral Don Carlos Carneiro."

Rav Menashe ben Israel said nothing. His shrewd eyes attempted to read the young officer's heart, to discover the reason for this visit. The Portuguese Inquisition was well known for its subtle plots. Perhaps they were having Don Carlos followed. Perhaps they'd had some word of dealings between the Portuguese admiral and the Amsterdam rabbi and had sent this spy to sniff out the truth. No! He would not give those evil men what they were after!

"Well?" the rabbi prompted cautiously.

"He was arrested two months ago. Arrested by the Inquisition." Pedro's emotion was impossible to hide.

The rabbi remained outwardly impassive. Involuntarily he bit his lower lip, and hoped that the young officer hadn't noticed.

"My young friend, I don't have any idea who you're talking about or what you're talking about. I am the rabbi of Amsterdam, versed in Torah and busy with my writings. What is it to me what happens in Portugal?"

The rabbi's words were spoken slowly and with a visible tension. Pedro sensed clearly that the rabbi was antagonistic to him, but didn't understand the reason why. Why was the rabbi denying all knowledge of his dear friend?

Pedro leaned forward in agitation. "I hope I won't sound disrespectful — but I *know* that the rabbi knows him! Don Carlos himself told me that he visited you here, in this house, several months ago. He told me this just after he was arrested, in the office of the Inquisition. And besides..."

Suddenly, Pedro broke off. He found himself utterly unable to say another word.

Not a muscle moved in Rav Menashe's face. This conversation was a total mystery to him. He sensed that every word he spoke was capable of bringing disaster, G-d forbid, to his friend in Lisbon. This clever young spy was trying to get him to say something that would lead to Don Carlos' imprisonment. He must send the man away as quickly as possible.

At the same time, he wished to pry from this officer everything he could tell him about Don Carlos, who was apparently in trouble. "First Raphael Chaim, and now Don Carlos," the rabbi thought sorrowfully.

"And besides...?" he said, repeated Pedro's last words. His curiosity overpowered his caution.

Pedro breathed deeply. Rav Menashe saw the emotion in his eyes. Was this young man a consummate actor — or could he, after all, be telling the truth? The rabbi could not make up his mind.

"And besides," Pedro said in a low voice, "besides, Rabbi, I was the one... who followed him from the... *Vera Cruz*... and saw him come here..."

Pedro wrung his hands in silent agony which he made no attempt to conceal. His eyes were cast down, or he would have seen the way the blood drained from the rabbi's face.

Quietly, Pedro added, "That's the only way I could have known the signal knock to use at the rabbi's gate."

Rav Menashe sprang up, quick as a flash. The color rushed back into his face, which was suffused with rage. He strode toward Pedro, grabbed him by the collar, and yanked him with all his strength up from his chair as he screamed wildly, *"Get out of my house this instant!"*

31

Pedro reeled from the totally unexpected attack. It was difficult to breathe with Rav Menashe grasping him so tightly by the collar. What had he said to so infuriate the rabbi?

But there was no time to think. He was fighting for his life — and for his uncle's life. He would not give up! He would not turn around and go back home after the long, arduous journey and all the dangers he'd faced to reach Amsterdam. He stopped struggling for an instant and then, bracing himself, heaved the rabbi away from him with all his strength. Twisting rapidly, he leaned against the door so that it could not be opened. He grasped the hilt of the sword that dangled from his left hip. Already the members of the household, alerted by Rav Menashe's cries, were attempting to enter. He heard loud, indistinct shouts from the other side of the door and tightened his grip on the sword.

Rav Menashe backed away some little distance, breathing heavily. Pedro said menacingly, "Rabbi, tell them to stop trying to break open the door... or there may be a tragedy here tonight."

To make his meaning clearer, he drew the sword several inches out of its scabbard. Rav Menashe, though clearly frightened, raised his voice and called out calmly enough, "Don't worry! Please move away from the door immediately. Nothing will happen to me." All the time he spoke, Rav Menashe never removed his eyes from the sword. Pedro heard the clamor subside on the other side of the door. His tension lessened. Slowly, in a manner calculated to draw attention to the act, he slipped the sword back into its scabbard. Then he threw a sharp look at the rabbi, on whose face rage and hostility were still very evident.

"Most honored rabbi," Pedro said in a tone which, though considerably softened, nevertheless yielded nothing, "does the Torah of the Jews have nothing that is comparable to the Christian ethic of forgiveness? I have no idea what I said that has angered you so terribly. Perhaps after I've had my say, I will be privileged with an explanation. But first I have something to confess. A man's life hangs on this confession, Rabbi!"

He paused to study the impact of his words on Rav Menashe. The rabbi, he saw, was still inflamed with anger. Rav Menashe held onto his theory of an Inquisition plot, whose instrument for his entrapment was this young officer. "Foul spy," he hissed through clenched teeth.

Pedro bowed his head. "True, *senhor*! Rabbi, you have no idea how true your words are. But it is precisely because of that fact that I — Pedro Alvares, a Christian and an officer in His Majesty's navy — have traveled to your home here in Amsterdam! You, who in my native land are considered a most dangerous heretic..."

Without waiting for permission, Pedro sank into a chair. His voice shook and his eyes burned with suffering as he added, "I testified against Don Carlos to the Holy Office. Because of my testimony he was arrested and will soon stand trial before the Inquisition. All Lisbon is in an uproar. His Majesty is furious at this apparent betrayal..."

There was still no reaction from Rav Menashe. Though the news had acted upon him as though a sharp sword had pierced his innards, he mustered all his resolve not to show what he was feeling. He must remain cautious.

"And it was then," Pedro continued in a near-whisper, "even before the official investigation began, that I learned the secret..."

Pedro subsided once more. He rubbed his eyes with the palms of his hands, which trembled uncontrollably. Rav Menashe tottered over to an armchair and sat. The knowledge that Don Carlos was imprisoned and facing an Inquisition trial had robbed him of his last strength. The downfall of all their operations in Lisbon was complete. First Raphael Chaim — and now, Don Carlos. What would the tiny Marrano community in Lisbon do now? The pain consumed him.

And as if that were not suffering enough, here was this foul traitor seated opposite him in his very own study. "If only I had a sword in my hand," Rav Menashe thought wistfully.

But he must be strong. He must conquer the anguish in his heart in order to extract from this strange young man every detail that could be gleaned about Don Carlos' arrest. With that knowledge, perhaps Hashem would give him the understanding and the strength to deal with the situation. He felt the power of the statement, "Hashem gives, Hashem takes away, may His Name be blessed." When he turned to Pedro, his manner was calm.

"I understand, young man, that you wish to tell me something. I see your agitation. Forgive me for wanting to throw you out of my house." Peering intently at Pedro, he asked, "What is the secret that was revealed to you?"

Pedro's hands still covered his eyes. When he made no answer, Rav Menashe rose and approached him. He placed a gingerly hand on Pedro's shoulder. It was an attempt to forge an atmosphere of trust and liking, so crucial at this moment.

"You can trust me, Pedro," the rabbi said softly.

Pedro rubbed his eyes. Without looking up, he said, "There, at that moment, I learned that Don Carlos is my uncle — brother of my father, who was burned at the stake many years ago by the Holy Office for being a Jew."

"What was your father's name?"

"Roberto da Silva. Professor Roberto da Silva. He was a lecturer at the University of Lisbon."

A fresh arrow pierced Rav Menashe's heart. He recalled that former tragedy clearly. More than once, in his conversations with Don Carlos, the topic of his brother's martyrdom had come up. Don Carlos had spoken especially poignantly about his brother's only son, who had been whisked away to a monastery at such a tender age. And now — what wonders Heaven performed! — in this strange and sorrowful manner, from the shell of Christianity in which he'd been reared rose this man, son of Roberto da Silva!

The miracle had been bought at a steep price... but who could judge Heaven's ways? Rav Menashe subdued the storm that raged inside him. His suspicions of the stranger had not yet been fully conquered.

"And then?" he asked.

"And then," said Pedro, "before he was taken away to his cell, Don Carlos asked me to flee to Amsterdam, as an atonement for my sins... too heavy to bear..."

Rav Menashe asked carefully, "Do you wish to return to the faith of your fathers?"

"No!" Pedro's answer was short and crystal clear. "I am a Christian, and Christianity is my faith."

Rav Menashe gnawed at his lower lip. What a good thing he hadn't rushed to embrace this lost son returned to his faith! His emphasis on self-control, learned during the years of battle against Christianity and the struggle to bring young forced converts back to Judaism, had stood him in good stead now. He removed his hand from Pedro's shoulder and resumed his seat.

"In that case, what is it you want from me?" Rav Menashe asked dryly.

Pedro sighed. "To help me save Don Carlos from his fate."

The rabbi permitted himself a bitter smile. "I don't understand. A devout Christian wishes to save a heretic?"

Pedro nodded his head vigorously. "Right!"

"Why?"

"Because he is my uncle."

"And how will you justify that to yourself, my young friend? Are you really willing to betray your faith for the sake of a family tie?"

Pedro didn't answer. The direct question went straight to the heart of his dilemma.

"I don't know," he replied finally.

Rav Menashe rose suddenly. It seemed clear to him that the young officer before him was an Inquisition spy. He extended a hand to Pedro and said, "Well, my young friend, you made a mistake in coming here. I regret the long journey you've made in vain. I don't know any Don Carlos. He has never visited my home. Naturally, my heart grieves for every Marrano who is exposed by the cruel Inquisition that terrorizes your land and robs men of their right to live by their own faith. The day will come when the G-d of the Jews will exact His just revenge on Portugal. But I cannot help. I am a Dutch citizen, with no power to interfere in your country's internal affairs. All I can do is pray that our G-d will preserve one of His sons from becoming a holy martyr to his faith.

"Good-bye, Pedro. May G-d guide you on the right path."

Pedro despaired. "He doesn't believe me!" he thought. "He is suspicious, and therefore lies without shame." He felt ready to explode with frustration.

His flung his head up. "Honored rabbi, I am not budging from this spot! You can do whatever you please with me, but I will not go!"

Pedro felt an immense resolve. He had made up his mind to what he must do. He turned his back on the rabbi and his proferred hand, still dangling in the empty air.

At that moment there came an urgent knocking on the door.

32

edro Alvares tensed like a coiled spring. In a flash he forgot his determination to remain rooted to the spot and leaped at the door in order to block it. But he was too late. The door burst open noisily, revealing two members of the Bais Yaakov congregation in Amsterdam. One was middle aged, with heavy features; the second was considerably younger. There was a definite family resemblance between them.

"Is everything all right, *Rabbino*?" the younger man demanded breathlessly.

Behind the pair clustered members of Rav Menashe's household. It was they who had summoned a neighbor, Dr. Roberto Gonzales, to come to the rabbi's aid as he was being held hostage in his own study. Together with his son Guilherme, the doctor had rushed to the house and broken down the study door. Guilherme held a stout wooden stick and was ready to do battle.

Rav Menashe smiled. "Thank G-d, all is well. There's no cause for worry." He shot a quick glance at Pedro, who stood stiff and tense in a remote corner of the room, hand poised on the hilt of his sword. He watched the newcomers closely. They had — literally — burst into his life at a most inopportune moment. Right now he had no idea how this episode would end, but one thing seemed clear. His chances to convince Rav Menashe that he was speaking the truth had just been reduced to zero.

"My poor uncle," he thought mournfully. "He will be burnt at the stake, and I, his nephew Pedro, will have been the one to light the fire."

Roberto Gonzales was not calmed by the rabbi's soothing words. "But the servant said there were screams of pain coming from this room. He told us that they tried the door, and it was locked!"

Rav Menashe's smile remained in place. He crossed the room to Gonzales and placed a hand on his shoulder. "Roberto, my friend, why all this fuss? Certainly there were raised voices — but cries of pain? Nonsense!" He turned to Pedro and added deliberately, "Am I not right, my young Christian friend from Portugal?"

Roberto stiffened. He tried to read Pedro's face, but the single taper provided too little light. With his hand still resting firmly on Roberto's shoulder, Rav Menashe strolled over to Pedro. The doctor was forced to come along with him. The last thing Rav Menashe wanted was an altercation between Pedro Alvares and Guilherme, Roberto's hotheaded son. When he reached Pedro, Rav Menashe said genially, "Please, *Senhor* Pedro, let me introduce you to my friend and neighbor, Dr. Roberto Gonzales. He is also a native of Lisbon!"

Roberto shook Pedro's hand, mumbling something — he hardly knew what — as he stared at Pedro. The young officer's face was familiar to him from somewhere, but at the moment he couldn't remember where.

"My name is Pedro Alvares, and I serve in His Majesty, the king of Portugal's, navy."

Pedro's voice triggered the recognition that Roberto had been groping for. The words burst from him emotionally: "If it were possible, I would think that you were the son of an old friend of mine from Lisbon. The same face! The same voice! Incredible!"

The doctor continued to stare mesmerized at Pedro's features, while their hands remained clasped together. As for Pedro, he relaxed slightly. The danger seemed to have been averted, if only for the moment. The rabbi, meanwhile, had retreated to the table, where he picked up the taper and handed it to Guilherme, tactfully taking the stick from him at the same time.

"What is your friend's name?" Pedro asked politely.

"My friend is no longer alive," Roberto replied. "He was burnt at the stake by some compassionate co-religionists of yours. His name was Roberto da Silva. He was a leading professor at the University of Lisbon."

Roberto would have spoken further, but he never got the chance. Pedro straightened suddenly. Gripping the doctor's hand until the bones nearly cracked, he exclaimed shakily, "*Senhor*, he was my father!"

Roberto was thunderstruck. He glanced helplessly at Rav Menashe, but the rabbi only inclined his head as if to say, "Yes, it's true. This Christian is the son of the holy Roberto da Silva."

Roberto Gonzales felt dizzy. Disjointed thoughts galloped through his mind like unbridled horses racing the wind. Heartbreaking images chased one another — images from the fateful day they'd put his old friend to death. They had placed Roberto da Silva in a cage and raised him on their shoulders to parade him before the cheering, celebrating crowd. The doctor remembered how he himself had been among that crowd, outwardly one of them, but inwardly weeping bitter tears. Among those he met that morning were numerous students of the eminent professor, who had learned much wisdom from him and now joined the rest in jeering and mocking the martyr. Roberto Gonzales had done everything he could think of to try and attract his friend's attention, so that even riding to his death in a cage Roberto da Silva would know that there was one caring heart accompanying him on his final journey. But da Silva never noticed him.

Gonzales recalled how the resolve had been born in him then, to leave Portugal forever. He swore that his feet would never again tread the ground of that accursed land. With much suffering he had managed at length to reach the safe shores of Amsterdam, and with no less suffering — and Rav Menashe's help — had finally been transformed into a Torah-observant Jew.

And now, his old friend looked out at him through the eyes of his son...

Blinking, Gonzales roused himself from his thoughts and tried to readjust to his surroundings. Rav Menashe, Pedro Alvares, and his own son, Guilherme, were watching him with great interest.

Pedro gently disengaged his hand from the doctor's. Sensing Gonzales' emotional turmoil, he decided to use it to further his own ends.

"And now," he said quickly, "my father's brother is in prison. My uncle, Don Carlos, admiral of the Portuguese navy. It was I who caused his arrest. I've come to beg the rabbi to help me free him — and the rabbi has refused! That was the conversation that so frightened the servants, *senhor*."

Roberto Gonzales was unable to answer. Still badly shaken from the encounter, and the terrible memories they had engendered — memories born in Lisbon some 18 years before — he staggered over to a chair and sat down heavily.

"I'm afraid," Pedro plowed on, "that the rabbi does not believe me. But I swear by all the holy martyrs of my own faith that I speak the truth! I swear by all that I hold sacred that I will never reveal anything of the help I receive here, out of the goodness of your hearts, to rescue my uncle. I plead with you, doctor, as a friend of my father's, to understand me and what I am feeling. After all, I'm prepared to act in opposition to my faith in this matter!"

Neither Roberto Gonzales nor Rav Menashe answered him. Pedro sensed something dark and mysterious in their silence. What were these Jews concealing? What did they think of his plea? Out of the corner of his eye he noticed that young Guilherme was shaking as though with rage. If he'd had his way, Guilherme would have long since dealt with this Christian officer who was toiling on behalf of the Inquisition!

Suddenly, Rav Menashe broke the silence. Very slowly, almost in a whisper, he said, "I do not know, Pedro, at this moment, who you really are. I do not know if you are speaking the truth, or if you have come here as errand-boy for the Inquisition, to pry from me some acknowledgement of a link with the unfortunate Don Carlos. I know your Lisbon friends' methods very well. So please do not be angry if I refuse to offer any help in this affair."

"But — " Pedro moved forward. Guilherme took a step toward him. Rav Menashe raised a hand and said forcefully, "Guilherme, are you prepared to obey me, and leave this room at once?"

Though the words had been couched as a question, they clearly constituted a command. A brief inner struggle ended with Guilherme slowly walking out of the room. His father watched him go.

"Don't interrupt," Rav Menashe said, as Pedro made to speak. "Pedro — or whatever your name is. I haven't finished what I wanted to say. Even if every word you've spoken is true, we still cannot help you. The cruel, fanatic leaders of your country will not listen to any request I might make, or that might come from the government of Holland, which offers freedom of religion to all its citizens. My country is looked down upon by your compatriots, who burn with a fanatical religious zeal that borders nearly on madness."

"But —" Pedro succeeded in squeezing in a sentence. "what about the underground? You could order it to —"

Rav Menashe and Roberto Gonzales exchanged a rapid, meaningful look.

"Underground?" Rav Menashe asked in astonishment. "What underground are you talking about?"

The rabbi looked genuinely interested, as though waiting to hear something new and fascinating. Pedro's heart sank. His mission looked more complicated than ever.

"The — the underground," he stammered, "that the Inquisition speaks of. They say that the Marranos operate secret cells..."

Rav Menashe laughed heartily.

"How could they? The Inquisition has spies everywhere — in every home and every family."

"I don't know," Pedro persisted, "but they say it exists. In fact, on the very day my uncle was arrested, they managed to rescue one of the Jews who'd been sentenced to death."

Though the news interested him intensely, Rav Menashe remained impassive. Dr. Gonzales inched his chair closer, the better to hear.

"The Inquisition people were very upset," Pedro continued. "This fellow, it seems, did not merely disappear from prison. There was a break-in — a well-planned operation. Guards were beaten and injured. The prisoner escaped."

"Interesting," Rav Menashe responded dryly. Roberto's eyes were glowing like a couple of torches. "All this is very interesting," the rabbi repeated with a shrug. "But it has no bearing on this matter tonight."

"But they say it exists! They say there *is* a Jewish underground!"

Rav Menashe snapped, "They may say what they like!" Then, almost by the way, he asked, "What was his name — the escaped prisoner?"

Pedro wrinkled his brow in an effort to remember.

"I think — if I'm not mistaken — that his name was Rodriguez. Arnaldo Rodriguez, I believe. They say he was the leader of the secret Jews in Lisbon."

Rav Menashe prayed with all his might that his face betrayed nothing of the excitement he was feeling. He could hear his own heart pounding, trying to leap from his chest in joy and thanksgiving to Hashem. Don Carlos had kept his promise — Arnaldo Rodriguez was free! Oh, why couldn't he jump up and embrace the bearer of this wonderful news?

Moving the taper a little so that his face was shadowed, the rabbi remarked, "The name is not familiar to me. In any case, Pedro, I cannot help you. I live in Amsterdam, thank G-d, and not in Lisbon!"

Pedro was devastated. Had he made the whole arduous journey from Lisbon for naught? He had deserted his post, told no one he was going away, traveled on little-used roads until he found a way to cross the border into Spain, and from there to France, Belgium, and then Holland. Where was he to turn now?

Rav Menashe saw his despair. Gently, he said, "I don't understand you, Pedro. If you are speaking the truth, you are prepared to oppose your own faith. Why? Because you recognize that to torture and murder your uncle simply because of his religion is a bad thing. How do you rationalize to yourself that the priests of your faith do such things enthusiastically? You are thinking of your uncle, languishing in prison and awaiting his doom. Why don't you stop and think of the thousands who have already perished at the stake? Or of the thousands more who are destined to die the same way? Your merciful faith has already been burning people for upwards of 200 years, for the crime of praying directly to G-d without asking for the intercession of your lord, whom I refuse even to name! Why are you prepared to oppose your faith for the sake of your uncle only? Perhaps, if crimes of this nature are occurring, there is some flaw in the faith itself?"

Roberto Gonzales burst out, "You — the son of Roberto da Silva! If only you could have seen your father on his last day, borne on a cage as the crowd around him cheered at the sight! The day was a festival in their eyes. If you could have seen it, you would have done what I did — fled that accursed land and settled here in Amsterdam, to start a new life and to honor your Father in Heaven with all your heart."

It was too much. The words that bombarded him from all directions raised a flood of tears that spilled over onto Pedro's cheeks, try as he might to restrain them. He felt as though he were drowning in those tears. Silently, he cried to the one who was not present, *"Don Carlos, my good uncle who has helped me so much! I tried to save you, but your wicked friends in Amsterdam have refused to help me!"*

Without a word to anyone, Pedro walked out of the room and out of the house to the street, where the darkness of sleeping Amsterdam and his own unknown fate awaited him.

33

Pedro ran headlong from the rabbi's courtyard into the street. Darkness beset him from all sides; he finally stopped running for fear of an unseen pit in the road that would send him sprawling. His entire body trembled with rage and frustration as he leaned, spent, against the wall surrounding Rav Menashe's house, breathing deeply in an effort to calm his jangling nerves. He must think clearly. There were decisions to be made. The Amsterdam street was enveloped in night from one end to the other, except for the faintest pale glimmer on the eastern horizon that heralded tomorrow. A chill pre-dawn wind began to gust.

He was at a loss. Alone in a strange city, he had no acquaintance to whom to turn. He could not believe, even now, that the rabbi had refused to help him. Even now, he half-expected Rav Menashe, or his father's old friend, to run after him to bring him back inside. But no one came. *"They don't believe me,"* he thought despairingly. *"Why?"*

Presently, he left the wall behind and began making his way slowly and cautiously up the dark street. In the profound silence, Pedro could hear the sound of his own footsteps keeping time with the beating of his heart.

"Why?" he asked himself again. "Why didn't they believe me? I was so open with them. I told them everything — even the fact that I was the one responsible for Don Carlos' arrest. Why didn't the rabbi understand how I've jeopardized myself for the sake of this mission, traveling so far from my home into the heart of enemy territory? The rabbi could have done anything he wished with me — even had me killed. That young hothead, standing there in the room with that stick in his hand, would have done it with joy. What more can I do to make them believe me — to make them search for a way to help poor Don Carlos?"

He reached the end of the street. From here there was only one direction to go: right, towards the harbor. The night he'd followed Don Carlos came to mind. It was here, down this very street, that he'd run after the admiral. Standing right on this spot, he had been able to see Don Carlos enter the rabbi's house.

Some persistent inner voice urged him to turn right, toward the harbor. The sea called to him. "Is that the only way out for me?" he thought wearily.

He threw a last glance over his shoulder at Rav Menashe's house at the far end of the street. At that precise moment, the door opened and light flowed out. Someone stood there, peering into the night.

"They want to make sure I've really gone," he thought bitterly. "But... maybe not? Maybe they're looking for me, want me to come back? Maybe I really should go back and try again?"

"NO!" The shout exploded from his lips into the silent street, frightening even him. Resolutely, he turned toward the harbor. His steps were quicker now. He was suddenly filled with a revulsion toward the rabbi. Rav Menashe's attitude toward Don Carlos seemed just one more proof of the Jews' typical lack of humanity. His hatred for the Jewish people, dormant for a time, received a powerful boost. "They don't care about each other a bit, those Jews. With them, it's every man for himself. They are a cruel and unfeeling people."

All at once, he stood stock still, struck by a new thought.

"If *they're* cruel and unfeeling, what, then, is the Inquisition? What are the citizens who cheer whenever any new heretic is burnt at the stake in the city square?" Every agonized cry, every lick of the devouring flames, only made the crowd cheer louder. "And they did it to my own father!

That's what Don Carlos told me. That's what Dr. Roberto Gonzales just described to me!"

It was a revelation. Pedro stood in the Amsterdam street, filled with thoughts he'd never had before. And suddenly, the full significance of the situation hit him with a tremendous impact:

"And I myself... am a Jew!"

It was as if a sharp sword had pierced his innards. The reality of his own Jewishness exploded upon him now with complete clarity. So long as he'd been immersed in the effort to save his uncle, Pedro had been able to avoid the knowledge, to push it away into a deep corner of his heart. But now that all seemed lost, it rose up before him in all its import. Despite the cold wind that blew from the sea, Pedro began to perspire. He lifted first his right hand and then his left. Gazing at them through the darkness, he whispered, pained and shaken, "These are the hands of... a Jew. I am a Jew. I... am... a... Jew!"

It was too much to bear. He began walking again, mechanically. Without realizing it he picked up speed, and was soon running. The more he thought about this awful new knowledge, the more tightly he was gripped by hatred — hatred for himself, for his father, for Don Carlos, for Rav Menashe, for the Inquisition, for Portugal, for the whole world. It seemed to his fevered mind, as he raced through the sleeping streets, that even the wind was shrilling in mockery:

"You are a Jew! You are... *a Jew!*"

≈)⌒

Panting, Pedro reached the harbor. Silence reigned here, too. The vessels tied to the dock were silent, their sails limp as though in mourning. Small waves slapped against the ships' sides and fell back again. It was not far from this spot that the flagship *Vera Cruz* had docked on the night Pedro had trailed Don Carlos to Rav Menashe's house. It had been an ill-fated night. So earnest had he been in his Christian zeal, so eager to serve the church and the Holy Office in ridding Portugal of heretics... and he had ended by falling into the very pit he'd dug for another. He had begun with a burning desire to reveal that Don Carlos was a Jew, and had ended by sacrificing all that was dear to him in order to save Don Carlos — and discovered that he himself was a Jew, to boot! Where was Heaven leading him?

Pedro found a boulder and sat down. His head felt heavy. He rested it on the palms of his hands. Presently the tears seeped through his fingers and made them damp...

⁊⸙

The city still slept, though here and there the first stirrings of the morning were beginning. A rooster crowed in the distance. Somewhere, a door slammed. Early risers passed quietly through the dim streets. Pedro rose to his feet and prepared to leave; he did not wish to be seen by anyone who might ask uncomfortable questions. But where to go?

He began walking, without direction or purpose. His empty stomach made its presence known. Pedro had not yet recovered from his failure at the rabbi's house, and his shoulders were still bowed from the fresh burden of his ancestry. Now, with the coming of morning, the outlines of the moored ships and of the nearby houses — houses he remembered from the trip he'd made with Don Carlos some months earlier — grew sharper.

Should he return to the rabbi's house — try one last time? Maybe this time they'd believe he was telling the truth.

Then Pedro grew angry at himself for even entertaining the thought. At the rabbi's house, everyone was more interested in turning him against Christianity than in saving the life of their fellow Jew in Lisbon. It was possible to understand their own anathema to Christianity, but why try to turn him away from it? What difference did it make to them what he believed in? Let each man go his own way!

He stopped walking — something he'd taken to doing these past hours, whenever his thoughts grew too pressing — and laughed at his own foolishness. "Here I am, complaining against them because they want to convince me with words — while my own church does the same thing to heretics, only with torture and killing." Without quite knowing the precise moment it had happened, Pedro realized that he'd begun to see his religion in a new light... by the light of the fire that had consumed his father.

Amsterdam, it seemed, had taught him much in the last few hours.

His thoughts turned to Don Carlos, and his wife Beatriz, and their children. He bit his lip, fighting back the anguish that threatened to choke him at the notion that it had been he who led them into their trouble. Who knew whether or not de Henrique was trying to hurt Don Carlos in retaliation for that other Jew, Rodriguez, the one who'd escaped? Slowly, he became aware that the fate of these hounded and persecuted Jews was beginning to touch his heart. Was this the will of G-d, guiding him back to the faith for which his father had died? Was the father's soul to know no rest until the son returned to the old beliefs — the beliefs he knew nothing about, and which he had been educated all his life to despise?

Even at this moment he felt no great love for that unknown faith. But as he stood in the Amsterdam street in the light of early morning, Pedro realized that he no longer fully believed all the things the Dominican monks had taught him as a child. He could not reconcile the ethic of love they had always preached with the cruel *auto-da-fé* that so delighted the masses of Catholics in Lisbon. And he had another question. Why had his uncle, Don Carlos, clung with such tenacity and secrecy to the faith of his fathers? Why did so many other Portuguese of Jewish descent stubbornly insist on abandoning Christianity to return to the old faith, despite the desperate dangers and the certain suffering that awaited them if they were found out?

Maybe there was something in this religion, something he didn't know about. Did it, perhaps, contain a kernel of truth, something that upheld its followers through all hardship and difficulty?

Confusion filled him, growing stronger each moment. What had Amsterdam done to him? The few people who passed him on the street gaped at him with wonder. How odd he must look, standing here immersed in his troubled thoughts. Odd enough, certainly, to attract all those curious stares! He forced himself to begin walking again. Of their own accord, his feet began to carry him back to the rabbi's house.

He banged on the gate. The serving lad peered out angrily.

"Tell the rabbi," Pedro said quickly, "that I've learned much this night. I want to tell him just one thing."

The gate closed. A moment later, it opened again.

"Enter," the boy said sulkily. "But don't keep him long. He has to hurry to *Shacharis* — the morning service."

Rav Menashe welcomed Pedro with a pleasant smile. Pedro asked for permission to sit: Exhaustion threatened to topple him at any second. Permission was granted. Pedro made a mighty effort to hide his rising emotion as he said simply, "*Senhor*, what must I do to make you believe me?"

The rabbi didn't answer.

"What must I do to convince you that I deeply regret having handed my uncle over to the Inquisition? I have just passed a night wandering through the streets of Amsterdam — painful hours of despair, hours that gave rise to many strange thoughts. Will it please you to hear, Rabbi, that I even entertained doubts about the leaders of my own faith?

"But at this moment, sir, I ask you — I beg of you — to believe what I say. I am prepared to take any test you might set me, in order to save Don Carlos from the flames of the *auto-da-fé*. Please — before it's too late!"

Rav Menashe saw a very different young man before him from the proud officer who had fled his house the night before. It distressed him to see Pedro now, eyes downcast and spirit broken. The doubts Pedro had mentioned, doubts about the religion he'd been raised in, admitted a gleam of hope.

Rav Menashe came closer and placed a hand on Pedro's shoulder. "Pedro, my young friend," he said, gentle as a father, "Pedro, look at me."

Pedro slowly lifted his eyes to the rabbi's. How often had he sat exactly thus before the priest of the Dominican Church in Lisbon?

"Pedro," the rabbi continued, eyes boring into Pedro's, "I will believe you, if you choose to stay here and begin learning about Judaism. If you try to learn to recognize your true faith. No one will force you if you end by rejecting it... though, if that should happen, we would all grieve deeply.

"But I know that will not happen. It has never happened yet with any young man who came to us from Spain or Portugal. The power of our Torah's truth is stronger than anything else!"

Pedro was surprised. He said nothing.

Once again, he heard Rav Menashe's quiet voice, asking, "Will you stay, Pedro?"

Silence.

⪢⪡

"Twenty years ago," the rabbi explained patiently, without removing his hand from Pedro's shoulder, "the Inquisition in Coimbra executed a young priest — a Christian from birth. His name was Bernardo Gimreines. He was not descended from Marranos, but despite that he studied our *Tanach* and used it as a reference point in studying the tenets of Christianity. And because he was an honest young man, he quickly came to the conclusion that Judaism is the one true religion, which Christianity has severely distorted. He came to this conclusion by his own abilities, and with the zeal for truth that burned in him he was not afraid to proclaim it publicly.

Rav Menashe paused to give Pedro time to absorb what he had heard. Then the rabbi continued:

"The church could not let that pass in silence. The religion of mercy and love can't bear it when someone isn't prepared to be merciful and loving in the way he is taught to be. The young priest was thrown into prison, just like your uncle. He suffered terrible tortures, but all attempts to bring him back to Christianity were futile. Bernardo remained true to Judaism — a faith he did not know, except for the fact that it is the Word of G-d that emanates to humanity.

"Pedro," Rav Menashe said softly, "listen to this. In prison, Bernardo decided to circumcise himself. With the aid of a sharp knife that came his way, he performed the circumcision and then, with the blood, wrote the following words on the wall of his prison cell."

The rabbi fell silent, watching Pedro intently. He went to his desk, opened one of its drawers, and drew out a large copper tablet.

"Read it, Pedro. Read the words that that young Christian wrote on his cell wall with the blood of his own circumcision!"

Pedro looked at the tablet.

"Read it out loud, my friend. Do you understand Spanish?"

Pedro nodded, then slowly read aloud, "*Contra la verdad noa ayi puersa*" ("Might cannot endure in the face of truth").

Rav Menashe pressed the tablet to his heart.

"Our holy Torah, Pedro, is the truth. Why do you think your father was prepared to place his position, and his very life, in danger? Why is your uncle Don Carlos prepared to undergo any amount of torture without turning his back back on his faith? Yes, I know Don Carlos. I know him well. He visited me here several times. And I helped him a great deal, so that he might be able to observe the *mitzvos* secretly in Lisbon and Oporto.

"My heart is crying in anguish because your uncle has fallen into the hands of those wicked men. But know this, Pedro: Don Carlos does not regret a single thing he did. I am sure of that. And do you know why? Because he has seen the truth. When the truth takes hold of a person, it doesn't let go. It gives his life a profound meaning, until living without it seems utterly pointless."

Rav Menashe fell silent. He felt drained by emotion. The serving boy appeared in the doorway and announced, "It's time to *daven Shacharis.*"

Rav Menashe nodded, then turned back to Pedro. "Christianity is not the truth! That's why they persecute us, the Jews, with such cruelty. As long as we're alive they know that a people exists that knows the truth, despite their own distortions and garblings..."

Pedro had found no words yet.

"Pedro!" the rabbi cried. "Does it not seem wondrous to you that the benevolent G-d has led you here by such strange paths — to me, rabbi of the Marranos who flee Portugal and Spain and wish to return openly to their Jewish faith? Is not that fact alone proof that you belong here?"

Turning, Rav Menashe went to his desk and replaced the copper tablet in its drawer. With his back still to Pedro, he asked again, "Will you stay?"

Pedro's eyes darted anxiously. "But what will become of my uncle — of Don Carlos?"

Rav Menashe ignored the question. "*Will you stay?*"

In his heart, Pedro knew that once he took the leap, there'd be no turning back. But the leap across the yawning chasm that had opened before him seemed impossible. Jumping from the faith he'd been raised in —

the religion that burned people who strayed from its tenets — to the faith of the people they despised most of all, seemed a hard and bitter thing. All he wanted to do was save his uncle. What was happening to him?

The rabbi said with great emphasis, "Your father, your holy father, is waiting for you here in this room!"

Yes, his father was waiting. If Don Carlos' words in the Holy Office were to be believed, he wished his son to take this step. His father, for whom — after Roberto Gonzales' tale last night — Pedro had begun feeling a closeness that with each passing hour was growing deeper and stronger.

He understood that he could resist no longer.

"Yes, sir. I will stay." His voice died away to a whisper.

Rav Menashe rushed over and embraced him. "Pedro — our brother!"

Pedro did not react. His thoughts were a confused tangle from which only one clear image emerged: a prison cell in Lisbon, and his uncle Don Carlos, whom he had not managed to save...

"You will live here, as my guest," Rav Menashe said. He rang a small bell that sat on his desk. The serving boy reappeared at the door.

"Take Pedro to the guest room, which will be his room from now on. Prepare him a light meal and see that he gets some sleep. I must hurry to shul for *Shacharis*."

Pedro rose shakily to his feet and followed the boy.

"By the way," the rabbi called after him, "we are already taking steps, in our own ways, to rescue Don Carlos from the Inquisition. Roberto Gonzales, I believe, will leave for Portugal within a few days to see what can be done."

Pedro whirled around. He felt new life coursing through his veins. The strength he'd lost in the night came back to him, and his heart beat a new rhythm of joy. With eyes brimming with profound gratitude, he gazed across the room at the rabbi, who gave him a wide, warm smile in return.

34

The *Vanderwalda*, a Dutch sailing vessel, was tied up at the dock. Roberto Gonzales stood on deck along with his fellow voyagers, leaning against the rail and watching the city of Lisbon spread out before him.

It was a beautiful day. Sunshine shone on the ship and the sea was calm. The passengers, hailing from Amsterdam, Hamburg, and Antwerp, were in high spirits and conversed loudly. In contrast, Roberto stood silently, hoping to draw as little attention to himself as possible.

Presently the passengers began to disembark but Roberto stayed back. He was anxious to see how the customs officials received those who had preceded him. From where he was standing, they seemed to be going about their business calmly and routinely. There was a chance that all would go smoothly. Roberto felt heartened.

His turn came. He approached the customs counter with a sure, unhurried step. A pair of young officials greeted him heartily: *"Bom dia, senhor! Bem vindo em nosso pais?* ("Good morning, sir! Welcome to our country!") What is your name?"

Roberto answered unhesitatingly, "Johann Van Sachlada." He paused, then added in halting Portuguese, "*Commerciante, commerciante* ("A businessman, a businessman")," as though to explain his reason for visiting Lisbon. Almost as an afterthought, he added, "Antwerpen."

The clerks smiled. With a cursory examination of his papers, they waved him through. Roberto was relieved. He had passed through unchallenged, and they had not asked to see the contents of the briefcase he held close to his body.

He wasted no time climbing into one of the carts lined up beside the quay, their teams facing the city. He had chosen a cart with an open leather roof. He wanted to see Lisbon as he entered — the city where he had been born 45 years earlier. There was more than mere sentiment involved here. The unobstructed view would allow him to pay heed to everything that was happening in the streets around him, and to discreetly monitor the passers-by.

"*Bom dia*," the cart-driver said with a toothy smile. "Where to?"

"*Bom dia*," Roberto answered. "*Por favor* (please), take me to Judge Fernando de Lima's house." Taking a slip of paper out of his coat pocket, Roberto read aloud, "Superior Judge Fernando Jorge Silvia de Lima." He spoke Portuguese with a dominant Dutch accent.

The driver nodded to indicate that he knew where the judge resided. He tugged at the reins to rouse his horses, then lightly plied the whip. The team started forward at a trot. Roberto sat back, trying to organize his thoughts and plan his next move. To his annoyance, he heard the driver shout above the noise of the clapping hooves and rattling wheels: "*Senhor* has visited Lisbon before? *Senhor* knows our city?"

Roberto tensed. In this city it was impossible to know who was asking the questions and with what intentions. Amsterdam was full of horror stories about Inquisition spies who roamed Lisbon's streets — spies who hunted down forced converts, or Marranos, with their seemingly innocent queries.

"*I must be careful*," he warned himself. Aloud, he asked, "Why do you ask?"

"It's just that the *senhor* speaks fluent Portuguese!"

Roberto laughed. *"Muito obrigado* (Much obliged)! But I've never been in Lisbon before in my life."

His words were untrue. Aside from the fact that he'd been born here, he had visited Lisbon a number of times in recent years. Always, his trips had been at the behest of Rav Menashe ben Israel, and had introduced him to Admiral Don Carlos, now languishing in an Inquisition dungeon. His missions had occasionally brought him to Judge de Lima's house as well.

The driver did not desist. "So where did you learn to speak Portuguese — and so well, too?"

Roberto made a dismissive gesture. "I learned a bit of the language in Amsterdam. There are many Portuguese emigrés there."

The driver made no reply to this, except to lash his whip at the horses' backs again. They picked up speed. Presently the driver asked, "Are there Portuguese Jews in Amsterdam?"

"Some."

The driver swung his head around to observe his passenger. Roberto evaded his glance, gazing instead at the city streets through which they were rumbling. He saw ornate villas and a smattering of pedestrians hurrying home for their afternoon repasts. With all his heart he longed to put an end to this uncomfortable interview.

The driver abruptly stopped the cart and swung completely around to face Roberto. "Tell me, *Senhor.* Who is Menashe ben Israel?"

"That's it! It's come!" Roberto thought, panicked. What did this cart-driver want from him? Was there anything about him that had aroused the other's suspicions?

"Menashe ben Israel?" Roberto repeated with all the casualness he could muster. His questioning intonation implied that this was the first time he was hearing the name. The driver never moved his eyes from his passenger. Suddenly, Roberto "remembered":

"Ah, yes. He's the Jews' rabbi in Amsterdam." He looked at the driver innocently. "Why do you ask?"

The driver turned back to his horses, whipping them mercilessly. Over his shoulder, he replied: "Oh, no special reason. There's been a lot of talk about him here lately." They drove on for a moment or two, then the driver added, "Tell me, why does he hate us so?"

Roberto shrugged. "I don't know. Who told you he hates you?"

"I tell you he hates us! The Inquisition speaks of him often. For some reason, he wants to harm Portugal. Travelers from Amsterdam say so, too."

Roberto held his tongue. Whatever he might say at this juncture could only hurt him. His best course was to simply agree with everything the driver said. He must reach Fernando de Lima's house in peace. In any case, in just a few minutes this man would have vanished from Roberto's life forever. Why get involved?

But the man wasn't finished. "Have you heard of Don Carlos?"

This time, Roberto had a difficult time hiding his agitation. In mounting excitement he thought, "Here's my chance to find out what's happened to Don Carlos." After all, he'd been sent to Lisbon precisely to see what could be done to rescue the prisoner.

"No, I haven't. Who is he?"

The driver eyed him in astonishment. "*Senhor* has really never heard of him?"

"No. What is there to hear?"

"You are from Amsterdam, *Senhor* — and you don't know who he is? Why, they say that the Jews of Amsterdam are praying for his deliverance night and day!"

"Who wishes to harm him? And who is he, anyway?"

The driver chuckled. "It's been years, *Senhor* — years! — since we've had a case that caused such a furor in Lisbon. This is the biggest case the Inquisition has had for a long time. Do you see, *Senhor*?" The driver lifted his whip to point at a large, grim building they were passing on their left. "That's the Inquisition building. He's sitting in that dungeon right this very minute, the great Don Carlos... the lowly traitor. The Jewish heretic!

"He was admiral of our navy. Three months ago, it came to light that he was really a secret Jewish pig. But what really makes me angry is that rabbi, that Menashe ben Israel, who encouraged him to betray his people, his country, and his faith." He paused. "Have you ever seen him?"

"Who? Don Carlos?"

"No — the rabbi of Amsterdam. What does he look like?"

Roberto shook his head. "No, I've never seen him... Actually, on second thought, maybe I have. I think I saw him once."

Roberto's eyes were riveted to the building they were passing. Every window, he saw, was covered with a thick curtain. He listened for the cries of Jewish prisoners from beyond the stone walls — cries bearing the pain of the entire Jewish people that at that moment would be heard by Hashem . Who knew what those wicked men had done to Don Carlos, in their evil efforts to extract from him the names of other Marranos? Had he managed to withstand the torture? Was his spirit, Heaven forbid, broken? Roberto fought back a strong urge to ask the cart-driver what had become of Don Carlos. Instead, he asked, "How did they catch him?"

The driver looked smug. "They know everything at the Holy Office! They know that he visited that rabbi's house in Amsterdam more than once. He was seen entering in the middle of the night. Isn't that enough?"

"It certainly is." Roberto's eyes closed of their own accord. After a few seconds, he forced himself to open them and ask, "And what's happening to him now?"

The driver laughed. "Rumor has it that next week, on Sunday, he'll be leaving this building."

"What do you mean, leaving the building? Is he being set free?"

The driver's laughter was loud and raucous, as though he'd just heard the joke of a lifetime.

"Set free? No! He's leaving this building and heading for Heaven... or rather, for Hell." He cast a knowing glance at Roberto, sitting ashen faced behind him. "I know you Dutchmen don't like it much, but on Sunday there'll be an auto-da-fé held here in the city square. Will you still be in Lisbon then? It will be well worth your while to come and watch the fun! There are several heretics waiting to be burned. What a bonfire we're preparing for them! This time, the king himself will be attending the ceremony. He wants to see with his own eyes his former friend Don Carlos tied to the stake. I tell you, it will be *fabuloso* (fabulous). You'd better come, *Senhor*. It will be a tale to tell back home."

Roberto felt faint. Dark thoughts crowded each other in his mind. This was Monday. He had five days in which to set a rescue plan in operation. Would it be enough time?

Past his troubled thoughts he heard the driver's voice again: "Here we are — Judge de Lima's house. A good man, the judge. He helps many people, especially poor people. A true Christian."

Roberto handed him a gold coin. "Here."

"B-but..." The driver could not believe his eyes. "Th-this is too much for the ride."

"It's all right. It was a pleasure riding with you."

Roberto jumped off the cart. He bade the driver a courteous farewell and waited until the cart had moved far down the street. Then he knocked on the gate that surrounded the judge's stately home. The knocks followed a pattern — the Marranos' signal.

A woman opened the gate. "Yes? Who do you want, Senhor?"

"Superior Judge Fernando Jorge Silvia de Lima. I have a message for him."

The woman scanned him, from head to toe, with a penetrating look. In Lisbon, one did not trust strangers very readily.

"Who are you, sir?"

For a moment, Roberto was at a loss for an answer. He wasn't sure if she was the judge's wife, privy to the secret of her husband's Jewishness. As her eyes remained fixed on his unwaveringly, he decided to take a chance.

"Roberto Gonzales," he answered quietly. "Roberto Gonzales from Amsterdam. Can I speak with your husband?"

The woman stiffened. "No!"

"But — why?"

"Because," she said grimly, "since this morning my husband has been at the Inquisition building."

Roberto felt as though he'd been delivered a death blow.

35

Roberto's eyes widened in fear. For several minutes he stood speechless with shock, gaping at the judge's wife while a spreading weakness overtook his limbs. Finally, he croaked, "He... was summoned... to the... Holy Office? To... the Inquisition?"

She did not answer immediately. His reaction, he saw, had startled her. At length she nodded "Yes." Her eyes were calm and she betrayed no fear. Where had she learned to mask her emotions so well?

They measured each other in silence. Roberto's knees felt on the point of buckling. If only he could sit down somewhere, drink some water, rest a little. But he was afraid of this woman, whom he did not know at all. So he remained standing adjacent to his friend Judge de Lima's house, pierced through with exhaustion, unmoving.

His thoughts were a confused tangle out of which only one question emerged clearly: What to do now? Where to turn? The long voyage from Amsterdam to Lisbon had been undertaken in vain. His ability to rescue Don Carlos had shrunk significantly. And it was very possible that the judge had been arrested as well. Why else had the Inquisition summoned him? Had Don Carlos broken under torture and revealed the names of the other secret Jews throughout the city?

Shooting pains shot through his chest. He was aware that the judge's wife was watching him closely. Surely she noted how her news had affected him. He must take care. Nevertheless, he asked, "They... followed him?"

"No! Why would you think that?"

Roberto didn't know what to say. Why was it so clear to her that her husband had not been followed? Could this be just another ploy on her part, another way to protect herself? Was she being excessively cautious? In Lisbon one was never sure exactly to whom one could speak, and on what topic. Inquisition spies were everywhere.

"I understand," he said at last, submissively. In all apparent innocence he asked, "When do you expect him to return?"

The woman spread her hands: "I don't know. I wish I knew! This is the first time he has been called there."

"Can I ask why they summoned him? What exactly did they say when they ordered him to appear at their tribunal?"

The judge's wife stepped back, so that she was partially shielded behind the door. "Who told you they summoned him to stand up in court? And as for that, what are all these questions, sir? Who are you, anyway? Roberto Gonzales, you said?"

"Yes," he replied quickly. At all cost, he must keep her talking.

After a moment, he added, "I am a friend of the judge's. A friend from Amsterdam." He waited for her reaction.

The door closed further. The woman leaned against it so that she was only partially visible. "A friend of my husband's?" She studied Roberto keenly. Had this stranger been sent by the Inquisition to spy on her and trap her in conversation? "Amsterdam, he said," she thought. He must want to witness her reaction to that. The Inquisition, she knew, was well aware of the strong ties that linked the Marranos of Spain and Portugal with Amsterdam and its rabbis. The very name of that city was, to the secret Jews, almost synonymous with the name "Jerusalem." She must be very careful. She must watch out for a trap. Her husband had been summoned to the Inquisition building — who knew for what purpose?

"A friend of my husband's?" she asked again, calmer but still in the same astonished tone. "Impossible! My husband has no friends in Amsterdam."

She spoke the final words forcefully, then slammed the door in Roberto's face.

Roberto closed his eyes in despair. He was standing on a quiet, pleasant side street in Lisbon — alone. More alone than he'd been just an hour before, when hope had still been his companion. What now?

His first step, he decided, was to leave the vicinity of this house as quickly as possible. One never knew what could happen — what the judge's wife might take it into her head to do. Don Carlos, it seemed to him, was as good as lost. He must worry now about saving his own life, of staying out of the Inquisition's way. May Hashem guide and protect me...

Fortunately, there were few pedestrians on Lisbon's streets at this hour. Nobody paid any attention to the man in Dutch clothing carrying a wide briefcase. Roberto began strolling the streets at a leisurely pace, outwardly unruffled. His target destination was the coast where, he hoped, he would find some remote corner in which to hide. There remained two days and two nights until the ship he'd arrived on was due to sail back to Amsterdam. What to do until then?

Many are the thoughts in a man's heart — and Hashem's plan will endure...

⥲〇⥲

The man he'd been awaiting had arrived.

Padre João Manuel raised his head. It had seemed to him that he'd heard the outer gate open. A moment later he caught the sound of the gate closing again. He was seated at the head of the table in the conference room of the Holy Office courthouse. A large tome was open before him. Upon hearing these sounds, he hastily closed it.

De Henrique sat at the table's other end, writing something with apparent indifference. The room was dim. Heavy curtains on the windows blacked the noon-time sun. Still, it wasn't hard to make out the expressions of the others who sat around the table. All of them were priests, and all were Inquisition judges. They were Bernardo Machado, Gabriel Monteiro de Silvia, and the head of the Dominican monastery, João Batista de Oliveiro. Garbed in their long brown cassocks, their expressions were uniformly grave.

No one broke the dense silence that hung like a pall over the room. Only their eyes, restless and impatient, darted here and there as though seeking some spot to latch on to. The tension derived from the fact that none of them as yet knew how this affair would resolve itself — the affair of Don Carlos.

From beyond the closed door came the tread of footsteps and the sibilant whisper of low-voiced conversation. The door opened. A young monk entered first, followed by the distinguished figure of Superior Judge Fernando Jorge Silvia de Lima.

Everyone present sighed with relief.

João Manuel rose and went forward to welcome the newcomer: "Good morning, Judge!" The others inclined their heads, smiling weakly in greeting.

Fernando de Lima scrutinized their faces, trying to discover why they had summoned him here in this fashion. Was it connected to Don Carlos whose sentence was expected to be handed down by these villains any day now? Or had Don Carlos, in a moment of weakness under torture, disclosed his name to the Inquisition interrogators?

De Lima had been forced to obey the summons: He'd had no choice. Had he tried to evade it with some excuse, he would merely have aroused all the suspicion that abounded in Lisbon these days. The judge was apprehensive as he watched *Padre* João Manuel, formidable head of the Inquisition, approach him with a warm smile.

João Manuel clasped de Lima's shoulder and led him to the table. His affectionate manner only deepened de Lima's apprehension. He sat on the chair that was indicated to him, beside João Manuel's.

The priest began speaking immediately:

"*Senhor*, we are indebted to you for answering our summons and hurrying here to this meeting of the judges of our Holy Office. Although by law we are obligated to bring this case to you in the High Court, we chose to proceed differently this time. We've asked you to come here —

in a moment you will understand why — in advance of our appearance before the High Court in the near future, to request approval of a certain sentence."

Padre João Manuel paused to allow for a build-up of tension. He loved having others hang on to his words.

"As head of the Holy Office, I must inform you that former admiral Don Carlos Carneiro has been found guilty of being a practicing Jew. Since the prisoner shows no sign of repentance, the Holy Office has sentenced him to death by fire. May his death atone for his heresy in betraying the holy faith, the king, and his people."

Not a muscle in de Lima's face moved. He had known from the moment of his friend's arrest that Don Carlos' chances of gaining his freedom were slim. Still, the news hit him hard.

With a celebratory cadence, de Henrique cried, "We hope to carry out the sentence, with the good lord's help, this coming Sunday!"

João Manuel cast a look of loathing at his secretary, who had spoken out of turn as usual. De Lima, feeling it incumbent upon him to say something, uttered only, "*Sim* (yes)." His voice was very low and seemed to him to shake slightly. He hoped none of the others noticed.

"The court," João Manuel continued, "has based its decision on the testimony of Pedro Alvares and on the heretic's own confession. It is a just decree, handed down in the spirit of our holy faith. The accused was afforded every opportunity to defend himself in accordance with the laws of our state and of the Holy Office."

"*Sim,*" de Lima said again in a cold, clear voice. He knew just how much store the Inquisition set by justice and due legal process, and exactly how assiduously the rights of each of their victims were guarded. He had heard many a horror tale of "legal" Inquisition practices. By law, every accused man was entitled to a defender. Don Carlos had had a defender — appointed by the Inquisition. The man had been de Henrique's lackey. Fernando de Lima smiled dryly when he heard João Manuel speak of the "law" that governed the Inquisition dungeons.

De Henrique could not contain himself. Jubilantly, he burst out, "This will undoubtedly be a great and joyous day for all loyal Catholics. And I stress — loyal..."

Between the folds of fat, the secretary's small eyes gleamed with evil satisfaction. De Lima noted that João Manuel was growing increasingly enraged at his inability to stop de Henrique from interrupting. "Nothing has changed between them," he thought. "Is there a chance we might take advantage of this situation to Don Carlos' benefit?"

"*Sim*," de Lima said quickly, in response to de Henrique's outburst. He wondered what form his own role in this farce was to take.

João Manuel cleared his throat. Shifting in his armchair, he searched for the right words.

"We called you here," he said, "because we have a problem. A small judicial problem. A triviality." He motioned as though waving away a fly. "A picayune matter that can probably be solved very easily. But we must find the solution."

"*Sim*."

"*Senhor* knows that, by law, when dealing with an accused member of the military, His Majesty, the King, is required to personally approve the sentence."

"*Sim*."

João Manuel peered in annoyance at the Superior Judge. De Lima's coldness struck him suddenly as strange. The reiterated "*sim*" — the only answer he'd vouchsafed so far — was irritating. The priest made a monumental effort to conceal his irritation.

"The king," he continued, "has approved the decree. However, he has not yet signed it. He is furious with Don Carlos, in whom he placed his trust and who betrayed him. The king won't hear a word in his defense. But his son, Prince Alfonso, is, as you will recall, a close personal friend of Don Carlos. He is trying with all his might to prevent the king from signing the sentence. He is making great efforts to postpone Sunday's scheduled auto-da-fé. He claims the sentence is illegal."

Judge de Lima felt an overpowering curiosity. "Why?"

"Because the witness, *Senhor* Pedro Alvares, never actually testified before the Holy Office tribunal. He disappeared under mysterious circumstances immediately after learning of his own close relationship with Don Carlos. We don't know where he is. Without witnesses, the prince argues, there is no case."

Fernando de Lima sat in prolonged silence. He broke it at last to say, "Yes, I see."

Instantly, he felt he'd made a mistake. The others around the table were all staring at him with daggers in their eyes. He must carefully weigh every word now. With Hashem's help, he might find a way to use this new information to save Don Carlos, or at least to postpone his execution. Cautiously he asked, "And Don Carlos himself confesses to his crimes?"

Once again, de Henrique was unable to restrain himself. "What do you mean, 'confesses'? Of course he confessed — in front of us all! Pedro Alvares' testimony, in my opinion, is valid. Two Holy Office judges, *Padre* João Manuel and myself, heard it with our own ears. Contrary to our illustrious leader, I don't envision any problem here at all!"

The others gazed at de Henrique in some alarm. Accustomed as they were to his disrespectful treatment of his superior, this time, they felt, he had overstepped the boundary.

João Manuel himself did not react, except to quietly gnaw his lip. But it seemed to Fernando de Lima that a raging fury burned in the priest's breast. His own mind raced at top speed, trying to arrive at a plan whereby he could turn this animosity to advantage for his friend, Don Carlos...

The scraping of the heavy key as it turned in its lock could be heard clearly down the dark corridor of the Inquisition dungeon.

Don Carlos did not stir when two young monks entered his cell. This was the first "visit" he'd been honored with in many days. It had been two full weeks since he'd been subjected to his last interrogation. He had no idea why they'd left him alone for this length of time. Had they given up on him? Had they finally realized that no amount of torture would elicit the information they wanted: the names of the city's other secret Jews?

He did not have any answers. He did not recognize this pair of monks.

He gave them the same look he'd given all the others: the aloof, proud glance of a Jew who knows that his G-d is with him even in the valley of the shadow of death.

Without a word, the monks tossed an orange robe at him. Don Carlos made no attempt to catch it, and the garment fell at his feet. The monks watched Don Carlos, testing his reaction to the sight of the robe. He remained still as a statue.

"This," he thought proudly, "is the way a Jew reacts to a gentile who is trying to destroy him! 'And Mordechai did not bend or bow...'" His face seemed carved from stone.

A moment later, in silence, the two monks turned and left the cell, locking it behind them. Only after their footsteps had faded completely into the distance did Don Carlos seize the robe with trembling hands.

He knew very well what the dreaded garment augured.

36

Don Carlos picked up the robe. His hands shook violently as they fingered the coarse cloth. He knew what this robe portended.

It was the robe worn by those who were sentenced to death.

He understood that the Inquisition judges had rendered their decision. For some reason they had avoided telling him directly, choosing instead to fling the telltale robe at his feet. He was to be burned at the stake. The orange robe would inform the thronging observers that he was a leper, a heretic, doomed to die in the flames.

It came as no great surprise. Don Carlos had known from the start that this would be his probable fate. He had witnessed his torturers' fanaticism and seen their evil smiles, de Henrique's the most ominous of all.

The Holy Office secretary had not personally questioned or tortured him; that dirty work had been left to others. However, he had visited the torture chamber on more than one occasion, to enjoy the spectacle of Don Carlos humiliated and suffering. At such times, Don Carlos had made a superhuman effort to conceal his pain. De Henrique would not see him broken! With the last of his strength he had sent the secretary a scornful look — the look of a man who is afraid of no one and of nothing, not even death. He had tried to stare directly into de Henrique's eyes. And each time, he had derived grim pleasure from seeing the other man look away first.

After a few minutes, de Henrique had slunk from the torture room. It seemed to Don Carlos that the sight was too much even for him. Perhaps he remembered the many favors Don Carlos had done for him in the past. Maybe, as he saw the former fleet admiral tied to one of the diabolical torture machines, he had called to mind the way Don Carlos had helped him advance in his own career, and had furthered his interests with the king.

And perhaps, Don Carlos reflected, all that he was suffering now was a just punishment from G-d, for befriending such a monster!

In the darkness of his cell, it was impossible to see clearly the drawing on the robe. He outlined it with his fingers, trying to make it out. Was it a picture of the devil? That was the image he had seen on the robes of other prisoners as they were led out to the auto-da-fé on the streets of Lisbon.

As he held the robe of death in his hands, the robe he would wear to the stake, Don Carlos recalled the awesome moment when he had taught the wicked de Henrique about the power of true faith. The torture that day had been more terrible than usual. Again and again, screams were torn from Don Carlos' throat against his will. His whole body was one searing agony. But the instant the secretary of the Holy Office walked into the room, Don Carlos had succeeded in appearing impassive to his suffering. He would not give de Henrique the pleasure of knowing how he suffered!

These had been supreme moments for Don Carlos. Though his flesh burned with the torture of his persecutors, though the unbearable pain licked and tore at him, he felt he had triumphed over the enemy. This, he thought, was the way Avraham Avinu must have felt when Nimrod had him flung into the flaming furnace because of his belief in the one true G-d. He had learned that story in Rav Menashe ben Israel's home in Amsterdam...

Don Carlos seated himself on the cold cell floor and threw the robe down. There was still a shred of hope. Just as he had triumphed over de Henrique and made him flinch under his own steady gaze — just as

Avraham Avinu had emerged victorious from the furnace — so he might yet win freedom from his fate. He believed with all his heart that his G-d would help him. His torturers had not succeeded in coming up with a single witness against him, nor had they managed to pry from him the name of even one secret Jew in Lisbon.

Apart from the note they'd received, they hadn't a shred of evidence. He had no idea why Pedro Alvares had not appeared in all this time to provide his testimony, as Inquisition law required. Why hadn't the Holy Office judges demanded that he appear? Don Carlos remembered asking them once.

"Why hasn't Pedro Alvares come to testify against me?"

Painful as it might be, Don Carlos longed to see his brother's son again. He nurtured a tiny hope that, were Pedro to see with his own eyes the state to which he'd brought his uncle, he might repent and rejoin the faith of his fathers... But *Padre* João Manuel had evaded his glance, offering no answer to his question. Only de Henrique had replied, scoffing: "It is not for an accused man to teach the Holy Office its job!"

"Something's happened to Pedro," Don Carlos thought. Where could he have disappeared to? Was it possible that Pedro had rescinded his story, and that the Inquisition itself was now the accusing party?

He remembered how Pedro had taken the news of his own Jewish blood and his relationship to Don Carlos. The young man had been deeply shaken. Was it possible... could it be... that Pedro had fled to Amsterdam?

If only that were true!

Abruptly, his spirits plummeted again. There was no sense in fooling himself with false hopes. With the robe of death flung into his cell in such a cowardly fashion, he knew that his fate was sealed. He must accept it. What had happened to Avraham would not happen to him. He would not be saved from the flames! It was G-d's will. Every secret Jew in Lisbon knew that the same fate could strike them, without warning or reprieve...

He began shaking uncontrollably. Where was Beatriz, his wife — and where were his precious children? What had those devils done with them? Even if there was a chance that he'd succeeded in turning Pedro Alvares back toward his Jewish roots, the price he'd paid was monumental. His children were to be educated in a monastery, transformed into loyal Christians — and he, Don Carlos, could not help them at all.

His eyes overflowed with tears held back too long. For many minutes he sat hunched on his cell floor, crying in the dark.

Fernando de Lima stirred uncomfortably in his seat. The Inquisition judges around the table waited for him to speak.

"So," he said at length, "what can I do about this matter? The testimony is illegal!"

The judges sat impassive, almost frozen, as though they had not heard what he'd said. Then, like a rising storm, de Henrique shot up. He paid no attention to João Manuel, who was glaring at him in open disapproval. With burning eyes de Henrique approached the Superior Court judge. Standing very close to de Lima, he hissed between clenched teeth:

"Your Honor, our good friend — I might add, our present good friend" — he raised a threatening finger to emphasize his point — "we don't care a bit about what you can or cannot do in this matter. Even the law, for your information, interests us not at all. The law was devised to assist men in achieving their goals. If the law doesn't serve our purposes, it can and should be changed!

"Right now, only one thing matters: that Don Carlos burn in the flames of the auto-da-fé on Sunday. Understand? That, and only that, is important to us here and now. You, as Superior Court judge, had better see to it that His Majesty, the king, signs that decree without delay! No young, inexperienced prince must be allowed to interfere with the workings of the Holy Inquisition. How you achieve this is your concern! That's why you studied the law." He paused to catch his breath, then snapped, "Is that understood?"

The other judges were stunned by this outburst. Fernando de Lima was one of Lisbon's most prestigious citizens. In a certain measure, even the Inquisition was subservient to the secular Superior Court. Rendered speechless, Bernardo Machado nervously fingered the silver cross that hung from his neck. Gabriel Monteiro de Silvia stroked his beard, and the Dominican, João Batista da Oliveiro, gazed at the ceiling and prayed that he'd be allowed to go home soon.

Fernando de Lima himself sat equally silent, consumed by rage at the way he'd been insulted. When he could trust himself to speak, he said softly, "What I understand completely is that the manner of your speech suits you to perfection, dear Paulo."

He had used de Henrique's given name deliberately, as a sign that he feared him not at all. Then he turned his back on the secretary and addressed *Padre* João Manuel. "I would be pleased to learn how the head of the Holy Office intends to safeguard the respect due to the Superior Judge of Portugal!"

João Manuel appeared chagrined under the judge's unwavering stare. When he didn't answer, de Lima pressed on:

"Am I to understand that I'm free to go now? Tomorrow, I believe, we have a date in court." He glanced witheringly at de Henrique. "You can be very sure, dear Paulo, that I will make a thorough examination of the laws which, as you so kindly reminded me, I once studied. I shall make my decision based on those laws. I must thank you, Paulo, for the very valuable lesson you've taught me today! It will remain with me always." He paused meaningfully. "It will be very interesting to hear the king's reaction to what happened here today."

De Lima rose slowly, bowed ironically to the judges sitting mute around the table, then turned and started for the door.

He had just placed his hand on the doorknob when a shout sounded from behind. "Your Honor! Halt immediately!"

De Lima hesitated. He did not turn his head to see who had shouted: He knew. What was not clear to him at that moment was how to react. Should he continue being affronted, unwilling to compromise the respect due to him — or respond to the call?

He had no time to decide. A soft hand landed on his shoulder.

"*Senhor*, on behalf of this tribunal, I would like to apologize to you for the secretary's outburst."

De Lima glanced back over his shoulder. Though he knew he'd won this round, he kept his expression severe and unyielding. João Manuel stood facing him, a hand still on the judge's shoulder. He had uttered his apology loudly enough for all to hear, especially de Henrique. He continued, "I hope you will accept the apology, *senhor*. You are familiar with that man's nature. You must not hold all of us accountable for his behavior."

Still de Lima did not react, other than giving João Manuel a small smile. Involuntarily, his eyes went to de Henrique — then quickly moved away. The hatred emanating from the man was frightening. There was no telling what that evil serpent was liable to do next.

Padre João Manuel spoke again: "However, all this has no bearing on the matter concerning us today. We must use the law to support our faith. Don Carlos must be put to death! We ask you to authorize the sentence we have handed down, so that the king will sign it as soon as possible. Time is growing short, Your Honor!"

De Lima heard the implicit threat in the priest's words. There was actually, he thought, little to choose between João Manuel and de Henrique.

"I understand," he said quietly. "Naturally, I will do what I can, *Padre*." He fixed João Manuel with a penetrating stare. "However, I make one request of my own. Please use the time I spend searching for a solution to your problem to improve the manners in your office!" He paused. "For my part, I will see to it that the king signs the death sentence."

Fernando de Lima turned and left the room. In his heart, he was determined to do everything he could to ensure that the king did not sign the Inquisition's decree. He still had no idea how, but prayed fervently that the G-d of his fathers would show him the way.

37

oberto Gonzales slowly wandered the narrow streets of Lisbon, always moving steadily toward the coast. His posture was slightly stooped and his eyes downcast. At all costs, he wished to avoid attracting the attention of curious passers-by. Presently he smelled the salt tang of the sea. It seemed to him that he could even hear the pounding of the surf. His heart was heavy with his failure. In despair he pictured the deeply disappointed and grieved welcome he would receive in Amsterdam. Though the Jewish community there had known how slim were the chances for the mission's success, nevertheless Rav Menashe had quoted from the Talmud to Roberto: "Even with a sharp sword poised on his neck, one must not despair of Heavenly mercy." The rabbi had gone on to explain: A person must not allow himself to see only what is before him at any given moment. Anything might happen. There is a Heavenly vigilance that surrounds us and effects change in our world.

It had been Roberto's belief in this truth that had led him to undertake the burden of his present mission, despite the faint hope it carried. And now he would be returning to Amsterdam with the additional bitter news that Fernando de Lima had been arrested as well...

His anguished thoughts and physical exhaustion combined to produce an overwhelming fatigue that drained his strength. Raising his eyes, he sought a bench or boulder upon which he might sit and rest for a short time. But at that moment he heard the approaching clip-clop of horses' hooves. Biting his lips, he adjured himself to continue walking. Whatever happened, he must not draw attention to himself.

He knew that his fears were exaggerated and tried to tell himself so; but as the hooves rang closer on the cobblestones, his tension grew. Roberto turned into a side street, empty at this time of day. To his dismay, the horses and carriage turned into the very same street, too. The wheels rattled loudly on the stones. Roberto kept walking. The carriage moved closer.

All at once, his heart stopped and his blood ran cold. As the carriage moved up beside him, he heard a voice call, clear as day, "Roberto!"

Against his will he stood stock still. Then, gathering his wits, he began walking again, as though to indicate to whoever might be watching, that the call could not possibly have been meant for him. Disturbing questions chased themselves through his mind. Who knew his name? What to do now? The carriage rolled nearer.

"Roberto! Roberto, stop!"

The carriage pulled up right beside him. The horses, coming to such a sudden stop, stumbled slightly and were still. Roberto pressed himself against the wall of a house and kept walking, waiting with pounding heart to see what would happen next. It took every ounce of his will not to glance at the carriage. He must act as though none of this concerned him.

A tall, sturdy man leaped from the coach. He ran after Roberto, grasped him roughly by the arm, and barked, "Quickly! Board the carriage and ask no questions. Quick!"

Roberto tried to pull free of the viselike grip. He struggled mightily, but the other was stronger and younger than he. In despair he found himself being dragged toward the waiting carriage.

He persisted in his struggle, kicking the man's leg and trying repeatedly to free his arm. "What do you want from me?" he screamed in Dutch. Then, unaware, he added in forceful Portuguese, "Leave me alone! I don't even know you! What have I done to you? Who are you?"

The stranger did not let go. "Quiet, Roberto. Stop shouting. You're liable to wake the people napping in these houses — and then it will be the worse for you, not me."

"I don't know what you're talking about! I'm just a guest in Lisbon! My name isn't Roberto! I come from Amsterdam, my name is Johann Van Sachlada. I don't understand what this is about!"

Roberto saw that the stranger was anxious not to attract attention. He wanted to effect this kidnaping quietly and without fanfare. Here, Roberto thought, was his chance. Raising his voice, he cried in Portuguese, "*Soccoro! Soccoro* (Help! Help)!"

The stranger tried to cover Roberto's mouth with one hand while the other continued to drag him forward. "Get into the carriage already, fool! What are you shouting about? Why are you looking for trouble?"

Roberto gave up the unequal struggle. His heavy baggage, weighing upon his shoulder, hampered his efforts at any serious resistance. All through his desperate efforts to free himself he never loosened his grip on the precious case, which held their hope of saving Don Carlos. "What's going to happen to me?" he wondered in silent anguish. "Save me, Hashem, for the waters have risen to engulf me..."

The stranger managed to drag him up to the carriage door. The door opened and a pair of strong arms reached out to pull Roberto inside. He was thrown to the back of the coach as though he were a parcel. He heard the door slam shut. He was a prisoner.

Roberto lay gasping on the carriage floor, shooting pains in every limb. The windows were covered with heavy curtains, leaving the interior of the coach dim as night. He could see nothing. He wanted to see nothing. Bitterly he regretted his decision to leave Amsterdam on this dangerous mission. He had failed even before he had properly begun.

A soft voice near him said, "Roberto, *meu bon amigo* ("my good friend"), why were you so obstinate? Why didn't you come with me at once?"

Roberto stiffened in shock. The voice was a familiar one. Opening his eyes, he tried to discern the speaker through the gloom. He couldn't see... But all at once, he realized whose voice it was that he had just heard.

An affectionate hand touched his shoulder.

"Come, get up, Roberto. Sit here beside me. I know that I frightened you just now — but remember, you are in Lisbon! I had to get you into this carriage with all possible speed, before anyone recognizes you in this miserable city. And you went and kicked up a fuss, shouting and drawing attention to yourself!" The voice paused, then asked, "What's happened? Why have you come to Lisbon?"

There was no further doubt. Roberto was absolutely certain.

The voice belonged to Superior Judge Fernando de Lima.

The fears that had been hounding him all day vanished in a flash. Almost groaning with the effort, and aided by de Lima's helping hand, he rose from the carriage floor and sat beside the judge. The two men exchanged a quick, warm embrace. Roberto's cheeks were wet.

"You're free, Fernando?" he asked incredulously. "You weren't arrested by the Inquisition? *Meu bon D-eus* ("My good G-d")! How did you know that I was wandering hopelessly through the streets? Who told you?"

The judge chuckled. He opened the curtains a crack, the better to see his friend, then quickly closed them again.

"No. I was not arrested. Why did you think I would be? I've just returned home from the Holy Office, and my wife told me about an unexpected visitor from Amsterdam. When she told me your name I understood at once that it was you. She couldn't tell me where you'd gone, so I went out into the streets to search for you — before it was too late."

"Too late for what?"

"Never mind! The important thing is that, thank G-d, you're in safe hands now. But tell me, what are you doing in Lisbon?"

Roberto glanced somberly at the judge. "Don Carlos."

De Lima was surprised. "Don Carlos? What do you mean?"

"They sent me here from Amsterdam to try and save him. Rav Menashe hasn't been able to sleep since he heard of the arrest. They sent me to see if I can do something."

The judge laughed bitterly. "What can anyone do? And how? Has Rav Menashe forgotten what the Inquisition is? It does not easily relinquish its prey. And ever since we freed Raphael Chaim, vigilance over the prisoners has redoubled. Many monks working for the Holy Office have been arrested on suspicion of helping Marranos." He shook his head gravely. "It is no simple situation, Roberto. We stand in need of a great salvation."

They fell silent. The carriage rattled along, swaying its occupants gently to and fro. Abruptly, De Lima broke the silence.

"How did Amsterdam learn of Don Carlos' arrest?" he demanded.

Roberto's reply was brief and to the point. "Pedro Alvares told us."

"What?" Fernando seized Roberto's hand emotionally. He was shaken to the core. "I don't believe it! Or rather, I don't understand it. Which Pedro Alvares?"

Roberto gently disengaged his hand and answered with candid joy, "Yes, yes — it's the same Pedro Alvares that you're thinking of!"

"And you're telling me that he made it to Amsterdam? The Inquisition has been searching for him everywhere!"

Roberto nodded in the affirmative. Like a man in a dream, de Lima murmured, "Who would have ever believed it? What a sweet revenge on the Inquisition. They need him to legally sentence Don Carlos to the auto-dafé." He broke off, marveling at the news, then added energetically, "How wonderful are G-d's ways! Through his own downfall, Don Carlos had succeeded in making his lifelong dream come true — bringing about his nephew's return to Judaism. Truly, our Creator's ways are mysterious!"

Roberto had no leisure at the moment for such musings. The miraculous reversal of his fortunes, just when all had seemed lost, made him more determined than ever to succeed in his mission. He asked his friend urgently, "Did I understand you to say that Don Carlos' sentence is not yet final?"

"That's right."

"Why?"

Fernando answered dryly, "Those devils have a problem."

"What kind of problem? Has Don Carlos refused to confess?"

"I'm not sure. I think not. We have no men in that accursed building these days — or rather, almost none. There's no one who can apprise us of the exact situation."

"Yes, I understand. But what's the problem?"

De Lima smiled. "The good news you just brought me. Pedro Alvares."

"I don't understand."

The judge filled his lungs slowly and then exhaled, as though to release an accumulation of tension. Only then did he answer: "He is the sole witness in this case. And he never actually testified before the Holy Office tribunal. His testimony was given privately, in the secretary's room. The law is not very clear here. Generally, it does not allow a case to rest on the accused's confession alone."

"And those criminals care about that?" Roberto was skeptical.

"You're right — they don't. Certainly de Henrique doesn't. But the king cares. The case must be clear and complete — or at any rate, His Majesty would like it to appear that way. That's why they called me in."

"What do they want from you?"

"All they have is the note Pedro Alvares wrote them — the note that described Don Carlos' visit to Rav Menashe in Amsterdam. They want me, as judge of the High Court, to decide that the note is admissible as testimony."

Roberto thought this over. "And what do you intend to do?"

De Lima threw up his hands in a gesture of despair. "I don't know. This is the biggest test Hashem has ever laid upon me. I'm in great danger. De Henrique has dropped a broad hint that I'd better do his bidding, or find myself in an Inquisition dungeon cell. On the other hand, the law can be interpreted differently, and the king would back me, I believe."

"But there's talk in the city of an auto-da-fé on Sunday!"

"I know. De Henrique is the one spreading that story. He wants, the wretch, to get the citizens to apply pressure on the courts to authorize the death sentence."

Another silence fell between them. Suddenly, Roberto turned to de Lima. "Please open the curtain."

The judge glanced at him in astonishment.

"A little air. I need a little air..."

"But it's dangerous!"

"Fernando, I want to show you something."

Wordlessly, de Lima drew back the curtain.

Roberto reached for his case and opened it. In the light from the window he found what he was looking for. He pulled a sealed envelope from the case. With de Lima looking on curiously, Roberto carefully opened the envelope and passed it to the judge.

"Read it!"

At that moment the coach stopped. The driver leaped down and opened the door. "Your Honor, we're home."

Roberto snatched the letter from the judge's hand. De Lima gaped at him.

"Not now," Roberto muttered. "I'll give it to you inside. No one is to know anything about this — not even your driver. I'm sorry, Fernando. It's just too dangerous."

⇒)⇐

The cell door opened once again. Don Carlos, seated on the floor in one corner of the cell, did not lift his head to see who had entered. He heard a sound of dragging, then a thump on the cell floor. There was a jangling of keys as they relocked the door, and then footsteps retreating into the distance. Absolute silence descended on the little cell again.

Only then did the prisoner look around. His eyes, long accustomed to the dark, came to rest at once on an object in the middle of the cell. It looked like a human form. What was happening?

He listened intently. It seemed to him that the body on the floor was breathing shallowly, the breaths punctuated by weak moans. It was unusual, though not unheard of, for the Inquisition to place two prisoners in the same cell. Why had they brought this tortured soul here? Who was he? Was this newcomer a spy, introduced into his cell in the guise of a fellow victim? Was this a last-ditch effort to extract from Don Carlos the names of Marranos in Lisbon? Anything was possible. He must be very cautious.

Then again, he might be mistaken. This might be a genuine Jew, immersed in genuine agony. Perhaps he needed a word of encouragement, of comfort, of faith, in this hopeless place...

Don Carlos crept soundlessly toward the prone figure. The man appeared to have fallen into a deep faint. He was young, possibly no more than 20. On closer inspection, Don Carlos noted that the young man's hands were trembling slightly — also his legs. He had apparently suffered severe torture... or was pretending. Be careful.

In spite of his misgivings, he placed a hand on the man's shoulder. He exerted a gentle pressure, as if to say that here was a friend. At his touch the young man began shaking uncontrollably. Don Carlos snatched away his hand and regarded his cellmate sorrowfully.

"I am an adult," he thought. "I've seen life and I've accomplished much, though never my true heart's desire: to lead a full Jewish life in Amsterdam. Still, my life hasn't been wasted. I can make my peace with my fate. But this youngster! Why?" His heart cried out to his Maker: "Why, merciful Hashem? Why him, too?"

He leaned forward to place his lips near the other's ear — speaking between prisoners was strictly forbidden — and whispered, "I am Don Carlos, former admiral of the Portuguese navy. Have you heard of me? Today you find me here, broken in body, but not in spirit. Just three months ago, I was well respected in this beloved and accursed land..." He fell still, then added even more quietly, "I had a wife and three children. Three children, two sons and an infant daughter... I... don't know... where they are..."

His voice choked in his throat. He was angry at himself for bringing up that painful topic. From the moment he'd been arrested he had resolved to spend the time remaining to him on this earth in perfecting his devotion to Hashem, Who was testing him with the supreme test of dying for His holy Name. Don Carlos believed with all his heart that everything Hashem sent was, in the final analysis, for the best... nonetheless it was a difficult task. So why had he brought up his wife and children now?

He knew why. This fellow sufferer was the first person in three months with whom Don Carlos was able to speak. His heart was near bursting with all the things left unsaid all this time!

Still, he had a feeling he'd said too much now. He fell silent.

The silence stretched. Don Carlos' eyes remained glued to his new cellmate. The fellow did not yet seem to fully sense his presence.

Don Carlos spoke again.

"I've told you who I am. Who are you? And from where?"

He had spoken idly, just for the sake of hearing a human voice, even if it was only his own. He had no real hope of raising an answer from the figure lying in a faint at his feet. To his astonishment, the youth turned slowly and painfully onto his side and said brokenly, "I am — from Amsterdam."

Don Carlos was stunned. He repeated disbelievingly, "From Amsterdam?" Then, in the same shocked tone, he added, "And you returned to this accursed place?"

"No... No! I did not return willingly." The voice was weak but clearer.

Take care! whispered a tiny voice inside Don Carlos. He did not know how to react. The man's words seemed insane. He'd come from Amsterdam? From Amsterdam, which boasted a thriving Jewish community where Torah was learned openly and *mitzvos* observed without fear? He'd returned from there — to here? Lisbon was one vast dungeon for Jews and Judaism. The story did not sit at all well with Don Carlos.

The suffering youth seemed to read his inner turmoil in his eyes. He said slowly, "My name is Yitzchak de Castro."

Don Carlos was in no hurry to reply. He pressed his hands to his forehead in an effort to remember. De Castro?

De Castro...? Was there a family in Amsterdam that bore that name? It was difficult to remember. It seemed to him that there was. He strained his memory further. His visits to Amsterdam had been few and far between, brief and cloaked in danger. De Castro? De Castro...?

Suddenly, he remembered. Yes, he had once met a fellow by that name in Rav Menashe's home. Yaakov de Castro. He'd been a prosperous merchant and a man of standing in Amsterdam's Portuguese community. It was hard to be sure, but he seemed to recall that the fellow had traded extensively in India and Brazil. Yes, it was coming back to him now...

Yaakov de Castro had made an impression on him: tall and broad shouldered, with eyes that shone like a pair of torches. His hatred for the Spanish and Portuguese persecutors of Jews had been almost fanatical. Don Carlos reminded himself a meeting he'd once attended at Rav

Menashe's house, to discuss the strengthening of the Marrano underground in Spain and Portugal. Yaakov de Castro had been one of the participants at that meeting. Don Carlos was certain he was not mistaken. Was this downtrodden lad a member of that family?

Leaning closer in his excitement, Don Carlos asked, "Do you know Yaakov de Castro in Amsterdam?"

The other made a restless movement on the cold stone floor. "Yes," he answered feebly. "He is my father."

And then, in the gloom that encased the dungeon, Don Carlos sensed a new trembling take hold of the unfortunate youth. It seemed to him that he also heard sobs, very soft and muffled, in the dark.

38

adre João Manuel stepped out of the Inquisition building, alone. His rage at de Henrique and the disgraceful scene he'd precipitated still burned within him. De Henrique, with his wild behavior, had managed to alienate Judge de Lima. There was simply no restraining that man! João Manuel had known this for some time, but today his anger was especially strong. He wanted to be alone with his thoughts.

"Go ahead without me," he told his driver, waiting outside with the carriage. "The air is particularly healthy and invigorating at this hour of the day, just before sunset. I'll walk home."

People he passed greeted him with a respect that was mixed with awe. This was the man who could do whatever he wished in Lisbon, the man everyone feared. João Manuel smiled inwardly: He loved the feeling of power that surged through him at such moments... Then he remembered, and the smile disappeared. The man who could do as he wished? De Henrique had just ruined all his plans with a single wild outburst!

João Manuel was decidedly apprehensive that he might not succeed in burning Don Carlos at the stake after all. This was something he had set his heart on doing, especially after Don Carlos — during their ill-fated talk on the beach — refused to help him implicate de Henrique. This morning, his plans had been dealt a serious blow. It was clear that Judge de Lima had been mortally offended. He certainly had the power to prevent the king from signing Don Carlos' death warrant; after all, the law was on his side. There were no witnesses, no testimony. Pedro Alvares had vanished. For all he knew, the Marranos themselves might have kidnaped and murdered him! They were capable of anything, those Marranos. Hadn't they managed to free Arnaldo Rodriguez from prison? What had he insisted on being called after his arrest? Ah, yes — Raphael Chaim...

It was to be hoped that the security measures with regard to Don Carlos were ample. If his people were not careful, those criminals might very well take it into their heads to try their luck again!

João Manuel strode forward, frowning in thought. The situation was a truly difficult one. Just a few days before the scheduled auto-da-fé, they still had no legal testimony. Even the prisoner's confession was not worth much: The judge could easily persuade the king that it had been extracted by torture. Nobody had been in the room with them when Don Carlos had admitted to the truth of Pedro Alvares' charges. He could always deny he'd ever said it.

He walked slowly. The first streaks of the setting sun were painting the houses of Lisbon pink and gold. Normally he loved this time of day, but he was not able to enjoy it right now. He had intended to win over the judge through careful flattery and a calculated show of respect. Every man, he knew, can be brought around if lavished with enough honor. And then de Henrique had proceeded to spoil everything! His uncontrolled behavior was causing the Holy Office untold damage. How to rid himself of that infernal nuisance?

A carriage appeared suddenly out of nowhere and bore down on him at great speed. In the nick of time, João Manuel managed to jump aside to avoid the galloping horses. As the carriage swept past, he caught a clear glimpse of its occupant. De Henrique!

It was impossible to mistake that evil smile. Had he really intended to run João Manuel down? To wipe away his archfoe in the Inquisition ranks, the one man who stood in the way of his own ambition?

Of course he'd intended it, the wretch!

The priest stood very still, breathing heavily. A belated shock set in, addling his thoughts. He must rest for a few moments before continuing on his way. Quickly he glanced around to see whether anyone had witnessed his humiliation. No, thank G-d — there was no one around at this hour. He began to breathe easier as his spirit gradually revived. At last he brushed the dust from his cassock, swept back his hair, retrieved his skullcap from the ground where it had dropped in his haste to evade the horses' hooves, and continued on his way home. All the pleasure had gone out of the walk — because of that fiend.

It occurred to him then that it might have been his anger labeling de Henrique's act purposeful. It might very well have been a genuine accident. Doubt entered his heart. He did not know what to think.

He did not know what to think about anything. How to proceed from this point, or whether Don Carlos would be tied to the stake on Sunday; even his standing within the church was no longer clear to him. He had no idea what was going on in the Inquisition building behind his back.

But mostly, he did know what course to take from here.

Night descended on Lisbon. João Manuel deliberately slowed his steps. The darkness calmed him, though his thoughts were still disordered. Tomorrow a formidable day awaited him and his fellow Inquisition men at the High Court. Instead of standing before a friend, as he had hoped, they would be confronting an enemy. Of course, Judge de Lima would give every appearance of cooperating in all areas, except when it came to permitting Don Carlos to grace the huge bonfire to be built in the square in front of the royal palace. In his mind's eye João Manuel could envision the way de Lima would speak, with the greatest friendliness and in a spirit of helpfulness. He would explain that he was prepared to employ all his power to aid the church and the faith — but what could he do? His hands were tied. The law was the law...

"And it's my dear secretary who's to blame!" he fumed aloud.

Several pedestrians turned their heads to see who had spoken. The priest, startled and abashed, smiled sheepishly and quickened his pace. Home was very near.

He approached his house and opened the front gate. Then, for some reason, he stopped in his tracks. A strange, inexplicable intuition gripped him. He was suspicious, though he knew not of what. Some inner counsel kept him rooted to the spot and prevented him from continuing on into the house.

He listened, but heard nothing. After long moments of total silence, in which even his breathing stopped, he took a few cautious steps in the direction of the house. He tried with all his might not to make any noise as he went. There was no sound from the house, only the wind whispering its secrets to the flowers, shrubs, and trees that filled his front garden. He tried to tell himself that he was being absurd, but the inner voice persisted: "There's someone in the house!"

Two steps away from the door, he paused again. He wished to first accustom his eyes to the darkness of the courtyard. Even here, he fumed, de Henrique was to blame. It was de Henrique who was at the root of the suspicion and fear that had crept into the very heart of the Inquisition's holy work...

João Manuel took a step, and then another. He grasped the doorknob and pushed gently. The tension mounted: The door was not locked...

Very slowly and cautiously, he pushed it open. Who could have unlocked it? Who was interested in his house at this hour of the night? A trembling took hold of him. Was it possible that, in his hurry to reach the Inquisition building and his meeting with Judge de Lima, he had simply forgotten to lock the door that morning? He shook his head fretfully. He couldn't be sure of anything anymore.

He entered the house. The gloom in the big front room was total. He groped toward the place where the lamp stood. He would light it, he thought, and put all these foolish fancies to rest.

Suddenly, he heard a rustling sound. He spun around, but all was quiet again. He could see nothing in the all-encompassing darkness. João Manuel was not a coward; on the contrary, he had a reputation for unusual courage. Ignoring his trembling, he strode toward the source of the sound.

At that, he distinctly heard a man erupt from his hiding place and make his way rapidly through the dark in the direction of the front door.

It happened very quickly. Breaking into a run, the priest managed to be the first to reach the door. He blocked the way out, trying to catch the intruder. The stranger raised his fists and rained blows on the priest's face, but despite the pain João Manuel did not relinquish his grip. The two fell to the floor, struggling feverishly. It was impossible for João Manuel to identify his assailant. His impression was that the other was a young man, possibly even very young, and that he wore a monk's robe.

"Who... are... you?" he gasped, as he tried to subdue the intruder. He succeeded in catching him by the throat. "Who are you?" he screamed. "Who sent you? What do you want from me?"

The young monk did not answer. With a wrenching thrust he managed to free himself from the grasp that held him. As João Manuel fell back, the stranger pounded his face with all his strength. João Manuel felt blood spurt from his cut skin. The stranger took advantage of the Inquisition leader's temporary lack of balance to flee the house.

Pain, deep and shattering, led João Manuel staggering to his bed. His entire body and especially his face ached from the encounter. He could not find the strength even to rise and wash the blood from his face. After a time, he realized that the wound was probably not serious; it had not shed very much blood.

He had no memory of falling asleep, but when he woke daylight was streaming through the window.

From his bed, with his eyes still half shut, he noticed a small package lying beside the front door. The intruder, apparently, had dropped it in his haste to be off. Groaning a little, *Padre* João Manuel rose from his bed and went to retrieve the package. He opened it.

Fear paralyzed him.

In his hand he was holding two *mezuzos*. Two *mezuzos*... such as those used by the hated Jews

39

ernando de Lima lit the candle that stood in the tall silver candlestick in the center of the table, and gazed affectionately at his unexpected guest from Amsterdam. His wife entered the room with a large bowl of fruit, which she set before them on the table. She neither looked at Roberto nor greeted him.

De Lima pushed the bowl closer to his guest. "Taste something, Roberto. In my house you can recite the *berachah* out loud. We're safe here." Then after a moment, he added soberly, "For now, that is. In Lisbon, everything is only — for now!"

It had been hours since Roberto had eaten. He took a fruit, which momentarily relieved his hunger. When he was finished, the judge thrust out an expectant hand. "The letter, please."

He spoke quietly, almost in a whisper, as though wary of being overheard. "Perhaps he is afraid of his wife, after all," Roberto speculated. She had made it abundantly clear that she was not pleased about the presence of this guest from Amsterdam in her house.

He drew the letter carefully from his case and passed it to de Lima. Fernando pulled the candlestick closer. Roberto watched the play of expressions on his friend's face as he read.

The judge took his time. At one point his face grew very grave and deep lines sprang onto his forehead. A little later a small smile played upon his lips — and then the grave expression was back. Roberto knew that his friend, at this moment, did not see him at all; his thoughts had wandered far away. He tried in vain to guess at those thoughts. Patience was his only recourse.

Abruptly, Judge de Lima rose from his seat and began to pace the room. Roberto remained silent, afraid to disturb his concentration. The letter, he believed, contained information that would be of assistance to them in their rescue attempt. He found himself clinging to that tiny kernel of hope. It had been a trying day.

Presently, Fernando returned to his chair. He looked directly at Roberto.

"Listen, *amigo* (friend). This morning, as I sat in the company of those Inquisition criminals, I had no idea what I could do to help Don Carlos. To rescue him, that is, without arousing suspicion against myself. Hashem, in his infinite compassion, has brought you to me at just the right moment. This letter can certainly help us. I already have the beginnings of a plan in my mind."

He reached across the table to hand the letter back to his guest. Smiling broadly, he said, "Come, I'll show you to a room where you can rest. It will be yours as long as you stay in Lisbon. I am going out this very night — to set things in motion for Don Carlos."

Roberto nodded his acquiescence. He asked no unnecessary questions. But as they were leaving the room, he grasped his friend's hand. "Wait!"

De Lima stopped in surprise. Roberto rummaged hastily through his case until he found a small bundle wrapped in silk. He held it out to the judge. "Here, take it."

Fernando accepted the bundle, a question in his eyes. Roberto explained, "This is a contribution by the Amsterdam community for expenses incurred in the rescue attempt."

Opening the bundle, Fernando saw the gleam of many gold coins. His eyes danced. "Oh, these will certainly help! Gold coins help everywhere. There's nothing which compares for opening every locked door and every sealed heart."

He accompanied Roberto to the door, where he paused and ended with a laugh, "It will help here in Lisbon, too, please G-d!"

Fernando de Lima stepped into the dark street and set off at a brisk pace. It was not long before he was knocking on the door of a large, ornate villa. The villa belonged to Gabriel Monteiro de Silvia, one of the judges he'd met with in the Inquisition building that morning.

Gabriel Monteiro himself opened the door.

At the sight of de Lima, he started. "What a surprise!" he exclaimed.

"A pleasant surprise, I hope?" de Lima asked sweetly. He waited alertly for Monteiro's reaction.

Gabriel chuckled to hide his confusion. "Pleasant? Naturally it's pleasant! But also puzzling."

Though Gabriel Monteiro de Silvia and Fernando de Lima were old friends, they were not in the habit of spontaneously visiting one another without prior arrangement. Gabriel wondered uneasily whether tonight's visit was linked to de Henrique's atrocious behavior that morning. He clasped de Lima's shoulder and led him into the house.

"Yes, I understand you well, Fernando," he said. "I was confused by de Henrique's outburst. Please forgive me for not rushing to defend your honor." He shook his head. "De Henrique is not an easy man to stand up to. He's dangerous."

De Lima waved a hand dismissively, as though the episode had hardly touched him. "Oh, we all know de Henrique. One simply does not permit himself to be insulted by him — just as one doesn't take offense from the slap of a horse's tail in the street. I wouldn't have come here tonight merely because of that."

"No?" Gabriel asked quickly.

He stopped walking, removed his hand from de Lima's shoulder, and peered into his face as though to read his purpose there. At last he asked bluntly, "In that case, what has brought you here tonight?"

Fernando de Lima did not answer immediately. He postponed his reply until they were seated in armchairs in the salon, and did not speak even then. Gabriel said impatiently, "We're already seated, Fernando. I'm curious. Very curious."

Fernando crossed his legs, folded his arms across his chest, and smiled at his host. In his heart he prayed that he would find the right words. It was always impossible to know the mind of an Inquisition man, or to predict his reaction. One minute he could be gentle and humane, and then, in a flash, revert to unspeakable cruelty. True, the man seated opposite him was neither one nor the other. Gabriel Monteiro was considered a weak man, a man who never held a firm opinion of his own — the type who generally agreed with the last person to have spoken. It was this trait that had led de Lima to try his luck with him first.

"It's nothing special, Gabriel," he said at last, in a quiet, pleasant voice. "As I recall, I am obliged to decide this Don Carlos matter by morning. It's a difficult decision to make. I thought it might be best to discuss the matter with someone who is well informed on the subject. Do you have any objections, Gabriel? Am I interrupting something?"

"No, no," the Inquisition judge assured him. "I shall be happy to assist you in any way I can." He grimaced. "Did you notice how excited de Henrique got? He hates Don Carlos with a passion. Frankly, I don't understand why."

Fernando shrugged. "That's not what concerns us at the moment. It is the law and justice that interests me right now, not de Henrique."

Fernando leaned closer to Gabriel, as though to whisper in his ear. "Understand me, Gabriel. As I see it, the whole case against Don Carlos is illegal."

Gabriel stiffened, staring at de Lima suspiciously. "Why do you think that?"

De Lima weighed every word. The real game was beginning now. He took a deep breath and looked the other man squarely in the eye. "Gabriel!" His manner was dry and very judicial. "I am responsible for seeing to it that the law is upheld in our land. You people have broken it. I don't see any other choice than to declare the sentence null and void!"

Gabriel shifted restlessly in his armchair. He knew full well that Fernando had not come here tonight solely in order to tell him this. He must wait patiently to learn what de Lima really wanted from him. He said mildly, "There's no need to exaggerate. The law regarding heretics is different."

"That's what you think. The king would not accept the validity of what you've just said."

Gabriel hesitated, then burst out with words he had not meant to say. "Is all this because of the insult you were tendered this morning, my friend?"

He regretted the question immediately, but it was too late to stem the other's anger. De Lima lunged to his feet, breathing deeply through his nose and demanding, "Have you also decided to insult me?"

Gabriel scrambled upright. Quickly he placed both hands on de Lima's shoulders and tried to press him back into his chair. "Calm yourself, my friend. This is no way to clarify a difficult subject. If I've insulted you, I apologize. That was not my intention."

Fernando acted as though he was regaining some measure of calm. Slowly he sat down. It would be easier now, he thought, to bring Gabriel around to listen to his request. He would be anxious to placate the friend he'd just insulted.

"His Royal Majesty," de Lima explained, "wishes to see justice done. While it is true that in cases of heresy the letter of the law is not always adhered to, that applies only in cases where the accused person's guilt is established beyond a doubt. As long as that guilt remains uncertain, the individual must be protected."

Fernando paused for a moment, and then added with emphasis, "And this is especially true when dealing with a figure like Don Carlos!"

Gabriel didn't like this. "Have you any doubt in your mind that Don Carlos is a heretic?"

"After the way de Henrique behaved this morning?" De Lima smiled coldly. "Yes, I do!"

Gabriel Monteiro directed a piercing glance at his guest, trying to figure out what Fernando was after and what exactly he wanted from him at this hour of the night. "Why do you think that?" he asked.

Fernando smiled. "I will tell you. You, like me, know that no actual testimony exists against Don Carlos. De Henrique knows it, too. And that disturbs him. In fact, it bothers all of you. True?"

Gabriel ignored the question. He reached for an apple that lay in a bowl at his elbow and began eating in a distracted way. At length he said, "There's still the note."

Fernando sighed lightly. "That's precisely it. There's only the note! You will agree with me, surely, that written testimony cannot lawfully be used to sentence a man to death!"

"How do we know when a letter or note is acceptable testimony," Gabriel argued, "and when it isn't?"

"It is up to me to decide that!"

"And what are you going to decide?"

Fernando's inner tension escalated, but he revealed no break in his outward calm. "In order to decide," he said, almost matter- of-factly, "I must see the note."

Gabriel Monteiro's eyes flew open. They searched his friend's face. Fernando sat at his ease, to all appearances totally relaxed. Gabriel said nothing.

Fernando let the moment stretch a little longer. Then he leaned closer and said quietly, in the tone of a command: "And that is why I want you to remove Pedro Alvares' note from your archives."

The two men's eyes locked as though in mortal combat. De Lima added firmly, "And I want you to bring it to me at home."

Gabriel was stupefied. A nebulous suspicion took hold of him. He had known the Superior Court Judge for years and had kept abreast of the many verdicts he'd handed down. These were always original and courageous. Often, they were based on ironclad reasoning and irrefutable logic that had occurred to no one else. However, it had not been easy to ascertain the precise degree of his loyalty to the church, and specifically to the Inquisition. On the one hand, he generally authorized the sentences handed down by the Holy Office tribunal. But, at the same time, he never came out with a burning zeal in favor of the war against heretics and suspect Christians. It was impossible ever to know what was truly in his heart.

Why was de Lima interested in seeing Alvares' note, and why didn't he rely on the Inquisition's judgment? Why had he come to him, to

Gabriel Monteiro de Silvia, tonight? Why was he asking him, in particular, for this extraordinary favor?

He broke a long, thoughtful silence to say, "All right. I will speak to my colleagues tomorrow and try to convince them to bring the note to court."

De Lima shook his head violently. "No! I must see it now!"

"Now? At night?" Gabriel's voice rose in disbelief.

"Yes!"

Gabriel's glance grew suddenly cold. The Superior Judge's request struck him as most peculiar. His excitable manner, too — his intensity and persistence — were odd. Most peculiar...

A heavy silence fell between them. Gabriel heard Fernando's voice past the turmoil of his own thoughts. It sounded gentle, as though eager to soothe the other's doubts. "I know how strange this must seem to you. However, if you wish to convict Don Carlos, there is no other choice."

Gabriel said obstinately, "I still don't see why!"

"Why don't you understand? I have until tomorrow morning to hand down my decision. By the time I am presiding in the courtroom my decision must be clearly formulated, at least to myself. And so, in order to help you, I must see that note. I need to see exactly what is written there. And perhaps..."

"Perhaps...?"

"Perhaps also... to examine the handwriting."

Gabriel cried, "What do you mean?"

"Never mind."

Fernando was afraid he'd gone too far. He waved dismissively, as though his words had been uttered nonchalantly. Gabriel sputtered, "But the note is in the investigation file."

De Lima spread his hands. "I never expected it to be anywhere else."

"I'm sure you didn't. But the file is located in our dear friend de Henrique's office! It will be almost impossible to gain access to that room."

"I understand." De Lima smiled. "But despite the difficulty, if you so desired, you could manage it." He gripped Gabriel's hand and said urgently,

"Help me to judge correctly! You know very well that should I uphold your judgment in this instance, no one will ever dare challenge you again."

As he waited for Gabriel's answer, Fernando was suffused with a rising tension. What thoughts were going through the Inquisition man's mind right now? Was he suspicious?

Finally, when Gabriel still failed to respond, Fernando rose from his seat. "My dear friend, I will be very happy if you will fulfill this one small request."

Slowly, he pulled a small purse from his pocket. Opening it, he extracted several shining gold coins. He played with the coins, and the sweet jangle reached Gabriel's ears. Fernando knew his friend very well. Gabriel Monteiro loved money. For money's sake he had already acted often in the past, acted in ways that were not always in strict accordance with the tenets of Christian doctrine. Fernando had managed to ease the lot of more than one imprisoned Jew through judicious gifts of money to Gabriel Monteiro. Naturally, the gifts had been transmitted through intermediaries. To this day, Gabriel had no idea that they had come from his friend, the Superior Court judge. Now Fernando stood revealed to him. He glanced down at the coins in his hand. Would the Inquisition judge succumb once again to the lure of gold? As he awaited Gabriel's reaction, Fernando distinctly heard the pounding of his own heart.

At last, he placed the coins openly on the table. Gabriel Monteiro took his hint. Fernando marked his heavy, emotion-laden breathing, but said nothing. His eyes flickered back and forth, from the gold to Gabriel's face and back again. He waited.

Gabriel finally broke the tense, prolonged silence to ask hoarsely, "When do you need the note?"

Fernando's chest expanded in the enormity of his relief. "I told you, I need it now. Tonight!"

Gabriel's eyes filled with discouragement. "How is it possible? How is it possible?" He hid his face in his hands. The hands, Fernando noted, shook slightly. "If I enter the Inquisition building at night, they will notice me!"

Fernando gave no answer. He merely began gathering the coins together, one by one, from the table. He replaced them in his purse, gently and very slowly stroking the silk covering.

It was more than Gabriel could stand. "All right. I'll go now. But I don't promise anything. I'll have to find the key, and without being seen. I shall have to think of a good excuse for visiting the building at night. You know that after the Marranos' successful rescue of Arnaldo Rodriguez, everyone at the Inquisition is suspicious of everyone else these days. We all know that the place is full of traitors. They mustn't suspect me!" His voice cracked. "If I don't return alive from this mission, my friend, please pray for the repose of my soul in Heaven!"

Fernando quickly tucked the purse of gold into Gabriel's hand, saying quietly, "Justice, truth, and the lovingkindness of our savior will help you."

Gabriel Monteiro closed his hand tightly over his purse and its precious contents. The men's eyes met for a moment in a deep look. They understood one another very well...

40

Suddenly, Don Carlos was not afraid any longer. Though fully cognizant of the Inquisition's foul methods of spying, he chose to disregard them. The youth's tears were utterly convincing in their sincerity.

Still, he did not understand why they had introduced young de Castro into his cell. Like Don Carlos, he was wearing an orange robe. Like Don Carlos, he was under the sentence of death.

Don Carlos' hand touched the youth's head gently. He felt an unaccountable sense of responsibility for him. Who knew whether Hashem had not sent de Castro here, to this cell, so that Don Carlos could guide his final steps on this earth? He was older and more experienced. He must arouse the young man to withstand his final ordeal with dignity and grace. The temptation would be powerful, in de Castro's last days and hours, to submit at last to the priests' demand — to convert to Christianity. Don Carlos knew that Hashem had set him a formidable task today: to keep this youth staunch in the faith of Avraham, Yitzchak, and Yaakov to the bitter end.

A trembling seized him. Was he at all certain that he himself would be able to stand firm in the face of the awesome test that awaited him in just a few short days? How awesome it was! How terribly awesome, in those final moments, when the flames would slowly lick at his body until it consumed it! And maybe that was another reason why young de Castro had been placed in his cell — so that each could strengthen the other in the terrible time that lay ahead for them both.

He wanted desperately to find the words to comfort Yitzchak de Castro. Instead, he asked merely, "How did you travel from Amsterdam to Lisbon?"

Something — the tone of his voice, the gentleness of his touch — calmed the youth. Opening his eyes, he tried to make out Don Carlos' face in the dark. He answered feebly, "It's a long story."

"I want to hear it."

De Castro tried to sit up, then slumped back. "I was brought here from Brazil."

"From Brazil? You left Amsterdam to go live in Brazil? With your whole family?"

"No. Just me."

Don Carlos was astounded. As a seagoing man he knew what it meant to cross the great ocean to Brazil. He had personal experience of the long, dangerous weeks aboard a storm-tossed ship. With something like anger in his voice, he asked, "How does a young man come to leave his home and sail alone to Brazil?"

Yitzchak de Castro found it difficult to answer right away. Physically, he lacked the strength to speak, and Don Carlos' questions were extracting their emotional toll as well. He could tell that his tale did not please his cellmate. He lay back on the stone floor, eyes wide open, and said, "We have relatives in Brazil — in Rio de Janeiro. My father also has a brother there... My uncle, Julio Castello Barnaco."

"So?"

"My father always spoke of them. He would tell us how much it pained him that his family over there were so far from their Jewish roots. He wanted to remind them of who they were and where they'd come from, but did not know how. Without some reminder, he was afraid they would eventually be swallowed up in the gentile world they lived in."

Don Carlos's curiosity grew. "And then...?"

"And then I decided to try and bring them back to our faith."

"What do you mean? Your father sent you?"

"No. My father didn't know."

Don Carlos snatched away the hand that rested on de Castro's shoulder. "What? You went without your father's permission?"

"Yes. I know now that it was a mistake, but when you're young you don't always calculate things to the outcome. I boarded a ship and sailed for Brazil. I left a letter with a friend, to be delivered to my parents only after I'd sailed a distance of some days from Amsterdam. In the letter I asked them to forgive me and tried to explain my reasons for going."

Don Carlos was silent. Young de Castro lifted a weak hand and tried to find Don Carlos' — but Don Carlos moved his hand out of reach. After a moment the youth gave up and allowed his powerless arm to drop to the floor. Hesitantly he asked, "*Senhor* is... angry?"

Through the dense silence Don Carlos heard tears in the young man's voice, mingled with his halting speech. "Don't be angry now. I need your help so much. I need your encouragement. Love, not anger. My mother and father are far away... and I'm going...to... die..."

A wave of compassion rocked Don Carlos. His hand reached out to stroke the youth's trembling shoulder again. De Castro sank back gratefully and continued his story.

"After sailing a month and a half, I arrived at Pornamboco, in northern Brazil. For a full year I lived in the city's Dutch quarter as a Jew. I sent a letter home to Amsterdam with every ship, filled with longing for my parents. I wanted to go home."

"Why didn't you?"

"So long as I hadn't even tried to bring my relatives back to Judaism, I couldn't go. I had to travel to them in Rio de Janeiro, a long and difficult journey. I awaited my chance.

"When it came, I traveled to Bahia. There, two days later, I was arrested. A Portuguese merchant who had been in Pornamboco recognized me. He testified against me to the Holy Office in that city, telling them that I was a 'new Christian' who had reverted back to Judaism. I couldn't convince those cruel judges that I was actually a Jew from birth. The Inquisition was not targeting that category of Jew in those days." He paused. With a sigh, he continued, "They tortured me. I suffered terribly. But I wouldn't 'confess.' They didn't believe me... In the end, they sent me here..."

After a moment, he cried, "And I never even managed to meet my relatives! I wish I might have at least told them something. To have given my uncle regards from my father. To have taught them something about Judaism. To have told them that my father is living openly today as a Jew in Amsterdam. I never even spoke to them..."

He broke off abruptly. Footsteps sounded down the corridor. A beam of light suddenly illuminated the wall opposite their cell. Then a key scraped in the lock and the cell door was flung open.

In the doorway stood Paulo de Henrique.

Don Carlos sat frozen in place. The visit was a total surprise. He had not expected to stand face-to-face with that evil man again. It took every shred of willpower he owned to school his face to impassivity. De Henrique brought his oil lamp closer to the prisoner's face, as though to scrutinize his every expression. Don Carlos did not move a muscle.

De Henrique stepped into the narrow cell, throwing a sharp glance at young Yitzchak de Castro lying motionless on the floor. With great disdain he pushed the prone youth with his foot, attempting to shove him into a corner. At the same time, he stooped to take a closer look at de Castro's face.

Then he turned back to Don Carlos. A jerk of his head signaled to the two monks who had accompanied him. The pair melted away into the darkness. De Henrique wished to be alone with his prisoner.

His eyes, cold and cruel, raked Don Carlos from head to toe. Don Carlos tried frantically to guess what De Henrique's purpose was in coming here today. The Inquisition tribunal had already sentenced him to death; what more could they want? But de Henrique remained silent. "It's hard for him, despite everything," Don Carlos thought, "to speak to me." The thought afforded him a smidgen of pleasure: one tiny revenge against a rabid enemy of the Jews.

"Stand!" de Henrique boomed suddenly.

Don Carlos was in no hurry to obey. He had nothing to lose now. The Inquisition was not in the habit of torturing men whom they had already sentenced to death.

"STAND!" de Henrique bellowed like a madman.

Slowly, Don Carlos pulled himself to his feet, carefully avoiding de Henrique's eyes.

"LOOK AT ME!"

The scream reverberated through the dungeon. From the other cells came a muted tumult. The prisoners, unaccustomed to hearing such ferocious cries, pressed their ears against their cell walls the better to hear further developments.

Don Carlos shifted his gaze to meet de Henrique's. An evil smile spread over the Inquisitor's fat-jowled face.

De Henrique's voice suddenly softened. "I've come to have a chat with you, Don Carlos — like in the old days."

Don Carlos's thoughts began racing wildly. "What does he want now?"

De Henrique moved away, leaning casually against one of the cell walls. "Your sentence has already been handed down. I'm sure you know what it is."

Don Carlos's face revealed nothing. De Henrique continued, "Yes, it's been handed down — but not yet signed."

No answer.

De Henrique came closer. Raising his lantern, he shone it full in Don Carlos' face again. The peaceful look he saw there enraged him. "I want you to pay attention to what I'm saying, do you hear? Don't make your situation any worse than it already is!"

"What should I pay attention to, Inquisitor?"

De Henrique relaxed somewhat. "The king has not yet signed."

Don Carlos nodded. It was better to avoid arousing the ire of the man who held his fate in his hands.

The secretary of the Holy Office smiled. "Ah, you're nodding your head. In your heretical heart you doubtless see this fact as a hopeful sign? Don't bother. Your doom is sealed!"

Abruptly changing tack, de Henrique barked, "You were a friend of Superior Court Judge Fernando Jorge Silvia de Lima?"

Don Carlos's heart missed a beat. A seeping fear melted his bones. What was this question? How was it connected to the matter of the king's signature? Fernando de Lima, he knew, was the one who must authorize the sentence before the king would sign it. What had happened? Was good Fernando using delaying tactics? Or — had something been discovered about him? In order to allay any suspicion de Henrique might harbor, he replied rapidly, "Friends? No. We were never friends. Acquaintances, that's all."

De Henrique regarded him murderously. He spun away as though to leave the cell, then whirled around again, eyes blazing. "Are you sure of that? You are not friends?"

The Inquisitor's furious breathing filled Don Carlos' ears. *What does he want? What are his intentions?* He tried to figure out what might be happening to his friend, the man who'd replaced him as leader of the small Marrano community in Lisbon. De Henrique would not rest until he'd accused every resident of Lisbon of being Jewish. Was he persecuting Fernando de Lima now?

"Why don't you answer?" de Henrique thundered.

"I didn't know I was supposed to answer," Don Carlos answered weakly. This frightening new suspicion of Fernando had sapped his courage.

"So what is your answer?"

Don Carlos breathed deeply. "I've already told you. I know him the way I know thousands of people in this city. But special friends? No!"

De Henrique closed his eyes. With his free hand, the one that was not holding the lantern, he rubbed them briefly. After a moment he opened his eyes again, an overly sweet smile on his face.

"Carlos, do you want your liberty?"

This time Don Carlos' heart stopped completely. The direct question threw him off balance. What diabolical trap was being set for him now? He must be extremely careful with every word he uttered.

"Well?" de Henrique repeated. "Do you?"

"I don't know. I am in G-d's hands. What He decrees will be done."

"Yes — but you can help G-d!" De Henrique paused, then added softly, "With my help, of course."

Then Don Carlos understood. De Henrique needed something from him, and to that end was even prepared to trick him into believing he would be set free. He decided to call the Inquisitor's bluff.

"I don't know if I want it. My honor is in shreds. My standing in the community is destroyed and my family has been stolen from me. Under these circumstances, death is preferable to life. That seems to be G-d's will." He shrugged. "Why fight reality?"

De Henrique said forcefully, "No, Don Carlos! I have the power to change everything. Your wife, Beatriz, is well. She is in prison, but until the investigation is complete nothing will be done to her." ("Thank G-d!" Don Carlos thought, elated.) "Your children will also be returned to you. So will your position with the navy, if you wish. Don Carlos, it is all possible! Only a portion of your confiscated wealth will not be returned. The investigation was a costly one, you understand."

The suspicion in Don Carlos' heart deepened. Even at this juncture, while trying to convince the prisoner that freedom was possible and a painful death could be averted, de Henrique's greed was unconquerable. The prisoner spoke up. "In that case, free me! What's the problem, if you really have the power to change everything?"

De Henrique caught the jeering note in Don Carlos' voice, but chose for the moment to ignore it. Moving very close, so that their faces were nearly touching, he whispered, "There is a price for your liberty, Don Carlos. Your liberty, and your life — they must be paid for. "

Don Carlos tried with all his strength to evade the Inquisitor's eyes. He was unsuccessful. Still locked in de Henrique's gaze, he heard him say, "And the price is... Fernando de Lima."

The words, spoken no louder than a whisper, crashed and echoed through Don Carlos' consciousness like the thunder of many drums. He felt his last strength ebbing and was afraid he'd fall. Only his fierce determination that de Henrique never suspect his weakness held him upright.

The last thing on earth he wished to do was hand his dear friend over to the Inquisition. De Lima, apparently, was working hard on Don Carlos' behalf, and had not yet signed the death warrant. De Henrique, impatient, was trying one of his dirty tricks. Not for an instant did it occur to Don Carlos to yield to his wishes, in return for his life and liberty.

He felt de Henrique's heavy breath on his face. There was a sour smell of wine. The brave Inquisitor, it seemed, had had to fortify himself with several glasses of wine before coming here to see him. Don Carlos heard the insistent whisper:

"What difference can it make to you if it is true that he's a secret Jew? You've already told me that he's no friend of yours, so why should you care? And if he's not a Jew at all, then you certainly don't care if we arrest and torture a true Christian."

Don Carlos felt a powerful urge to vomit. Dizziness attacked him, and a strong pain in his stomach forced him to screw up his face. The priest's foul wickedness was having a real physical impact on him.

He shook his head to clear it. "No, de Henrique," he said wearily. "I'm not the right person to come to for such dark doings. The One Who gave me life is the One Who will take it from me, when He so desires. He despises such twisted plots — certainly when directed against a person one is acquainted with, and also against perfect strangers. And even — thought I know you'll find this hard to understand — against men of a different faith. It is only the Christian religion that advocates killing and burning people who believe differently."

De Henrique shook himself wildly, like a mad dog, and stepped back into the middle of the cell. His eyes darted flame. With his right hand he dealt Don Carlos a ringing slap. Don Carlos reeled and fell onto the icy cell floor.

"Even in your last moments on earth you dare malign the holy faith you've betrayed?! Don Carlos, you know that your death sentence has not yet been signed. As long as the king does not authorize it, the Holy Office may continue its investigations." He paused to let the import of his words sink in. "Yes, we may continue to investigate your case by any means we choose... Especially the means you've come to know firsthand these past few months."

De Henrique remained in place another moment, then turned in anger and stalked out of the cell. He noisily locked the door. Before long his heavy tread had died away in the darkness of the corridor. Don Carlos remained lying on the floor for a long time, just as he had fallen.

41

abriel Monteiro pulled himself out of his armchair and stood looking down at his visitor. "Go home now, Fernando," he said quietly. "I will come to you later tonight — that is, if I succeed in laying my hands on the information you want."

Fernando de Lima shook Gabriel's hand warmly. "Thank you. You are assisting the cause of true justice — not the sort that your dear secretary espouses."

"He poses a problem for all of us, *Senhor*, not just you."

"I know."

The two stepped out into the night. It was dark, with no moon to illuminate Lisbon's narrow winding streets. At the gate each turned, without another word, in a different direction.

Fernando stopped at the corner and hid behind a tree. He wanted to check whether Gabriel was indeed on his way to the Inquisition building, or if he would merely wait until Fernando had passed into the distance before returning home.

His suspicion was unnecessary. Even in the darkness, he was able to catch the outline of Gabriel's figure as he toiled steadily onward in the direction of the accursed Holy Office headquarters.

Gabriel Monteiro walked slowly. The darkness in the street was total, except for the odd, infrequent ray of light from some gap in a passing window or door. He tried to stay close to the walls of the houses in order to be as inconspicuous as possible. This was the first time, in all his years of service in the Inquisition, that he was bent on such a mission. Tension coursed through him with every step. The fear of what he might expect on the heels of failure dominated his every thought. There was great danger in this unscheduled night visit to the Inquisition building. He had not yet determined the tale he would spin if he were challenged.

Not far from his destination, he suddenly glimpsed a figure moving toward him. It was too late to hide: The stranger had already seen him. He had no choice but to continue on his way.

"Oh, my, what a surprise! *Padre* Gabriel Monteiro," the other greeted him. Gabriel's heart stood still.

"*Boa noite* ("Good evening"), *Padre* Paulo de Henrique," he answered. There was a tremor in his voice.

"What's wrong, *Padre*? Can't you sleep?"

"Yes... Yes, that's it. The stresses of the day rob the night of its sleep. It happens, no? I decided to stroll about the city a while. Are you suffering from the same problem tonight, sir?"

De Henrique laughed heartily.

"No, of course not... Well, honestly, yes. I couldn't fall asleep. That Superior Judge angered me this morning. I have no liking for him. He doesn't understand his job. He's trying to avoid doing what he must to help us dispense justice in this land." He paused, then added meaningfully, "I returned to the Holy Office to check the archives. I wanted to see what information we have on him."

Gabriel Monteiro felt suddenly faint. How fortunate that the darkness hid his face! More than anything, he wanted to turn around at that moment and retrace his steps homeward. All at once it had become abundantly clear to him how risky this escapade was. Why, de Henrique would stop at nothing! He was not even afraid to accuse the eminent Fernando de Lima of being a Jew. The man was the scourge of Lisbon!

Then he remembered the gold coins that Fernando had so tantalizingly dangled before him. He didn't want to lose them. He must go on. Apprehensively, he asked, "And did you find anything against him?"

"No." De Henrique shook his head, then corrected himself. "That is, not yet." He laughed again, as heartily as before. Gabriel understood the meaning of that laughter. He joined in.

"You keep this city interesting, de Henrique. First Don Carlos, and now even the Superior Judge..."

De Henrique placed a hand on Gabriel Monteiro's shoulder. Still smiling broadly, he said, "We are only trying to do our job, *Padre*. Our faith has many enemies. If only the public would appreciate our efforts as they deserve to be appreciated!"

The secretary's false humility irritated Gabriel. "Why do you feel they're not appreciated? Everyone knows how assiduously you work."

De Henrique heaved a deep sigh and murmured, "Not everyone, my dear man. Not everyone."

Gabriel Monteiro wished de Henrique would leave. The conversation struck him as exceedingly strange. At the moment, however, he had no choice but to continue taking part in it. He asked, "What makes you think that? Who doesn't appreciate you?"

De Henrique laid a second hand on Gabriel's shoulder. "Our illustrious leader, for example — *Padre* João Manuel! You saw how he behaved today at our meeting with de Lima. What an uncultured boor!"

Gabriel Monteiro was taken aback. Even in the darkness there was no mistaking the rage on de Henrique's face. He marveled at the way the secretary had managed to turn the situation on its head. Everyone who had been present at the unfortunate meeting that morning had seen just who was the boor. Now here was de Henrique, calling João

Manuel the uncultured one. Why, next he might decide to call João Manuel a Jew!

Limply, he answered, "Yes, yes, you're right."

De Henrique slowly removed his hands from the judge's shoulders. Once again he was laughing, and parting from Gabriel Monteiro with wishes for a good night...

Only when Gabriel had seen de Henrique melt into the night did he proceed to the Inquisition building. The gate, naturally, was locked. He tried carefully to open it, but his efforts were fruitless. He rapped on the metal.

The monk on duty woke, startled and dazed. "Who — who's there?"

"It is I, Gabriel Monteiro de Silva. Please open the gate."

The guard lifted his oil lamp so that the light fell full on Gabriel's face. Gabriel smiled pleasantly. Only after he had ascertained that the newcomer was indeed a member of the Inquisition staff did the guard do as he'd been bid. Glancing cautiously around, Gabriel slipped through the gate.

"*Muito obrigado* ("Much obliged"). I'm sorry if I woke you. I accidentally left my prayer book behind today, and I leave for Coimbra at daybreak. Thanks again."

The drowsy guard smiled. "That's all right."

Gradually, Gabriel's eyes readjusted themselves to the darkness of the courtyard. Now he must cross that broad expanse and then climb all the steps into the building itself. There would be a second guard to contend with at that point. He turned back to the young monk.

"My friend, lend me your lantern?"

The guard hesitated. "*Senhor o Juiz* ("Your Honor") knows that it is forbidden for me to remain here in the dark. I must be able to identify everyone who approaches the gate. There is no moon tonight."

Gabriel Monteiro raised his voice peremptorily. "I am no longer young. My vision has deteriorated lately."

"But what do you need to see in the dark, *Padre*?"

Gabriel laughed nervously. "Naturally, there is nothing to be seen in the dark. But I'm afraid of bumping into a stone or some other obstacle on my way. Understand?" As he spoke, he patted the guard's arm in a friendly way.

The young monk capitulated to the subtle pressure being exerted upon him by his superior.

"Here it is, then. But I beg you," he said, "to make haste. Don't leave me here long without a light. It's forbidden. *Padre* Paulo de Henrique has begun instituting random night checks... You understand, *Senhor*."

"It will be all right." Gabriel noted that the guard refused to be soothed. Curiously, he asked, "Why are you so worried? Are you that afraid of the dark?"

"Not of the dark, *Senhor* — of unexpected guests. Especially since..." The guard broke off.

"Especially since what?" Gabriel prodded.

"Especially since those heretics succeeded in spiriting away the prisoner Arnaldo Rodriguez. And now, as Your Honor knows, we have Don Carlos down there."

"Yes," Gabriel acceded. "I understand. I'll try to make all possible speed." With that, he moved off, lighting his way with the lantern.

Suddenly, he halted. A new idea had flashed upon him. Turning around again, he said, "My young friend, you don't want to be alone and without a light. I'll send you the guard who stands at the building entrance himself. He'll keep you company."

He heard the young monk's voice calling through the night, "With pleasure!"

Gabriel approached the wide stone staircase. Using the lantern to light his way, he climbed heavily up the stairs with slightly labored breathing. I'm past 60, he thought with an inward smile; every day the stairs get a little steeper.

"Who goes there?" shouted the guard at the building entrance.

"It is I — Gabriel Monteiro da Silva."

There was a perceptible relaxation in the guard's voice as he answered, "*Boa noite* (Good night)! What are you doing here so late at night?"

Gabriel Monteiro moved closer to the door and raised his lamp to illuminate the monk's face. "Ah, it's you, Jorge Machado! How are you? You must be surprised to see me at this late hour."

The guard hastened to refute this. "No, no! The judges come here at all hours — sometimes even in the middle of the night." Jorge Machado tried with this obvious untruth to mask his own confusion.

Gabriel passed over this lightly. "You see, I left my prayer book behind this afternoon. That is — I'm not certain I left it in the building, but it's missing and I'm troubled. It was hard for me to fall asleep tonight." He smiled, adding sentimentally, "That prayer book was a present from my mother. It's a family heirloom, you understand?"

"Oh, yes."

"Then open the door for me, please."

The guard hastened to comply.

Gabriel smiled. "*Muito obrigado* ("Much obliged"), Jorge. I shall remember you in my prayers." With his left hand he patted the young monk's cheek. The monk smiled bashfully.

"You know what, Jorge? The guard down at the front gate is alone. I have his lamp here. It's not very pleasant being all alone in the dark, is it? Perhaps you would be so good as to stay with him until I return. All right?"

The guard nodded his acquiescence. In an instant he had vanished down the stairs.

Gabriel Monteiro took a deep breath. Now there was no one to observe his movements inside the building. The first stage had been successfully executed. He could hear the clink of the gold coins echoing in his mind.

He entered the building and went directly to his own room. Placing the lantern in the center of the table, he dragged the table itself closer to the window that looked out on the courtyard. He pulled aside the curtains and opened the window wide.

Anyone passing by would clearly see the light from outside. And the two guards, if questioned tomorrow, would be able to testify that Gabriel had been right here in his room the entire time.

42

Roberto Gonzales was alone in Judge de Lima's house. Exhausted by his travels and by the myriad adventures that had beset him on his first day in Lisbon, he was grateful for the chance to rest.

He was very tired, but content. Hashem was guiding him in the proper direction, just as He had guided Eliezer, Avraham's servant, to find the right wife for Yitzchak. He locked the door of the room Fernando de Lima had appointed as his own for the duration of his visit, and fell onto the bed. His eyes closed of their own accord.

Just as he was drifting off to sleep, a loud knock sounded on his door. His eyes refused to open. The knock was repeated again and again, louder each time. He grew worried. Who could it be? There was no choice — he must get up and open the door. He unglued his eyes and climbed from the bed. Stumbling with fatigue, he crossed to the door.

The judge's wife stood there. Her steely gaze did not spell good tidings for Roberto.

Without asking his permission, she stalked past him into the room. "Where is my husband?"

Roberto was nonplussed. He recalled that de Lima had spoken to him earlier in an undertone, effectively eliminating the possibility of his wife overhearing their conversation. Throughout, the judge had cast quick looks at the kitchen door as if to make certain his wife wasn't listening. And now she was standing before Roberto, demanding an answer. What to say?

His silence only served to further enrage her. The guest from Amsterdam was clearly hiding something from her — something she very much wanted to know. She moved closer menacingly.

"I asked," she repeated forcefully, "where Fernando went?"

Unconsciously, Roberto took a step back. "I am a stranger in this city, *Senhora*. How can I know?"

"He never leaves home at night. I believe you've sent him somewhere."

Roberto shook his head, but she pressed, "*Where?*"

What was he permitted to tell her? He had no idea to what extent, if any, this woman was involved with the Marrano community.

"What do you want from him?" she almost screamed. "Who sent you?"

The best method of defense, Roberto decided, was to go on the attack himself. Coldly, he said, "I would have thought, madame, that you'd have greater respect for your husband. You saw how warmly he welcomed me into his home. I am his guest. I don't understand why you're insulting me!"

"I respect my husband very much. That is why I want to know why you're here. I'm afraid that something could happen to him. Understand?"

"No!"

She fell silent, gazing at him in perplexity. Roberto felt satisfied: Now it would be up to her to explain what it was she was so afraid of. In that way, he would be able to ascertain just how much she knew about secret Jewish activity in the city. He repeated, "No! I don't know what you're talking about!"

His hostess maintained her silence. At last, with an appraising glance at her mysterious guest, she asked, "*Senhor* is... from Amsterdam? Really from Amsterdam?"

Roberto relaxed a little. "Yes, *Senhora*. This afternoon, when I first arrived, I told you from where I had come."

She sat abruptly on a chair and asked, with open hesitation, "*Senhor* is... a Jew?"

Roberto's laughter did much to dispel the tension. "Now I understand. Yes — I am a Jew!"

The woman began wringing her hands on her lap. There was a certain despair in her eyes. "Where, then, has my husband gone?" she asked again, pleadingly. "I know that you've come to ask for his help in a matter concerning the Marranos. But you have no idea how dangerous it is! We are still reeling from what happened to Don Carlos. Spies are everywhere. Yes, I am afraid for my husband. I beg of you, tell me where he's gone! He is an important man, a man whom the spies will follow very closely."

Roberto considered his reply. It was clear from her words that she was also a secret Jew and that she knew exactly where her husband stood in relation to the Marrano community in Lisbon. He must say something.

"Rav Menashe ben Israel sent me," he said carefully. A flash of something — respect? — glinted momentarily in her eyes. But she asked only, "For what purpose?"

He thought another moment before answering honestly, "To try and rescue Don Carlos."

His hostess jumped up from her chair, shaking violently. "Do you want to bring tragedy upon us all?" she cried. "Don't you realize that the good Don Carlos is lost? In just a few days they will tie him to the stake! He'll be burned in an *auto-da-fé*! What makes you think you can do anything for him?" Her voice rose in a frenzy. "Where has my husband gone? *Where?*"

Roberto wished he knew the right words to say. "Calm yourself, madame. Nothing will happen. G-d will help."

He might as well not have spoken. In anguish she wailed, "You keep avoiding my question. Where has Fernando gone? On what dangerous mission have you and the rabbi of Amsterdam sent him? Yes, he would do anything for you — even risk his life and the lives of his children. For that rabbi's sake he would totally forget all about me!"

"I truly don't know where he went. We spoke a while, and then he decided to go out."

Like a snake lunging at its prey, she charged at the the door and wrenched it open. "Go!" she shrieked. "Leave my home! You have come to destroy my family. You've come to destroy our lives — to drag my husband into matters that can have no positive results and can only harm him. Go, and return to Amsterdam at once — before I betray you to the Inquisition!"

Roberto silently rued the day he'd undertaken this mission. He had been prepared to face danger, but not for this sort of revilement. An instant later, however, he regretted the thought. In performing the all-important task of saving a Jewish life, one must be ready to face the worst kind of scorn and abuse, if necessary.

She shouted again, intruding on his thoughts. "Leave at once!"

Roberto hastened to gather together his belongings. He thrust them any which way into his case, locked it, and turned to the door. All his efforts were directed at avoiding the woman's malevolent gaze. He prayed for his friend Fernando's quick return. Only he could rescind Roberto's banishment.

No such fortuitous event occurred. Roberto left the house, slowly walking out into the night. All the anger and humiliation he'd felt that afternoon returned now, redoubled. For several minutes he stood near the gate, irresolute. Where to turn? With a pang he noted the warm light in the windows, and remembered his longing to pass a peaceful night's sleep in a comfortable bed. Exhaustion made all his limbs heavy as lead, and the burden of his suitcase made him twice as weary. Filled with despair, he began to make his way in the direction of the harbor. He would hide there day and night (*And what about food?*), until the ship sailed for Amsterdam.

He had not gone more than a dozen yards when he suddenly stopped. He set the heavy case down with a thump. No! He must not leave. He must wait for Fernando — to give him the letter. With it, his friend had a chance of saving Don Carlos from the flames. Leaving it with Fernando's wife was unthinkable.

He groped in the darkness for a large boulder to sit on. After some time he located one, and sank down gratefully. He wound his hands tightly around the straps of his case as his eyes closed.

⇌

Roberto sat up with a start. He had no idea how long he'd been sitting outside on this stone, in the cold and the dark. In dismay, he became aware of the thing that had roused him from his sleep. Someone was tugging at the straps of his case.

It was impossible to make out the man's features, but he was dressed in a long cassock. Roberto leaped to his feet and drew himself up to protect his precious cargo. Seizing the case with both hands, he held it against his chest.

"Who are you?' the figure demanded in the voice of authority.

"A passing visitor, sir. I merely sat down on this rock to rest a little." Roberto could hear the fear that permeated his own voice.

The stranger retained his hold on the straps of Robert's case, asking brusquely, "Where are you from?"

Roberto hesitated. "Er... Uh... I am from... Eldorado. I entered the city at a late hour, and sat down here to rest my legs."

He knew he hadn't convinced the other man. On the contrary, his stammerings had doubtless only reinforced the stranger's suspicion.

"And I say that you are a thief!"

"I swear by our savior that I am not a thief. I am innocent!"

"Whose house have you just left with your loot? The judge's? Speak!"

Roberto tried in vain to discern the other's features in the darkness. The priest moved closer, pulling at the straps. "Show me what you have in that case!"

A deep terror pierced Roberto. He knew he must battle to keep his case, even if it resulted in his own death. With all his might he tried to push the man away from him.

"These are my... personal belongings, sir," he said, as he tried to free himself and his case from the stranger's grip. "I am not... required to show them to you. Let me be, sir!"

"I have no mercy for thieves or Marranos. Now show me!" He hauled on the straps.

The man was strong, but Roberto held his ground. Any minute now, the two of them would fall struggling to the ground. His own strength was quickly ebbing. The man must not get hold of his case!

The two were fiercely engaged in their tug-of-war when a new voice thundered, "What is the meaning of this uproar near my house?"

Both combatants whirled around to face the newcomer. With unspeakable relief, Roberto recognized his friend Fernando's voice. The stranger straightened, let go of the case, and turned to the judge.

"On my way home I chanced to pass your house, Fernando, and I've caught this thief!"

It was the voice of Paulo de Henrique.

Fernando's brain worked furiously. What was de Henrique doing near his house at this time of the night? Why was Roberto outside? When he'd left home, his guest had been about to go to bed. What had happened?

Fear held him in its sway. He did not know what to answer or how to act. His heart still burned with the insults de Henrique had hurled at him that morning. He breathed slowly and deeply, trying to calm himself and gather his wits. Finally, in a tone as cold as the tomb, he asked, "What is the secretary of the Holy Office, Paulo de Henrique, doing near my home tonight?"

He had named de Henrique deliberately, in order to warn Roberto to be careful of every word that issued from his mouth. Fernando was completely in the dark about what exactly had transpired here between his guest from Amsterdam and the Inquisitor.

De Henrique answered quickly, soothingly, "I told you, I was on my way home. I stayed at the Holy Office very late today. I am glad we met, so that I can apologize to you for my behavior this morning."

Fernando knew de Henrique well: He was a man who never apologized. Just what that monster intended to do next was a mystery to him.

Fernando decided to ignore his conciliatory words. In the same cold voice he asked, "And what is the meaning of this tussle outside my door?"

This time, Roberto decided to take the initiative. He replied, "*Senhor*, I am a stranger in this city. I am from Eldorado. I sat down on this rock to rest and must have fallen asleep. Now this gentleman accuses me of being a thief. I am not a thief, *Senhor*! He tried to take my case away from me. I did not let him have it. I am an honest man, sir — truly!"

In this way, Roberto tried to transmit to his friend the salient facts of the story he'd told de Henrique. Fernando understood — and also recognized the magnitude of the danger into which they'd fallen. Inside Roberto's case lay the letter that could help save Don Carlos' life. Woe betide them if that letter fell into de Henrique's hands! But how had they come to meet here? What had taken Roberto out of the house? And what to do next?

The judge approached Roberto slowly. In a crisp, harsh voice, he said, "My name is Fernando Jorge Silvia de Lima. I am the Superior Judge in this city. I cannot simply dismiss this honored clergyman's accusations. Give me the case. I will take it inside and inspect it thoroughly."

Roberto sighed in relief. This seemed the best way out of their predicament. However, he did not hand over the case at once. To lull de Henrique's suspicious mind, he began to plead plaintively, "But why won't you believe a poor, unfortunate traveler? In the name of all that is holy, I am prepared to swear that I am innocent of any wrongdoing!"

With a quick movement of his arm, he thrust the case behind him and began inching backwards.

Fernando de Lima snapped, "I would suggest that you hand over the case for inspection, without delay. I say this for your own good."

As he spoke, he moved closer to Roberto. But de Henrique was quicker. He fell on Roberto, dealt him a crushing blow, and seized the case. With an air of triumph he handed this over to the judge.

Now that he had the case in his own hands, Fernando began walking rapidly toward his front door. Over his shoulder he tossed back ironically, "Thank you, de Henrique, for being so vigilant near my home." And to Roberto he added, in a raised voice, "You may wait here until I've checked your case. Understand?"

But Roberto, recovering from de Henrique's blow, raced after him, crying, "I do not consent, sir. That is my private case! I beg of you, return it to me. I am not a thief, sir!"

De Lima paid him no attention. He continued along the path to his home, with Roberto on his heels. When Fernando opened the door and entered his house, Roberto burst in after him.

De Henrique stood in the street, watching this farce. He saw the judge pause at the door to try to eject the intruder. Something told him to remain alert.

As Fernando pushed Roberto from his door, he whispered in his ear, "How did he find you? He's the one we're striving against right now!"

Roberto, trying to retain his grip on the door, whispered back, "I don't know. I fell asleep on that rock, and he woke me."

Fernando persisted, "But why did you leave the house? Didn't you know it was dangerous?"

"Yes. I know."

"Then why did you do such a thing?"

"Your wife, Fernando. She told me to leave."

In his astonishment, Fernando stopped pushing Roberto. He paled. "My wife, you said?"

"Yes."

Suddenly, he remembered de Henrique, standing outside and observing their every move. His confusion grew. Had de Henrique noticed them talking? Without warning, he roared, "Leave my house at once! You will wait outside until I return your case — that is, if I decide to return it to you at all!"

In a whisper, he added to Roberto, "Now really go! Both for the benefit of the monster outside, and for my wife in the house. I will call you when it's safe."

Roberto stepped back into the garden, and Fernando slammed the door in his face. Once again, black night covered the scene.

Roberto chose to remain close to the house rather than step back into the street. He had no desire to meet de Henrique again. His anxious eyes strayed repeatedly to the front gate, to see whether his opponent had left or if he was still standing there, awaiting developments.

De Henrique had not budged. From his vantage point on the street he had watched the bizarre struggle at the judge's door. Something seemed wrong. An inner voice whispered to him that the two were not actually strangers to one another. He didn't know why he thought that, but think it he did. The way they had fought and shoved each other by the door had not looked genuine. He decided to wait.

Perhaps here, at the very entrance to de Lima's house, he would find the evidence he needed to condemn the judge. Only an hour ago he had attempted to goad Don Carlos into testifying against de Lima, and had failed. But de Henrique did not give up so easily. The Superior Judge would pay heavily for the humiliation he had inflicted on him that morning.

He squinted into the dark, trying to make out the figure of the traveler he'd accosted outside the judge's house. There was no sign of him. De Henrique had hoped that the man would step out into the courtyard, where he could have a good look at him, but no one came. No doubt he was afraid to come any closer.

De Henrique decided to try a ruse. He would pretend to leave. In a voice that carried he called, "*Adeus* ("Good-bye"), wretched thief. You have fallen into the hands of the Superior Judge. I hope he will treat you better than I would have."

There was no answer.

De Henrique waited another moment. When there was still no sound, he shouted, "Did you hear me? I'm saying good-bye to you!"

De Henrique closed the gate noisily and began whistling a merry tune. The melody grew fainter and fainter as he moved away at a rapid clip. The moment he stopped whistling, however, de Henrique stopped, wheeled around, and reversed course. He concealed himself behind a tree opposite Judge de Lima's house. As far as he was able, he quieted his own breathing. Patiently and in silence, he waited.

Some minutes later, he saw the front door open. The oil lamp that had lit the front hall threw a beam of light into the courtyard. Clear as day, he saw the stranger move toward the door and enter it. De Henrique's heart began to pound with painful excitement in his chest. It had not been

Judge de Lima who'd opened the door, in order to return the stranger's suitcase. It must have been the stranger who had let himself in, once he'd felt sure that de Henrique was gone — which meant that he and de Lima did know each other! De Henrique felt a powerful urge to know the true identify of that traveler — and more to the point, what he had hidden in his case that was worth fighting so strenuously to hide.

De Henrique remained at his post a good while longer, busy turning over possible schemes that would allow him to penetrate the house. He would need a good excuse to pay a call on the Superior Court judge with whom he'd embroiled himself that morning. This would be no simple matter.

Abruptly, he decided that he had no choice. There was no sense waiting for the morning. If nefarious deeds were being perpetrated here tonight, tomorrow would be too late. The clever judge would find a way to cover his tracks. He must enter the house *now*. When the time came, he would find the right words to say to the judge and his mysterious guest...

De Henrique left his hiding place behind the tree and began making his way stealthily toward the house. An instant later, he halted. He heard the sound of footsteps moving through the quiet night. At lightning speed, he flung himself back behind the tree's broad trunk. He must wait until the passer-by was out of sight.

The steps proceeded slowly. The darkness was so complete that de Henrique could not see the walker. His ears, sharpened by this night's events, clearly heard the footsteps, and even the walker's labored breathing. He was not far away now. De Henrique heard him open the gate of de Lima's house and walk with confidence right up to the door. The sound of the man's knock came clearly. The door opened.

In the doorway stood Fernando de Lima, welcoming his late-night visitor. De Henrique thought that he would faint from the shock. The visitor was none other than Inquisition justice Gabriel Monteiro de Silvia...

What was going on at the judge's house tonight? Was all this connected to the death sentence for Don Carlos, waiting to be handed down in court tomorrow?

De Henrique had no idea. But there was one thing he did know: He must act — and act quickly.

43

abriel Monteiro passed quickly through the doorway into the well-lit room from which Roberto had just hurriedly escaped. It was imperative that the Inquisition judge know nothing at all of de Lima's visitor from Amsterdam. He must not suspect anything untoward. Gabriel must be made to believe that he was aiding the Superior Court judge in the pursuit of justice. Moreover, he must be persuaded that his efforts would provide the evidence necessary to convince Crown Prince Alfonso of the soundness of the Holy Office's judgment.

Fernando de Lima welcomed his guest tensely. "Have you brought it?"

Gabriel shook his head. "No."

In his heart, he had already parted ways with the lovely gold coins he coveted. The mission for which he had been paid had not been accomplished. He put his hand into his pocket, reluctantly drew out the bundle of bribe money, and placed it on the table.

De Lima was oblivious. A rage had seized his soul — rage, combined with a searing sense of his own helplesslness. Without the note in hand, he could not proceed with Don Carlos' rescue plan. Was Gabriel telling him the truth?

"Why didn't you bring it?" he demanded.

Gabriel spread his hands in a gesture of despair. In his eyes de Lima read a genuine pain of failure.

"I went to the Holy Office," Gabriel said, downcast, "and even before I went inside there was a surprise waiting for me. De Henrique came out of the building. He noticed me near the gate. That, of course, was not good."

Fernando was aghast. "De Henrique? So late at night?"

"I was also surprised. I even asked him about it."

"What was his answer?"

Gabriel Monteiro remembered vividly what de Henrique's response had been, but he had no wish to repeat it to Fernando. Instead, he said shortly, "That's not important. The point is, I managed to enter the archives room..."

Fernando saw through these evasive tactics. "Wait a minute!" he broke in. "First, I want to know what de Henrique told you. I sense that you're hiding something from me. What is it?"

Gabriel shifted uneasily in his armchair. "Why are you pressuring me? I have no desire to embroil myself in your dispute with de Henrique — or to broaden it."

"Am I to understand from this that he said something about me?"

Gabriel hesitated. Under the Superior Court Judge's penetrating gaze, he found himself muttering, "More or less."

Fernando de Lima rapped the table with his knuckles. Without removing his eyes from the Inquisition man's, he said quietly, but in the tone of greatest authority, "Tell me everything — now!"

Gabriel paled slightly. At moments of stress he tended to lose control of his facial muscles; right now he felt his lower lip begin to tremble uncontrollably. Hoping that Fernando would not notice, he answered reluctantly, "He said that you had angered him. Therefore, he was checking what was written about you in your records in the archives... Surely you know that everyone of any standing in Lisbon has a dossier in the Inquisition building."

Masterfully suppressing all signs of the dismay he felt, de Lima produced a light laugh. "What? He's trying to make a Jew of me, too? What a joke! I tell you, the fellow's gone completely mad."

Leaning closer, he winked at Gabriel and whispered, "So, did he find anything on me? What did he say?"

"No. He didn't tell me anything. I think he said he didn't find anything... But I'm not sure those were his exact words."

Smiling all the while, Fernando grimly faced two bald facts. The first was that he must exert every possible precaution whenever de Henrique was concerned. And the second was that he must get hold of Pedro Alvares' note soon — before it was too late. With the note in his possession, there was a chance that he could save Don Carlos from the bitter fate that awaited him. And apart from that, it would be an act of priceless revenge against de Henrique. He could just picture the secretary's face when he discovered that his prime — in fact, his only — piece of evidence was missing.

"You're right, Gabriel," he resumed. "I really shouldn't have asked you anything about de Henrique right now. The important thing now is why you didn't bring the note."

"As I told you, I entered the building without any problem. I reached de Henrique's office and, after some effort, managed to open the door. A short search brought to light Don Carlos' file. But the note wasn't there! All the other documents are neatly in place, but the note is missing. I tell you, it's gone!"

Fernando plucked a fruit from the bowl on the table. "What do you think this means?"

"Someone has apparently taken the note out."

Fernando's fury broke through his nonchalant facade. Balling the fingers of one hand into a tight fist, he slammed it into his other palm. This helped reduce his tension enough to let him speak almost normally as he asked, "Who could have been interested in that note?"

Gabriel Monteiro was startled by de Lima's livid face. He had never seen the judge so angry. Gaping, he hurried to answer, "De Henrique himself, perhaps?"

Fernando didn't answer. Gabriel was not even sure he had heard what he'd said. Hesitantly, he added, "I suppose I must return the gold to you."

Fernando de Lima made a dismissive gesture. "Keep it! The important thing now is for you to make every effort to locate that missing note, and to discover who took it." He paused, then added almost as an after-thought, "At any rate, I won't be issuing my decree tomorrow."

Gabriel's eyes widened in astonishment. "What?"

"It is my privilege," Fernando said quietly, "to see all relevant documents before I hand down a judgment. It is not possible that the most important piece of evidence in a case like this simply vanishes from the file. I am taking the Inquisition staff's honesty for granted — with the exception of de Henrique. I have no idea how much control he exerts over the rest of you, or how much you are all willing to yield to his wishes, even in the face of the truth."

Fernando de Lima rose. The conversation was over. Gabriel stood up too, and de Lima clapped him on the shoulder. "I believe you, Gabriel. Leave no stone unturned in order to bring me that note. It is not advisable for the king to learn that this most valuable piece of testimony is mysteriously missing."

Gabriel bowed. "I will do what I can, *Senhor*. But please, do not post-pone Don Carlos' judgment."

Fernando was filled with disgust for this Inquisitor, who apparently also lusted for the blood of an innocent man. Forcing a pleasant smile to his lips, he said softly, "That's up to you, Gabriel. Bring me the note, and Don Carlos' case will speed to a conclusion."

Gabriel opened the door and went out into the night. Fernando, suddenly overwhelmed with weariness, closed the door after him and leaned against it for a long moment.

Presently, he roused himself and went along the corridor to Roberto's room. He knocked.

Almost immediately, Roberto opened the door. The men's eyes met — and said everything.

"What's going to happen now?" Roberto asked. Bitter disappointment was stamped on his face and in his voice.

Fernando clasped his hand warmly. "Remember this, my friend: G-d's salvation can come in the blink of an eye!"

44

In an effort to calm himself, de Henrique wrapped his arms around the tree trunk that hid him and held on tightly. With squinting eyes he tried to make out the judge's house in the dark. His heart thumped violently in a mixture of excitement and fury. Some dark plot was being hatched at this very moment in Judge de Lima's house; he knew that as surely as the night was black. How to find out exactly what was afoot?

He was certain of one thing: It would be fatal to wait for morning. With sunrise, those wily birds might well have flown the nest! And tomorrow, no one would believe him when he described the secret meeting he'd witnessed taking place at de Lima's home. They would attack him for daring to accuse Inquisition judge Gabriel Monteiro de Silvia of paying a midnight visit to Fernando de Lima's home. Gabriel Monteiro would deny it emphatically; he might even bring a complaint to *Padre* João Manuel. He, de Henrique, would be opening himself up to all sorts of difficulties. He knew how little he was liked in the corridors of the Inquisition.

In particular, it would be impossible to make them believe his story without a witness to corroborate it. He bit his lip, remembering that other case of a missing witness. Pedro Alvares had vanished without a trace, before testifying officially about Don Carlos' clandestine visit with an Amsterdam rabbi. The interview in de Henrique's office, in which Don Carlos revealed the truth about his relationship with Pedro Alvares — a story that de Henrique, for one, did not believe for an instant — had clearly shaken the young man deeply. So deeply, that he had escaped the necessity of testifying against his alleged uncle. Only the note was left — the note that Alvares had slipped into de Henrique's door one morning, and which had raised the first finger of suspicion against Don Carlos.

Now, with the Don Carlos case nearing its successful conclusion, de Henrique was filled with misgivings. He hadn't liked Judge de Lima's attitude that morning. The judge had not seemed overly enthusiastic regarding the true course of justice — that is, Holy Office justice. If de Lima wished, he could disqualify the note as admissible evidence of Don Carlos' guilt. Prince Alfonso, the king's son, had been a close personal friend of Don Carlos. It was he who was responsible for pressuring his father to delay signing the death sentence. Judge de Lima had only to express a doubt about the written testimony's validity, and the king would not sign.

What was really astonishing, de Henrique thought, was the fact that the prince would continue to support a professed Jew. Prince Alfonso continued obstinately to maintain that the case was one of pure libel, and that Don Carlos' confession had been extracted by torture. Was this any way for a prince to talk, when every effort was being made to eradicate those who betrayed the true faith? And he the son of a Catholic king, in a Catholic country! Scandalous!

As de Henrique stood outside Fernando de Lima's door, his apprehension grew stronger. A cold sweat broke out on his brow as he tried to think. What to do?

Involuntarily, his hand slipped into the pocket of his voluminous cassock. Yes, the note was still there. It represented his sole hope in this case. Only this note had the power of consolidating the death sentence against Don Carlos — or so he hoped. After the disastrous meeting with de Lima that morning, de Henrique had felt disturbed enough to take the note into his own personal safekeeping. Should someone else make off with it, there would be not be any evidence against Don Carlos. Neither the king nor Judge de Lima would sign the order of execution then. De Henrique's hand, in his pocket, clutched the note tightly. He felt more confident when he could touch it.

What to do now?

He decided to draw closer to the house. If he hid under one of the windows, he might overhear some of the conversation taking place between the three conspirators. Two of them — Fernando de Lima and Gabriel Monteiro de Silvia — were known to him. But who was the third, the unknown man he'd found sitting on a rock near the judge's house, case in hand? He recalled how strenuously the stranger had fought when de Henrique tried to relieve him of it. He'd fought like a lion! What did that case contain, and why could de Henrique not shake the impression that de Lima knew the man, despite all the pushing and shouting at his door? It had seemed to him, and it still seemed to him, that it had all been an act concocted for his benefit. He had no proof, but his instincts — finely honed by years of hunting down Marranos — told him otherwise. He was rarely wrong in matters such as this. What was going on in that house? Did it have anything to do with Don Carlos?

Gradually, his grip on the tree trunk loosened. He breathed deeply of the cool Lisbon night air. Taking small, careful steps, he approached the house. The silence was profound. All of Lisbon slept. Only the wind in the trees made a sad, soft melody. The surrounding houses were dark — except for de Lima's. Strain as he might, de Henrique could catch no sound from the house.

He tiptoed closer, turning often to make sure no one was watching — though the night was so dark that this was unlikely. When he reached the gate, he opened it cautiously. It squeaked. Appalled, de Henrique threw himself behind a large bush, waiting to see if anyone in the house had heard.

Minutes passed without any reaction. De Henrique straightened up, slipped through the half-open gate, and made his way toward the lighted window.

Suddenly, the front door opened, spilling light into the courtyard. De Henrique held back a gasp and shrank into the shadows. A broad-trunked tree planted alongside the path shielded him from view. As he watched, Gabriel Monteiro de Silvia exited through the door.

Seeing him — the traitor! — de Henrique was consumed with a yearning for vengeance. Gabriel Monteiro stepped into the courtyard — and then halted in confusion. When he'd entered a short time before, he'd made sure to latch the gate behind him. Now it was open. Was someone following him?

Fearful and suspicious, his eyes swept the area. They halted at the tree behind which de Henrique was hidden.

45

Don Carlos lay on the cell floor, dazed, injured, and sapped of strength. Satisfied though he was with his reaction to de Henrique's infamous proposal, he ached too much to truly savor the triumph. The Inquisitor's ringing blow to his face still smarted. When he fell, his head had struck the stone floor, and he was experiencing some dizziness. His ears felt as though a hundred church bells — the bells that were heard throughout the air of Lisbon on Sunday mornings — were clanging inside them. He sensed a wet spot on the back of his neck but the cell was too dark to permit him to see whether or not it was blood. Don Carlos continued to lie without moving, eyes closed with an all-consuming weariness.

His mind drifted back to the final minutes before de Henrique had stalked out of the cell, his mission unfulfilled. He had asked Don Carlos to betray his friend, Fernando de Lima. Don Carlos remembered the exact words of his own answer:

"No, Paulo de Henrique! I am not the one to turn to for such dark doings. The One Who gave me life — the great G-d above — is the One Who will take it from me, when He so desires. G-d, may His Name be blessed forever, despises such foul plots. He would not forgive me if I did such a thing to a friend, and would also punish me if I were to act against a stranger. And — you will perhaps find this hard to believe — He would stamp me with the same guilt were I to act against a member of a different faith. The G-d of the Jews is not Christian, Heaven forbid! *He* does not advocate burning and murdering men of other faiths."

Now, in the deep silence of the Inquisition dungeon, Don Carlos felt proud of the way he'd flung the truth into de Henrique's face. Where had he found the inner strength to utter those words? How had he managed to say them without trembling in fear, without pleading for his life? He did not know. But he would be prepared to reiterate them, even at the cost of hearing de Henrique's menacing reply once again. Losing control completely, the priest had shrieked:

"Even in your last moments on earth you dare malign the faith you've betrayed? Don Carlos, you know that your death sentence has not yet been signed. As long as the king does not authorize it, the Holy Office may continue its investigations... Yes, we may continue to investigate your case by any means we choose — especially the means you've come to know firsthand these past few months..."

Don Carlos took his enemy's warning to heart. De Henrique could easily carry out his threat. The thought of undergoing further excruciating torture made Don Carlos break out in a cold sweat. He was afraid — very afraid. And still, not for a single second did he regret his decision to spurn the priest's appalling deal.

Something touched his left arm. A rat? A snake? He wanted to move, but could not yet muster the necessary strength. A surge of fear ran through him as he felt a tug at his sleeve. Then he heard the soft sound of breathing — human breathing. Young de Castro, apparently, had crept in silence across the dark cell to where Don Carlos lay.

"I heard everything!" Yitzchak de Castro whispered, lying beside his cellmate on the stone floor.

After a moment, Don Carlos asked, "And you understood?"

"I think so."

"What did you understand?"

"What I've known for a long time."

A silence fell between them, punctuated only by their ragged breathing. It was hard for Don Carlos to speak. At length, he asked, "And what have you known for a long time?"

Yitzchak de Castro turned heavily onto his side. "What you, too, know all the time."

After a while, Don Carlos sighed, "True."

With a tremendous effort, he dragged himself to the nearest wall and struggled into a sitting position. Weakly he leaned against the wall, gasping from the exertion. Presently he was breathing almost normally again. He gazed across with compassion at his companion.

"You are right, my young friend. We have just been shown further proof of the falsity and lies practiced by these Inquisition priests. They masquerade as pious individuals whose burning faith leads them to track down and execute heretics. And the peasant in his village, the man on the city street — simple, everyday Catholics — believe them! They believe that those accursed serpents are holy! You have just seen to what lengths the secretary of the Holy Office himself is prepared to go in order to exact revenge on a worthy citizen who won't jump to do his bidding. I don't know what's happened between him and the High Court. But he has offered me — *me*, his greatest triumph! — my liberty in exchange for consenting to accuse an innocent man of the heinous 'crime' of being a Jew. He is eaten up by greed, and a lust for honor and vengeance. De Henrique does not really believe in his own Christianity!" He peered through the dark at de Castro. "Do you understand what I'm saying?"

De Castro smiled. "Of course I understand. Do you think Portugal is the only place where they act in this manner? In Brazil they also arrest people to further their own ends. Their victims are usually the rich. They don't care whether the man is really a secret Jew or a devout Catholic; the criteria is to get their hands on his property."

The young man paused. In the ensuing silence the voice of the prisoner in the adjoining cell filtered through clearly to them:

"A curse on those torturers and murderers! I am a Christian. A Christian from birth. And now, here I am in an Inquisition dungeon! My wife, in a moment of anger, went to the authorities and told them that I'm a secret Jew. And those devils believed her!"

Don Carlos asked in a quiet voice that echoed through the dungeon: "Have you confessed?"

"Of course I 'confessed' that I am a Jew, and that I observe the *mitzvos*. Believe me, to this very minute I have no idea what the Jews' *mitzvos* even are!"

Don Carlos did not reply. Da Castro grasped his hand and held it so tightly that it hurt...

Suddenly, the silence was shattered by a raucous cry from the staircase: *"What is all this talking?"*

In every cell, the prisoners scuttled away from the openings that had allowed them to listen to the short exchange. They flung themselves onto the stones and pretended to be asleep.

There was a noise of heavy feet descending the stairs. Someone had decided to investigate what was happening down in the dungeon.

❧

Roberto freed his hand from Fernando's clasp, saying, "I too believe in Hashem's salvation. Still, we must do something! We must act! Why didn't he bring the note?"

Fernando answered quietly, "He claims it was missing from the file. It's possible that he's lying. At the same time, it is also possible that he's telling the truth. I don't know! You can't trust anybody in this city. Maybe someone has paid him more than I did."

Roberto pointed at his suitcase. "There's a large sum of money in there. The Inquisitor's love of gold is common knowledge in Amsterdam. Fernando, take as much as you need. I will bring more if necessary. We must rescue Don Carlos at any price. This is more than just a matter of saving a life — it will also deal a severe blow to the Inquisition. Just as Raphael Chaim's escape did."

"I need the note. With it, I can achieve a great deal through the High Court. The letter you've brought can change the whole picture. But without the note" — Fernando spread his hands helplessly — "I don't know what I can do."

"So how will we find the note?"

"I don't know."

All at once they froze in their places. Someone seemed to be observing them through the window. They dashed over and opened it as wide as it would go.

In the darkness, they saw nothing. But it had seemed to both of them that they'd heard footsteps running in the direction of the front gate and vanishing into the night.

46

abriel Monteiro de Silvia glanced apprehensively at the tall, broad-trunked tree that stood to his left, in the center of the courtyard. He was standing immobile on the path that led to the outer gate and the street. The darkness was complete. However, though he could see nothing, his fluttering stomach was sending him unmistakable signals: Danger was near.

Something or somebody was hiding behind that tree, watching him. Was it an animal — a dog or cat, perhaps — or a man? The last possibility made the fluttering in his stomach grow markedly stronger.

Gabriel bent slowly and picked up a stone, never removing his eyes from the tree. Without warning, he jerked back his arm and hurled the stone with all his might. It hit the trunk and fell harmlessly to the ground. The noise of its impact disturbed the quiet night, and Gabriel waited anxiously to see what sort of reaction it would elicit.

There was none. Nothing moved or cried out. This frightened Gabriel more than anything else. A cat or dog would have taken to its heels at the sudden sound. His worst fears appeared to be well founded: There was someone hiding behind that tree.

Who could it be? A thief on his way to plunder the house? A drunken passer-by resting after a night's carousal? Or — this thought terrified him — was someone following him? Had anyone seen him enter the judge's house? And if so, who was he, and who had sent him?

A sudden weakness assailed him. He tried to calm himself, but the fearful imaginings had taken too firm a hold on his mind. His first instinct was flight. He could run over to the gate as fast as his legs would carry him, lock it behind him, and then take off into the night. Whoever was following him — if anyone really *was* following him — would never see where he'd gone. Under cover of the impenetrable darkness, Gabriel would rid himself of his watcher. Tomorrow could take care of itself.

But for some reason, he did not run. Something prompted him to remain rooted to the spot. Then another urge — it may have been nothing more than curiosity, growing stronger by the minute — arose in him: to approach the tree and see for himself. Breathing deeply, he stepped off the path and into the garden.

With both hands he lifted the hem of his cassock so that the fabric would not get caught on thorns or enmeshed in the shadow-shrouded flower beds. He took one cautious step forward, and waited. When the silence continued unbroken, he walked a little further, every one of his senses alert for possible danger.

When he was only a few steps away from the tree, he called softly, "You there — why don't you come out and show me who you are?"

Nobody answered. But in the silence, it seemed to Gabriel that he could hear a man's shallow breathing. Or was it only his own breath, rising and falling in a mad, ragged tempo?

Once again he called softly into the night, "Are you afraid? Do you have something to hide?"

Charged with fresh tension, Gabriel fell back, ready to do battle. For he'd heard what he'd been waiting for, or rather, dreading: the sound of a figure rustling behind the tree.

There was a man standing before him.

He was impossible to identify in the darkness. Then he spoke, throwing Gabriel into complete confusion and panic.

"No," he said, just as softly. "I have nothing to hide. Can you say the same?"

A stifled cry burst from Gabriel's throat. There could be no mistake: He knew the voice well.

It belonged to Paulo de Henrique.

⤙⤚

He regretted not having run away, but it was too late for that now. He must gather his wits about him to deal with the next difficult moments. In trepidation, Gabriel saw the figure detach itself from the shadow of the tree and move toward him. Drawing a breath, he decided to take the offensive. "What are you doing here at this time of the night?" he demanded shakily.

De Henrique laughed. "What interests me far more, my dear Gabriel Monteiro, is what you are doing here. Not right here, in the garden, but in the Superior Court judge's house."

Gabriel hastened to answer, "I was visiting a friend, sir!"

De Henrique's laughter grew heartier, though there was no missing the underlying menace. "Hm... a strange hour to be seized by the sentiment of friendship. Interesting... very, very interesting!"

"It is not strange at all — for someone who actually harbors such sentiment in his heart."

De Henrique caught the barb in Gabriel's answer, but chose to ignore it. "But was there really a need for such haste, my dear Gabriel? Was it so vital for you to visit Judge de Lima's house at such a late hour?"

"Yes! Otherwise I would not have come."

De Henrique took a step closer to the other priest. They were face to face now. De Henrique whispered, "Was it connected to Don Carlos?"

Gabriel was appalled. His voice choked in his throat as forced the words out: "No, not at all."

"Really? Nothing to do with the fact that tomorrow Judge de Lima hands down his decision with regards to Don Carlos' case? The truth, please!"

"*Senhor* Paulo, shall we leave this garden and continue our discussion out in the street?"

"No. I still have some unfinished business in this house. Some very interesting business."

Gabriel Monteiro swallowed hard, and quavered, "I did not come here about Don Carlos. My visit was connected to... you, Paulo."

"*Me?*" De Henrique's blood boiled. "You were plotting against *me*?"

"Plots, Paulo, are *your* hobby and pastime. I myself have no great love for them."

He paused, then added, "And neither, as far as I know, does Fernando de Lima."

De Henrique chewed his lip. He did not know where this upstart priest found the courage to insult him this way, but his day would come. This was not yet the moment... Aloud, he said sarcastically, "Thank you for your assessment of my personality, Gabriel. However, you did mention that your visit here tonight was connected to me. What else might that be referring to, if not for a sweet little plot?"

"If you want the truth, you shall have it. I came here, Paulo, to apologize to de Lima. To tell him that we, the Inquisition judges, wished to dissociate ourselves from your behavior this morning. I wanted to show him that my friendship for him remains unchanged."

"Nice. Very nice," de Henrique chortled. "May Heaven be blessed — at least one person in this fair land of ours zealously guards the precious jewel of friendship! However" — His voice dropped menacingly — "I had thought that you were even more loyal to the church, to our faith, and to our holy task of rooting out the heretics in our midst!"

"I see no contradiction between the two, Paulo."

"That," said de Henrique, "is precisely your problem. It is a problem that is shared by other members of the tribunal, and even by our leader, *Padre* João Manuel, who sometimes forgets his duty in the call of his nobler feelings." Venom dripped from de Henrique's voice.

"Again, I don't see your point, Paulo. And it's interesting to hear that you are the only one who is loyal to the cross and the church."

Suddenly, de Henrique seized Gabriel's arm. "Are you blind or deaf?

Haven't you paid attention to the fact that Fernando de Lima has refused to authorize Don Carlos' death sentence? You were one of the judges who issued the sentence! Don't you care?"

De Henrique's grip was too tight for comfort. Gabriel said quickly, "No, I noticed nothing. Why are you so suspicious of him?"

"For good reason. *Senhor* Fernando is entirely too indifferent about this case. Even when we spelled out for him what Don Carlos had done, he hardly reacted."

"And so...?"

"And so, who knows whether or not that indifference is real or feigned? Perhaps our friend Fernando regrets the fact that Don Carlos is slated to die in the very near future. Who knows whether or not Fernando himself is not a member of the *Cristão Novo* (New Christian, or Marrano)?"

De Henrique shook him as though he were a lowly servant instead of a respected Inquisition judge. Bringing his face very close to Gabriel's, he hissed, "And you visited the home of a secret Jew."

Fury blazed up in Gabriel's breast. Pulling his arm away, he cried, "Is this your newest plot? We all know how many loyal Christians you have already had put to death through the good offices of the Inquisition."

"Quiet!" de Henrique commanded, darting a look over his shoulder. "If we're caught out here, you will find yourself in very great trouble."

He was right, Gabriel was forced to acknowledge. If they were seen here, there would be many questions asked — asked of *him*, not of de Henrique. He paled. The secretary's intention was clear to him. That master plotter hoped to implicate him, Gabriel Monteiro, with being a secret Jew, too. The man was mad... And dangerous.

"Are you threatening me?" he asked, with quiet intensity that did nothing to mask his anger. "Are you hinting that *I* am to be your next sacrificial victim? I will fight you, Paulo. You will not easily ensnare me in your twisted web of lies and schemes. I know exactly what happens in our celebrated dungeons. I know what happens in our interrogation rooms. It will not be pleasant for you if I decide to speak. Do you understand me, Paulo de Henrique, illustrious secretary of our Holy Office?"

De Henrique was not to be intimidated. In a low, silky voice, he replied, "It's up to you, my friend. You will decide what happens."

"What do you mean?"

Even in the dark he could feel the other's penetrating stare. "Are you prepared to tell me the name of the man who was with you in de Lima's house?"

"There were only the two of us there. No one was with us." Gabriel was bewildered.

De Henrique shook his head violently. "Just a short time before you came to the house, another man went in. He never left it. Who is he?"

"I saw no one, Paulo — in the name of all the holy martyrs!"

De Henrique reacted promptly. "I believe you. I believe that you didn't see him. Now, come. I want to show you something."

Head spinning, Gabriel turned and began to follow de Henrique as he walked quietly and quickly toward Fernando de Lima's house.

47

De Henrique stepped quietly and with care toward de Lima's house, using the protection of the trees that filled the small square. Gabriel Monteiro was drawn after him like a pin to a magnet. Gabriel experienced a pang of renewed fear as he realized that he was in de Henrique's power. He must do as the secretary bid, or suffer unknown but assuredly bitter consequences. Inwardly he prayed that he would never have to confess to de Henrique the precise nature of his business at Judge de Lima's house this night. Perhaps, if he followed de Henrique now and obeyed his instructions, he would be freed from suspicion.

De Henrique halted at a small distance from the house. Gabriel stopped, too. In the garden, hidden by the sheltering arms of a tree that grew near the house, they were able to see — though not look through — a lighted window.

At first they heard nothing. Then, gradually, as their ears accustomed themselves, they heard a door closing, and then soft voices talking together inside the room. De Henrique raised a finger to his lips to adjure Gabriel to silence. Leaving the protection of the tree, he tiptoed closer to the house.

The window was a little too high for him. De Henrique began searching the ground for pieces of wood, which he gathered swiftly into a pile beneath the window. At last, with extreme caution, he climbed to the top of the pile. Balancing himself carefully, he raised his head to the level of the window sash and peeked into the room.

An evil smile overspread his face. What he saw satisfied him deeply, because it confirmed his suspicions.

Seated at the table with Judge Fernando de Lima was the stranger whom he, de Henrique, had suspected of thievery just a short time ago. The violent struggle between the judge and the stranger at de Lima's front door had been nothing but a huge farce, then, enacted for de Henrique's benefit. The two had their heads together and were whispering earnestly. What were they talking about?

He clambered down the woodpile and gestured for Gabriel Monteiro to take his place. Gingerly, Gabriel obeyed. Standing on tiptoe, he looked through the window into the lighted room — and began to tremble. De Henrique had been right. There *had* been another person in the house while he was there. Who could he be? Could de Henrique have been correct, too, when he'd asserted that the two men were plotting mischief? And if so, would he, Gabriel, be believed when he asserted his own innocence? De Henrique was liable to have him thrown into prison and handed over to the interrogators... His trembling increased.

Suddenly, to his dismay, he slipped. The pile of wood lost its precarious equilibrium and crashed noisily down in a heap, with Gabriel on his hands and knees among them, breathless and bruised. The noise brought Fernando and his guest to the window. At the sight of those two faces pressed to the glass, Paulo de Henrique took to his heels. Despite his bulk, he reached the gate in record time, and vanished through it.

Gabriel scrambled to his feet and followed. Where he found the energy to run so quickly at his age he didn't know, but run he did. Fervently he hoped that Fernando had not recognized him in the dark.

He reached the gate. Now he could slip away to his own home. De Henrique, he guessed, must have also decided to abandon this place as rapidly as possible. It would not do for word to reach Lisbon that he personally had spied on the Superior Court judge tonight. Pausing to catch his breath, he glanced back over his shoulder at the house, to see whether Fernando had opened the door for a glimpse of the intruders.

The door was closed. Peace reigned all around. The window where, a moment ago, two faces had peered out, was dark now. The judge, it seemed, was also afraid. Lisbon had become a city of fear... And he, Gabriel Monteiro, was afraid, too. Who knew what his friend was concealing in his house? Had Fernando really wanted the note in order to authorize Don Carlos' death sentence — or the opposite? He felt frightened and confused. He had allowed himself to be sucked into a quicksand that could endanger his very existence. And for what? For a few pieces of gold! He must distance himself from this affair as quickly as possible. He wanted nothing to do with either Fernando de Lima or Paulo de Henrique. What business had he, an Inquisition judge, to embroil himself in the sudden quarrel that had erupted between two such important and powerful figures?

Passing through the gate, he stepped out into the street. However, he had not proceeded more than a few paces before a strong hand grabbed his arm and propelled him toward the stone wall that surrounded de Lima's courtyard. De Henrique had caught him neatly in his trap.

All of Gabriel's will to fight evaporated in a surge of black despair.

"Did you see him?" De Henrique hissed in his ear.

"Y-y-yes..."

"So what do you have to say to that?!"

"I - I - I d-don't know."

De Henrique seized Gabriel by the throat and began shaking him. Under cover of the night and the empty street, he abused and humiliated the judge, who actually ranked above him in the hierarchy of the Inquisition.

"You don't know who that man is?" he screamed softly. "You did not sit with him when you were in that house? Speak! What's going on in this city? Tell me everything!"

Gabriel made a choking sound. "Let me go! I can't talk! I can't breathe..."

Far from letting go, de Henrique tightened his hold. He regarded the terror in Gabriel's eyes with satisfaction. Let there be no mistake about who was master here! After a few seconds, he loosed his grip slightly, and said, "Well? What do you have to say in your defense?"

Gabriel's voice was raw and rasping in his painful throat. "Paulo, I promise you... in the name of all the holy martyrs... there was no one in that house when I was there. No one! Believe me! I didn't see him... I don't know him... And Fernando said nothing to me about any guest."

"And you expect me to believe you?" de Henrique snarled.

"It's the truth! I saw no one, I heard no one, and there was no sign that anyone else was in the house with us."

De Henrique relaxed his hold. A measure of relief, and with it renewed courage, came to Gabriel. He asked, "Tell me, Paulo — how did you know there was someone in the house?"

"The same way I knew that you were there." De Henrique's bark of laughter was short and sinister.

Tension gripped Gabriel's heart once more. "What do you mean?"

"I knew you were in there because I'd followed you."

"What — What do you mean, 'followed me'?!"

"I believed," de Henrique said, eyes dancing with glee, "that it was necessary for me to do so."

Unconsciously, Gabriel wrung his hands. "But — *why?*"

De Henrique was in no hurry to answer. Even in the darkness, he could sense Gabriel's frantic impatience. In a voice suddenly low and pleasant, he asked, "Perhaps you can tell me why one of our hardworking Inquisition judges takes it into his head to stroll through the city so late at night, first in the direction of the Holy Office, and then reversing course to visit the Superior Court judge? Do you think you can clarify this for me?"

At this recital of his itinerary, the words died in Gabriel's throat. De Henrique was everywhere; he knew everything. What sort of stories would the secretary spread about him tomorrow? Gabriel had only been trying to further the cause of justice, as Fernando had explained it to him. Had his friend deceived him?

Only one detail appeared to have escaped de Henrique: He seemed to be unaware of the fact that Gabriel Monteiro had left home tonight only after receiving a visit from Fernando de Lima. Discovery of that fact would certainly hasten Gabriel's doom...

Or was the wily secretary merely playing a cat-and-mouse game with him? Did de Henrique actually have that fact in his possession, and was concealing it from him only to heighten Gabriel's subsequent discomfiture? At that moment, Gabriel berated himself intensely: *"Why did I ever set foot out of my house tonight?"*

"I'm waiting for your answer, Gabriel." De Henrique's voice had hardened. Gabriel drew a deep breath and decided to tell the truth.

"Paulo, please believe what I'm about to tell you. My friend Fernando de Lima asked me to help him prepare for tomorrow's sentencing."

"Hm. Interesting!"

"He's come to me for help many times in the past," Gabriel embellished untruthfully.

"Go on."

"After what happened at the Holy Office this morning — after you shouted at him, Paulo — he began to wonder whether this case had been conducted according to the strict letter of the law. He simply asked me if I could get him the note on which the case rests. He wants to help, Paulo. You know that the prince is standing in our way, while Fernando is loyal to us. Your tirade today was really out of order..."

De Henrique's hand shot out again to seize Gabriel's cassock. His small eyes blazed with fury.

"You're naive, Gabriel! A fool! My 'tirade,' as you call it, was definitely in order. I am an expert at sniffing out those who've strayed from the true path. Didn't you notice how indifferent de Lima was when we told him about the sentence we'd passed? He betrayed no joy at all at the news that we've managed to expose the traitorous Jew, Don Carlos. He should have shown his revulsion at the thought of a man like that reaching such a prominent position in Portugal, while charading as a loyal Christian!"

De Henrique paused, then added through clenched teeth, "He'd be a good deal happier at our triumph if he himself were not a secret Jew!"

"Surely you're exaggerating, Paulo."

"I am not! Have I ever failed? Has anyone I've accused ever been set free? No! And do you know why not? Because I have a good sense of smell. I can smell a heretic from far away. Do you understand?"

"After the tortures of your interrogation rooms, anyone would confess. Even I would."

De Henrique shoved Gabriel violently against the wall, saying, "One day you *will* confess to me."

On this menacing note, he turned and melted into the night. Gabriel Monteiro stood rooted to the spot, unable to move a muscle. He strained to hear the secretary's last, faint footfalls, as his heart sobbed silently within him.

48

Late as it was, de Henrique hurried back to the Inquisition building, where he went directly to the sleeping quarters of the younger monks. He roused a few whom he knew to be loyal to him with orders to meet him in his office at once.

"I have a job for you," he ordered, his voice sharp with urgency. "You must hurry to Superior Judge de Lima's house. Don't delay for even a minute! Surround the house on every side. Seek out every possible exit, and guard each one well. Keep an eye on the house and mark down everyone who leaves or enters it. You will remain in place there until the carriage comes to take the judge to the Superior Court in the morning."

"And what are we supposed to do?" one sleepy monk asked, unsuccessfully trying to stifle an enormous yawn.

"First of all, don't yawn — and don't fall asleep!" de Henrique thundered.

"Yes, but what do we do if we see someone leave the house?"

"If he is a member of the judge's household, you are to seize him and bring him to me at once. Is that understood?"

"Yes, *Senhor*. We understand."

De Henrique waved away the drowsy monks. After the last of them left his office, he ran over to the door they had just closed behind them, flung it open, and shouted out one final instruction:

"After the judge leaves home in the morning, you are to keep the house under observation. Only one of you will return here to report to me. And remember: No one must notice what you are doing. Your surveillance must be extremely discreet. Understand?"

He returned to his room. He would spend the remainder of the night right here.

But his attempts at falling asleep in his armchair were futile. He was pent up, filled with nervous tension which successfully chased away any possibility of rest. Tomorrow, he knew, would be a fateful day for him. It would bring either his triumph — or his undoing. It would be a day of battle, of grappling with powerful enemies. De Henrique loved conflicts and the excitement that accompanied them. But this time his enemies were truly formidable — and very, very clever.

He saw them clearly in his mind's eye: *Padre* João Manuel and Fernando de Lima. The pair were obstacles standing in the way of his achieving final and total victory over Don Carlos. Such a victory would win him the acclaim of all of Portugal, as a true crusader for the holy faith, for his people, and for his country. And who knew? Perhaps, as the flames licked Don Carlos' body, someone in the royal palace would bethink himself to promote the hero, de Henrique, in the Inquisition hierarchy... It was a tantalizing thought.

Gradually, he increased the light from the oil lamp that sat on his desk. The light dispersed some of the shadows in the room. From his pocket he withdrew the note upon which Don Carlos' case rested. He held it in both his hands, a bitter smile creasing his heavy features. This was what Fernando de Lima had wanted to lay his hands on tonight. Why? What use was the note to him in the middle of the night? De Henrique could make no sense of it. Unless... Could he have wanted to destroy the note? To destroy it, so that no evidence would exist against Don Carlos apart from the verbal confession extracted under the tender ministrations of his torturers? With the note gone, de Lima would be able to severely undermine the Inquisition's death sentence against Don Carlos, and might even be able to have the entire case thrown out of court. Aha! And Gabriel Monteiro had agreed to help him — the lowly traitor!

De Henrique rose from his chair and began to pace the narrow room restlessly. How to vanquish the judge? Impatiently, he opened the door and peered down the dark corridor. He decided to step out into the courtyard for a breath of air and a calming glimpse of the moon and the star-studded sky.

The sound of his quiet footsteps echoed in the empty courtyard. It was hard for him to believe that the judge would willingly endorse the death sentence for Don Carlos. But he, de Henrique, was determined: De Lima would not snatch his victory from him! Don Carlos would die. If de Lima refused to authorize the sentence, or even if he delayed his decision, de Henrique would organize all of Lisbon to demonstrate its displeasure. And as for de Lima himself, de Henrique swore that the eminent judge would meet his end in the exact same way as Don Carlos would next week.

All he needed was patience, and cunning. Gabriel Monteiro de Silvia would be a big help. He would speak out! And he would say what de Henrique wished him to say. He'd been frightened enough when de Henrique caught him coming out of the judge's house. Fear of an Inquisition interrogation would be enough to ensure that Gabriel Monteiro cooperated with everything de Henrique wished. Everything!

He left the deserted courtyard and returned to the solitude of his room. He would wait to hear the news his young accomplices brought him in the morning. In besieging the judge's house, perhaps they would unravel the riddle of the stranger's identity. Where had the man come from, and what connection did he have to the Don Carlos affair? Was there any connection at all?

De Henrique chuckled deep in his throat. And if the man wasn't linked to Don Carlos, did that really matter? A link would be created! Let the young monks bring him here, and de Henrique would know what to do with him. In his dungeons, everyone said what they were supposed to say.

But the suspicion against the man was substantial. His sudden appearance near de Lima's house, on the very night that the judge was trying to obtain possession of an important confidential document from the Inquisition archives, was enough to excite all sorts of suspicion. He must wait for morning, and then act quickly. Quickly — before the Inquisition tribunal, headed by *Padre* João Manuel, appeared before the Superior Court judge.

Ah, yes, *Padre* João Manuel. De Henrique had a score to settle with him, too. He had not yet ascertained whether young Salvador Gimreines had returned from the mission on which he, de Henrique, had sent him. Had he succeeded in planting the two Jewish *mezuzos* in João Manuel's house, as he'd been instructed? If he had, de Henrique could order a search of João Manuel's home as early as this very morning, before the Superior Court session.

≈⧀

Roberto Gonzales was seized with panic. He stared anxiously into Fernando de Lima's eyes.

"What could that have been?"

"I don't know," Fernando answered slowly. "I'm afraid someone's been watching our every move."

"Who might it be?"

The judge's laugh was bitter. "In Lisbon, that's no question. To our misfortune, it was de Henrique himself who saw you enter my house. And he is a very suspicious-minded man."

Fernando sank into his thoughts, then roused himself to add, "Besides, he will no doubt want to use your presence here as a weapon against me."

Robert said despairingly, "So what will we do?"

"First of all, you have to disappear from this city with all possible speed."

Roberto was surprised. "But how can I? I can't return to Amsterdam now — the first ship leaves Lisbon only at the beginning of next week!"

"I didn't mean for you to leave the country. I meant only to leave Lisbon."

"How?"

Abruptly, Fernando stood up. Grasping Roberto by the forearm, he drew him deeper into the interior of the house. Roberto followed without a word, not forgetting to take along his case. They descended to the basement. There, in one dim corner, Fernando stooped and removed a stone from the wall. He reached inside and groped for a moment, until his hand touched a cold iron ring. With all his might, he pulled it. Slowly, inexorably, the whole stone wall began moving inwards, toward them. Roberto saw a black tunnel yawn suddenly ahead of them. In the light of Fernando's single candle, he saw narrow steps winding down in the darkness.

"Go in. Don't be afraid. Take the steps slowly, one at a time. Don't worry about the dark; the steps are smooth. Help yourself along by keeping one hand in contact with the wall and keep moving forward. After a while you'll feel an obstruction in the wall and won't be able to continue. Wait there. Someone will come and take you out of there." Fernando smiled grimly. "No one will be able to testify that there was a stranger in my home."

Roberto Gonzales burst out, "Not even your wife?"

By the light of the candle, he saw his friend's face blanch. Both realized that, in this case, the judge's wife represented a real danger. At length, Fernando said, "The important thing now is to save Don Carlos. So you wait patiently. One of my men will tell you what to do next."

Roberto Gonzales cast a penetrating look at his friend, then turned away and began carefully descending the stairs. Fernando watched him go in silence. Just as Roberto was swallowed up by the darkness, Fernando called softly, "Don't be anxious, my friend. De Henrique's day will come. If Hashem will help us, his downfall might come as early as tomorrow — in the Superior Court."

The wall closed. The Superior Cour judge hasted back to his room, to rest for a while in preparation for what the morrow would bring. It promised to be a difficult day.

≈≫

Padre João Manuel stood at the entrance to his home, shaking with rage.

The sun's first rays were tipping with gold the treetops that adorned his garden. This, he knew, would be a difficult day for him. In his hand he still held the two *mezuzos* that his uninvited visitor had flung into his house last night. To his chagrin, the intruder had managed to escape before João Manuel could catch a good look at his face or ask him the questions he burned to have answered. He'd worn the clothing of a novice monk; that much, João Manuel knew for certain. But who had sent him, and for what purpose?

Then he laughed inwardly — a bitter laugh. As if he didn't know exactly who had sent the young monk, or why! The diabolical plot — sending someone to "plant" the *mezuzos* in his house so that a search could be instigated later that would implicate João Manuel — could have sprouted only in the brain of one man: his dear secretary, Paulo de Henrique.

As the priest stood looking out on the new day with the Jewish symbols in his hand, fury replaced his initial panic. This, then, was de Henrique's response to his, João Manuel's, effort to placate Judge de Lima yesterday. To accuse the most respected man in Lisbon of being Jewish, and to topple him from his position of honor and power — that would be the form of revenge de Henrique most enjoyed. Had his secretary been standing before him at that moment, João Manuel would have had no compunction about strangling him with his bare hands...

He turned and entered his house. This morning he must appear in the Superior Court on the Don Carlos case. Yesterday's abortive meeting had definitely sabotaged their chances of success today. De Henrique, too, was required to appear. What would happen when the Inquisition secretary and the Superior Judge met again?

In any case, João Manuel must hurry and prepare the necessary documents for the hearing. The results were shrouded in doubt. Would de Lima endorse the tribunal's death sentence, and in such a way that His Majesty, the king, would do the same? He was no longer sure. Yesterday's stormy encounter between de Lima and de Henrique had muddied the waters; certainly, it boded no good. The judge's incisive questions had revealed the trend of his thoughts: He was none too eager to grant his stamp of approval to the Inquisition's decree.

The *mezuzos* were still in his hand. Catching sight of them, the priest trembled. He must act quickly. He must hurry to the Inquisition building before that serpent, de Henrique, had time to organize any action against him. He knew exactly what he was going to do about the *mezuzos*. He would publicize the tale! This morning, he would tell everyone what had happened when he came home last night. He would ask every monk he met whether he knew anything of the matter, and if he could help identify the nameless novice who had perpetrated this crime. Naturally, the same question would be posed to de Henrique — preferably, before witnesses. It would be very interesting to see how the secretary reacted...

João Manuel though could venture an accurate guess. De Henrique was a hardened liar with the hide of an elephant. Nothing fazed him. He would doubtless utter more bald-faced lies in response to questioning. Nevertheless, his plans would have suffered a setback.

But that was not enough. There was no longer any choice: He must work to oust de Henrique from the Inquisition. He must stop that dangerous man in his tracks before it was too late! And who knew whether it was not already too late? De Henrique could be lightning swift in his reprisals. João Manuel would not have been surprised to learn that his secretary had already plotted a hideous vengeance against Judge de Lima as well. No one was permitted to wound de Henrique's self-esteem — on pain of death!

The *mezuzos* seemed to scorch his fingers. Who knew how many innocent men de Henrique had had thrown into the Inquisition dungeons, through precisely these methods? How many pairs of *mezuzos*, *tefillin*, and the like had been introduced into the homes of men upon whom de Henrique wished to exact revenge? This was not the first time such thoughts had tickled João Manuel's conscience, but it was the first time the notion had been allowed to burst into his full awareness. He deeply regretted now that he had not acted to prevent such maneuvers in the past. He had not acted, and now de Henrique was trying to use the same tactics against him.

Rousing himself from his thoughts, João Manuel went out the door, locked it behind him, and began with a firm and vigorous stride to walk to the Inquisition building. He would deal with de Henrique today, even before the Superior Court appearance.

Don Carlos cowered silently in his corner. So did Yitzchak de Castro. And so did all the other prisoners, each in his own corner. The guard's heavy tread came closer. He walked slowly down the corridor, the lantern in his hand illuminating each tiny, dank cell in an effort to uncover the source of the talk he'd heard. But he found nothing. The silence was complete. Every man pretended to sleep.

The guard reversed direction and went back to the stairs leading up to the building proper. When he reached the bottom step, he turned and barked:

"Make no mistake, my dear men. An investigation will be held tomorrow morning, to discover who disrupted the peace and quiet down here — who broke the rule about talking in the prison... It will not be a very pleasant investigation."

The guard climbed the stairs.

In their cell, Don Carlos stroked Yitzchak's hand in a soothing way, as if to tell him not to be afraid.

49

Don Carlos woke suddenly. He had no idea whether night still reigned over Lisbon, or if the sun was already shining over the city that had betrayed him. There was only perpetual darkness in the depths of the Inquisition dungeon.

Above his head were the sound of dull footsteps. They came from the long, dim corridors of the Inquisition building. It must be daytime, then.

Don Carlos turned over onto his back. The stone floor was uneven and bore painfully into his ribs. Squinting upward in the dark, he strained to hear the noises coming from overhead. There were heavy footsteps, and lighter, quicker ones. Did the heavy ones belong to de Henrique, from whom Don Carlos was expecting another visit at any time?

Remembering the ominous conversation they'd had the night before, Don Carlos shivered with fear. He knew that the cruel secretary was perfectly capable of renewing his torture, even though Don Carlos had already been sentenced to death. He did not have the strength to bear it. There was little left of the strong, proud admiral who had walked the streets of Lisbon before his imprisonment, interrogation, and torture. Moreover, he was weary of life. He'd made his peace with his fate — to die in the sanctification of G-d's Name. But to be tied again to the torture machines — to feel red-hot coals beneath his feet — to be stretched on the wheel until his bones were broken — that he could not stand any longer.

He crawled slowly to the corner where Yitzchak de Castro lay.

"Yitzchak? Are you awake?"

The answer was low in the darkness. "Yes."

"I'll be leaving you today," Don Carlos whispered.

"Why?"

"Don't you remember what de Henrique said?"

"Yes, I remember. But what do you mean, you're leaving?"

"You don't know him as well as I do. He will fulfill his promise to renew my torture. I've seen him at work among Lisbon's citizens for many years now."

De Castro was silent. After a sorrowful pause, Don Carlos sighed and said, "It's hard for me to believe that I'd be able to withstand such torture again."

Stretching out his hand and resting it gently on his cellmate's head, young de Castro murmured, "Hashem will help you."

Don Carlos shook his head. "No. No, Yitzchak. My body is weak. If he really does keep his promise, I am certain that my soul will leave me on the torture wheel." He added with a bitter smile, "May Hashem's Name be blessed forever and ever. At least, that way, de Henrique will be cheated of his great drama. He won't be able to burn me before all of Lisbon."

He heard Yitzchak's whisper: "You've forgotten something. They also burn the dead bodies of 'sinners.' He'll have his pleasure in either case."

A profound silence fell between them. Then Yitzchak de Castro burst out explosively, "That accursed evildoer!"

He removed his hand from Don Carlos' head and huddled deeper into himself. Don Carlos continued to lie motionless, eyes fixed on the ceiling. From the adjoining cells came disjointed sighs and mutterings.

Abruptly, de Castro sat up and stretched. "Don Carlos!" he whispered in a supplicating tone.

"What?"

"Do you really think they'll take you up for interrogation again?"

"Yes."

"And what will become of me? Will I remain here alone?"

Don Carlos did not reply. His young cellmate had grown accustomed to his company. No doubt he felt more confident with the older, more experienced man nearby. Now he would be alone again. Don Carlos did not know which words to say to comfort him. Finally, he whispered, "David, king of Israel, said in *Tehillim*: "Even if I walk through the valley of the shadow of death, I will fear no evil because You are with me."

Yitzchak de Castro crawled to the wall and tried to sit with his back leaning against it. "True. But... it's hard."

"Hashem gives a man the strength to face the tests he's given. He will not abandon you."

"Nor you, Don Carlos. He will grant you the strength to withstand the tortures that man may inflict upon you."

Don Carlos smiled sadly at the young man's naiveté.

"You did not understand me, Yitzchak. We were saying that Hashem gives a man the strength and faith that he needs to face his tests. But there's no guarantee that he'll come out of them alive!"

"But maybe — if that wicked man comes and takes you away with him — you will find the strength to live through the torture and return here?"

Don Carlos hesitated, then decided to be soothing. "Maybe."

"And then, you'd be with me when... when..."

De Castro choked on the next words. Don Carlos understood what he'd mean to say. He wanted Don Carlos to be with him when they tied him to the stake, and the fire was ignited that would consume them both to the cheers of the watching throng.

≈⌒

Padre João Manuel arrived at the Inquisition building. The gate swung open to admit him. He stood in the center of the busy courtyard and motioned imperiously for all who were present to surround him. In his hand he grasped the bundle containing the two *mezuzos*.

The monks stopped, drawn by the obvious excitement in his manner. Curiously, they came nearer. With trembling fingers, as they watched uncomprehendingly, João Manuel slowly opened the bundle.

De Henrique chose this moment to walk by.

"What is this?" João Manuel screamed at the startled secretary, waving the *mezuzos* in front of his face. "What is this supposed to be?"

De Henrique's eyes narrowed. He knew instantly that his plot had failed, but permitted no trace of that knowledge to show on his countenance. His glance swept the gathering crowd, then went back to his superior. He registered surprise.

"Why are you shouting, *Padre*?" he asked innocently.

Crimson with rage, João Manuel cried, "I asked you something! *Now, what is this?*"

De Henrique smiled to cover his uncertainty. "Is this a test, *Padre*, to see how much I know about Jewish practices? Those are *mezuzos*, which you know as well as I do."

The monks surrounding the two Inquisition leaders began to feel uneasy. Though they were aware of the conflict between the two, they had never seen it erupt into open hostility before. They gazed with wondering eyes on the head priest, who was waving a pair of Jewish *mezuzos* in the air and arguing vehemently with the Holy Office secretary.

In a voice shaking with suppressed fury, João Manuel turned to the spectators. "Let me tell you what happened last night. Perhaps you will be able to explain it to me." As he paused for air, de Henrique began moving away from the circle of onlookers, muttering, "After the way you just abused me in public, *Padre*, I have no desire to hear your stories."

But João Manuel was not ready to let him go. Grasping the secretary by the arm, he snapped, "You will remain here until I finish, is that understood?"

The monks were appalled. The quarrel between their two superiors seemed to have escalated to unheard-of heights. They still did not understand what was happening. What, exactly, was this all about?

"Maybe it was one of you," the *padre* thundered at the small crowd. "One of you who broke into my house last night. His face was masked, but he was a young monk. The wretch entered my house when I wasn't there — and tried to plant these there!"

The men glanced at each other in open stupefaction, eyes darting from João Manuel's furious red face to de Henrique's frozen one.

"When I tried to stop him, he struck me. *Me,* head of the Inquisition! Do you hear?"

Only now did his audience note the jagged red scar on his face. No one uttered a syllable. De Henrique was silent as a tomb.

Padre João Manuel felt privately satisfied with the way things were going. He knew that the story would spread. From this building it would eventually disseminate to all of Lisbon. Everyone would hear of the foul plot — and of who had been behind it. Perhaps it would even come to the ears of the king and his advisors. Such a story could only assist João Manuel in his struggle against the secretary.

"The young monk," he added softly, "would not have dared to undertake such a thing on his own initiative. Someone must have put him up to it."

His audience continued to listen in silence. They simply did not know what reaction would be most appropriate at this moment. Those who stood at the outer edges of the circle began inching discreetly away. But de Henrique's booming voice reached even them:

"I promise you that an investigation will be launched. The truth must come out!"

To his astonishment, *Padre* João Manuel broke into a broad smile. In a voice that was suddenly friendly, harboring no trace of his anger of a few minutes earlier, he said, "My dear Paulo, perhaps you are willing to conduct the investigation on my behalf. You, I am certain, will succeed in unearthing the whole truth." Breaking into laughter, he ended mockingly, "Yes, yes, Paulo. You're the only one who can unearth the real story!"

With that, he turned to the wide staircase that led into the Inquisition building. The other monks hurriedly melted away. Only de Henrique, after a moment's shock, followed João Manuel. He caught up with him halfway up the stairs.

"You devil," he hissed into João Manuel's ear, too quietly for anyone else to hear. "You will pay dearly for your attempt to humiliate me in front of the other monks."

"We shall see who will pay," João Manuel answered calmly, but with a dangerous glitter in his eye. "Did you really think I wouldn't figure out who had tried to plant those *mezuzos* in my house? Do you really think the good lord does not see all the miserable things that you perpetrate, you — you criminal spiller of innocent blood!"

He shoved de Henrique lightly but with great scorn. But the secretary, by catching hold of João Manuel's cassock, managed to regain his balance and save himself from the ignominy of a fall.

⇒⤆

Roberto Gonzales ran his hands along the walls of the tunnel beneath Fernando de Lima's house. He walked slowly in the pitch darkness. The air seemed thinner and it was difficult to breathe. He knew he must continue straight on until he reached the rock wall opposite, as the judge had instructed him. The going was hard. The floor was pitted, causing him to trip and pitch forward time and again. Each time, he rose with pounding heart and forced himself onward. In one of these falls he hurt his foot, and managed the rest of the journey at a limp. On his back he bore the case with the gold coins remaining in his possession, and the letter on which their hopes for Don Carlos' rescue rested.

It was hard to tell how much time had passed. It felt like days. Just when Roberto was feeling utterly drained from the difficult underground trek, his nerves stretched to the screaming point, his hands encountered the wall he'd been waiting for. There was no way to go on from here.

He sat down on the floor to wait. In the pitch blackness he had no idea what his surroundings looked like. Somewhere not far away he heard the trickle of water. Something crawled over his leg. Robert shook it off and leaped to his feet, despite his injury and his weariness. Had it been a snake? He must be careful. Impatiently he peered into the impenetrable darkness. When would Fernando's man come?

He was beginning to regret that he'd undertaken this dangerous mission. When he'd left Amsterdam, he had not dreamed that he'd meet up with such adventures. Here in this cold, clammy, midnight-black tunnel, he felt anew the beauty of his Jewish life in Amsterdam. Would he ever see it again?

Suddenly, he felt a trembling all around him — like an earthquake. Without stopping to think, he murmured, *"Shema Yisrael, Hashem Elokeinu, Hashem Echad."* It took him several moments to realize that it was only the rock upon which he was leaning that had begun to move. Roberto leaped backward. The rock face yawned open. A beam of weak light penetrated the black tunnel. Roberto closed his eyes.

When he opened them, he saw a man standing before him. He was dressed in the garb of a Dominican priest.

50

Fernando de Lima woke unrefreshed from a troubled slumber. The early sunshine creeping over the walls of his room told him that in just an hour or two the Inquisition tribunal was due to appear before him.

He felt his upcoming decision as an enormous pressure. Today he must decide whether or not to endorse Don Carlos' death sentence. In past years of presiding over the Superior Court, he'd often had no choice but to uphold such sentences. In his heart he had wept each time he was forced to sign the death warrants of his fellow Jews. He knew he had no choice, and that the Inquisition would find other means of murdering their victims, even without his authorization. On occasion, he'd managed to use his exalted position to save a life — and he swore to himself that he would try to do the same for Don Carlos.

He must succeed! Don Carlos was too important to the small Marrano community in Lisbon to be lost now. Roberto Gonzales' arrival from Amsterdam, and the important letter he'd brought with him, had ignited fresh hope in Fernando. This time, it seemed, the Inquisition judges themselves were not sure of their ground. Even according to their own evil laws, they always attempted to demonstrate that theirs was an authentic justice. The victim's confession was important, but the main thrust of their case lay in the testimony of neutral witnesses who had caught the accused practicing Judaism. In Don Carlos' case — and the Inquisition men knew this well — such testimony simply did not exist.

The only thing that did exist was the note...

Fernando rose from his bed and dressed. The carriage would be here soon, to convey him to the ornate hall that housed the Superior Court. He must be ready to leave. He went into the kitchen and ate breakfast — some small pastries he found on the table – while his mind mulled over Gabriel Monteiro's failure to find the note for him.

The question had haunted him all night: Where could the note be? He must lay his hands on it at any price. Without that note, he would find it impossible to set in motion the plan he'd devised in the wee hours of the morning. There must be a reason it was missing from the investigative file. Where was it?

His thoughts turned to de Henrique. He felt certain that the cunning priest was hiding something from him. De Henrique, he knew, would battle like a lion for the pleasure of seeing Don Carlos tied to the stake. Why did he hate the man so much? Perhaps, Fernando thought, it stemmed back to the fact that it was Don Carlos who'd been instrumental in helping de Henrique obtain the post of Holy Office secretary. Human nature was ungrateful, often returning bad for good... but to this extent?

Fernando folded his papers and thrust them into his leather briefcase before making his way to the front door. His wife was still asleep, and he saw no reason to awaken her merely to say good-bye.

The carriage had not yet arrived. The sky was blue, and in the boughs of the trees, birds twittered their morning song. But Fernando was in no mood for enjoying the beauties of nature. The day's events loomed ahead of him with troubling uncertainty. He only hoped that Jose de Melo would fulfill his part of the plan. Right now, Jose de Melo represented Fernando's great hope.

All at once, he stiffened in surprise. Every other thought fled as he stared at the place where, a second earlier, he had distinctly glimpsed a man's head. The head had promptly disappeared behind the broad trunk of a tree as soon as Fernando fixed his eyes on it. Suddenly he noticed a young man strolling, apparently aimlessly, in the street in front of his house. And a third was watching him from the roof of a partially constructed building on the other side of the road...

"Something's happened," he thought. Had Gabriel Monteiro talked? Had he told anyone what Fernando had asked him to do?

His first instinct was to rush back into his house. But it was too late...

⁓⦆⦆⁓

Roberto Gonzales stood paralyzed at the sight of the Dominican priest standing by the steps leading to the tunnel. Who was he? Had the Inquisition had him followed? He recalled now that Fernando had never told him just who would meet him at the tunnel's end. Had he deliberately sent a priest? A more awful thought struck him: Had — had it been a mistake to trust the judge? Had Fernando himself betrayed him?

No! Impossible! Roberto rejected the idea vehemently. As for Fernando's wife, though, it was definitely possible. She'd been furious enough at his visit to her house...

"I am Jose de Melo," the man said softly.

Roberto Gonzales kept quiet. He still did not know who the man was. Jose de Melo? The name told him nothing.

The other man sensed his fear. "You have nothing to be anxious about, *meu irmao* (my brother). Our brother in faith, Fernando de Lima, sent me here to you."

He extended his hand to Roberto. After a brief hesitation, Roberto took it and allowed himself to be led upward. He found himself presently in the central room of a well-furnished house, with an expensive chandelier dangling from the ceiling. The chairs and cupboards, too, spoke of great wealth. He looked around, while Jose de Melo watched him closely.

"Is this your house?" Roberto asked.

"No."

"Where am I?"

Jose smiled. "At a great distance from the judge's house. You are safe here and have nothing to fear."

Robero was still not satisfied. "To whom does this house belong?"

Again Jose smiled. "It is ours."

"What do you mean, 'ours'?"

"Ours — the Jews'."

"Yes," Roberto said impatiently. "But who lives here?"

Jose de Melo explained, "No one lives here permanently. This house is located at the edge of the city. There are tunnels from many other homes that all lead here. It is an easy place from which to flee the city in times of danger. Do you understand?"

"Am I to understand from this that I'm not staying here?"

"Apparently not. It depends." De Melo paused. "Fernando described your interesting letter to me. May I see it?"

Tension gripped Roberto once again. Involuntarily, his fingers massaged the leather of his case, as though afraid it would be taken from him again. It was only with great effort that he managed to master his fear.

Jose quickly crossed to the door and locked it. He drew the curtains, plunging the room into near-darkness. Then he lit the oil taper that was waiting on the table. The flickering light cast a faint illumination over the whole room.

"I don't want to attract any attention," Jose explained. "We must remain here until nightfall. Then we will leave, traveling north."

"North?! Why?"

"We must rescue Don Carlos. Traveling northward is part of the plan."

"Is that what Fernando ordered?" Roberto asked in surprise.

"Yes, yes, he's given me his instructions."

"Why? And how is this connected to Don Carlos?"

"Don't worry! We will be coming back from there. The G-d of the Jews will come to our aid."

Roberto peered into Jose de Melo's face, trying in vain to read something there. "I don't understand."

"You will." Jose gestured towards a pair of chairs drawn up to the table. "And now, if you please — the letter that you brought from Amsterdam."

≈⟊⟊

"Quiet — they're coming!"

Don Carlos moved quickly to the other side of the cell, while Yitzchak de Castro rolled into his corner. The dark corridor was suddenly lit by torchlight, piercing the gloom from afar. Heavy, confident footsteps descended the stairs to the dungeon. The footsteps moved closer. The prisoners waited.

Then two monks were standing just outside their cell.

For Don Carlos, the next few moments seemed to stretch into eternity. He closed his eyes, the better to conquer the terror that seized his heart at the prospect of further torture.

He heard the scrape of the iron key in the lock. The hinges squeaked as the door was pulled back. He knew that the priests must be standing inside the cell now. With clenched fist, he made a silent vow never, never to betray his friend Fernando de Lima to de Henrique. No pressure in the world could make him do that. De Henrique would probably try once more to extract information from him before sending him on to the torture room. Don Carlos made up his mind not to yield. He would not betray his friend, or his G-d!

"Don Carlos?"

Don Carlos stopped breathing.

It couldn't be — the voice he'd expected to hear. No. It wasn't de Henrique's voice... He opened his eyes slowly, and in the light of the torch he saw, standing above him, the familiar figure of the Inquisition head himself: his former friend, *Padre* João Manuel.

"Don Carlos?"

"*Sim, padre.*"

"I wish to speak to you, in your final days of life on this earth!" João Manuel turned to the monk who had accompanied him and said, "Wait outside. I will not be long."

The monk left the cell and retreated down the corridor. Don Carlos wondered what was coming next.

The question, when it came, took him by surprise. "Has de Henrique visited you here recently?"

At first, Don Carlos did not know what to answer — or rather, which answer would serve him best.

At last, with difficulty, he murmured: "Yes."

51

The three monks who had kept a watchful eye on the de Lima residence for the past few hours charged forward to intercept the judge. They wore long black cassocks. On their heads each wore a hood that concealed most of the face. Two slits allowed a pair of dark, suspicious eyes to peer out.

Fernando knew who they were. These men were part of a special corps that de Henrique had organized to do the sort of work that was illegal, even by Inquisition standards. Their job was to stalk respectable citizens — especially those who enjoyed the protection of the king.

They were a fierce, cruel band. These monks feared no one and no thing, and would not hesitate to act even against the heads of state themselves. They were completely anonymous. Because it was impossible to identify them, it was also impossible to lodge a complaint against their activities. De Henrique always vigorously denied that the men were his, but no one believed him. The city held him in considerable fear because of his band of loyal henchmen; and because of that fear, de Henrique had gained considerable power in the capital city.

They swooped at Fernando de Lima, who was running with all his might in the direction of his house. On the path, just in front of the front door, they caught him. De Lima struggled only a moment. He was older and less fit. He could not defend himself against these sturdy, hooded monks.

Two of them grasped him roughly by the arms, while a third came to stand in front of him. Fernando began to regret that he'd attempted to flee. He should have stood his ground, giving them the proud, haughty stare of a man who knew his own worth. His instinctive break into a run had raised the finger of suspicion against him. Any fear he betrayed could only benefit them.

Fernando decided to do what he could to salvage the situation. With a sudden jerk, he freed his arms from the monks' grip. His hand shot out to seize the hood of the monk closest to him and tried to pull it off so that he could identify the man. Before he could do more than lift it an inch or two, a second monk dealt his hand a heavy blow. Immediately, his arms were pinioned again, more tightly this time, and twisted behind his back. An intense pain shot through him Shaking with rage, he cried, "You devils! Have you forgotten who I am?"

Their only response was to twist his arm further. Fernando felt himself utterly humiliated. "Do you think this crude attack will be permitted to pass unchallenged? You are mistaken!"

They said nothing, and their grip never slackened.

"Do you think I don't know who sent you here? He will soon feel the strength of my arm!" Fernando thundered.

The frightening silence continued.

"I will speak to His Majesty, the king, this very day. You will rot in jail."

Still the monks did not react. The one standing in front of Fernando signaled to the other two, who began pushing him toward the front door of his house, and through it.

Inside, they sat him down and then released him. The hooded trio stood in a menacing semicircle around Fernando. Keenly aware of his helplessness, he waited to hear what they had to say.

"We wish to speak with the stranger you've brought into your home." The speaker's voice was muffled behind the hood he wore.

Fernando was stunned. How did these men know about Roberto Gonzales? Apparently, de Henrique had told them. After catching the "thief," the trickster must have remained near the house, observing everything that transpired here last night. He had seen the "stranger" — that is, Roberto Gonzales — enter Fernando's house...

And perhaps it was he, too, who had peeked through the window and seen Roberto seated at Fernando's table? Fear crept into his heart. If that was the case, the situation was not good. If the face at the window — the one who had seen Roberto in his house — was de Henrique himself, the situation was, in fact, ominous. Fernando was near despair.

But his captors saw nothing of his inner turmoil. His impassive countenance held only scorn.

"Now I understand!" the judge said. "I knew immediately that you'd attacked the wrong person. I'll be glad to elaborate further, in person, to the man who sent you here — Paulo de Henrique!"

"We made no mistake," the lead monk said fiercely. "We know exactly whose house we are in. And we know exactly whom we are seeking. Where is he?"

"But there is no stranger here."

"You're lying!"

Fernando lunged furiously to his feet, but strong arms pushed him back down. "You're calling me a liar, you wretched young fool? Aren't you ashamed to lay such an accusation at the door of your country's Superior Court judge?"

"No, I'm not ashamed! I have nothing to be ashamed of — because you are truly a liar. Where is the man who visited this house last night and has not, as of this moment, left it yet? Who is he, and where is he from?"

Fernando recognized these tactics. These men were accustomed to speaking with the greatest disrespect even to the nation's elders. Some of them had once spoken thus to the king's son himself. The royal palace had placed great pressure on the Inquisition to oust those particular monks from the organization's ranks, and they had served long prison terms.

"I must ask you to remember, dear young men: My name is Fernando Jorge Silvia de Lima, Superior Court judge. If you didn't know that fact yet, know it now, and try to speak more courteously." He made a conscious effort not to infuriate the monks too much. He knew how dangerous they could be.

"Where is the man?" asked the apparent leader.

"Which man?"

"I will repeat myself: A suspicious stranger is concealed in your home. We wish to ask him a few questions."

Again, Fernando leaped to his feet in anger. "I am not prepared to accept such a blatant disregard of the due process of law! If you have proof to back up your allegations, go ahead and search for him. You may search in the house, in the basement, in the attic, wherever you wish... lawbreakers."

Immediately, the monks left him to disperse throughout the house. Fernando's mocking voice followed them: "When you find him, bring him to me. I would like to have a look at the fellow too!"

⌇

For a long moment *Padre* João Manuel was silent, looking down at Don Carlos. The prisoner was lying on the floor, clad in the orange robe of death.

Other images rose up in the priest's mind, images from Don Carlos' life: the much-admired admiral, riding through Lisbon on his tall white steed. Don Carlos, glory of the navy, intimate of the king. Now here he lay, helpless on the cold cell floor, his body tortured and broken.

João Manuel held his lantern closer, the better to see the face of the man condemned to death. Don Carlos closed his eyes tightly. He had no desire to gaze on the man who had once been his friend and who had betrayed him, throwing him into this dungeon cell on de Henrique's advice. A spark of pity glowed in João Manuel's heart — and was quickly suppressed.

"Don Carlos!" This time, the priest's voice was slightly less harsh.

Don Carlos heard the call clearly, but decided to ignore it. He said nothing.

After a brief hesitation, João Manuel lowered himself to his knees beside the prisoner. He placed his torch on the stone floor. Every line in the prisoner's face was etched clearly in the light.

"How he's aged in these last months," João Manuel marveled inwardly, with a touch of sadness. He called again, softly, "Don Carlos!"

Don Carlos did not open his eyes. If João Manuel wished to speak to him, he would not make it easy for him. Slowly, almost invisibly, he nodded his head as though to signal that he'd heard. João Manuel whispered, "What did de Henrique want from you?"

Don Carlos opened his eyes for an instant. An enigmatic smile touched his lips. The smile enraged João Manuel. Was it meant to signify that he himself had been the topic of de Henrique's conversation in this cell?

"Did he mention my name?" the *padre* asked. He spoke calmly, but Don Carlos detected the tension in his voice.

"No," Don Carlos said slowly, with difficulty. "This time he spoke about the Superior Court judge, Fernando de Lima." After a pause to catch his breath, he added, "That was yesterday. Your Paulo said he would return. Maybe next time he will speak of you."

He felt rather than saw João Manuel start. He was pleased; he'd frightened the priest a bit.

"What business has he with de Lima?"

"He wanted me to testify against him — to accuse him of being a secret Jew. He promised to free me from prison if I did."

João Manuel was agitated. Before he could speak, Don Carlos went on, "What do you think my answer was, *Senhor Padre*?"

The priest did not reply. He suddenly recalled the stroll the two of them had taken on the beach, just days before Don Carlos' arrest. He had told Don Carlos then that the Inquisition was harboring grave suspicion against him. There at the seashore, far from any witnesses, he had suggested that Don Carlos join forces with him against Paulo de Henrique. He had asked Don Carlos to sign a false document accusing de Henrique of the very crimes for which he hunted down others. The document had been calculated to oust the traitorous secretary from the Inquisition ranks forever.

And Don Carlos had declined. While agreeing to work with all his might against de Henrique, he had refused to do anything false or dishonest. In that case, he would obviously not have agreed to cooperate with any plot of de Henrique'.

João Manuel got to his feet, his eyes never leaving Don Carlos. Though he hated the man, he felt a grudging respect for him.

"I understand," he said finally. "But tell me. Today, after all that de Henrique's done to you, don't you regret that you didn't help me get rid of him?"

"No!" Don Carlos was surprised at his own vehemence.

João Manuel regarded him another moment, then turned and left the cell, taking the light with him.

Jose de Melo read Roberto's letter with great interest. When he was done, he rose to his feet, smiled and said, "Wonderful! With G-d's help, I think we will succeed!"

Going over to a built-in cupboard in the wall, he pulled out a novice priest's robe. "Put it on," he ordered Roberto Gonzales.

"Why?"

"Because, my friend, these next few days you are going to be a priest. Do you still remember your Catholic prayers?"

"What must I do?"

Jose de Melo ignored the question. He continued issuing his instructions: "Right now, it's dangerous for you to leave during the daylight hours. Tonight a carriage will come to convey us to Oporto, in the north. Don't worry, I'll be traveling with you."

"I understand. But what is the purpose of the trip?"

"The Inquisition has eyes everywhere. From what I hear, they are looking for you already. You must disappear as quickly as possible from this area. Oporto's Marrano community will look after you."

"And what of Don Carlos? And the letter?"

"I do not yet know how," de Melo answered, "but a solution will be found." He paused, then added softly, "The plan is to send the Bishop of Oporto with the letter. He's one of ours."

Jose de Melo regarded Roberto with laughing eyes, eyes that seemed to whisper: We know many secrets...

52

The trio in black dispersed rapidly throughout the house. Fernando heard them overturning furniture and opening cupboards, before running down in the direction of the basement. He himself remained where they'd left him, in the center of the room. He was still reeling at the gall of those young men, breaking openly into his home. De Henrique's hand, he thought grimly, was clearly at work here.

The Holy Office secretary had decided, apparently, to come out openly against him. Fernando could follow his reasoning in sending his henchmen here today. Their job was to frighten him, to break his spirit, to undermine his confidence as Superior Court judge. In this way, de Henrique doubtless hoped in his black plot-ridden heart, he could intimidate de Lima into signing Don Carlos' death sentence, with no questions asked.

Fernando wondered — he shivered at the thought — what would have happened had the men in black actually discovered Roberto Gonzales in his house. The probable scenario was not hard to envision. De Henrique would have used the incident to publicly denounce him, possibly even to the point of accusing him outright of being a secret Jew. To his own great good fortune — or so, at any rate, he fervently hoped — Roberto was presently in safe hands.

Still, the situation was troubling. A creeping exhaustion overwhelmed him. Life in the city was growing daily more fraught with danger. Where would it all end?

With a resounding crash, the bedroom door opened. His wife ran out, eyes wide with a rage that almost bordered on madness. The men in black, it seemed, had not awakened her gently.

"It's all because of the strangers you let into our house!" she screamed.

Fernando went over to her quickly and placed a strong hand over her mouth, hissing, "Quiet now! They're still here, in the house!"

She subsided at once, groping for a chair and literally collapsing onto it. It seemed to her husband, observing anxiously, that she was on the point of fainting. Instead, she covered her face with both hands and sobbed quietly, "Why are you doing this to us? Don't you know that they follow you more often than any other person in this city?"

Fernando regarded her with deep compassion. It was a pity that, because of her profound fears, she was unable to accept the fact that Fernando was obliged to carry on the job that Don Carlos had been forced to relinquish when arrested... and that observing the Torah and *mitzvos* in secret was worth more than everything else — sometimes even more than life itself. When would she finally understand that the existence of the Jewish people must continue at all cost?

He cocked an ear, but could not discern any sound that would tell him where the searchers were at this moment. He knew that they would find nothing that could incriminate him. Not even the secret tunnel, leading from his home to a house at the city's edge, bore any trace of his hidden identity. The sole pair of *tefillin* that Lisbon's tiny Marrano community owned was well hidden in the hills outside the city, an hour and a half's ride away. From time to time, Jews would slip out there in pairs, one hurriedly donning the *tefillin* while the other kept watch against unexpected company.

Apart from the *tefillin*, the community had one portion of a Torah scroll, which Fernando de Lima's father had rescued from the flames to which a hate-maddened populace had consigned the contents of an extensive Jewish library. This portion lay hidden today in the Inquisition building itself — locked inside a secret cupboard in the room belonging to Alfonso, in charge of the dormitory of young novice monks. No one would ever dream of searching there.

Once a year, several days before Pesach, Alfonso would remove it from its hiding place and carry it to a concealed spot in the hills outside Lisbon, where the Marranos secretly gathered to conduct their Pesach *seder*. The *seder* always took place three days before the actual date on the Jewish calendar: The Inquisition spies knew very well which was the actual date. On that day, their eyes were peeled for any citizens reported missing from their work places, or immured mysteriously inside their homes.

Despite his attempts to reassure himself, Fernando's heart remained weighted with worry. Where were de Henrique's goons now? The house was not especially large; they ought to have completed their search by this time. Had they managed to locate the entrance to the tunnel?

From behind the hands that concealed her face, his wife's muffled voice came again: "Why, Fernando, are you not more careful? Why? Why? Why? You'll be the ruination of us!"

Once again, Fernando signaled forcefully for silence. If the enemy heard her, the end would indeed be upon them.

At that moment a noise came from outside. Fernando froze, and even his wife stopped her wailing to listen. It was the sound of horses' hooves and the rumble of coachwheels. In his shock at this morning's events, Fernando completely forgot that he'd been waiting for the carriage to take him to court.

He roused himself abruptly. "Come quickly!" he called aloud to his wife. "We must go at once to the Superior Court."

She gazed at him in bewilderment. She had never traveled to court with him before, and in general rarely left the house at this time of day. But Fernando did not wait for her reply. Seizing her by the hand, he virtually dragged her after him, muttering, "If you stay here, they're liable to arrest you. Don't you understand?"

"Why?" she gasped.

"They won't find the visitor from Amsterdam. When that happens, they might try to take revenge on you — especially when they see that I've left the house as well."

They reached the outer gate. "L-let go of my hand," she said breathlessly. "You're hurting me."

"I'm sorry. Now hurry — into the carriage!"

Just before she entered the carriage, she managed to whisper, "But when did he leave, that nemesis of ours, your visitor from Amsterdam?"

Fernando was angry at the way she'd worded the question, but he made no reference to it. Instead, as he climbed after her into the coach, he answered, "He did not leave the house. You know very well where he is."

She threw him a quick look of comprehension, and fell silent.

Fernando locked the carriage door. The coachman lifted his whip, flicked it lightly over the horses' backs, and they began galloping forward.

The ride, a brief one any day, was rendered even shorter this morning. The horses did their job faithfully, bringing Fernando to court in record time. He did not wait, as was his custom, for a courthouse lackey to open the door for him. Instead, under the startled eyes of various courthouse staff, he leaped from the carriage like a much younger man. "Wait here," he called softly to his wife.

He turned to the nearest man. "Quickly!" the judge commanded. "Bring me Manuel Soarez Lagrates!"

Manuel Soarez Lagrates was the king's appointee in charge of internal security in Lisbon. Together with a small elite corps, he maintained order throughout the city. Lagrates and his men were at hand wherever any disturbance of the peace was expected.

Fernando hurried to his office. Barely taking the time to sit, he unscrewed the lid of his inkwell, dipped in the gold tip of his quill, and began rapidly and smoothly filling the page lying before him on the desk. From the courtyard, he heard the thunder of hooves. Going to the window, he saw Manuel Lagrates leap off his horse and dash into the building. Just moments later, the two men clasped hands in a firm handshake.

Fernando handed Lagrates the paper he'd been writing on. "This," he said grimly, "is an official arrest warrant."

Manuel Soarez Lagrates took it from him impassively. "Against whom?"

"I wish I knew! If you hurry, you'll catch them. Three men dressed in black are rampaging through my house. They also attempted to harm my wife and me."

"I will do my best, *Senhor O Juiz* (Your Honor)!" Manuel Lagrates clicked his heels together and bowed respectfully before de Lima.

Soon after, Fernando saw ten young horsemen gallop away in the direction of his house. Inwardly, and with great fervor, he prayed that his enemy's evil plot would be foiled.

≈⊃⊂

Paulo de Henrique sat alone in his office, tense and irritable. *Padre* João Manuel, it seemed, had seen through his little trap. How? Had the monk, João Batista, performed as he'd been ordered? He must meet up with his underling quickly, in order to learn exactly what had happened in João Manuel's house last night.

Meanwhile, his superior had succeeded in humiliating him in the Inquisition courtyard, in front of all the monks and priests who had come there to pursue their work and their studies. Today, the victory had been João Manuel's. But it would be a brief victory! De Henrique clenched his fist and swore to continue fighting until he'd conquered them all. All!

In just an hour they were due at the Superior Court. De Henrique had good reason to hope that Judge de Lima would not be presiding with his usual arrogant self-confidence. De Henrique's plan was to bring along to the court the stranger he'd seen in de Lima's house the night before. He'd sent some of his most talented men to the judge's home, and was certain they'd do the job right. He smiled now, picturing de Lima's shocked face when he saw his archenemy in the company of that man. He, de Henrique, would be master of the situation. De Lima would do exactly as he was bidden. He would endorse Don Carlos' death sentence without delay.

And after that, de Henrique thought with anticipation, he would think about what to do with the great judge himself...

He struggled to his feet and went to the corner cupboard to fetch Don Carlos' dossier. It was very thick, containing every detail of the investigation, including a copy of the text of the note he'd received from Pedro Alvares, Don Carlos' aide.

He went back to his desk and seated himself, but the anxiety would not subside. "João Batista!" he whispered aloud. "What have you done to me?" The failure of his grand plot against João Manuel gnawed at his heart. By bad luck, João Manuel had found the *mezuzos* that were meant to have been planted in his house. De Henrique had planned to have the cleaning woman 'find' them. She would then testify to what she'd discovered, and the wheel of accusation would be set in motion!

Now all was lost. *Padre* João Manuel would be more careful in the future. And who knew what stratagem João Manuel would now devise against *him*?

He couldn't sit still. Again, he rose from his chair. It was growing late, and his men had not yet returned from de Lima's house. Impatiently he drew aside the heavy curtain at the window to see if they'd arrived.

The outer gate was wide open and a carriage was speeding wildly through. De Henrique rejoiced to see it. He saw his men leap down to the ground and sprint for the stairs leading into the building.

Then he stopped smiling. His henchmen were alone. Where was the stranger they'd been set to catch and bring back? Where was the man he'd seen in Fernando de Lima's house? What had happened?

Had his plans been foiled again?

53

Outside the cell, *Padre* João Manuel felt the full force of his anger against Don Carlos. He waited a moment to regain his self-control, then slowly turned back and stepped inside the cell again. Haughty eyes gazed down his nose at the prisoner, prone on the cell floor. To Yitzchak de Castro, huddled in his corner, the priest paid no attention at all. But de Castro, for all his seeming indifference, was keenly aware of the scene being enacted in his cell. He followed with interest the strange conversation between the Inquisition head and the imprisoned admiral who was slated to be executed a few days hence.

"You were known as a clever man, Don Carlos!" The words emerged from João Manuel's mouth like stones, sharp and hard. "And now, in these most fateful moments of your life, you stand revealed as a man without sense! A fool! *Nao acredito!* (Unbelievable)!"

Though Don Carlos had decided to reject any offer of cooperation with João Manuel — especially if it involved bearing false witness — he was extremely curious. What, in fact, did the illustrious priest want from him?

Don Carlos had decided long before that, as a Marrano in Portugal, and particularly because of his high profile as admiral of the navy and an intimate of the king's, it would be difficult for him to observe the *mitzvos* between man and G-d as fully as he would have liked. But at least, he'd vowed to himself, he would do everything in his power to observe the *mitzvos* that obligated him toward his fellow man. Not even at this critical juncture would he save his life by trespassing on Hashem's commandments. As he had understood from his reading of *Tanach* — and also from Rav Menashe ben Israel's *Consoliador*, buried in his garden back home — it was G-d's will that a person act with righteousness toward his fellow man. Thinking of this, he blurted a few carefully chosen words that he knew João Manuel would recognize: "*Midvar sheker tirchak* (Distance yourself from falsehood)!"

The *padre* gripped his blazing torch until his fingers hurt. Rage threatened to consume him entirely. In his imagination he pictured himself hurling the torch into the prisoner's face, in a private *auto-da-fé* three days ahead of schedule. His anger was kindled further by the peace he saw in that face. Did Don Carlos think he wished to return to that talk on the beach, when João Manuel had urged him to forge a document that would accuse de Henrique of being a secret Jew?

"*You* talk of lies? You, master trickster that you are, enveloping your whole life in a tissue of lies! Pretending outwardly to be a loyal Christian, while secretly being an accursed Jew! Is *that* not lying? Is *that* not trickery?"

João Manuel was shouting, his voice reverberating along the corridor that was normally deathly silent. Yitzchak de Castro cowered more deeply in his corner. It was not wise to infuriate their cruel captors like this. He glanced apprehensively at Don Carlos.

The priest's heavy breathing cut through the ensuing silence. For several long minutes no one spoke. The tension was palpable in the tiny cell. The burning torch threw tongues of light onto the wall, where they played like waves in a gentle sea.

At last, João Manuel broke the silence: "To destroy the lie that is destroying this city — that is no lie! That is truth!" He spoke more quietly now. "To destroy the enemy of Lisbon's citizens is no sin. Our 'friend,' Paulo de Henrique, is indeed such an enemy. Do you hear me? An enemy! By his actions, he has terrorized the city, turned every man into a betrayer of his neighbor, and wiped the joy from every heart. Even in the royal court they tremble before him. He has set fear loose to rule our lives. Do you know what that is like, Don Carlos?"

Don Carlos still did not answer. What arrant nonsense the man was talking. They'd imprisoned him, tortured him, and were due to burn him alive in a few days' time — and João Manuel spoke of the fear that ruled the city? Why had he not remembered that fear and de Henrique's part in it when they'd brought him, Don Carlos, to trial? Why hadn't João Manuel rescued him then from de Henrique's powerful arm? Where had his compassion been? And besides, wasn't the head of the Inquisition equally guilty of terrorizing Lisbon?

He would not ask these questions aloud.

Don Carlos tried to sit up. Leaning against the cell wall, a sharp pain shot through his chest and traveled down to his feet. His eyes tried to gaze directly into João Manuel's. A small smile played deliberately about his lips. The smile was meant to tell the priest that his spirit was not broken, though his body might be. He remembered the question he'd been asked earlier: "Did de Henrique mention my name?" Something had happened. *He's afraid*, he thought. João Manuel obviously felt that de Henrique was operating against him. How to learn more?

He asked, "Has Paulo accused you of being a Jew? As... As he accused me?"

Padre João Manuel reacted quickly. "No! Why do you think that?"

The secret smile crossed Don Carlos' face again, as he replied, "Because you are afraid. You are afraid of him!"

"That is a lie, Don Carlos!" The fury was back; Don Carlos had understood him only too well.

"I see." Don Carlos spoke in a placating manner. João Manuel's overstrong reaction proved his theory. The great master trembled before his wily secretary. This was a dangerous moment. He mustn't enrage João Manuel any further. At the same time, Don Carlos felt a twinge of satisfaction at seeing the dread leader of the Inquisition tasting a little of the terror he inflicted on the populace.

Without warning, João Manuel wheeled around, flung open the cell door, and, for the second time, stalked angrily through it. Don Carlos called softly after him: "*Padre!*"

The priest hesitated. He turned, but did not re-enter the cell. Through his teeth, he hissed, "*Sim*(Yes)?"

As he spoke, he moved the torch closer to Don Carlos' face. Don Carlos squeezed his eyes shut against the sudden bright light. However, he recovered rapidly. He said, "*Padre*, you did not come to see me in order to gossip about de Henrique. We've both known what he is like for a long time now. What did you really want from me?"

João Manuel relaxed slightly. He took one step toward the cell. Standing in the doorway, he said softly, "As a clever man, I came to ask you for advice."

"Advice about what?"

"About how to stop de Henrique."

As Don Carlos considered this, João Manuel whispered, "If you'll help me, I'll make sure you're set free."

Then, as Don Carlos continued to keep silent, the priest added, "And if you *don't* help me with some sound advice, you'll be taken back to the torture chamber."

"I was already promised that," Don Carlos answered wearily, "by de Henrique."

"So tell me what to do!"

The silence seemed to João Manuel to stretch for a long time. Finally, Don Carlos said, "I will think about it. Perhaps my G-d will help me — the G-d Who is with me even here, in your dungeon."

Without a word, the *padre* turned away and locked the cell door. Once again, Don Carlos' voice floated back to him.

"*Padre?*"

"*Sim?*"

"*Padre* — where is Pedro Alvares?"

João Manuel's breath caught in his throat. He understood fully well why Don Carlos had asked the question. Pedro Alvares was the only witness against him; now that he'd disappeared, testimony against Don Carlos did not, in fact, really exist.

Up until now, in the interrogation and torture rooms, whenever Don Carlos had inquired into the fate of his nephew, neither he nor de Henrique had answered him. Now João Manuel decided to speak. Perhaps, this way, he would more easily win Don Carlos' cooperation.

"He's disappeared."

"Without... Without testifying against me?"

The *padre* weighed his response. "He vanished immediately after the two of you met in Paulo's office. We have not seen him since. We've searched diligently throughout the country, but it is as though the earth itself has swallowed him up."

Quickly, in order to distract João Manuel from this topic, Don Carlos asked, "Where is my wife? Where are my children?"

"In a safe place. Your wife is in prison. She has not been interrogated yet. We await the outcome of your trial."

"And the children?" Don Carlos persisted.

"In good hands — in the Dominican monastery at Eldorado. Don't worry about them."

But worry was just what Don Carlos did do. João Manuel saw tears roll involuntarily down the prisoner's hollow cheeks.

"*Padre*," Don Carlos said with difficulty, "I have promised you to think about it." He wanted to end the conversation.

With a final glance, João Manuel left. Silence and darkness returned to the cell. The only sound was a slithering one, as Yitzchak de Castro crawled across the floor to Don Carlos' side and stroked his hand gently, as though to offer a meager crumb of comfort in this comfortless place.

<hr />

The men in black burst breathlessly into de Henrique's office. They removed their hoods and breathed deeply, trying to fill their lungs with air so that they could speak. Their eyes, however, spoke volumes.

De Henrique asked in trepidation, "What happened? Speak to me! Why haven't you brought the man back with you? What happened? Why don't you speak?"

One of the trio gestured toward the window. "They... They..." he gasped, then finished, "They're... coming after us."

De Henrique jumped up as though bitten by a scorpion. He rushed up to the monk who had spoken, seized his cassock at the throat, and screamed, "Who are 'they'? Tell me!"

Again, the monk waved ineffectually at the window. At last the words came: "*Padre*, you must save us. We..."

He never got the chance to finish. The door burst open. In the doorway stood Manuel Soarez Lagrates, sword unsheathed, with several of his elite corps behind him. The men in black stopped breathing. There was a moment of utter silence. Manuel Lagrates seemed dumbfounded to find himself in the presence of Lisbon's most powerful figure.

Slowly he returned his sword to its sheath. A few brisk steps brought him face to face with de Henrique. The two men measured each other. Lagrates said in the voice of cold authority, "These three men are under arrest, in the name of the law."

De Henrique pulled himself up. The conflict was truly upon him now.

"Which law, *amigo* (friend)?"

Manuel Soarez Lagrates held up the letter with the arrest order. De Henrique reached out as though to take it from him, but Lagrates pulled his own hand back: He did not want the other to see Superior Judge Fernando de Lima's handwriting on the warrant. De Henrique bristled, fighting down his anger. The eyes of the two men clashed, cold steel on cold steel.

Lagrates snapped, "What were your men doing in the house of His Honor, Judge Fernando de Lima?"

"My men?" de Henrique blustered.

"A fish will swim to deep water when he is in danger. A child will return to his mother's lap... And the men in black run straight into the arms of Paulo de Henrique." Lagrates made no attempt to disguise the mockery in his voice.

He repeated, "I asked you: What were they looking for in the Superior Judge's house?"

Infuriated, de Henrique stepped closer. "I am afraid, my young friend, *Senhor* internal security officer, that you have overstepped your bounds. You have forgotten, it seems, who I am, what my job is — and most especially, what sort of power I hold."

"*Padre*, I have forgotten nothing. At the same time, nothing can justify breaking the law. Did Don Carlos' exalted position help him when he broke the law? No! And so..."

De Henrique broke in roughly. "You are also on Don Carlos' side, just like... like..." He stopped himself just in time. He'd been about to say, "Just like the Superior Judge," but remembered that Manuel Lagrates was very close to de Lima. In fact, his job fell under de Lima's jurisdiction.

Suddenly, a frightening thought struck him. "Did Judge de Lima write out the arrest order?"

But Lagrates was too angry to hear the question. "First of all, *Padre*, what do you mean by accusing me of being on Don Carlos' side? May I have an explanation? How did you reach this conclusion? Do you want to accuse me of being a Jew also, like..."

Now it was Lagrates turn to bite his tongue. He did not utter the name he'd been about to throw at de Henrique. Some three years previously, de Henrique had a good friend of his arrested, the son of one of the city's most prosperous citizens. It had been a false arrest: Lagrates' friend, Jose Consalves Salvador, had been a good Christian all his life. He'd been accused of being a Jew, thrown into prison, stripped of his honor, robbed of his freedom, and tortured long and terribly.

His crime? A *mezuzah* had been "found" in his house...

In the end, Salvador had been released. Manuel Lagrates had sat at his friend's bedside for two days, learning what the Inquisition was really all about. His friend had died before his very eyes...

From that day, Lagrates had hated de Henrique.

The three men in black tried unobtrusively to slip away, but Lagrates' men prevented their leaving. They were pushed rudely back into the center of the room.

The situation, de Henrique realized, was a perverse one. He searched for a way to come to terms with the secular law, but Lagrates' inflexible attitude showed him that any attempt at finding a compromise would be futile. He glanced at the security men by the door. There were four of them, plus their captain. He had his three monks. There was no choice but to fight. He would not surrender to Fernando de Lima's men for the world!

He waved a fist in Lagrates' face. "No one will be arrested in my office! I demand that you leave the Inquisition premises before it's too late!"

Manuel Lagrates' hand shot to his sword hilt. His men did the same.

"That's too bad," Lagrates said harshly. "Your men are coming with me."

"No!"

54

P*adre* João Manuel turned his back on Don Carlos' cell and-walked slowly away down the dark corridor. The steps at the end of the corridor would take him back to the Inquisition building proper. As he went, a burning rage consumed him — a rage directed mostly at himself.

How could he have allowed himself to expose all his deepest fears to that traitor, Don Carlos, a man sentenced to death? Why had he sought out the prisoner at all? What imbecility! Hot shame filled his heart. How would Don Carlos view him now — the head of the Inquisition, the man supposedly all powerful, trembling before him like an autumn leaf? In his fear of what de Henrique might be plotting against him, he had sought the advice of a prisoner. What had made him think Don Carlos could help him?

João Manuel sighed, a deep, shuddering sigh. It was too late to rectify his mistake. It was done. His embarrassment was all encompassing.

He paused at the foot of the stairs to gather his wits, and to fill his lungs. Very soon now, he must appear at the Superior Court alongside the other Inquisition judges, to conclude the Don Carlos case. Superior Judge Fernando de Lima would be presiding. De Henrique would be there too...

Suddenly, a strange desire took hold of the priest: to work for Don Carlos' release, simply in order to balk de Henrique. He smiled bitterly to himself. "A grand idea," he thought. "But Don Carlos must be punished — if only for rejecting my plea for help on the beach that day." Vividly, he recalled the scene so recently enacted in the dungeon cell. "No, Don Carlos must die. He must not live to remember how I humiliated myself before him."

He began climbing. The upper part of the staircase was illuminated with daylight from above. When he reached a point about 10 steps from the top, he came to an abrupt halt. His ears strained to make sense of what he was hearing. There was noise —a tumult — a medley of cries completely alien to the stately halls of this building, in which all were expected to conduct themselves with the reserve and dignity due to their calling.

Slowly he resumed his climb, listening all the while. From what he could make out, some sort of squabble seemed to have erupted among the monks. At the very head of the stairs, he paused uneasily. It seemed to him that there were unfamiliar voices mingled with the others. Had strangers entered the building? What was happening?

Padre João Manuel straightened his shoulders. He must exude an air of authority. His appearance must inspire respect and confidence. Quickly he smoothed the folds of his cassock and brushed away the dust of the prison cell. Last, he adjusted the jeweled cross that hung upon his chest. The dejection that had engulfed him from the moment he'd left Don Carlos suddenly vanished. He must appear every inch the leader.

Unconsciously he held his head high as he stalked through the door into the building. The tension that had held him fast just moments earlier had dissipated. The old self-confidence surged in his veins. With every step, the commotion grew louder.

At first he saw no one. The corridor was deserted. He could not even hear the usual hushed footsteps of the monks as they passed to and fro on their various tasks. From where, then, was the disturbance coming? His pace quickened.

Gradually, the sounds grew more distinct. Among them, he distinguished the clash of metal on metal. Swords? João Manuel felt a clutch of fear. Sword fighting — in *this* place?

The noise was very loud now. Just another turn in the corridor and he would be upon its source.

Shouting voices came to his ears. "This order is like an order from the king himself, *Padre!*"

João Manuel could not identify the speaker. The words had been uttered harshly and with great force.

"On Inquisition premises," Paulo de Henrique's voice came back clearly, "Fernando de Lima's orders have no weight at all!"

"*Fernando de Lima?*" João Manuel was astonished. "*Is he here? Impossible!*"

He trod silently now. Clearly, something dramatic was taking place near the door of de Henrique's office. What was that serpent up to now? He could hear the heavy breathing of men within. There was a gasping cry: "You won't arrest me, *Senhor!*"

And again, the other voice, just as forcefully: "Your men must come with me at once, *Padre!*"

"Lisbon will rise in flames before you arrest my men, you foul lackey of de Lima's!"

"You are insulting His Majesty himself, *Senhor* de Henrique. That is extremely serious!"

"I command you and your men to leave this building at once! You will meet your punishment yet, for daring to disrupt our holy work. The Inquisition is immune from this sort of harassment!"

The answer was quick and sharp: "Not in this case, *Padre*. We are dealing with a criminal act. I want these men to come with me now. Otherwise, I will send for an entire company of soldiers. Do not humiliate the Holy Office in the eyes of the citizenry."

"ENOUGH!"

The shout burst from João Manuel's lips like an explosion, and echoed along the empty corridor. Silence descended like a curtain. Every head turned in surprise. *Padre* João Manuel stood before them, eyes darting icy arrogance and scorn. The scene that met his eyes was not at all to his liking. What he saw was the plump figure of de Henrique, secretary of the Holy Office, engaged in a shoving match with leader of the King's guards, Manuel Soarez Lagrates.

He tried to divine, without asking, what had led to this disgraceful scene. He took in the guards with drawn swords, and wondered how and why they came to be there. Ranged beside de Henrique were a number of young monks whom João Manuel recognized.They had taken up defensive positions, though whether they were attempting to defend themselves or de Henrique was unclear. The only thing that *was* clear to him — he had gathered as much from the impassioned shouts he'd heard reverberating through the corridor — was the fact that the king's guards had come to arrest somebody. But who?

One of the monks? Perhaps even de Henrique himself! For an instant he allowed himself to taste the joy of such a development... Then, hastily, he banished the foolish thought from his mind.

João Manuel strode toward the group. No one spoke; all waited to hear what he had to say. He smiled.

"*Bem vindo, senhores* (Welcome, gentlemen)! I see we have some important guests today."

No one spoke. Even de Henrique held his tongue.

João Manuel's tone grew slightly more acerbic. "The arrival of guests is very pleasant, but why all the commotion? Eh?"

The men hid behind their silence, as though recognizing the sting that underlay the *padre*'s polite words and broad smile.

"*Senhor* Manuel Soarez Lagrates, have my people not welcomed you as they ought? Has our secretary, Paulo de Henrique, not extended the proper greetings? I find that hard to believe!" And still, his face was stretched in the same scornful smile.

Suddenly, his tone hardened. "Why does no one answer me? I want to know what has been happening here!"

Manuel Soarez Lagrates bowed. Taking up João Manuel's cross, he caressed it reverently.

"*Padre,*" he said, gesturing toward the black-clad monks, "this morning these men broke into the home of His Honor, Superior Judge Fernando de Lima. They threatened him and treated him abusively. The judge fled from his house and ordered me to arrest them. Upon arriving at his home, we found the men attempting to escape. We caught up with them here, in the secretary's office."

Padre João Manuel's eyes darted fire at de Henrique. If he could have done so with impunity, he would have killed the man on the spot. To desecrate the holy church in this way — to heap shame upon the entire Christian faith!

"Here is the signed arrest warrant, *Padre.*" Lagrates held out the order that de Lima had signed. João Manuel did not bother to read it. His eyes remained locked on his dangerous adversary. Then his glance swept de Henrique's three henchmen, who squirmed uncomfortably beneath his scrutiny.

Unexpectedly, João Manuel burst into loud and startling laughter. He fixed his gaze on de Henrique once more.

"Paulo, my friend," he said silkily, "was it one of these men, perchance, who visited my home last night in order to leave me a gift — a *mezuzah*? Or do you have other helpers in this building?"

The men reacted to his words with visible shock. Lagrates blurted incredulously, "Not only the Superior Judge's house — but yours, too, *Padre?*"

As soon as the words had left his lips, Lagrates regretted them. They had only served to heighten the tension. He saw de Henrique's fist clench with fury and nearly rise to João Manuel's face before subsiding at his side.

"*Padre,*" de Henrique hissed between clenched teeth, "I see that everything is to be laid out on the table between us. You have apparently reached the conclusion that the entire city must know of your decision to hound and humiliate me — to cast false aspersions on my name and on my valuable work in the Holy Office."

Again, a scornful smile twisted João Manuel's features. "If that is your wish, Paulo, then so be it. Perhaps, indeed, it would be best if everyone finally heard of your nocturnal activities. Maybe then the honest citizens of this city would learn not to hold you in such awe."

He turned abruptly to Lagrates. "May I see the arrest order?"

Lagrates handed it to him. João Manuel read it through carefully, sighed, and said, "Yes, there is no question about it —the law is on your side. I must authorize the arrest of these men."

The trio of black-clad monks reacted with an anger that was heavily mixed with fear. They turned beseeching eyes on de Henrique. But the secretary's face was shuttered. Only his lips, mouthing inaudible words, betrayed any reaction.

João Manuel continued: "I hope it will ultimately be proved that your men are guiltless. That will remove a great potential embarrassment from the Holy Office. Right now, however, we have no other option than to accede to the law."

Though his face remained impassive, João Manuel's heart was rejoicing in triumph. This was indeed a sweet victory against de Henrique! The latter stood immobile as Lagrates' men seized the monks' forearms and marched them out of the building. The corridor was empty once more, and silent. João Manuel and de Henrique remained alone.

João Manuel's face reflected his satisfaction, but de Henrique did not see it. His own eyes were riveted to a remote corner of the ceiling.

"Paulo," João Manuel said softly. "You understand that I was forced to let them take the men. It would be dangerous to anger Fernando de Lima right now."

De Henrique did not answer, nor did he meet his superior's eyes.

João Manuel's eyes were bright and mocking as he purred, "In fact, we're due to see him very soon. You remember the Don Carlos case, I'm sure?"

At that moment, de Henrique felt as though he would gladly give the world for a chance to clobber the Inquisition leader over the head with all his might!

55

ernando de Lima stood at the window of his chambers, looking out on the broad street leading up to the courthouse. Though he stood as if carved from marble, there was little peace in him. This morning's episode outside his house had reminded him with cruel emphasis how unbearable the lives of the Marranos in Lisbon were becoming.

It had always been necessary to exercise extreme caution in practicing even the few *mitzvos* they were able to observe. But lately it seemed to him that they sat on the summit of a veritable volcano — one that was likely to erupt, Heaven forbid, at any moment. The city's gentile population had not yet recovered from the shock of discovering that Don Carlos was a secret Jew... Or so, at any rate, the Inquisition opinion-makers and Sunday morning preachers would have them believe.

As Superior Court judge, Fernando de Lima was ever careful not to pour oil on already troubled waters — not to feed the hatred that simmered against the Jews in Lisbon. The attack by the black-clad monks near his home this morning boded ill for the future.

He breathed deeply, never shifting his eyes from the street below.

Captain Manuel Soarez Lagrates and his men should return at any moment. Had they succeeded in arresting de Henrique's henchmen? The wait was growing intolerable. And still, the street remained devoid of all but a few stray passers-by, intent upon harmless business of their own. The trees that lined both sides of the street blocked the view farther up.

Impatiently, he left the window and began pacing the length of the spacious room. He walked with his head down, staring unseeing at the thick rug that muffled his steps, and allowed his racing thoughts to charge through his mind unimpeded. Had it been a mistake to call the king's internal security guards into action? In doing so, he had openly contested de Henrique's authority. What would his reaction be? He must not forget for an instant that, despite his outward guise of Catholicism, he was in reality a secret Jew, and so in constant and imminent danger of exposure.

The pretense was meticulous. Fernando faithfully attended church every Sunday. He regularly confessed to his priest — though not, naturally, his greatest "sin" of all — observance of Judaism! He taught a course in religious philosophy at the local university, and had even traveled to Rome to see the pope. And yet, Fernando knew that no one was immune from suspicion in these dark days. Look how they'd caught Don Carlos!

He came to the conclusion that calling in Lagrates' men had been the right move. If they succeeded in catching the monks red-handed, it would be a heavy blow, maybe even a mortal one, for de Henrique. Perhaps G-d, in His mercy, would even arrange for de Henrique to be removed from his exalted post! Many people — and loyal Christians among them — would breathe easier the day de Henrique stepped down from the Holy Office.

Abruptly he paused in midstride, eyes glued to the ornate gold chandelier hanging from the ceiling, though he saw nothing. He thought of his wife, whom he'd sent to the home of a friend in the city with strict instructions to stay away from their home. Would it be best if he sent her out of the city entirely before the situation worsened? They had a pleasant residence near Coimbra, a vacation home that no one in Lisbon knew about. She could hide there, and if it became necessary he could flee there, too.

A light rap at the door interrupted the train of his thoughts. A young man entered. He stood before de Lima without speaking, expectant.

"*Bom dia* (Good morning), Orlando," Fernando greeted him in a perfectly natural voice that gave away nothing of what he'd been thinking this past hour.

"*Bom dia, Senhor O Juiz* (Good morning, Your Honor)," the young man responded politely.

"Orlando?"

"Sir?"

"Prepare suitable seating arrangements for our honored guests. The illustrious Inquisition delegation is about to arrive. Oh, yes — and bring the law books you'll find on the upper shelf of the archives room."

Orlando heard the mocking overtones in the judge's "honored guests" and "illustrious delegation." Fernando could permit himself a little liberty in his presence, for the young lawyer was the newest member of Lisbon's Marrano community. It had been Fernando who found him this job with the ministry of justice.

Orlando threw the judge a keen, curious glance. "Is this about the Don Carlos case at last?"

"Yes. Don Carlos — at last!"

They exchanged a last, hurried glance that said more than scores of words could have done. Orlando understood that there would be no more postponements, no further delays: Don Carlos' judgment would be handed down today. He knew how very difficult this ordeal was for de Lima, who not only respected Don Carlos as leader of their small band of Marranos, but also loved him as a dear and longstanding friend. And now, in a cruel twist of fate, it was the Superior Judge's job to authorize the heartless decree sentencing Don Carlos to be burned at the stake!

The young lawyer left the room without another word. Finding himself alone once more, Fernando permitted himself the luxury of sinking into an armchair and closing his eyes. Though it was still morning, he was exhausted. He thought again of Lagrates. Today's summation of the Don Carlos case would be considerably eased if he and his men had managed to apprehend the monks in black. De Henrique would be weakened. His attitude would be far less strident and aggressive if he knew that Judge de Lima had won this round. Yes, an arrest would certainly be helpful...

It might, he thought doubtfully, be possible to push off judgment yet a little while longer. He needed time, time to put into action the plan he'd been weaving ever since he read the letter Roberto had brought with him from Amsterdam. For the plan to succeed, he needed a few more days at a minimum.

Right now, though, he couldn't see how he might be able to buy that desperately needed extra time.

And if Lagrates had failed in his mission? If those monks had successfully evaded arrest, de Henrique's arrogance would be increased tenfold! At that prospect, a sharp pain shot through Fernando's stomach. In that case, he would need to call on Hashem's mercy as never before.

He rose and crossed the room to the window. The street below lay empty and quiet. Where was Captain Lagrates? What had happened at his house? Had there been a fight? On the outcome of that fight, Fernando knew, hung — literally — life and death.

He paused, one hand frozen on the window sill as he listened. His ears had picked up the faint *clip-clop* of approaching horses. He narrowed his eyes, the better to see. For a long, agonizing moment he waited, every muscle tense, every nerve quivering.

No. It was not Lagrates. Now he could see three noteworthy carriages. He identified them at once: the Inquisition delegation.

The carriages came to a halt near the courthouse. From each, a coachman jumped down to open the door. Out of the first carriage stepped *Padre* João Manuel, leaning on a young monk's arm. After him came two of the judges who had met with de Lima yesterday, in the Inquisition building.

From the second coach only Paulo de Henrique descended. Fernando waited, but there was no one with him. De Henrique had apparently traveled alone.

The third carriage was carrying a contingent of young monks, all carrying heavy dossiers: the investigative material on the Don Carlos case. Fernando noted with interest that João Manuel made directly for the courthouse door without waiting for his "beloved" secretary to accompany him. He did not even turn his head to see if de Henrique followed.

Then he noticed something else. Judge Gabriel Monteiro da Silvia was not among those present. What had happened? Had Gabriel been caught leaving his house last night? Fernando remembered that Gabriel had left just about the time that de Henrique's men (or had it been de Henrique himself?) had peeked through his window, catching sight of Roberto Gonzales at the table with him.

Or could Gabriel have simply opted not to accompany the delegation this morning — out of anxiety, perhaps, that his nervous manner would arouse suspicion against him?

Fernando didn't know what to think. And in any case, he had a matter of far more pressing concern to occupy his mind just now. *Where was Lagrates?* Could de Henrique have had a hand in his disappearance? Had he had Lagrates and his men arrested? Fernando whispered a short but fervent prayer for salvation to the G-d of Avraham, Yitzchak, and Yaakov, then started slowly for the door. It was time to greet his guests.

In the meantime Orlando had arranged the meeting room to his satisfaction. On a small table beside the judge's dais he arranged the law books Fernando had requested. He filled the judge's inkwell and provided the special parchment on which the judge would render his judgment. De Lima entered the room in advance of the Inquisition men, and stepped up to his place.

As he took his seat, he suddenly wondered where Roberto Gonzales was at this moment, and what he was doing. This was another thing to charge to de Henrique's account. Because of him, Fernando had been forced to leave home in a hurry this morning, before his messengers had the chance to bring news of Roberto. Had he made it to the end of the tunnel? Had the plan been put into execution? Whether or not they would see it through depended in large measure on how successful he, Fernando, was today in stretching out the Don Carlos case.

The tramp of feet sounded outside the door. Orlando hurried to admit the Inquisition group. Those of higher rank entered first, followed by the young monks with their heavy records. All wore expressions of somber gravity, as did Judge de Lima. The memory of yesterday's meeting in the Inquisition chamber hovered phantom-like in the air, contributing to the strained atmosphere.

Gazing down from his dais, Fernando valiantly fought down his feelings of deep anger and loathing. Nothing showed in his face but a preparedness to engage in his life's work of upholding the law.

The delegation found their seats, de Henrique taking his at the far end of the table, at an angle to the judge. He made every effort not to meet de Lima's eyes. His fury knew no bounds. De Lima had foiled his plans: He'd managed to spirit away the stranger he'd been harboring in his home, and had dared call out the king's guards to arrest his, de Henrique's, men. He gritted his teeth, fists clenching and unclenching under the table. He would show this judge just who really ruled Lisbon!

"Christianity will conquer," de Henrique whispered triumphantly in his heart of hearts.

≋

Don Carlos sat sunk in thought. The profound silence that had again enveloped his cell allowed him to muse undisturbed on the doings above his head, in the Inquisition halls. The battle between João Manuel and Paulo de Henrique had apparently reached a head. And somehow, he gathered, his friend Fernando de Lima had become embroiled in the fight. Though João Manuel had made no mention of the judge, de Henrique had been prepared — or at least had said he was prepared — to release Don Carlos in return for his testimony against de Lima.

There was more. João Manuel had, for the first time, openly admitted that Don Carlos' nephew, Pedro Alvares, had never actually testified against him. Don Carlos knew that without direct testimony they were not legally empowered to burn him at the stake. Could the quarrel upstairs possibly revolve around that point? Was his friend, Judge de Lima, making things difficult for them — and was that why de Henrique wished to have him removed from his post?

Perhaps. But de Henrique's concerns did not seem to matter much to *Padre* João Manuel. Why, then, had he visited Don Carlos' cell and supplicated so strangely before him? Strange talk from the mighty Inquisition leader!

Don Carlos rolled over onto his side and peered through the gloom at Yitzchak de Castro. His young cellmate, he saw, was watching him closely. Perceiving that he had Don Carlos' attention, his eyes lit up. Don Carlos extended a hand, and Yitzchak seized it. For a time they remained that way, unmoving and silent.

Then the young man whispered, "How can you help him?"

"I don't know."

"But why does he believe that you can help him?"

"I don't know."

"Why does he want you to help him?"

"I don't know."

"Don Carlos?"

"Yes?"

"Tell me something that you *do* know!"

Don Carlos found himself smiling. He couldn't blame Yitzchak for his curiosity. He had witnessed strange doings here in this cell, and the "all-knowing" Don Carlos refused to tell him what it all meant. He had seen something that surpassed all belief: the dread leaders of the Inquisition, coming down to the dungeon to beg for the help of a man condemned to death! No wonder his young cellmate was bewildered!

"Don Carlos?"

"*Sim?*"

"Are they so unsure of themselves? How can that be?"

Don Carlos answered slowly, "A person who has evil in his heart, who weaves plots and acts in treachery and deceit — though he may succeed for a time — will not derive any pleasure from his actions. Joy and contentment are locked away from him. Uncertainty and fear are his constant companions."

Silence. Then the young man burst out, "Why? Why is it that way?"

Don Carlos patted his hand. "Because only the pure of heart merit G-d's blessing. Only to them does G-d grant peace of mind, genuine happiness, and true security."

"Security... Does that mean, having faith that all will turn out well? That we will be saved from the *auto-da-fé*? That... That we will not be burned at the stake?"

Don Carlos gripped young Yitzchak's hand will all his meager strength. "The poor boy needs so much encouragement," he thought. Aloud, he said, "Yitzchak?"

"Sim, Senhor?"

"Yitzchak, faith in Hashem does not necessarily mean that he will save you. No one alive knows why things happen to him. Having faith means believing that everything comes to us from His hand — and that it comes to us for our good! This kind of faith engenders the kind of security I mean, Yitzchak: the kind that brings peace of mind and true content. Do you understand?"

Yitzchak hesitated, then whispered, "Does that mean that it is forbidden to try to save one's life? Because... Because that is against G-d's will?"

Don Carlos sensed the other's violent trembling. As his impending death loomed ever nearer, the Dutch youth was growing more and more troubled. Don Carlos heaved himself closer to Yitzchak's side: The boy needed to feel his presence, his closeness, now as never before. "We are permitted to do everything we can in order to save ourselves," he said forcefully. "Everything except breaking Hashem's laws. Understand?"

"A — a little."

"Well, what don't you understand?"

The words burst out: "Why can't you help the Inquisition head? Maybe he will help us in return!"

"Because he's asking me to lie! He is demanding that I falsify my testimony, that I say things that aren't true. Our G-d despises falsehood. Haven't you ever heard Rabbi Menashe ben Israel teach — you, Yitzchak, who had the joy of living in Amsterdam?"

Yitzchak de Castro did not answer. Don Carlos heard the soft, heartbreaking noise of his muffled weeping, the only sound in the silence of the cell.

56

Fernando de Lima gazed down on the Inquisition delegation and knew that the battle for his friend's life had truly begun.

Suppressing his anxiety, he opened the proceedings calmly enough. "*Senhores muitos honorarios* (Very honored gentlemen)."

The other men responded with slight nods. Fernando continued: "The case we are called upon to adjudicate today is one of crucial significance to Portugal. Our allegiance to His Majesty, the king, requires us, in judging this matter, to rise above any personal feelings or considerations that might obscure the true course of justice. Today's judgment will have its influence on our realm. If the decision is rendered to burn Don Carlos at the stake in the name of justice and our holy faith — after clearly establishing his guilt, of course — that fact will have a positive impact on the faith of our Portuguese masses. Let us, therefore, make a valiant effort to remove from our minds what must be removed, and to judge the case that the good lord has set before us, in accordance with the tenets of honesty and justice that must always guide our steps."

He paused to breathe and to peer at the Inquisition men, whose veiled eyes met his with blank stares from which he was unable to discern anything.

"*Senhores,*" he finished quietly, "one more thing. I have forgiven what occurred yesterday. My heart is free of pain and shame." Involuntarily, his gaze met de Henrique's. The contempt he read in the other's face told him that de Henrique did not believe a single word he'd just spoken. While the others sat as though carved from stone, de Henrique had shifted restlessly throughout Fernando's speech. Now it was he who spoke out: "Your Honor, the judge!"

Everyone present swiveled around to look at him. Once again, de Henrique had disregarded etiquette and spoken out before his superior. Etiquette, however, had never stopped him before; and it did not stop him now.

"I understand that the honored judge's comments are directed at my own behavior yesterday in the Holy Office courtroom. I deeply regret if, due to overhasty speech, I insulted His Honor, and the honor of law and justice in our land. It is my hope that this apology — tendered at this important moment when the fate of Don Carlos Carneiro is to be decided — will facilitate the smooth course of justice for which we are all hoping."

With a brief nod in the direction of the judicial dais, de Henrique lapsed into silence. Fernando had watched the man closely as he spoke, and had noticed the way de Henrique squinted and shifted his eyes repeatedly so as not to meet his own. The interpretation was not difficult to arrive at: De Henrique was lying. He clearly hoped to gain something from the insincere apology he'd just offered.

Yes, Fernando thought gravely. The war between them had truly begun.

He turned a forgiving face to de Henrique. "Yes, this is an important moment, Paulo. Certainly I accept your apology. It is a sign that we are about to embark on a solemn matter with a sense of high purpose and courage. Yes, courage. It is well known that there is serious opposition in royal circles to the sentence you've handed down against the admiral."

"That is your job," *Padre* João Manuel hastened to state. He would not leave the stage entirely to de Henrique.

Fernando assumed a wounded expression. "I know, *Padre*. I know that it is my job. And now — to the matter at hand."

João Manuel rose. "Most honorable Superior Judge of the realm, I believe the tale of Don Carlos' betrayal of Portugal is well known to you."

Fernando repeated, "Betrayal of *Portugal?*"

"Yes. In Portugal, there is no separation of state and religion. Betrayal of our faith is tantamount to betrayal of His Majesty, Don João IV."

Fernando nodded thoughtfully, while inwardly cursing the man. "Continue," he ordered.

"Accordingly, he was arrested after it came to light that he had secretly visited the home of a rabbi in Amsterdam, the heretic Menashe ben Israel. He has confessed to this."

"Confessed?" Fernando challenged.

"Yes, confessed!

Out of the corner of his eye, Fernando noticed signs of de Henrique's increasing agitation. He lifted a restraining hand, and de Henrique sulkily resumed his seat.

"May I see the protocol of his confession?"

"Certainly, Your Honor." *Padre* João Manuel signaled to two of the monks presiding over the files behind him. One of them brought a dossier up to Judge de Lima's podium and opened it. The monk flipped through a mass of papers until he arrived at the section that dealt directly with Don Carlos' confession of his Judaism.

Fernando could scarcely contain his excitement. He'd been anxious to get a look at his friend's records for a long time. Among other things, he wished to ascertain what, if any, details Don Carlos had confessed about the Marrano underground in Lisbon and throughout Portugal. A deep unease had plagued his Jewish friends since Don Carlos' arrest; indeed — why deny it? — he himself had felt it, too. This morning's intrusion by the monks in black had only served to strengthen Fernando's fear that Don Carlos had broken under torture and revealed their secrets...

He began perusing the documents spread before him. He read of Don Carlos' proud bearing throughout the confession, and the repeated, "Yes, I am a Jew!" The protocols also described the tortures he'd undergone. But Don Carlos had not broken.

"I was a Jew only for myself," he insisted over and over, despite his suffering. "Not even my wife knew that I was observing Jewish *mitzvos* in the cellar of our home.... Jewish friends? I had no friends!"

A contradiction arose on the question of his clandestine visit to Rav Menashe in Amsterdam. At first Don Carlos seemed to admit to the visit. In subsequent interrogations, however, he denied it emphatically. Fernando did not understand what had prompted his friend to do this; nor could he ask the Inquisitors seated before him.

He turned to the very beginning of the documents, where the case began. There was the name of the witness who had seen Admiral Don Carlos enter Rav Menashe's house: Pedro Alvares. The witness had disappeared before actually submitting his testimony — that is, the story he'd offered in his note. It was imperative that Fernando see that note, in order to implement the plan he'd concocted with Roberto Gonzales.

After studying the protocols for a long time, he lifted his head and faced João Manuel. "*Padre*, the information here speaks for itself. Don Carlos' confession of Judaism and observing Jewish practice are clearcut. However, *Padre*, you are as familiar as I am with the amendment to the Inquisition Law that was passed 12 years ago, after the trial and burning of Manuel Jorge de Oliveira. Only later, after his death, did the truth emerge: He had been a loyal Christian all his life, and only the intense pressure of interrogation and the terrible pain of torture extracted a 'confession' to things he'd never done.

"The amendment states clearly that without witnesses there is no case. And believe me, after reading these protocols, there is no doubt in my mind of his guilt."

De Henrique shot to his feet, but was waved down by the judge: "You will have your turn to speak. Permit me to finish."

De Henrique sank into his seat, muttering unintelligibly under his breath. Fernando resumed: "The only thing that can help here would be to show clear proof of guilt, in a way that will be acceptable in the royal court..."

"The royal court? *Senhor* means, surely, the prince!" The words had burst from de Henrique.

With difficulty, Fernando forced himself to answer quietly. "No, Paulo. This morning I was informed that the king himself now shares his son's position. Apart from that, I must ask you for permission to complete my thoughts without interruption. Out of respect for the court, please!"

He allowed a moment to elapse before continuing.

"Therefore, the only thing that can help us here would be, at the least, to provide the incriminatory note referred to in the investigative file." His tone sharpened. *"Where is that note?"*

He had intentionally directed the question at *Padre* João Manuel, though he knew from Judge Gabriel Monteiro de Silvia that the note was actually, for some reason, in de Henrique's possession.

João Manuel was stymied. Where *was* the note — and why wasn't it in the file?

Fernando repeated his request patiently. "The note is the only document that can bring conclusive proof of the prisoner's guilt. Why wasn't care taken that it remain in the file?"

No one in the room looked at de Henrique, though each man privately thought the secretary most likely to be responsible for the note's disappearance.

De Henrique sensed their subtle pressure, but ignored it. He had prepared a little surprise for the judge.

⇌

Orlando, the young lawyer in Fernando de Lima's employ, left the room without attracting attention. But no one could help but notice the way he re-entered the room moments later. Rushing breathlessly up to the judge's dais, he whispered in excitement, "Manuel Lagrates has returned! He arrested them!"

Fernando did not react. His expression remained as impassive as his heart was jubilant. This timely arrest, he hoped, would be a severe blow to de Henrique. Glancing sideways at the end of the table, he noted the way de Henrique strained to hear what was passing between him and Orlando. *He's nervous,* Fernando thought. *Good.*

Orlando retreated to his place at one side of the room. Fernando picked up the thread of the proceedings where he'd left off.

"Well, we seem to have come to a standstill, gentlemen. I've already told you that I'd like to help, as I've often done in the past."

"*Here* is the note!"

De Henrique's voice rang out in triumph. The reaction was everything he might have hoped for. Every eye was trained on him in surprise and anticipation. Standing by his seat, he waved the note over his head like a pennant.

"Here's the note," he repeated. "And who knows better than His Honor why it was not left in the archives?"

Anger rose up in Fernando, threatening to choke him. With difficulty, he reminded himself that his only hope of victory lay in total control and icy calm.

"I have no idea what you're talking about, Paulo," he said coolly. "You must know how seriously the law looks upon the removal of official documents from an investigatory file."

De Henrique laughed mockingly. "Yes, yes, *I* know it well, Your Honor. But do *you*?"

Padre João Manuel was unable to contain himself. "Once again you disrupt the proceedings! We are able to conclude this matter quickly. What are you trying to do?" His eyes radiated pure hatred.

To the astonishment of everyone present, de Henrique's reply was to turn on his heel and walk out of the room. He quickly returned, accompanied by a frightened-looking priest. It was Gabriel Monteiro de Silvia. De Henrique was smiling.

Fernando paled. He had fallen neatly into de Henrique's trap. Gabriel Monteiro had betrayed him. He had told de Henrique everything. And now, Gabriel was prepared to testify against him.

A charged silence filled the courtroom. Every eye was riveted in astonishment on Gabriel Monteiro. What was he doing here? For that matter, where had he been until now? And what did de Henrique have up his sleeve this time?

De Henrique said smugly, "Now do you understand, Your Honor, what I meant before? Could I have safely left the note in the file?"

Fernando felt his strength drain swiftly away from him. De Henrique had won.

57

Gabriel Monteiro de Silvia took a few steps forward. His eyes were cast down; never once did he raise them to meet Judge de Lima's. He bowed. The onlookers watched him expectantly — curiously. Other spectators, habitual haunters of courthouses, drifted into the court in ones and twos, filling the benches that lined both sides of the room.

Gabriel stood before the judge's dais, head bent. Fernando watched him, his heart pounding so furiously he was sure it must be visible to all. Had Gabriel given away the secret of his midnight mission?

The silence was shattered by a single sharp command: "Speak!" The command came from Paulo de Henrique.

When there was no immediate response, de Henrique barked again, "Speak, Gabriel!"

Gabriel spoke. In a stiff, wooden voice, he said, "I confess that I did not behave properly last night. I surreptitiously entered the secretary's room at the Holy Office, for the purpose of removing the incriminating note from the Don Carlos file."

Not a muscle twitched in Judge de Lima's face, though inwardly he wept. Voices whispered insistently in his ear that all was lost. He himself would shortly become another victim of the Inquisition. He knew de Henrique's methods well: First came the personal public attacks, steadily undermining the victim's self-confidence, then the spreading of rumors throughout Lisbon, and finally, the "revelation" of the victim's secret life, and imprisonment. The persecution had begun. And Gabriel Monteiro de Silvia, it seemed, was to be the first weapon in de Henrique's arsenal...

De Henrique's rough voice rang out again. "Why did you want to steal the note?"

Fernando roused himself as if from a trance. "I am the one who gives the orders here. *I* will ask the questions!" He made no effort to conceal his anger.

De Henrique suppressed a broad smile. Bowing low and ironically before the Superior Judge, he murmured, "Your Honor wishes to interrogate the witness? Please! Only make sure to ask the most important question of all: Who asked the Inquisition judge, *Senhor* Gabriel Monteiro de Silvia, to remove the note from the archives?"

Fernando bit his lip, as de Henrique's eyes danced with triumph. Then the judge drew himself up and spoke so that his voice filled the room. "And so... who asked you to take the note? Speak!"

And the answer came — the answer that Fernando had been dreading above all.

"It was his honor, the Superior Judge, who asked me to take the note."

The words fell upon the audience like a thunderbolt. Muffled exclamations filled the spectators' benches. The Inquisition delegation, headed by *Padre* João Manuel, sat electrified with shock.

Fernando did not stir, except to lightly pound the dais with his gavel for silence. How to extricate himself from the pit into which he'd fallen? *Ana Hashem hoshiah na!* Please, G-d, save me!

Suddenly, he began to smile. He crooked a finger, beckoning Orlando. His young assistant approached the dais at a sprint. Fernando bent over to whisper something in his ear.

Orlando did not waste a second. He ran from the courtroom, and returned again very shortly — accompanied by Captain Manuel Lagrates of the king's guard.

Lagrates approached the judge's dais, bowed low, and said exactly what Fernando had been hoping to hear.

"Your Honor, a short time ago, in the Inquisition building close to Secretary Paulo de Henrique's office, we arrested three young monks. They are now in prison."

"Why?" the judge rapped out.

"We found them ransacking your house, Your Honor. They managed to escape to the Inquisition building, where we caught up with them. In accordance with the law which permits the arrest of a priest — or any employee of the Holy Office — caught in a criminal act outside the precincts of the Inquisition building, we arrested them."

"Who had sent them on their criminal mission?"

Manuel Lagrates hesitated. "I'm not sure, Your Honor... But, judging from the way the Holy Office secretary defended them, I believe it was he who sent them."

Once again, a wave of babble engulfed the spectators' benches. This open battle between the Superior Court judge and secretary de Henrique was beginning to look very interesting indeed. Which of them would emerge the victor?

Fernando de Lima did not cast so much as a glance de Henrique's way. Instead, he addressed himself to *Padre* João Manuel. He was fighting for his life.

"*Padre*," he said, in a tone that managed to sound authoritative despite his inner quaking, "are you beginning to see a connection between the tissue of lies spouted by Gabriel Monteiro de Silvia here today, and the illegal entry of the three black-clad monks into my home — the home of the Superior Judge of the realm?"

João Manuel was uncomfortable. The presence of the curious spectators was especially galling. The facts that were emerging publicly about de Henrique's secret activities would bode no good for the Inquisition's image. As it was, a good percentage of the population already disliked the Holy Office and its methods. Today's revelations would only further demean its reputation.

João Manuel rose, glancing right and left uncertainly. It was clear that de Henrique had some plot up his sleeve against Fernando de Lima. But where did Gabriel Monteiro de Silvia come into the picture? He would have to call the man into his office soon to clarify the matter.

Meanwhile, he must try to terminate this hearing as quickly as possible — before any additional damage was done.

He began to make his way up to the judge's dais, walking very slowly because he had not yet decided what to say. This complication with the note infuriated him. Then, all at once, he made up his mind. The first priority was to cleanse the Holy Office of the stigma de Henrique had placed upon her. He would answer the judge's question — but, in the main, he would address the listening crowd.

"Your Honor," João Manuel said, weighing every word and speaking so quietly that the audience had to strain to hear, "without intending to, we seem to have stumbled into some very complicated — and very troubling — territory."

He paused. With a glance directed first at the spectators' benches, he continued: "When I came upon members of the king's guard in my building this morning, Your Honor, I experienced one of the most difficult moments of my life. With my own eyes I had seen a serpent, coiled and dishonest, slithering into the holy bastion of our faith."

Again he paused. Even the least discerning listener could see that speech was difficult for him. No one uttered a syllable. Finally, in a slightly trembling voice, he said, "But even more difficult was the knowledge that the evil that has infiltrated our beautiful building has been directed also against me. Those monks in black visited my home, too, Your Honor. The home of the Inquisition head! A hooded, black-clad monk tried to plant a Jewish artifact in my home — a *mezuzah*, they call it. And why? So that, afterwards, his friends might search my house and find 'proof' of my Jewishness. Just as they were trying to do to you, *Senhor* Fernando de Lima." He shook his head. "Who bears the responsibility here? I do not know. But the pain is sharp as a two-edged sword."

João Manuel fell silent, closing his eyes. Not a soul in the courtroom spoke. Every person there knew exactly whom João Manuel was accusing.

"And now" — the words burst from the priest with surprising force — "hand that note over to the judge! We wish to convict Don Carlos!"

De Henrique did not budge.

The judge's gavel came down hard on his podium. "I am calling a recess for an hour. The note will be handed over after that hour. A conviction is dependent on de Henrique's immediate compliance with the court's order to hand over the note he illicitly removed from the investigatory file."

Whispering and murmuring, the crowd rose to its feet. As they filed from the courtroom, the whispers turned into a frenzied babble as they went over every nuance of the incredible scene they had just witnessed.

"Wake up!"

Roberto Gonzales slumbered on. Jose de Melo shook him by the shoulder. "Wake up! We're leaving now."

Roberto opened his eyes. "Whe-where am I?"

"Hurry up. You're with me. And we're leaving for Oporto right now!"

Roberto tried to will himself into a state of alertness despite the shroud of sleep that still entangled him. Rising heavily, he grasped the case that had been propped near his bed and slung it over his shoulder.

Suddenly, he stopped.

"You said we'd be leaving at night. You said it was dangerous to leave by day. It's still daylight now!"

"True — but we have to hurry. I've just received a message from the courthouse. It said that Fernando de Lima is about to authorize Don Carlos' death sentence. He has no other option. He asks us to leave immediately, despite the danger, so that there will still be a chance of saving Don Carlos' life."

Roberto came thoroughly awake.

58

In the large waiting area, de Henrique was intent on avoiding everyone's eyes: those of the excited crowd of spectators as well as of his fellow Inquisitors. It was *Padre* João Manuel who was responsible for all the animosity being directed against him. The moment of truth was speedily approaching between himself and his Inquisition superior. The explosive confrontation was not far off. It was unavoidable now.

He saw João Manuel, who had been conversing in a corner with Judge de Lima, turn and begin to make his way toward him. The secretary tensed. He could hand over the note if he wished; it was useless to de Lima now. The crowd that had witnessed the recent scene in the courtroom would spread the word throughout the city. No one would believe that the eminent judge, Fernando de Lima, would be naive enough to try to filch a document of which the entire city was aware! No, the note would do him no good now.

Still, he hardened his heart. De Lima would not get the note from *him*. Nor would he hand it over at João Manuel's command. Once word circulated about João Manuel's attack on him in the courtroom, de Henrique's powerful standing in the city would be severely damaged.

João Manuel approached rapidly. De Henrique saw the rage in his eyes — a rage directed at him. Normally, de Henrique delighted in this kind of power struggle; today, he would far rather have avoided it, sought a compromise. He had no desire to engage in battle when his opponent unquestionably had the upper hand. What to do?

When he was still a short distance away, João Manuel halted. Their eyes met. João Manuel gestured brusquely for him to come closer. Flushing, de Henrique walked slowly in the head priest's direction. Every step caused him untold humiliation. But right now he had no choice but to submit.

João Manuel stepped over to a corner of the large room. He would speak to his secretary privately, far from the many listening ears of the curious. He did not want any of them to hear what he was about to say to de Henrique.

⁕

"Tell me about Amsterdam " Don Carlos tried to distract the younger man's thoughts.

But Yitzchak de Castro was silent.

"Why don't you speak, Yitzchak? You were in Amsterdam. You know the city!"

Yitzchak understood his cellmate's motives, but he was afraid. He was afraid that talking about Amsterdam would arouse unbearable longings — for the city itself, for his parents, for his friends. He did not feel strong enough to endure that right now.

"Now, I," Don Carlos continued, "was never in Amsterdam longer than just overnight." Then he remembered: "No, I was once there during the day, too."

Yitzchak roused himself. "Did you *daven* at our *shul* — *Kehillas Bais Yaakov*?"

"No, no, I was in Rav Menashe ben Israel's house and didn't step outside all day, for fear I'd be recognized. But many people came to the house that day, just to chat, or to inquire after their relatives in Lisbon."

They both heard it at the same moment: footsteps descending into the dungeon. In a twinkling, complete silence enveloped their cell as each man sat huddled in his own corner.

~⊃⊂~

Padre João Manuel looked at his secretary with open disfavor. He began speaking sharply and at once. "Have you decided to ruin everything, Paulo? Do you have some sort of pact with Don Carlos, so that you're doing everything in your power to save his life?"

De Henrique replied coldly, "Your clever words mean nothing. It is the Superior Judge who is trying to free Don Carlos. You could see that yesterday. Instead of putting him in his place, you chose to humiliate me, to damage me in the eyes of my fellow Inquisitors."

"Oh, is that why you tried to conceal a *mezuzah* in my home? That's why you sent your henchmen to ransack Judge de Lima's house?" João Manuel's voice was heavy with sarcasm.

De Henrique began to breathe quickly. His eyes glazed over with fury and there were specks of foam on his thick lips. Another explosion was on its way, João Manuel realized sourly. With so many interested watchers peering their way, it was best to avoid such a scene.

"Calm yourself, Paulo," he said curtly. "We will make our own accounting some other time. What is important now is to give the note to the judge. We must have the sentence handed down today. Understand?"

De Henrique did not calm down; however, contrary to his usual practice, he spoke quietly. "First of all, I did not send anyone to hide a *mezuzah* in your house! You will suffer for that libel against me!"

Their eyes clashed like swords. João Manuel knew that de Henrique was lying, and de Henrique knew that he knew it.

"And what of the search of de Lima's house?"

"You heard what Gabriel said! Don't you believe him?"

João Manuel said coolly, "Actually, I'm not sure. Maybe I do, and maybe I don't. The man undeniably loves money."

"Exactly! Fernando de Lima gave him money, a lot of money, to bring him the note. And why do you think it was so vital for him to get his hands on that note in the middle of the night? To destroy it, I tell you — so that there would be no evidence against Don Carlos!"

João Manuel was not convinced. "On the other hand, perhaps Gabriel received money, a lot of money, from *you* — to tell that story. It would not be the first time you've operated in such a fashion, my dear Paulo. You are besmirching the Inquisition's good name."

"Just who is hurting the Inquisition and who is protecting the faith among the masses, you or I? That still remains to be seen, João."

It was the first time he had dared use the priest's first name. For de Henrique, it was the only way to express the anger that was building up inside him, without exploding. He saw *Padre* João Manuel grow pale, but he was beyond caring. He continued unconcernedly, "But right now, that's not important. It's Don Carlos who matters now — Don Carlos, and his good friend, Fernando de Lima, our so-called Superior Judge."

João Manuel was still speechless. The secretary pressed on: "By the way, did you know that a stranger was staying in de Lima's house last night?"

"Who told you that?" Curiosity had conquered João Manuel's fury, if only for the moment.

"What do you mean, who told me? Gabriel Monteiro de Silvia! We saw him through the window!"

"You saw...!"

De Henrique recognized his mistake. "Did I say, 'we saw'? Slip of the tongue. Gabriel saw him." He crossed his arms sneeringly. "Well, head of our illustrious Inquisition? Who do you think that stranger might have been?"

João Manuel was silent. De Henrique's "slip of the tongue" had served to re-arouse all his own suspicions against his secretary. The man, it seemed, never ceased his plotting.

But this was not the time.

"All this is not important just now, Paulo. I will be speaking to the king, and perhaps also to the cardinal in Rome." He held out a hand. "And now, Paulo — the note, if you please."

Roberto Gonzales straightened his cassock and followed Jose de Melo outside. The sound of horses' hooves told him that their carriage had arrived. The daylight seemed full of inquisitive eyes.

De Melo carefully locked the door behind him, and both men took stock of their surroundings.

No one was visible. The carriage door was open for them. There would be no need to spend more than a bare minimum of time on the street, a prey to every curious passer-by. De Melo and Roberto walked quickly up the path through the courtyard. When they reached the carriage, de Melo signaled for Roberto to enter first.

Just as his own feet were touching the carriage stair, a voice spoke at his back, freezing his blood:

"*Padre* Jose — *Padre* de Melo, *boa tarde* (good afternoon)!"

De Henrique shook his head. "I won't give you the note."

"Do you want Don Carlos released?"

"No. I think *you* want that."

João Manuel was at a loss. "But without the note, there is no case!"

"If the note lands in de Lima's hands, there will surely be no case. Understand me well, João!"

João Manuel swallowed the insult. In a very low voice, he said, "We must find a compromise, a solution... Or all is lost."

59

The curiosity of the crowd was an almost palpable weight on the two priests' backs. Both João Manuel and de Henrique noted the way the onlookers were inching slowly but steadily in their direction. It was imperative, João Manuel thought, that they conclude their business at once, before all these curious people overheard ... and spread the news to the rest of the populace.

"Paulo!" he whispered urgently. "We must finish this up now. Propose something!"

It was a pleasant moment for de Henrique. His superior, head of the whole Inquisition, was pleading with him. He decided to be benevolent.

"I am prepared to hand over the note to some important and respected person, someone who is not directly connected with the law. Someone who will remain loyal to me and able to withstand whatever pressure Fernando de Lima may try to put on him." The small eyes narrowed. "I don't trust him, that judge. You should know that Gabriel Monteiro de Silvia was speaking the truth!" He paused, then moved a step closer and hissed, "This time, you must believe me!"

Casting a hasty look over his shoulder to make sure no one could overhear, he added, "In the name of all the saints, believe me. I was there myself last night, near de Lima's house. I myself caught Gabriel leaving the house. Apart from that, a stranger, dressed like a northern European, was in the judge's home."

Astonishment nearly overcame *Padre* João Manuel. He made it a practice never to believe his secretary, but this time it seemed to him that de Henrique was telling the truth. Making a mighty effort to subdue his surprise and curiosity, he answered, "All that is not to the point right now. We must conclude the Don Carlos matter. Arrangements for the *auto-da-fé* have already begun. The builders are putting up the dais and the stake. I hope Judge de Lima will agree to the note's being entrusted to a third party. Whom do you suggest?"

De Henrique answered slowly, "I'm not sure. Perhaps... Perhaps someone from the royal house."

"Prince Alfonso?"

"Out of the question!" De Henrique turned purple. "*He* is not a devout Catholic. Don Carlos has remained his friend."

"Then who?"

De Henrique hesitated. "Don Luis de Sauza, the minister of the treasury. He is loyal to me."

"Very well. I agree."

Judge de Lima had returned to his dais. As *Padre* João Manuel hurried up to him, he noted the judge's impassive face, which looked as though it were carved of stone. "What is he thinking about?" João Manuel wondered. De Henrique had succeeded in planting a seed of doubt in his heart about de Lima's loyalty to the faith.

"*Senhor altissimo* (Most honored sir) Fernando," the priest opened. "I believe it would be useful at this point to entertain a compromise. I know it will not find full satisfaction in your eyes, but this is neither the time nor the place to settle our accounts with our mutual enemy, Paulo de Henrique."

He waited for a response, but the judge made none. Fernando's eyes remained on João Manuel's face, waiting. The priest continued, "There is no choice, Your Honor. We must submit to him this time. I must have that note."

Fernando had no intention of reacting until he knew just what João Manuel was proposing in de Henrique's name. It seemed clear to him that João Manuel was finding it difficult to present the proposal. Why?

The judge's lack of response seemed to João Manuel a rejection of any thought of compromise. Tension gripped him and weakened his hold on his patience. He rushed on, "Paulo, you understand, is reluctant to hand the note over to the court. He doesn't believe that... He thinks..." He broke off with a short laugh. "Never mind, there's no need to analyze de Henrique's thoughts or motives here."

"What, then, is the compromise that you are suggesting, *Padre?*"

João Manuel straightened, took a deep breath, and said, "To entrust the note to a third party — namely, to Don Luis de Sauza."

Fernando considered. The suggestion was decidedly disrespectful to the court, but he did not see that he had much choice. He had as little desire as João Manuel to engage in open battle with de Henrique right now — especially not with Gabriel's confession to tilt the scale.

He nodded once, and said in a voice of dry officialdom: "Agreed."

João Manuel could hardly believe his ears. He had been sure it would take all his powers of persuasion to elicit the judge's consent. Instead, he had agreed at once. Was this an indication that de Henrique had, after all, been lying about him? João Manuel was thrown into confusion.

Fernando summoned his assistant, young Orlando, and asked him to fetch Captain Manuel Lagrates once more. When Orlando had gone, the judge drew a sheet of paper close and dipped the tip of his quill into the inkwell.

When Captain Lagrates stood before him, his bearing proudly and militarily erect, Fernando handed him a folded letter, sealed in wax.

"This is to be delivered personally to the minister of the treasury. Afterwards, please return here as quickly as you can."

Captain Lagrates bowed formally, clicked his heels together, and turned around. A moment later, everyone in the courtroom could hear his horse galloping away at top speed.

Don Luis de Sauza, the minister of the treasury, was strolling in one of the king's gardens. Accompanying him were several of the country's wealthiest citizens, whom he had invited to negotiate a significant loan for the royal house. The loan was needed for a pressing cause: to defray the cost of building new warships to fight the pirates that persisted in launching surprise attacks from their bases in northern Africa against both Spain and Portugal. Some believed that those pirates were really Jewish Marranos, seeking revenge on their enemies, the Spaniards and the Portuguese. Don Luis de Sauza was seeking a substantial infusion of capital to support the new offensive.

The pounding of horses' hooves came as a startling interruption to this serious conference. A noble steed stopped right beside the men, and Captain Lagrates leaped off its back. He stood directly in front of the minister and held out the letter.

"This is for you, sir."

Don Luis de Sauza took the note, his astonished eyes searching Lagrates' face. "The Superior Judge sent me," the captain explained.

Don Luis de Sauza quickly broke open the seal. As he read, he saw with dismay that his hands were trembling. He fervently hoped that none of the others had noticed.

Jose de Melo, one foot on the bottom step of the carriage, debated the wisdom of ignoring the voice at his back. He could leap inside and speed the horses on until they'd put a considerable distance between him and the speaker.

But before he could make up his mind to act, the man was right behind him. "*Padre, boa tarde* (good afternoon)."

There was no choice. Jose turned his head and smiled warmly. The newcomer exclaimed, "*Padre*, I was just on my way to see you! I have something important to discuss with you."

Jose recognized the man. His name was Luis da Menzes, a merchant. He was a member of the church where Jose de Melo served as priest. Luis da Menzes was a zealous Catholic who never missed mass. Jose did not know how to react. To betray even a flicker of impatience could arouse suspicion in these dark days.

"Yes?" he asked politely. As he spoke he fingered the cross hanging on his chest.

"I have a confession to make, *Padre!*"

Jose thought he would burst with frustration. It was imperative that he hurry north; Don Carlos' very life hung in the balance. And now, this man with his confession...

"Perhaps," he ventured, "we can delay the confession until tomorrow. I will be back tomorrow morning. All right?" He turned swiftly to board the carriage.

But Luis da Menzes was nothing if not persistent. He grasped Jose's cassock lightly but firmly. "Please, *Padre*. This thing has been weighing on me all week. I am afraid of hellfire!"

Slowly, regulating his breathing in order to maintain control, Jose de Melo removed his foot from the step and placed it on the ground. He turned back to face the supplicator.

"It is not possible for me to return to the church at this moment to hear your confession. I am in a hurry. You can make your formal confession to- morrow... However, in order to ease your mind, you may tell me about it now."

Stubbornly, the man shook his head. Encountering the implacability in the priest's face, however, he yielded. "All right, *Padre*. Let's move away from the carriage, so that no one will be able to hear us."

They walked around to the back of the coach. Luis da Menzes dropped to his knees and bowed his head. "It's been a week," he said, "that I've been carrying around this terrible secret. I can't do it any longer."

Jose tried to erase every trace of impatience from his voice. "And what is this terrible secret?"

The other man hesitated. "Last week I was visiting the home of my good friend, João Mauricio, and he whispered to me that he knew for a fact that the Superior Judge, Fernando de Lima, is a *'Cristãogo novo'* ('New Christian'). He once came to Judge de Lima's house on a Friday night and saw him wearing a white shirt. He also noticed a few other things, things that definitely point to an observance of Jewish practices."

Jose de Melo felt the blood drain away from his face. He bit his lip with all his strength before asking quietly, "And why doesn't your friend reveal his suspicions to the Holy Office?"

"That's just it, *Padre*. He doesn't want to, because Judge de Lima once saved his father from the Inquisition. He refuses to turn him in now." Luis looked beseechingly into Jose's face. "What am I to do, *Padre*?"

Jose pondered. As the silence had stretched just a little too long, he sensed the other man's questioning gaze. In the present climate in Lisbon, questions could very quickly turn to suspicion. He answered with superb gravity, "*Senhor* Luis, this is truly a serious matter. I must ask you not to speak of this to anyone just yet. Tomorrow we will sit down and decide how best to proceed."

The man rose from his kneeling position, bowed to his spiritual advisor, and without another word walked away.

He had not gone more than a few steps, however, before he suddenly stopped short. Turning, he called back to Jose, "And who, *Padre*, is the man sitting in your carriage?"

60

Don Luis de Sauza lifted his eyes to Captain Lagrates, but could learn nothing more from the face of the man who had brought him the judge's letter. Lagrates' expression was shuttered. De Sauza could not even tell whether or not the captain of the guards knew the letter's contents. This frightened him.

He rubbed his eyes, which had been troubling him ever since his return from the spas of France some time ago. His vision tended to blur at times, especially if — as in this situation — he grew excited while reading. De Sauza brought the letter closer to his face to reread the letter and make sure he had understood it correctly.

As he read, his lips moved silently and his heart screamed within him. The hands that held the letter shook. What had happened to him? Wasn't this the sort of thing he had been prepared for?

Luis querido ("my dear"), he read.

> *I am in great trouble. That serpent, our dear friend Paulo de Henrique, has once again emerged from his poisonous pit. This time, I am his target.*

Some of his men broke into my home early this morning, while I was still there. I fear that he is stalking me now the way he successfully hunted down our beloved Don Carlos.

I do not know how much time is left me before he succeeds in finding the evidence that will allow him to throw me into the dungeon below the Inquisition building — that place of "truth," "mercy," and "compassion." Don Carlos' downfall heralds, I fear, that of our community as well.

Don Luis de Sauza could not go on without pausing to collect himself. His breathing was labored. Apprehensively, he glanced at his illustrious guests, hoping his agitation was invisible to them. They had moved politely to one side and were waiting for him to finish — although not without a certain amount of inevitable curiosity.

He continued reading.

The suspicion which presently surrounds me is making it extremely difficult to postpone Don Carlos' death sentence. The "holy" men of the Inquisition are now seated in my courtroom, pressing me to authorize that foul sentence — a sentence, incidentally, that is practically without legal backing. But it is difficult to fight them now. I fear lest I be forced to do the worst thing of all: to authorize the death sentence quickly, in order to divert their suspicion from me — a suspicion which could bring calamity down on all of our heads. This is the bitter fate that the G-d of Avraham, Yitzchak, and Yaakov has prepared for me, because our fathers yielded to their desire for life in this world and betrayed their faith..."

Again, Don Luis de Sauza stopped. All the usual precautions, second nature for a Marrano pretending to be a loyal Christian, deserted him now. He began walking to and fro, oblivious to the watching eyes.

"*Senhor*, can I help you with something?"

The voice roused de Sauza from his thoughts. Fear gripped him. How could he have forgotten where he was? With a valiant effort, he smiled at the speaker, one of his guests.

"No, no, my friend. Everything is all right. Sometimes one comes upon unexpected news in a letter — but *graçhas a D-eus* (thank G-d), all is well."

Quickly he immersed himself in his letter.

> *And now, I turn to you, my friend. The evil Paulo has in his possession the sole testimony against Don Carlos, and the basis upon which the entire case against him rests. I refer to the note in which someone relates how, on his own initiative, he followed Don Carlos to the home of our teacher, Rabbi Menashe ben Israel in Amsterdam. Do you understand? On the basis of this note alone, which could possibly even be a forgery, the Holy Office has based its case against our dear friend and leader. De Henrique now refuses to hand the note over to me. Before many witnesses he has hinted that he suspects me, that I am liable to destroy the note in order to try and free Don Carlos from prison.*
>
> *However, I have decided that, come what may, I will not endorse the death sentence until I have all the incriminating evidence in my possession. And so, we have arrived at a compromise. Instead of handing the note over to me, it will be given to a third party, someone who is trusted by both sides. Your name was put forward, and I have agreed. You, my friend, are still in the good books of these men in cassocks. May it long remain that way.*
>
> *Please come at once to the courthouse. It pains me deeply that you will also have a part to play in helping Don Carlos join the many, many others who have given their lives for the sanctification of G-d's Name.*
>
> *Come quickly!*

Don Luis de Sauza raised his eyes. For some reason, he was less agitated now. Perhaps he had taken the first tiny step in coming to terms with his fate, which might be the same as that of Don Carlos. A measure of self-control returned to him, enabling him to radiate strength, authority, and inner peace despite the turmoil that still raged within.

He folded the letter over once, then began tearing it into small pieces. When his hand was filled with bits of torn paper, he regarded them solemnly for a moment, then opened the hand wide. The wind plucked the papers away and cast them into the air on every side. He bowed politely to his guests and begged their pardon.

"To my regret, I must cut our important discussion short. No man can know what the future holds for him each day. I have been summoned with some urgency to the Superior Judge, Fernando de Lima. I will be pleased to meet with you again later today."

He turned to where Captain Lagrates was waiting. To his surprise, a coach had already rolled up and was standing open for him.

After the carriage had disappeared from view and even the sound of the horses' hooves had faded completely, one of the minister's guests stooped and began gathering up the torn scraps of paper. He wished to learn the contents of that letter at all cost...

⋙⋘

Jose de Melo, stunned, did not reply immediately. The other man smiled, a seemingly stupid smile, and asked again, "*Padre*, who is the man sitting in your carriage?"

Jose de Melo abandoned self-control. "You dolt! You have seen that I am about to embark on a journey, yet I took the time to hear your story, as befits my priestly duty. And still you stand here interrogating me like those black-robed assistants of our Holy Office secretary. I will not answer you! I am not required to answer you!"

De Melo leaped aboard the carriage and slammed the door so hard that the horses sprang forward even before the whip cracked above their heads.

Inside, de Melo turned to Roberto Gonzales.

"You are from Amsterdam. You are simply incapable of understanding what we must go through here, every single day."

He mopped his brow, his whole body still trembling with rage. He could never know whether the man had been an Inquisition spy.

For a few moments they rode quietly. De Melo used the time to compose himself. Then he thrust his head through the coach window and bellowed at the driver, "Faster, man! Faster! A man's life is at stake!"

⋙⋘

The cell door opened.

"Yitzchak de Castro, stand up!"

Yitzchak lifted his head and blinked at the torches held by two young monks. Between them stood a man he had never seen before. He looked neither Spanish nor Portuguese, and was clothed magnificently. Who was he?

"Yitzchak de Castro! We have ordered you to stand!"

The prisoner struggled to rise, but all his bones, particularly those in his back, ached. Don Carlos tried to help him, but was pushed roughly away by one of the monks.

"One prisoner is not permitted to help another!"

At a signal, the two young monks stepped up to help Yitzchak to his feet. When he was standing, albeit feebly, the order came sharply to his ears: "Yitzchak de Castro, look at the Honorable Monsieur Lasnier, French Ambassador in Lisbon!"

Yitzchak tried to lift his head. Taking a good look at the ambassador, he saw a face that was softer and less harsh than those of the men who had had him under their power these past few years. The ambassador, in fact, was the first outside person he had laid eyes on since his arrest by the Inquisition in Bahia, Brazil.

The monk continued, "Yitzchak de Castro, the ambassador would like to appeal to you, in these last moments of your life, to return to the true faith. Because your heretical family lived in France for several years, where you studied philosophy and medicine at the universities of Bordeaux and Paris, he feels a certain responsibility for the fate of your soul."

Yitzchak directed his reply at the ambassador. "Most honored sir, I am not interested in speaking to anyone on this subject."

"That is not up to you!" barked a monk, still grasping him under the arm. "You will talk to whoever we order you to talk, understand? You will not insult the honorable ambassador!"

The monks winked at one another. "There's the tragedy of it," one "confided" to the other. "He's imprisoned in a cell together with an older heretic who assuredly has a bad influence on him. And so" — The monk turned to Yitzchak — "from now until you are tied to the stake, you will occupy a solitary cell. There you will meet with whomever the Holy Office deems best."

Without further ado, the pair dragged de Castro out of the cell and quickly disappeared with him round a curve of the dungeon. The ambassador followed quietly behind.

Seated alone in the darkness, it was Don Carlos' turn to cry.

61

The carriage sped northward. It soon left Lisbon behind and turned onto the road leading to Oporto. The driver flicked his whip over the horses' backs almost continuously; and they, as though sensing the urgency of this particular trip, raced along as never before.

Inside, Roberto Gonzales and Jose de Melo gripped their respective handholds in an attempt to diminish the effects of the coach's swaying and bumping. They scarcely exchanged a word during the long trip.

For two hours, perhaps three, the horses swept along the road without pause. Then the two passengers sensed a slackening of the pace. Some 10 minutes later, the horses had slowed to a trot. And 10 minutes after that, the carriage came to a complete and unexpected stop.

The two exchanged an anxious glance. Drawing aside the window curtains a fraction, they saw that they had pulled up in the center of a town. Around the central square were a number of inns and taverns. The driver slid off his seat and opened the carriage door.

"*Padre*," he said, "the horses are a little tired. There is still a long way ahead of us. I've decided to let them rest and feed here."

"Well done," de Melo returned warmly. "It will also give us a chance to rest up a bit. I am unaccustomed to being knocked about in a carriage."

The coachman bowed and added, "*Padre* will surely not be angry if I drink a glass of something in one of these taverns." He gestured around the square and smiled bashfully. "I am also in need of some refreshment for the miles ahead."

"Very well, Andre." After all, Jose thought with resignation, what else could he do, now that Andre had chosen to stop in the middle of a bustling town without asking his leave?

Roberto turned to Jose, a question in his eyes. What to do now? How to pass the time in the least dangerous fashion?

The townspeople streamed toward the central square. A few audaciously flicked aside the carriage curtains and peeked inside. Upon seeing the two priests within, they quickly withdrew.

"Roberto, there's no choice. We must get out and stroll about the square. The longer we sit in here, the more suspicion we will arouse. Only one person need suspect that we're hiding, and our troubles will begin. Come, let's leave, and the G-d of Avraham and Moshe will be at our side."

Taut and tense, they stepped down from the coach. Every ounce of concentration was focused on giving the appearance of confidence and serenity. They strolled through the square with even, unhurried steps, responding with polite nods to the greetings and genuflections of the people they passed.

"Here's a bench," Roberto said presently. "Let's sit down. See, there are fewer people in this area. We can talk about the things that really interest us."

They took their places on the bench, all the while watching — without seeming to watch — the passers-by for signs of any unusual interest in their activities.

"The preparations," Jose de Melo remarked, "are already well under way."

"Preparations for what?"

"The *auto-da-fé*!"

Roberto was silent for a long time. Then he said, "I thought the burning of heretics takes place only on a Sunday. Today is Wednesday."

"No, there's been a change. That viper, Paulo de Henrique, became fearful after what happened to our friend Arnaldo Rodriguez — that is, Raphael Chaim — whom our people successfully rescued from prison."

"What is he afraid of?"

"He worries that a similar armed rescue attempt will be made on Don Carlos. He knows that our people are everywhere, just like his own dark henchmen."

"And so...?"

"And so, he has succeeded in advancing the day — to this coming Friday."

Roberto's eyes widened in horror. "*What? In just two days?*"

"No, my friend." Jose de Melo shook his head sadly. "Not two days anymore. We are already approaching Wednesday evening."

Roberto struggled to maintain his composure. This was no place to display the fear and anguish that wracked him. "So what will happen?" he whispered.

"I don't know. It partially depends on us — on the success we have in Oporto."

"Perhaps Fernando de Lima will manage to postpone the sentence."

"Perhaps. But I don't believe it. De Henrique doesn't like him, and de Henrique knows how to apply pressure. He is even more powerful than *Padre* João Manuel."

"He isn't human! He has the heart of a serpent, twisted and black!" The words burst out of Roberto in a furious hiss.

Jose shrugged.

"How can I return to Amsterdam," Roberto wondered aloud, features contorted in pain, "without having saved Don Carlos?"

"Who says we won't save him? Maybe G-d above will help us. Why despair already?"

Roberto clenched his fist. "What is obvious is that we must hurry!"

"Yes," answered de Melo, and rose from the bench. Peering ahead, he saw their coachman emerging from a tavern on the square. "We must return to the carriage."

Roberto got to his feet in silence. They had not taken more than two steps before a noise from behind made them both turn. From the copse of trees behind the bench burst a youth. As they watched, horrified, he raced away toward the nearest group of houses.

Still staring, Roberto asked, "Do you think he overheard us?"

Jose shook his head slowly. "I don't know. I hope not."

But both their hearts told them that the boy had heard everything. And those hearts pounded with a terror that threatened to choke the very breaths from their throats...

≈⌒≈

A short ride brought Don Luis de Sauza to the Superior Court. Without vouchsafing so much as a glance at the ever growing crowd of the curious, he hurried directly into the courthouse. Excited murmurs rose up on every side, but he determinedly ignored them.

He walked directly up to the judge's dais and bowed. The eyes of the two Marranos met for a fraction of an instant — but in that instant, they said all that needed to be said.

Fernando de Lima picked up his gavel and pounded three times. Silence fell upon the crowded courtroom. Every face was turned to him expectantly.

"Decision of the court!" Fernando called. The silence deepened.

"Because of the difficulties that have been encountered between this court and the Inquisition — or rather, to be more precise, between this court and the esteemed secretary of the Holy Office, *Padre* Paulo de Henrique — a compromise has been agreed upon. By the terms of the compromise, His Majesty Don João IV's most honorable Minister of the Treasury, Don Luis de Sauza, is viewed as a trusted friend to both the secular court and the religious one.

"Therefore, the documents incriminating Don Carlos Carneiro, former admiral of the Portuguese fleet, will be given by the Inquisition secretary to the minister. It is the minister's duty to guarantee the safety of these documents and see to it that they come to no harm." Fernando frowned from his dais. "While the court is at a loss to understand the exact nature of the Holy Office's apprehensions, it has agreed to this compromise — solely in order to expedite the conclusion of this case."

He fell silent. The air of expectancy was, if anything, sharper now. His insides fluttered with tension.

"I now call upon the Holy Office secretary to pass the documents touching on Don Carlos Carneiro's alleged transgressions, to the most honorable Minister of the Treasury, Don Luis de Sauza."

Now all eyes were directed at de Henrique. He did not hurry to rise. This was a moment of extreme pleasure for him, and he wanted to savor it to the full. All of Lisbon waited for him!

"It is my desire to conclude this case *today*," Fernando called sharply. "The secretary will hasten to comply with the court's request."

De Henrique pulled himself heavily to his feet and lumbered over to Don Luis de Sauza, still standing beside the judge's dais. Though he smiled at the minister, he assiduously avoided Judge de Lima's eyes. Withdrawing an envelope from the pocket of his cassock, he passed it solemnly to the minister. He then returned composedly to his seat.

Don Luis de Sauza opened the envelope, his right hand trembling slightly. He could feel his lower lip involuntarily doing the same. Inside was the notorious note, written by Pedro Alvares on his return from Amsterdam on Don Carlos' ship, in which he described the way he had trailed the admiral to the rabbi's house.

Reading it, de Sauza's heart was wrung with anguish. This was the very document that would send his beloved friend and leader to the stake. "It is G-d's will," he thought sorrowfully.

He climbed the few steps to the judge's dais, note in hand, and passed it to Fernando for his perusal. The courtroom was abuzz. Both men were keenly aware of de Henrique's fierce gaze on them.

"May Heaven's curse fall upon him," Fernando whispered almost inaudibly to de Sauza.

"Amen," answered the minister, just as quietly.

They both understood that the resolution of Don Carlos' fate was rapidly approaching. Fernando de Lima would not be able to postpone judgment even for a short time on some legal pretext. Though de Henrique's men in black had been arrested, there was no telling what consequences their visit to his home that morning might yet bring in its wake. Victory might still belong to de Henrique. If he spotted even the slightest inclination on Judge de Lima's part to favor Don Carlos — after the entire city had been incited to thirst for the former admiral's blood — Fernando might find himself languishing in an Inquisition dungeon cell, on that or some other pretext.

Why had Hashem brought this punishment upon him? Why must he be the one to authorize the death sentence of one of his people's truly righteous men?

He pounded with his gavel three times, and quiet returned to the courtroom.

"The court has reached its decision!" The judge's voice rang out clear and strong. Only Don Luis de Sauza, standing beside him, saw the way his friend's fist, out of sight of the spectators, was clenched until the knuckles turned white.

"This is no ordinary decision," Fernando said. "We are dealing with one of our country's foremost citizens. It is not easy for this court and for the nation as a whole to absorb the depths of this man's treachery — this man who was a national hero and an intimate of the king's. We must all applaud the men of the holy Inquisition for their zealous safeguarding of our faith, and for bringing this man to justice.

"After studying the relevant documents, it is clear that the case has been conducted flawlessly throughout. Don Carlos enjoyed all the protection that he deserves from the Inquisition tribunal, which desires not the death of suspected heretics, but their full-hearted return to the fold. In the course of his interrogation, Don Carlos never expressed a desire to take this step. We have also not found any basis for the prisoner's complaint that he was subjected to excessive torture which forced the confession from him. From this perspective, the Inquisition has conducted matters just as it ought.

"However —"

He paused. His eyes swept the now enormous crowd that filled the courtroom. He felt nothing but contempt for them, these people who relished the burning of living men. They were no better than the most primitive of cave dwellers. At last his gaze rested on de Henrique, who had been listening throughout with his plump chin resting on his palm, a victorious grin on his face.

"However," de Lima continued, "we have a small problem. This is the first case in recent years that is based on something other than direct witness testimony. In other words, on the oral evidence of living men who step forward to testify that the suspect has indeed engaged secretly in religious Jewish practice.

"According to the law of our land, which is binding on the Inquisition as well, it is forbidden to condemn a man solely on his own confession, without witnesses to speak out against him. There are no such witnesses in the Don Carlos case."

De Henrique started. Red-facedly, he jumped up and opened his mouth. But before he could utter a word, the judge continued: "I will ask the secretary to calm himself. The court has not finished its summary. This unseemly haste is not in keeping with the secretary's honorable office."

Murmurs of agreement rose up throughout the packed room. De Henrique slowly resumed his seat, fury stamped all too clearly on his heavy-jowled face.

"All we have in our possession is a note. The note was written by a man who intended to testify, an aide to Admiral Don Carlos Carneiro by the name of Pedro Alvares. With his own hand he wrote down the incriminating evidence against Don Carlos."

He breathed deeply and turned to face de Henrique directly.

"*The note is not enough.* I cannot accept the position you stated to me yesterday — namely, that the law is intended to uphold the faith and must be subservient to it."

The judge raised a hand and said quickly, "I must ask the secretary once again to be seated. The court has still not finished its say about Don Carlos itself. Right now we are discussing the difficulties attendant on this case."

De Henrique was seething. Reluctantly, he resumed his seat once again, but did not refrain from carrying on an audible conversation with those seated nearby. The judge was heaping insult upon his head! He was depicting the secretary of the Holy Office as a man who scorned the law and used it only for his own ends. But he found few supporters in the courtroom. All were eager to hear what the judge had to say.

The gavel came down with unaccustomed force.

"With all this, I would like to point out the fact that the absence of the witness, Pedro Alvares, is not the Inquisition's fault. Various factors prevented him from appearing at the tribunal. He has simply vanished. I believe the Inquisition when it tells me it has made every effort to locate Alvarez so that he could provide his testimony about what he witnessed in Amsterdam, in accordance with our law.

"Accordingly, after much thought, and after reading the incriminating note — though I still fail to understand the secretary's aim in concealing that note from this court — I have decided that, in this case, it is appropriate to accept the note in lieu of personal testimony, as corroboration to Don Carlos' own confession.

"The decision of the court, therefore, is to pass on the sentence of death by burning for approval by His Majesty, the king."

De Henrique sat disbelieving. The crowd around him whispered excitedly, but his own joy was not complete. Several times in the course of rendering his decision, Fernando de Lima had insulted him publicly. De Henrique chewed his thick lower lip, eyes glinting with a hatred directed at the judges on the dais.

Fernando did not vouchsafe de Henrique so much as a glance. He stepped down from his dais and walked to his office. Inside, he locked the door and reclined on a small sofa there. Tears trickled from his eyes, and he made no attempt to dry them. An inarticulate prayer welled up in him. Gradually, his thoughts drifted to Roberto Gonzales. Where was he now?

Back in the courtroom, bedlam had erupted. Every person there was intent on leaving as rapidly as possible, in order to spread the news throughout the city. Voices rose higher and higher as the excitement spread. Only de Henrique remained glued to his seat. To the congratulations he received he returned only an absent nod. The insult he had suffered at the hands of Fernando de Lima gnawed at him unceasingly.

Don Luis de Sauza left the courtroom quietly, without attracting any notice. He had had a direct hand in the outcome of the sentence this morning. He decided to head straight home, where he could sit alone and brood on the bitterness of his fate.

62

Deep night shrouded the port city of Oporto as the carriage from Lisbon entered it. Silence reigned in the sleeping streets, where the streetlamps had long since been extinguished. Here and there, in isolated pockets, yellow lamplight gleamed through a shutter in contrast to the vast majority of black windows. Jose de Melo was pleased: the fewer who were awake to witness their passage, the better.

The carriage wound its way slowly through the narrow streets. As though they sensed the need for secrecy, the horses ambled quietly, their hooves making scarcely a sound on the smooth cobblestone.

The carriage stopped, and the coachman jumped from his perch.

"Excuse me, *senhor*," he whispered through the window. "I don't know the way. Where are we going?"

"We must reach Cardinal João Batista Tenorio's house."

The coachman stood mutely, scratching his head. It was clear to Jose that he had no idea which way to go. "Drive straight," he instructed, "until you reach the city's central square. There you will turn left into a long, tree-lined avenue. At the end of this avenue you will find a narrow side street, on the right. Stop in front of the second house on the left."

The driver nodded, then turned to clamber up to his perch. A whisper from Jose stopped him: "You don't know who *Padre* João Batista is?"

"No!"

Impatience and astonishment mingled in de Melo's voice as he snapped, "He is the cardinal here in the north!"

It was no wonder that Jose was surprised at the coachman's ignorance. *Padre* João Batista Tenorio was famous throughout the land, and was held in high esteem even by the heads of the church in Lisbon and the royal court.

The driver duly followed the directions he'd been given until, some half hour later, he pulled up before the cardinal's house. Jose descended first, then Roberto Gonzales, both walking as quietly as they could. The cardinal's house was dark. De Melo had no idea how late it was, but it was surely past midnight. Softly he tiptoed toward a gate set in the fence that circled the house, opened it without a sound, and crept over to the front door. He hesitated.

Finally, he raised his fist and knocked twice, then twice more. After a moment he knocked again, three times.

There was no answer.

Roberto Gonzales had sidled up to stand behind him. One of the horses, snorting suddenly, startled them. De Melo tried the prearranged knocks once more, a little louder this time. Pressing his ear to the door, he thought he could hear a faint noise within. After a time, a faint, flickering light showed at the window. Joy and relief flooded him. He had managed to rouse the cardinal without waking the neighbors.

The door opened. In the doorway stood Cardinal João Batista, his expression apprehensive, wearing a nightshirt and carrying an oil taper. He squinted into the night, trying to make out the identities of the visitors who had disturbed his sleep. Catching sight of Jose de Melo's face, the cardinal's eyes lit up.

"*Boa noite, amigos* (Good evening, friends)," he murmured, with an inviting gesture. "Please come in. Oporto can be cold at night."

"This is my guest," Jose said quickly, pulling Roberto into the light where his host could see him. The cardinal closed the door and locked it. They could speak more freely now.

João Batista bowed slightly to Roberto.

"A guest from Amsterdam," Jose clarified.

The cardinal gave Roberto another glance, a keener one this time, filled with curiosity. "What is your name?" he asked.

"Roberto. Roberto Gonzales."

"No — what is your Jewish name?"

"Ah! It's Yitzchak. Yitzchak ben David."

João Batista's eyes grew soft. "Please step in here, gentlemen. Such important guests — especially the honored gentleman from the 'holy' city of Amsterdam!"

They were soon seated in plush armchairs. Jose broke into speech without preamble. "The situation in Lisbon, *Padre*, is not good."

"I understand what you're talking about, but explain it to me anyway."

"I am talking about our friend Don Carlos."

João Batista inclined his head sadly. "I knew it, my friend. I knew it. What happened in court?"

"I understand, from speaking with Fernando de Lima, that he will not have much choice."

"Choice?"

"To avoid authorizing the Inquisition's death sentence."

"Why?"

Jose did not answer immediately. The sound of his breathing filled the room. João Batista understand that fresh troubles had come upon them. At last, de Melo murmured, "They are following him, too."

"Who is?"

"Can't you guess who, *Padre*?"

"Paulo?"

"Yes. Paulo de Henrique."

"That serpent!"

De Melo shrugged. "Calling him names won't help us much now."

"True. Have you made the long trip from Lisbon to Oporto because of this matter?"

"Yes."

"And our friend here, from Amsterdam, is connected?"

"Exactly!"

For a long moment the room was plunged into silence, as each of its three occupants sank into his own thoughts. The first to emerge was Jose de Melo.

"We must save Don Carlos."

João Batista lifted his hands in a gesture of despair.

"No, João! We have come to you because you can help. Perhaps you are the only man who can."

João Batista's head jerked up. "*I*? How can I help?"

De Melo signaled to Roberto. Roberto reached into his case and pulled out the letter he'd brought with him from Amsterdam. He placed it in de Melo's outstretched hand, while João Batista looked on with interest.

"Here," said Jose, pointing at the letter, "is how we might find the solution."

Just as de Melo had done a moment earlier, João Batista extended a hand for the letter. But Jose was in no hurry to give it to him. The hand remained hanging in the air as he said, "I trust, *Padre*, that you are fully briefed on the Don Carlos case?"

"Meaning — what?"

"You know what led to his arrest?"

"Yes, of course. His aide made the accusation against him."

Jose de Melo thrust the letter at him. "Then read!"

The cardinal opened the letter and began reading. His two guests watched his face for his reaction. It was soon clear that his primary response was one of pleasure. Presently he lifted his eyes to his guests.

"Yes, very nice! But where do I come in?"

Jose de Lima answered, "Our Superior Judge, Fernando de Lima, requests that you come to Lisbon — with the letter!"

João Batista considered this. Quietly, he asked, "Why me?"

"You are a well-known church figure. You are respected; people listen to you. And... you are not a resident of Lisbon."

"Why is that important?'

"Lisbon is poisoned. No one can trust his neighbor. Everyone is under suspicion these days, and men of standing most of all, if Paulo de Henrique has his way. He particularly delights in toppling men who enjoy lofty positions in society. Everyone, from government ministers on down, is afraid of him. You, on the other hand, live in a distant city. You're 'clean.' No one would suspect you of being a secret Jew."

João Batista absently flipped the letter over and over in his hands as he stared at a point on the ceiling. Finally he said, "I don't know. But there is a definite possibility that it would work. And for even a possibility of saving Don Carlos' life, isn't it worthwhile placing my own in danger?"

He stood abruptly and strode back and forth through the room to dispel the last shreds of sleep. At the far end of the room, he whirled around with sudden decision. "You are right. I will come with you to Lisbon."

"Can we leave now?"

João Batista made a negative motion. "How can we? I can't sneak out of town like a thief. With daylight, I can bid a formal farewell here. Then we will leave for Lisbon."

"But *Padre*, the road is long. We'll lose precious time! We may even be too late..." The words burst from Roberto Gonzales.

"I understand," said the cardinal. "But what will we gain if I, too, fall under suspicion?"

He strode toward the hall, which led to a series of smaller rooms. "Here are your bedrooms," he said, pointing at two open doors. "Tomorrow, with first light, I will wake you and we will leave at once."

The two young monks half-led, half-carried Yitzchak de Castro along the gloomy corridor. Yitzchak made no objection: He had no strength left in him to object. And yet, the resolve hardened in his heart not to succumb to any blandishments that might be offered about conversion to Christianity. The short time he had spent in Don Carlos' company had done much to strengthen his will.

They reached the stairs leading up from the dungeons. Yitzchak was surprised. He had assumed he was to be placed in another cell, in solitary confinement. And here they were, leading him up into the building proper. Could it be... Could it possibly mean... another bout in the torture room?

"Oh, merciful G-d," he prayed inwardly. "Not that!" He would never, he was certain, withstand another encounter with the sadistic men in charge of interrogation.

He was taken to a well-lit room, lavishly furnished as though belonging to an important personage. In the two years since he'd been in the clutches of the Inquisition he had passed through its corridors many times, on his way to and from interrogations. Yet he had never seen this particular room. Whose was it? And why were they bringing him here?

He sat gingerly on a comfortable armchair. After long months lying on stone floors, the chair felt heavenly. At the same time, every limb was tensed almost to the point of trembling. What did his accursed captors want from him now?

Opposite him, in an equally comfortable easy chair, sat Monsieur Lasnier, France's ambassador to Portugal. Lasnier gave him a pleasant smile and motioned for the two monks to leave the room. Nervously, Yitzchak waited.

"I asked to speak to you," the ambassador began, "out of a feeling of responsibility. For a number of years you and your family lived in France — in Tours. Do you remember France?"

Yitzchak hesitated. Despite his youth, he understood what the man was after. The smile that accompanied his apparent concern was assumed, but for all that Yitzchak decided to treat him respectfully. Maybe, just maybe, Hashem would take pity on him and bring his salvation through this man. Maybe — miracle of miracles — Yitzchak would once again be free to return to his home in Amsterdam. Stranger things had been known to happen.

He nodded affirmatively. He remembered France, especially the cities of Tours and Avignon. A small smile indicated that he missed that country.

"It is truly a pity," Lasnier continued, "that you ever left France. A pity you abandoned your studies of medicine and philosophy in the university there. You might have been a successful young Catholic today."

Yitzchak de Castro lifted his head sharply. "No, sir. My parents were forced to convert to Catholicism, but not me! They inadvertently neglected to have me baptized. I've always been Jewish, and so — according to its own laws — the Inquisition has no right to judge me. Only converts who return to Judaism may be tried by the Holy Office, not those born Jews who never converted."

Monsieur Lasnier chuckled. It seemed to Yitzchak that he was taken aback, perhaps because of the strident tone Yitzchak had adopted, or because, as a Frenchman, he had no liking for the practice of burning people alive at the stake. Yitzchak had no way of knowing.

"My young friend," Lasnier said pleasantly, "you know very well that the investigators of the Holy Office have not substantiated your story. They have discovered that your parents, who were born in Portugal, left this land and their true names, which are Christoban Luis and Isabel da Paz. Your name in France was Tomas Luis — and you *were* baptized as a Christian! When your heretic parents fled France for Holland, they threw off the yoke of the true faith and returned to their former Judaism, and you along with them! Isn't that the truth?"

"No!"

Lasnier lifted a hand. "Relax, my friend. You have tried to save yourself from your fate as a heretical Christian by concocting this pretty little story about never having been a Christian at all. It will not succeed. But let's not speak of that now. As ambassador of France, the land of your birth, my desire is to save you. I pity you."

Yitzchak's heart leaped upward and began pounding furiously. The ambassador wanted to save him? How? Never mind — Hashem had His ways. Nothing was beyond His powers. Nothing!

He smiled eagerly at the ambassador. "Monsieur wishes to save me? But how? Will *Padre* Paulo de Henrique agree?" His heart tolled within him like church bells on a festival day.

The ambassador smiled back — a sad smile. "You misunderstand, my young friend. I wish to save your soul. As for your bodily existence, I'm afraid it's too late for that."

The words struck Yitzchak like a hammer blow. He almost literally felt his heart shatter into tiny pieces. How could he have believed, even for an instant, that anyone was prepared to spare him from the stake? The ambassador was only an accessory to this crime.

Then, in a flash, he understood. The Portuguese Church wanted to save his soul, and had asked the French ambassador to step in with pleasant smiles, hoping that these would succeed where torture had failed. Yitzchak de Castro lifted his head. Every ounce of his remaining strength went to his eyes, which directed a look of utter scorn at the ambassador. He would not, for any price, betray the way his heart was breaking inside...

Suddenly, the door opened, and Paulo de Henrique entered.

63

All of Lisbon was talking. The news of the Superior Court's authorization of Don Carlos' death sentence spread like wildfire, and the *auto-da-fé* was always the first topic of conversation throughout the city.

"Have you heard?"

"What?"

"They've advanced the *auto-da-fé* to Friday, instead of Sunday, as originally scheduled!"

"Why did they do that?"

An interested crowd began to gather around the pair in the central square. The man who'd brought the news swelled up with self-importance: He knew something the others didn't know.

"Well," he said, "it's like this. The secretary of the Inquisition..."

"*Padre* Paulo de Henrique."

"Yes — don't interrupt me. Anyway, the secretary of the Holy Office is afraid something might go wrong at the last minute."

The man had his sources of information. His cousin's son, an Inquisition judge, would, from time to time, share with his family glimpses of the activities which took place behind the formidable stone walls that surrounded the Inquisition building.

A voice called from the small crowd: "What could go wrong? The Superior Court has authorized the sentence, His Majesty, the king, will sign it, and that's that!"

The news bearer directed a look of withering contempt at the questioner, as though to say, "What would *you* know of these things?"

"You've heard of young Alfonso?" he snapped.

"Of course I've heard of him."

"I'm talking about Prince Alfonso, the king's son."

"Yes!"

"Well, he is still trying to prevent the death sentence from being carried out. He is a friend of Don Carlos."

"But what can he do at this point?"

"You never know. Paulo de Henrique is afraid that the prince will manage to influence his father, the king. So he's advanced the *auto-da-fé* to tomorrow at noon."

"*Graçhas a D-eus* (Thank G-d)!"

One person cried this out with great feeling, and he was echoed by quieter murmurs of assent from the rest of the group. Here and there came a fervent "Amen."

"Listen — you haven't heard everything yet!"

The crowd pressed closer to the speaker, ravenous for news.

"Apart from Don Carlos, there will be others burned in the *auto-da-fé*."

"Heretical Jews."

"Yes. Thirty-four of them."

"Unbelievable! Thirty-four Jews?"

The crowd muttered and marveled. The speaker said in a know- it-all tone, "Yes, yes. Thirty-four Jews."

"All of them from Lisbon?" someone asked.

"Yes, all of them from Lisbon — except for one young man. They brought him over from Brazil."

"From *Brazil?*"

"Yes, yes, from Brazil! His name is Yitzchak de Castro. He is not an insignificant heretic; only 21 and stubborn as anything. He is not prepared to repent."

The faces around him reflected amazement and disapproval. "How did they catch him?" a man wanted to know.

"What do you mean, 'how'? Agents of the Holy Office in northern Brazil discovered him. From then on he's been in prison."

Now the faces shone with pride in their Inquisition's abilities.

"Where will they burn them?" someone asked.

"Don't you live in this city?" he was asked in annoyance.

"No, no, I am from Eldorado. This is my first visit to Lisbon. And I thank all the holy saints that I've come just in time for the *auto-da-fé*. So where is it to be held?"

The crowd relented. "Do you see, *Senhor*? There, in the Triero da Paso, the big square near the royal palace. Over there. The laborers are already preparing the stake, with special seats for the king and his entourage, and the priesthood. Don't forget to come tomorrow morning. It's an awesome sight!"

Gradually, still discussing the news with animation, the crowd dispersed. Two among them had been silent the entire time. One was dressed in priestly garb, the other wore the demeanor of a high government official. They threw each other a quick glance before going their own ways.

Half an hour later, they met again in one of the quieter streets of the city.

Don Carlos felt slightly revived, although his new solitude oppressed him. After months of solitary confinement, the few days spent together with Yitzchak de Castro had been a blessing. He had been able to speak to another human being, to a Jew, and not just to the four walls.

Those few days had provided him with much encouragement. He had been especially moved at the spectacle of the young man, little more than a young man, who had been prepared to risk his life to travel to the end of the world, to Brazil, in order to try to bring his family back to its heritage. Don Carlos had also been impressed with young Yitzchak's moral fortitude, and his readiness to die for the sanctification of G-d's Name.

He missed his cellmate sorely. Turning painfully over on the cold hard stones, he wondered where Yitzchak was now. From what he'd gathered, the Inquisition was making yet another effort to return this "stray sheep" to the fold of Christianity.

But — would they resume the torture? Would they destroy the little that was still left intact in the young man? Good G-d, no! Please, he prayed, have mercy on all your loyal, devoted followers. Have pity on Yitzchak!

Calling on reserves of stamina he didn't know he possessed, Don Carlos pulled himself to his feet. He grasped the bars of the small window set in the metal door of his cell, and looked out. All was darkness. There was nothing at all to be seen. He heard a single muted groan from a nearby cell, then silence returned.

His lips whispered, "Yitzchak, my dear Yitzchak, I am praying for you — that you stand firm, that you succeed in repelling all attempts to turn you from the faith of your fathers. Be courageous against our enemies! Turn a deaf ear to their lies and their promises. Your fate is sealed. They will kill you either way, whether you persist in clinging to your own faith or, Heaven forbid, abandon it at the last moment.

"Stand firm in this last challenge you are about to face, before you will be able to bask in the glory of the King of heaven and earth. Let your death and mine serve as an atonement for the sins of our fathers, who did not succeed in passing their own tests and underwent forced conversion to Christianity.

"I beg of you, Yitzchak — stand firm! Your parents demand it of you. Rav Menashe ben Israel demands it of you."

His lips ceased their murmuring. For a long time he stood quietly, his thoughts with his young friend. Suddenly, he cried out with all his might, shattering the stillness of the dungeon: "*Yitzchak! G-d Himself demands it of you!*"

He stepped back from the door and sat down on the floor, leaning against the cell wall. His head fell forward onto his chest. In the storm of his own emotions, he failed to notice the subdued turmoil issuing from the other cells. Prisoners moved restlessly about their cells, muttering disjointedly or banging on their doors. Only when a pair of monks with torches appeared in the corridor did the noise abate.

One of the monks shouted, "What is this disturbance? Who was it that cried out?"

Nobody answered him. Only silence on all sides — the silence of the graveyard.

After a moment, the monks turned and made their way back up to the Inquisition building. Behind them, the silence continued unbroken.

⟞⟝

Alfonso, the young prince, kneeled. His head bowed and his clasped hands touched his lips. Then he lifted his head and looked up at his father, the king, who gazed back impassively.

Alfonso rose, adjusted the sword that hung from his left hip, and took two steps toward the table where his father sat, awaiting his lunch. A flicker of surprise crossed the king's face at his son's strange behavior. Alfonso had never kneeled to him before in the privacy of their chambers. The king had never demanded it of him. What was his purpose in doing so now?

Alfonso came closer to the table and sat down. Contrary to his usual practice, he did not take his place at his father's right hand. The king noted this, then ordered curtly, "Speak!"

Alfonso hesitated, searching for the right opening words. At last he said gravely, "The honor of the crown and of the royal house are in danger, Father."

The king, starting on his first course, did not so much as raise his eyes to his son. "Really?" he asked, supreme indifference in his voice.

"I think so." With difficulty, Alfonso suppressed his irritation.

"And why is that?"

"Because — because the honor of the crown rests on honor and integrity, and in justice to all its citizens."

The king continued with his repast, just as if his son were not sitting beside him. He knew quite well what Alfonso was referring to — and Alfonso knew that his father knew. The name "Don Carlos" was not spoken aloud between them.

The king reached for a piece of bread. "And is justice not being served?"

"I am afraid that it is not, Father."

The king pushed his plate away and finally lifted his head to meet his son's eyes. "How dare you make such a judgment? And all because of a personal friendship!"

"No, Father."

"Are not the honor of the royalty and of your father important to you?"

"Of course they are!"

"And yet you do not seem to care about a gross betrayal of our crown, our country... and me, personally!"

"Of course I care! Your honor, Father, is more important to me than anything else! But who says there was any betrayal?"

"He confessed," the king said shortly.

"Paulo de Henrique, Father, is capable of dragging a confession from a dead man! And from stones and trees, for that matter."

"That has no bearing on this matter!"

Alfonso sensed that his father was beginning to grow angry. He moderated his own tone.

"Remember all of his major accomplishments for our country's sake. Remember how he succeeded in bearing our fleet to victory against the pirates from northern Africa, those who had so sorely damaged our merchant vessels. Remember, Father, the excellent treaty he negotiated with Holland just a few months ago, which allowed for the free movement of our ships despite the dispute over settlements in Brazil. He did not betray you, Father — even if Paulo de Henrique is right."

His Majesty Don João IV rose from his seat and stood at his full height. He looked coldly down his nose at his son, still seated at the table.

"My son, one hour ago, I signed the death sentence that was authorized by the Superior Court."

Alfonso started up as though struck in the face. He stared wildly at his father. His mouth opened as if to speak, but the king's eyes were cold and cruel. A terrible weakness overcame the prince. Stumbling to his feet, he managed a shaky bow, clicked his heels together, then turned and left the room. His right hand unconsciously clutched the hilt of his sword, as though he longed to smite down the invisible enemy who had created this impasse, who had decreed the death of his good friend, Don Carlos.

On second thought, the enemy was not so invisible after all. As he strode down the palace steps, Alfonso found himself cursing Paulo de Henrique and *Padre* João Manuel under his breath. He mounted his white horse and fled blindly toward the sea.

There on the sandy shore, he rode aimlessly for hours as his brain searched for some way to rid his land of the Inquisition's strangle hold — the clammy embrace of death.

≈)⊂

A new day dawned on Oporto. That important port city in the north of Portugal woke to its hectic daily round, and the tolling of bells from its many churches roused the last sluggards from their beds.

Cardinal João Batista Tenorio woke his guests and served them a hasty breakfast, consisting of bread, codfish, and substantial dishes of olives. As they ate, he leaned close to Jose de Melo and asked, "The coachman? One of ours?"

"Yes."

"Can he be trusted?"

"Absolutely!"

"Then we will make a stop on the way to Lisbon."

Though Jose looked at him questioningly, the cardinal did not elaborate.

It was nearly noon by the time they set out. Jose and Roberto had tried in vain to hurry him into departing earlier. They had intimated urgently that any delay might result in their arriving too late — after the king had signed the death sentence, or even after the *auto-da-fé* itself. But the cardinal would not be rushed. By nature a slow-going man, time never meant much to him. And now, Jose fumed, he wanted to make a stop along the way...

The carriage traveled slowly through Oporto's streets toward the city gates. But when they reached the beginning of the high road to Lisbon, the cardinal leaned out of his window and ordered the coachman to turn east.

64

The carriage proceeded through the fields east of Oporto. Jose de Melo was absorbed in thoughts of his own, most of which centered around the question: Where was the cardinal taking them? But João Batista Tenorio offered no clues.

The carriage stopped. The coachman clambered down to ask, "Where am I to go? I can't just keep driving through fields!"

The Cardinal answered mildly, "There — do you see the orchard at the foot of that hill?"

"Yes..."

"Well, that's it! There's a track to the left that will lead you directly to that orchard. But slow down, so that the carriage will arrive after the farmers have already left for the day."

The driver climbed back up and drove the horses in the orchard's direction. What did the cardinal want there? No one had a clue — neither the coachman, nor Jose de Melo, nor Roberto Gonzales, who had fallen into a deep sleep immediately upon entering the coach.

Presently, the carriage pulled up near their destination. Just ahead of them lay the orchard, peaceful in the late-afternoon sun.

"No, my friend," the cardinal called softly. "Go around to the other side. We mustn't stay here, in plain view of the city and the fields."

When they were finally positioned to the cardinal's liking, he led the way out of the carriage and asked the others, including the coachman, to follow him. They entered the orchard, which was so thick with trees as to nearly obscure the sun. The cardinal felt the ground carefully with his feet until he found the spot he wanted.

"Here!" he cried suddenly. He turned to the coachman. "You are the youngest of us. Lift the cover!"

The coachman did as he was told. The cardinal leaned over and peered into the hole. "Do you see? There's a ladder inside. It's attached to the wall of the hole. Please go down. At the bottom, you will find a box. Bring it up here. But hurry — we don't have much time."

Cautiously, the coachman began to descend the ladder. Several minutes passed before his head became visible again. One hand groped for the lip of the hole, while the other held fast to the box he'd brought up with him. The cardinal quickly took this from him while the others helped him climb out. A satisfied smile broadened the cardinal's already round face, and a gleam of triumph brightened his eyes.

"We are about to set out on a dangerous journey," he said. "You do not yet have any idea just how dangerous it may be for me. Therefore, I have decided to ask for a blessing for the road..."

He opened the box with care. Inside was a pair of *tefillin*. They were old and worn — but they were *tefillin*!

João Batista wasted no time donning them. Quickly he recited the *brachos*, then removed the *tefillin*. It was Jose's turn next, then Roberto's. Interestingly, it was the latter who seemed most moved of all. In Amsterdam he had donned *tefillin* regularly, but had not done so at all for the past two weeks since he'd been sent on this rescue mission. To bring *tefillin* into Lisbon would have carried the risk of death. Rav Menashe had instructed him that trying to save Don Carlos' life took priority over wearing *tefillin*.

And yet now, even here in Portugal, Roberto had merited the privilege of performing this special *mitzvah*, if only once.

The cardinal's thoughts seemed to parallel his own. "We've performed a *mitzvah*," he whispered to his guests. "In its merit, may we be successful in the job at hand!"

The coachman hastily did as the others had, then the *tefillin* were replaced in the box, the box lowered into its hole, and the cover set above it. In single file, the group left the orchard for the carriage and the patient horses.

The coachman flicked his whip lightly over their backs, and the carriage set out on circuitous paths for the high road to Lisbon.

⊸◠

Yitzchak de Castro could not prevent the fear from springing into his eyes at the sight of the Holy Office secretary, Paulo de Henrique. He did not understand why this heavyset man with the cold, cruel eyes hated him so. Not every Inquisition prisoner was privileged, as Yitzchak had been, to be personally tortured at this man's eminent hands. The reason eluded him. From snatches of conversation with other prisoners, he knew that de Henrique enjoyed torturing those important scions of Lisbon society who were unfortunate enough to fall victim to him. He liked to show them that he was the conqueror — and the destroyer. But what interest could de Henrique have with him, an anonymous youth of 21 who didn't even have the distinction of being a resident of Lisbon?

He quickly lowered his eyes. "What does he want with me now?" he wondered apprehensively.

"And how is our young friend?" de Henrique asked in an incongruously pleasant voice. Behind the seeming gentleness, the mockery in his words was blatant.

Yitzchak did not answer. De Henrique turned to the French ambassador. "Monsieur Lasnier, have you succeeded in finding an opening of faith and mercifulness in this heretic's armored heart?"

Monsieur Lasnier shook his head in the negative. In two strides de Henrique was at Yitzchak's side. He placed a finger roughly under the young man's chin and lifted it, so that their eyes were forced to meet. He continued to lift the chin until Yitzchak's neck began to ache and a silent prayer started up inside him. Traces of wicked laughter were visible at the corners of the secretary's mouth.

"What is it like to be so young, and so heretical?"

Yitzchak did not answer.

De Henrique's finger pressed down hard on Yitzchak's throat. The pain was sharp, and breathing became difficult. He began to wonder if his final hour was upon him.

"Answer me!" The scream curdled Yitzchak's blood. Out of the corner of his eye he saw the same momentary panic grip the ambassador. What to say?

"Well?" de Henrique prompted sharply.

How Yitzchak hated him at that moment! He knew that his doom was at hand. He would most likely be tied to the stake and burned alive sometime soon. And still, this loathsome creature wished to see him crumble and yield in his final moments. He would not do it! If only in his innermost heart and in the words he spoke, he would not surrender to the church that stood ready to snatch away his very life.

"*Senhor Padre*," he answered slowly and with a valiant effort at calmness, "Do you think that only adults are able to see through the tissue of lies in the Catholic faith? As *Senhor Padre* can see, even youngsters can reach the same conclusion..."

The slap came before he could finish. It flung him from his seat and hurled him across the room. Hardly had he landed on the floor when the next attack came, in the form of a vicious kick. De Henrique stood over him, fists clenched, breathing hard. Red-faced, he stared down at the doubled-up figure for a long moment, then turned away. Without a word to the ambassador, de Henrique stalked from the room. The door slammed furiously behind him.

Monsieur Lasnier rushed to Yitzchak's side. He had not liked what he'd just witnessed. Though an ardent Catholic who despised heretics, in his heart of hearts he could not bear the cruelties practiced by the Portuguese Church on those suspected of Jewish observance.

He helped the trembling youth to his feet and, with his own handkerchief, mopped the droplets of blood that had gathered on one broken lip. When Yitzchak was seated again, Lasnier asked resentfully, "Why do you persist in angering that man? Haven't you suffered enough?"

Yitzchak spoke thickly. "Yes, I've suffered from him. And this is my tiny revenge — to make him suffer a bit, too. He suffers because I won't give in to him, won't do his bidding!"

Lasnier was silent. He was remembering his task here: to try to restore this strayed sheep to the fold of the faith before his death. He had hoped to persuade his young compatriot with gentle persuasion — until that monster came along and spoiled everything.

Yitzchak felt Lasnier's hand stroke his head. He had no liking for the French gentleman, but at that moment the compassionate touch was beneficial. He could imagine that the hand was that of his own loving mother, in faraway Amsterdam. His mother and Amsterdam... he would see neither one again. Tears gathered in his eyes and he made no attempt to brush them away.

"Monsieur," he asked, low voiced, "do you know when it will happen?"

The ambassador knew exactly what Yitzchak was referring to, but his heart quailed at telling the young man that tomorrow, Friday, would be his last day on earth. Instead, he hedged, "It has not yet been finalized. But why won't you have pity on your soul? Why don't you even try to think again about the true faith?"

Yitzchak stirred uncomfortably. The ache in his middle, where de Henrique had aimed his kick, was still pronounced. His back, too, was sending out daggers of pain.

He looked up at the ambassador. "I do pity my soul, Monsieur."

"What do you mean?"

"I pity my soul — and it is this compassion that gives me the strength to bear what they're doing to me and not to abandon the faith of my fathers."

Lasnier was not yet angry, but a definite impatience had crept into his manner. "My young friend, are you really sure you know what you're doing?"

"With your permission, Monsieur, I will explain to you just what I think I am doing."

I've failed in my mission, Lasnier thought. He experienced a growing desire to end this conversation quickly. Why had João Manuel ever asked him to undertake it? He had come to Lisbon on a diplomatic mission, not as a churchman. Pressing his lips into a tight line, he said shortly, "Speak."

Without hesitation Yitzchak said, "As long as I retain possession of my senses, Monsieur, I will live joyfully and peacefully with the laws of Moses. That is because I am convinced that these are the best laws in the world. I understand and accept the fact that non-Jews may save their souls by observing certain natural laws, but I — and all the other descendants of the 12 tribes of Israel — can only do so through observance of the commandments. That is why I am prepared to give my life for those commandments."

"I think I understand," the ambassador cut in. He had no wish to listen to any additional heretical talk.

But Yitzchak continued. "How much time, *Senhor* — excuse me, honored sir — is left me? Won't you let a young man whose life is nearly over speak what is in his heart? Had you been Portuguese, and especially a citizen of Lisbon, I would not have asked you for such a big favor. But you are a French gentleman, and a Frenchman's heart is more compassionate."

He rushed on without waiting for Lasnier's reply. The Frenchman felt helpless to stem the tide of young de Castro's words.

"You must understand, sir ambassador, that I believe in the Creator of the world — a single creator without any partners — and I am pledged to fulfill His laws as meticulously as possible. I pray three times a day and I fast on the Jewish fast days. I try not to do any unnecessary actions on the Sabbath — that is, when I know when the Sabbath is. This past year, in prison, I fasted three days in a row because I lost track of which day was Yom Kippur. I was filled with grief because I could not celebrate the festivals of Succos and Pesach as they are meant to be celebrated — as I used to celebrate them back home..." His breathing suddenly became difficult — "back home... in Amsterdam..."

The last words were uttered in a feeble whisper. It seemed to Lasnier that Yitzchak was about to fall out of his chair with the force of his own emotion. Hastily, the Frenchman said, "I heard you. I've listened patiently, my young friend, although it has not been easy for me. But I respected your wishes. Now I ask you to listen to me."

When Yitzchak did not react, the ambassador hurried on:

"In the name of our savior, I ask you to open the eyes of your soul, if only for a minute! We know that the prophecies recorded in the Bible were about him. They foretold his appearance in the world. My young friend, he is the savior. The proofs are numerous. If you like, I can have the monks come and explain them to you."

"That is not necessary, honored sir. All during my imprisonment, they tried to convince me of all this. I can read the prophecies in their original language. I know how your explanations distort the true meaning of the text. And I know full well that they would have treated me more mercifully had I agreed to accept what you're telling me now about the truth of the Catholic religion. But — I pity my soul. I will not lie to it. And so, I will not deny my own Jewish faith." Yitzchak paused. "Have I hurt you, Monsieur Ambassador?"

Lasnier shook with rage. "Yes, you have hurt me. I have tried to help you, and this is your response! I will not spend any more time talking with you. I see now that those who claimed it would be a waste of my time were right. Just know that you are cutting yourself off from the salvation of our savior!" Lasnier ended his little speech on a note of deep emotion.

Yitzchak raised his own voice. "But he's dead! He was crucified at least 1640 years ago!"

"He will return. He promised that he will return!"

Yitzchak gazed at the ambassador with compassion-filled eyes. "This is a very serious time for me, Monsieur. It is no time for jokes."

Lasnier shook visibly. De Henrique had been right in slapping him!

"You are right," he said furiously. "This is a very serious and very tragic hour for you. You are to be burned tomorrow morning! *Burned alive.* Because even at this crucial moment in your life, you are drowning in your heresy."

Lasnier left the room at a near-run. At once, the two monks came in and seized Yitzchak by the arms. In short order, he was brought back downstairs and flung into a solitary cell in the dungeon.

65

hurch bells throughout the city tolled long and loud on Thursday afternoon. The pealing sound traveled the city streets and drifted out into the fields. Pedestrians stopped in their rounds to listen, and in their homes people lent an ear to the unusual ringing and wondered what it portended.

There were many who already knew. They had followed events tensely during the past few days, agog with curiosity to learn the fate of the once-illustrious Don Carlos.

"The king has signed!" a woman whispered to her daughter as they kneaded dough for the family bread.

"The king has signed!" another woman called across the street to her neighbor.

"The king has signed the sentence!" The man's voice rose above the others in the city square, where a large throng had gathered, listening to the bells.

The central gates of the vast Inquisition building burst open, and ten riders galloped through them into the street. They were magnificently dressed, and on their heads were bright yellow hats with red tassels. They rode out of Lisbon into the surrounding countryside, to spread the news in all the villages there. The Inquisition wanted everyone to witness the spectacle the next day — to see the heretic Don Carlos receive his just punishment at last.

The riders dispersed in every direction, the thunder of their horses' hooves nearly as loud and insistent as the music of the church bells.

⁓〇⁓

Armando Batancur, a junior monk, left the Inquisition building shortly afterwards. He greeted the gatekeeper in a friendly fashion, then walked unhurriedly up the street.

His walk was apparently aimless — until, at a certain house, he stopped. Cautiously, he opened the gate and went up to the front door. He knocked: first twice, then three times, then four more. Between each set was a pause of ten seconds or so. Without waiting for an answer, he returned to the street and resumed his walk.

Several more minutes brought him to another street, and another house — this one on the corner. Once again he knocked: twice, then three times, then four. This time, too, he did not wait for any reply. But before hurrying away, he took a moment to hastily scan his surroundings to see whether his activities had attracted undue attention.

Armando breathed in silent relief. Lisbon's citizens, intent on their own affairs, were passing by without taking the slightest notice of him. He continued on his way.

He covered many streets, from time to time pausing to repeat his knocking ritual. In the end, he had stopped at nine houses in all.

Two hours later, as night began to spread her cloak of darkness over Lisbon, ten men met at the seashore. Armando was one of them. Each was mounted on a horse, and all were pointed northward. Together they rode at a leisurely pace, as though they had nothing more on their minds than a pleasant moonlight outing.

Not a word was exchanged until they reached a certain dark, deserted hut.

Minister of the Treasury, Don Luis de Sauza, could not calm himself. In extreme agitation he paced his house, thoughts and emotions in a turmoil. His hand still clutched the accursed note, which seemed to scorch his skin. With his free hand he formed a fist and struck his forehead a mighty blow. It hurt, but that was what he wanted. He simply could not forgive himself.

Just a few hours before, with his own hands, he had helped bring about the authorization of Don Carlos' death sentence... Don Carlos, the best of men, leader of their tiny Marrano community, the one who had clung tenaciously to the laws of their G-d and had taught his people to do the same.

"What do we do now?" he asked himself in anguish.

As one of the king's ministers, his attendance at tomorrow's *auto-da-fé* was mandatory. To his grief, he had already been forced to witness other Jews being burnt at the stake, and the experience had caused him great suffering and nightly terrors. But this time would be worst of all. To see Don Carlos rise to his death enveloped in tongues of flame would be like... like seeing his own son burnt alive.

"How will I be able to survive after that?" he cried out in despair. The four walls of the room remained dumb, unresponsive.

Suddenly, an idea blossomed in his disordered brain. He stopped in the center of the room, then dashed over to the window. The idea took further shape. He considered it again, this time flinging himself into a deep armchair first. Before his inner eye rose the cast of characters in this tragedy: Don Carlos, *Padre* João Manuel, Paulo de Henrique, Fernando de Lima... and now, he himself had been drawn in, too. Lisbon surely had a curse upon her!

Don Luis de Sauza stood up decisively. His idea had entirely taken over his being. He went to the door, passed through it, and locked it behind him. His official carriage, placed at his disposal by the king, stood near his house. Without waiting for the coachman's assistance, he climbed inside.

The coachman, on his high perch, bent closer to the carriage window to receive his orders.

The minister's voice was clear, if slightly weary: "To the Superior Judge's house!"

The driver nodded.

"As quickly as you are able!"

The whip cracked over the horses' backs and the carriage sprang forward. So faithful was the coachman to the minister's command that no more than 10 minutes had passed when he drew up before Fernando de Lima's house.

⭤

Padre João Manuel did not return home, but elected instead to remain in his office at the Inquisition. Pulling the window curtains aside, he looked down at the courtyard. Even at this hour, as dusk approached, there was an air of heightened activity there. Monks dressed in cassocks of brown, black, or orange moved purposefully through the courtyard, making various preparations for tomorrow's *auto-da-fé*. It seemed to João Manuel, watching them from above, that they bustled about like ants around a crumb.

Now, why, he wondered, had that particular image occurred to him?

Could it be because, in his heart of hearts, he was not fully reconciled to what was slated to happen tomorrow to his one-time friend, Don Carlos?

He steeled himself. No! He did not regret Don Carlos' demise. Had he wished, Don Carlos might have helped himself by abetting João Manuel to get rid of the Marranos' greatest enemy — the enemy, indeed, of Lisbon's citizens and of the Inquisition itself: Paulo de Henrique. The plot João Manuel had unfolded at the seashore, featuring a forged letter condemning de Henrique, had seemed perfectly valid in his own eyes. But Don Carlos had rejected it. He had been prepared to sacrifice his life rather than stoop to a lie. What a strange man!

The priest leaned against his desk, right hand playing with the cross at his chest. After tomorrow, Lisbon would never be the same. An exalted figure, a leader and statesman, would die for his heresy. What effect would that have on the populace? João Manuel had no way of knowing.

To be honest, it did not worry him very much. What did worry him — and frighten him, too — was the fact that, after tomorrow, de Henrique would soar on the crest of a power he had never yet enjoyed. He had been victorious in his battle for Don Carlos' life. He would be hero of the rabble that swarmed Lisbon's streets. And de Henrique, João Manuel knew, would play that victory for all it was worth.

With the fading day came a strengthening of his anxieties. The planting of the *mezuzos* in his house, by de Henrique's agents, still gave him no peace. And what little remained of his peace of mind vanished at the thought of those monks in black, de Henrique's fanatical young henchmen, bursting into the Superior Judge's home in broad daylight. Would he himself, or Fernando de Lima, prove the secretary's next victim? It seemed that even the royal house held the man in fear!

Abruptly, he rose to his feet. He lit a taper, and the soft yellow light dispersed some of the gloom that had gathered in the room. Taking his place again at his desk, he took up quill and paper, dipped the former in ink, and began writing quickly by the taper's light. A few moments later, finished, he brought the page closer to his eyes and read what he had written.

He nodded once, and sprinkled a pinch of ash over the page. When the ink had dried, he slowly folded the letter, which he placed into a pocket of his cassock. He extinguished the taper. With his usual measured step and air of self-importance, João Manuel left the room, passed along the corridor, and arrived at the entrance to the building.

Out here, activity had slackened but not ceased completely. One carriage, he saw, was still standing harnessed and ready beside the gate. With a slightly quickened step, he approached it. The coachman greeted him deferentially.

Padre João Manuel climbed into the coach without returning the greeting. Above, the coachman fumed silently at this unexpected errand, just when he'd been about to unhitch his horses and settle them for the night. Through the gathering darkness, he heard the *padre's* clear voice calling up to him.

"Take me with all possible speed to the home of Superior Judge Fernando de Lima. And remember... hurry!"

Along the high road leading southward from Oporto galloped the ornate carriage belonging to cardinal João Batista Tenorio. The large cross emblazoned on its gilded doors informed all passing coaches of the Eminence that rode within.

During most of the long journey, the three passengers did not exchange many words. The Cardinal sat peacefully, his face a portrait of contentment and serenity. In stark contrast, Roberto Gonzales was a screaming bundle of nerves. Would they arrive in time? Would the cardinal succeed in doing what he'd been asked to do? The questions tormented him without pause.

Roberto glanced at the cardinal, whose air of calm infuriated him. How could he sit there so serenely when Jews were slated to be burned tomorrow? Roberto was forced to admit to himself that he disliked the man. Perhaps, if their mission succeeded, his feelings would change.

He transferred his gaze to Jose de Melo. To his astonishment, Jose was fast asleep. How could he sleep at a time like this?

But perhaps, he thought, this was the way these men protected themselves, and their own sanity. As Marranos, they lived with extraordinary tensions all their days. Coming from free Amsterdam, Roberto had no legitimate right to judge them...

A sudden jerk straightened the cardinal's back and woke Jose de Melo in confusion. The carriage was swaying alarmingly from side to side. Almost before the passengers could begin to wonder what was wrong, the wheels passed rapidly into a ditch at the side of the road. The coach jerked and swayed again, and then overturned!

Paulo de Henrique lit a taper in his bedroom. Taking down a Latin prayer book, he knelt by his bed, genuflected, and began murmuring a prayer. After a few minutes he closed the book, closed his eyes briefly as though in concentrated thought, and rose heavily to his feet.

He was tired. It had been a difficult and nerve-wracking day. Fernando de Lima had done exactly as de Henrique had wished: authorized the death sentence. But, in the process, he had intentionally humiliated de Henrique before a large crowd of citizens. That was unforgivable!

And the slight had not been directed at him alone. It had been an insult to the entire Inquisition, to the church, to the Catholic faith — an insult perpetrated in public!

The secretary was particularly incensed because the judge had destroyed his well-deserved pleasure in his triumph over Don Carlos. This was so despite the fact that De Henrique knew himself to be the most powerful man in Lisbon today. He was well on his way to realizing his goal: to rule the Inquisition, and through it, the whole city. He would easily manage to depose the foolish João Manuel. On the day de Henrique made his move, João Manuel would not represent any real obstacle. But what of the judge? By now, everyone in Lisbon, including the king himself, knew of de Henrique's abortive attempt to search de Lima's house for a man who wasn't there. This made it difficult for him to harm the judge, to send him into hell along with Don Carlos. It would be necessary to be cautious, to move slowly and indirectly against de Lima. It was also unlikely that the judge would remain silent and not make his own move against de Henrique.

And then there was Alfonso, the spoiled royal prince...

Still, de Henrique was inclined to pat himself on the back. Tomorrow was the big day! With Lisbon freed of Don Carlos, the way to the king's heart would be free and clear...

But what of Fernando de Lima? His was a voice that was heeded in the royal court. How to rid himself of this stone in his path — the one man who had the power, even before tomorrow's *auto-da-fé*, to ruin de Henrique's chances with the king?

His eyes opened wide. A new thought had struck him. It would not be an easy plan to put into action. But on the way to conquest, it was some-times necessary to do unpleasant things.

Blowing out the taper, he threw on his cassock, placed his monk's skullcap on his head, and left the house. His steps took him in the direction of the Superior Judge's house.

66

The 10 riders trotted gently up to the hut, the sound of their horses' hooves making scarcely a sound in the star-studded night. They tied the reins to several thick, long hooks protruding from the outside walls. Without a word two of the men moved away from the others, going around the back of the dark structure. The rest waited in their places.

The two soon returned. To the questioning looks they returned quick, negative headshakes, as if to say, "Nothing. We saw nothing suspicious."

Armando Batancur, who had summoned them all to this urgent meeting, was not satisfied. He signaled the others to untie the horses. Two of them grasped his intention. Rapidly, they freed the horses, then led them by the reins into a nearby copse of trees. The horses dispersed throughout the copse and behind it. It was better that they remain out of sight of the hut. The more pains they took to avoid suspicion, the better it would be for everyone.

Armando opened the door of the hut and the others streamed quickly inside. They did not light tapers. Darkness was preferable for the discussion that would take place here tonight. When Armando saw them all seated on the cold floor, he spoke.

"The question is: What to do?"

A voice answered him from the darkness: "The question is: Is there anything we *can* do?"

"That's the sort of question we would not have expected of Luis!" another voice retorted sharply.

Silence fell. Everyone present remembered Luis and his group. Their last and most spectacular success had been the dazzling rescue of Raphael Chaim — Arnaldo Rodriguez — from the Inquisition dungeon. They had spirited Raphael Chaim away on a ship to Brazil. Certain of the great danger of being discovered, Luis and his men had elected to sail away on the same ship — a ship in Don Carlos' fleet...

The first speaker had his answer ready. "What Luis would not have asked, we do have to ask! It is doubtful whether we could accomplish the things Luis might have."

"What, then?" Armando demanded. "Are we to abandon any thought of saving Don Carlos? To simply participate in tomorrow's loathsome spectacle and watch him burned at the stake? And afterwards, tell our Father in Heaven, 'We are not to blame! There was nothing we could do!'?"

This time the silence was heavier, and lasted considerably longer. Armando finally broke it by pressing, "Is that what you're suggesting?"

Someone answered softly in the darkness: "Well, for that matter, what do *you* suggest?"

"That's why I summoned you all from the city! To listen, to think, to be advised!"

They were all young men, all bearing positions in the Inquisition, the church, or the government. They all belonged to Lisbon's dwindling Marrano community. After Luis and his band left Portugal, these men had decided to organize themselves to help those unfortunates caught in de Henrique's web. The Marrano monks who worked in the Inquisition building would smuggle food to the Jewish prisoners. On occasion they would bring in some news, or even a letter from a prisoner's family on the outside.

But their most daring escapade had never actually taken place. The plan had been to kidnap Paulo de Henrique one night and throw him into the river. It had been worked out in meticulous detail. On the day in question, they were to have received word of de Henrique's schedule from Armando. Masked and mounted, they would lie in wait to ambush the secretary's carriage on some deserted street corner. According to the plan, two of the riders were to overtake the carriage, overpower the coachman, gag and bind him, take the reins from him, and drive the carriage out of the city. Their chances of success, at night when illumination was at its weakest, had seemed fairly high.

But the plan had never been implemented. It had been scheduled for the tense and difficult days immediately preceding the conclusion of the Don Carlos case. The Superior Judge, Fernando de Lima, had been the one to prevent the plan from going forward. In his opinion, de Henrique's disappearance would arouse enormous suspicion throughout Lisbon, ending with the decision to execute Don Carlos as de Henrique had wished. At that time, too, De Lima was still hoping to avoid endorsing the death sentence, either via legal means or through the king's intervention.

And now, one week later, they were here in the darkened hut. De Henrique was alive and well, and Don Carlos had a mere 12 hours left to live. Armando, for one, bitterly regretted ever having heeded de Lima's advice. They should have proceeded with the plan, despite the judge's foreboding.

He had no idea what they should or could do now — but he did have a strong conviction that they should act.

"Maybe," came a hesitant voice from among the group, "maybe tomorrow, when the procession is moving toward the site of the *auto-da-fé*, we can start a riot of sorts and try to free Don Carlos from his cage?"

"There are only 10 of us capable of action. Ten are too few to stage a riot."

Another man stood up in the dark. "It's useless to speak of it! Even if we were to free him, what then? Where would we take him? Apart from that, wouldn't the many soldiers — not to mention the crowd itself — tear us to pieces?"

There were several sounds of agreement. "True!" someone cried. "We must do what is possible — not the impossible!"

"If we wish to destroy our small community," someone else said gravely, "then we must act as our friend Armando wishes. We must attack the procession bearing the prisoners, create a riot, and let ourselves be killed for our Torah... But, no. I don't think that is exactly what our faith demands from us. To our sorrow, Don Carlos' fate is sealed. It is G-d's will. Our job is to continue where he left off, to continue observing the *mitzvos*, and to keep his memory alive in our prayers."

No one refuted this. With one accord, the men began scrambling to their feet. It seemed to them that the meeting was over.

Armando stayed where he was. He stood facing his friends, though he could not see their faces nor they his. But all could hear his rapid, furious breathing. They understood that the fury was directed at them.

"All right!" Armando snapped. "I can understand your despair!"

"It is not despair, Armando. It is simply facing reality."

Armando hissed, "All right, my friends, go home. I will act alone. I will find no comfort in this world if Don Carlos is burnt at the stake tomorrow and we, his faithful followers, did not lift a finger to save him!"

"Just don't act foolishly, Armando!"

Another added, "Don Carlos would not be happy if, in trying to save his life, our entire community were destroyed."

And another: "Armando, calm yourself. This is his fate. It is our payment for the way our fathers sinned and abandoned their faith. We are doomed every few years to see a number of our beloved friends obliterated in the Inquisition's merciful flames. Will you fight your fate?"

Armando did not answer. He stood silently, unmoving, as his friends tried to dissuade him from attempting to rescue Don Carlos. Finally, without a word, he elbowed past the others and burst through the door. His friends heard him race towards the copse. Moments later, the sound of his horse's hooves came clearly to their ears. They stood still, listening, until the last echo of the hoofbeats died away and silence had returned.

Then, slowly, they filed out of the hut, located their horses, and rode wearily back to the city.

≈)(≈

Don Luis de Sauza burst into the judge's house, so wrapped up in his thoughts that he forgot to knock. Fernando de Lima started in fright, then grew even more frightened at the sight of his friend's wild, pale countenance.

"What's happened to you?" he demanded.

The words had a magical effect on de Sauza. The frenzied look left his eye, and he smiled. Vaguely, he felt that he hadn't behaved with perfect propriety, and that his unannounced entry had probably panicked his friend.

"Nothing, my friend," he answered quietly. "I'm just so distressed by the death sentence that you were forced to endorse. It's very hard for me to accept."

Fernando, in his turn, relaxed slightly. He rounded his desk to sit in an armchair and motioned for the minister to take his place opposite him. When de Sauza was seated, Fernando asked, "What do you want from me?"

"Only your company in this difficult hour. And to believe that you, too, are suffering over the fact that you have sentenced our friend to death."

Fernando's expression took on a frozen rigidity. His eyes, fixed on de Sauza, seemed sightless. The minister did not know what he had said to bring that look to his friend's face.

Fernando spoke in short, clipped syllables, his lips moving as though made of lead. "I-did-not-sentence-Don-Carlos-to-death."

Da Souza realized that he had made a mistake, but was helpless to correct it. Fernando went on, "My job, my dear friend, is to either endorse or reject the sentences of the accursed Holy Office."

"Yes, yes, I understand," de Sauza said hastily.

"No, you don't understand." Fernando's tone cut across the space between them, sharp as knives. "You don't understand, because you are not familiar with the laws of this land. You don't understand because you don't know that I, apparently, am to be Paulo de Henrique's next sacrificial victim. In his quest for ultimate power in this city, he will stop at nothing. And he will succeed! Anyone who stands in his way finds himself accused of being a secret Jew, with 'witnesses' to bear out that accusation."

In the face of de Sauza's silence, Fernando shook his head. "Yes," he murmured. "Apparently, my turn is next." There was a note of despair in his voice.

Da Souza said gently, "Fernando, my friend, we have been living like this for several generations, ever since our fathers converted to Christianity on the order of Portugal's king. From the day we're told we are Jews we carry with us the knowledge that there's a good chance we will not live out our days like other people, in a peaceful old age, surrounded by our families and offspring. You speak of your doom. Didn't you expect it to happen to you one day?"

"Of course I've thought of it. But why do you bring it up now?"

Da Souza moved in his chair, groping for the right words. "I bring it up because of the despair I sense in you now. Why despair? This is no sudden development. You knew it could happen, and have prayed for strength to stand up to this test."

Fernando chuckled lightly. "You've forgotten, it seems, how you burst into this house just now. You, too, know what it is to be afraid... to fear an unknown fate."

Da Souza considered this, then answered, "My fear was for what is supposed to happen to Don Carlos tomorrow — may G-d preserve him from harm."

Still Fernando laughed. "And didn't he know this could happen to him one day, and didn't you know that it could happen? You tremble for his fate, yet demand that I greet my own with equanimity!"

"You're right," de Sauza whispered in deepening distress. "It is possible to know much, to expect the worst — but when it comes, you're confused and afraid. We're only human."

The judge straightened in his armchair, some of his old authority flowing back. "You're right. We are only human. But it was Don Carlos himself who taught us more than once that beautiful lesson he heard in Amsterdam from our great rabbi, Reb Menashe; the story of *akeidas Yitzchak*. We have been in the position of *akeidas Yitzchak* for several hundred years already. We must be strong, my friend. Don Carlos demands it of us. Tomorrow, with bitterly grieving hearts, we will have to be present. You'll see with your own eyes how they burn Don Carlos at the stake. He will sanctify G-d's Name."

"Are you trying to tell me something?" Don Luis de Sauza wrinkled his brow.

"Yes. I'm asking you not to search for signs of despair in the words I say. I'm not a hero. But I do try to accept whatever Hashem decrees for me, without complaint." Fernando sat back. "That's all I wanted to say. Do you understand?"

For a long time de Sauza did not reply. His eyes roved the walls restlessly, moving from one oil painting to the next. At last he blurted, "Forgive me. Please."

Fernando nodded, as if to indicate that the request had been noted and accepted.

Don Luis de Sauza stood up. It had been a profitless talk about a hopeless situation in an unbearable city. Still, sharing one's woes with a fellow sufferer was comforting. He extended his hand in farewell. Fernando took it without rising.

Da Souza was already at the door and about to leave when he paused. He turned around and returned to where his friend sat.

"Fernando, what should I do with the note you gave me?"

"What do you mean? That's an official court document."

"Yes — but what do I do with it?"

"Tomorrow, after... You return it to de Henrique for the file. That accursed file of his."

Fernando saw the gleam that sprang into the other's eyes. Da Souza retreated a few steps, then took the folded note from his pocket and dangled it before the judge. "I think I'll tear it up."

Fernando jumped. "Why?"

"Because... because... if I tear it, it might help somehow. Later."

Fernando crossed the room quickly to his friend's side. "What do you mean?"

"Simply this: We cannot prevent Don Carlos' death. That is his fate, G-d's decree. But in a few months we can demand a new investigation into the matter. If the note is gone, there will be no witnesses. Perhaps then it will be possible to get rid of de Henrique at last. Now do you understand?"

"Not exactly." Fernando kept his eyes trained on the note.

"Criticism of de Henrique will be sharp. He will have ordered the death of a brilliant military commander without proof. The people will hate him, and the possibility of ousting him will be real. *There will be no witnesses*. Understand?"

Fernando grabbed de Sauza's hand. "No, don't do it! At least until after the *auto-da-fé*, don't touch that note. You are required to hold onto it until then. Those were my instructions, the instructions of the Superior Court!"

"Yes — but why?"

"Don't ask me that." Fernando's thoughts flew to Oporto. Had the cardinal agreed to the plan? Had they set out for Lisbon? Would they arrive before Don Carlos was consigned to the flames?

"That's an order," he said forcefully.

Don Luis de Sauza hesitated, then reluctantly agreed. He replaced the note in his pocket.

Moving tiredly now, he left the house and closed the door behind him. In the darkness of the courtyard, he sensed a living human presence very close by...

From every direction leading to the capital city of Lisbon came a steady stream of horses and carts. There were riders on horseback and even those who walked the roads on foot. All were hastening to arrive early at the Triero da Paso square, where workers were laboring to finish the scaffolds and stakes for the burning of Don Carlos.

⇒)(⇐

The coachman was the first to regain his footing after the carriage from Oporto overturned. He heard groans from inside. Clambering over the side of the coach, he managed to open the door and help the passengers out.

When they had cleared their heads, the group stood on the empty high -road. It was devoid of life.

Jose de Melo asked, "What do we do now?"

"We must wait until someone passes by who can help us lift the carriage back onto the road," the coachman opined.

"What are the chances that someone will come along soon?"

The coachman peered along the road at the setting sun. Slowly, he answered, "I don't believe that anyone will pass here before morning."

"NO!" Jose cried. He thought of the *auto-da-fé* scheduled for the next morning. They *must* reach Lisbon in time!

67

The two stood very close, by the door to Fernando de Lima's house, but did not see each other at first. Then, in the same instant each realized that he was not alone. The surprise encounter startled them both. Fear kept them silent for a long moment.

Don Luis de Sauza recovered first.

"Who are you?" he demanded.

The answer shot back at him: "And who are *you*?"

De Souza gasped. He had recognized the voice. It belonged to *Padre* João Manuel. Disjointed thoughts chased themselves through his mind. What was the head of the Inquisition doing here? What would he think of the fact that the Minister of the Treasury was visiting the Superior Judge after the harrowing day at court?

Then a new and chilling notion struck the minister with fresh dread: Was it possible that Fernando de Lima was not as loyal to the Marranos as he had thought? Could he be working hand in glove with the Inquisition?

No! His heart screamed the answer almost before his mind had articulated the question. It was just not possible! Why was he entertaining such thoughts? Where did these doubts come from?

All this took only seconds to pass through his mind. Heart still pounding with shock, de Sauza said, "*Padre*, don't you recognize my voice?"

As he spoke, João Manuel did recognize him. He moved closer and asked, "What are you doing here?"

The questioner's peremptory tone angered de Sauza. "I might ask you the same thing. I beg of you not to forget who I am!"

João Manuel was angry in turn, but controlled himself. In the dark, the minister could not see the spasm that crossed the priest's face. João Manuel said, "Sir Treasurer, you have no need to ask me such a question. I am concerned with various legal matters on behalf of the Holy Office. If you recall, today we dealt with the case of Don Carlos." He paused. "If you must know, I've come here to drink a toast with Judge de Lima, to celebrate our victory! And now, what is your business here?"

There was something indefinably menacing in his tone.

Don Luis de Sauza did not believe a word of the *padre's* explanation. There would be no celebratory toasts drunk here tonight. Why, then, had João Manuel really come? He strained his mind for the answer, but none came to him.

"I have come," he said smoothly, "for the same purpose — to raise a glass in honor to this great success. Or have you forgotten, *Padre*, that I, too, am involved in this case? Who was entrusted with the note? Who was called a friend of the court, in contrast to the complete lack of trust in you Inquisition people? It was I, that's who! I've come to thank Judge de Lima for the faith he demonstrated in me, and to congratulate him for rendering a just decision today."

João Manuel sensed the mockery behind the minister's words. Seething, he listened as Da Souza continued, "As for your threatening manner and your desire to know what I am doing at every moment, if I had not recognized your voice, *Padre*, I would have been sure you were the Holy Office secretary, de Henrique — the man who, as I am sure you know, essentially rules this city."

Before João Manuel could answer, de Sauza turned on his heel and hurried away. He left the furious priest behind, together with a reminder of what João Manuel would much rather have forgotten: that de Henrique's power was greater than his own, and growing greater every day.

He made a fist and slammed it into a tree trunk, eyes probing the darkness that had swallowed up the minister.

⟋⟍

Jose de Melo stood in despair at the edge of the highroad. Not far away the Cardinal fumed. He was beginning to regret that he'd ever agreed to participate in this adventure. It would not save Don Carlos and would only increase the risk of exposing his own Jewish identity. Here he stood in full view on the public road beside an overturned carriage, like some wretched beggar.

As for Roberto Gonzales, he had seated himself on a boulder at the roadside and was praying quietly to his G-d. His thoughts wandered away to Amsterdam, to his congregation "Bais Yaakov," and to Rabbi Menashe ben Israel. Would he ever see them again?

Meanwhile, the coachman was trying to unharness the horses from the carriage. They were not cooperating. The pressure of the overturned carriage was causing them much discomfort, but in their frightened snorting and plunging they did not allow the coachman to ease their situation.

Suddenly, a wild reckless spirit seemed to infuse the horses. They began moving spasmodically along the ditch, dragging the carriage sideways after them.

"*Senhores! Senhores, depressa* (Gentlemen, hurry)!" the coachman shouted. "This is our chance! Help me right the carriage while the horses are moving it. Come quickly!"

After a moment's astonished stare, all three gentlemen climbed down into the ditch. Working in tandem, they grasped the coach's side as it was lifted slightly by the exertion of the horses. Running slowly alongside, they strained mightily to tilt the carriage onto its wheels. It was the work of many minutes until they finally succeeded. Both men and horses stood panting.

"*Graçhas a D-eus, graçhas a D-eus* (Thank G-d, thank G-d)," came from every pair of lips. Even in the dark, with only the faint starlight to illuminate their faces, each could see the shine of joy in the others' eyes.

Then, without warning and to their intense horror, the horses plunged forward. They broke into a gallop, leaving their honored masters behind in the dust...

≈⌒≈

Armando Batancur returned to his room in the Inquisition building bitter and weary. He was grievously disappointed in his friends' refusal to join him in a violent confrontation, the kind Luis and his band had advocated. The men were loyal to the Marrano community, but — unlike their predecessors — also anxious to take good care of their own skin. They were searching for the easy way out. Though willing to risk their lives to observe the few *mitzvos* they knew — an observance attended by self-sacrifice and grave personal danger — the violent rescue of Don Carlos was apparently beyond them.

Armando went out into the courtyard for a breath of fresh air. Around him all was silent, asleep. Until a short time ago, the place had reverberated with last-minute preparations for tomorrow's *auto-da-fé*, but that was over now. The only light came from the watchman's booth at the gate. The guard was softly singing Portuguese folk songs to pass the time.

Armando strolled aimlessly to and fro. Below him, in the dungeon, Don Carlos lay awaiting his death. Why, for all he knew, he was standing directly above Don Carlos' cell this very minute! Armando stopped his pacing and lifted his face to the sky. Millions of stars hung there, casting their everlasting magical spell. At such moments it was easy to feel

Hashem's presence very near. He prayed without making a sound, but he knew that the G-d of Moshe heard him very well:

"Please hear the prayer of Your simple servant, and make a miracle. See how the remnants of Your nation, scorned and oppressed, are trodden down into the dust year after year for centuries — and see how, despite it all, we are prepared to give our lives for the holy faith we inherited from our fathers. Make a miracle, so that the accursed de Henrique will fall. Make a miracle like the one You made for Raphael Chaim, whom Your good messengers, led by Luis, rescued from this place" — Amando stamped with his feet on the ground — "from this cruel dungeon of death.

"There is no Luis now, there is no one to devote himself to such a rescue. I am left alone. Please, G-d of the heavens and the earth, G-d of Avraham and Moshe, make a miracle, and save Don Carlos so that Your Name may be sanctified forever in this wicked country!"

Armando stood transfixed in the center of the courtyard for a long time, eyes closed, completely immersed in his silent, heartfelt plea. He had forgotten where he was as his thoughts traveled ever upward, toward his Creator.

He woke abruptly from his far-fetched dream when a soft hand landed on his shoulder. Armando began to shake.

⁓)⌒

In the square outside the royal palace, the work did not cease all night long. Laborers moved through the darkness, aided only by the flickering light of hundreds of flaming tapers. Using long, heavy boards, they erected a dais from which the king and his entourage would view the proceedings. Other boards formed a barrier to hold back the expected horde of spectators. The reasons for this were many. For one thing, some pious Portuguese citizen might take it into his head to injure the heretics with his own hands. Also, it was not beyond the bounds of possibility that some relative of the doomed prisoners, or perhaps a daring Marrano, would try to disrupt the festivities. Several monks worked at readying the site of the burnings themselves.

A number of interested onlookers from Lisbon and the outlying villages gleefully observed the preparations. The workers waved genially at them. In the east, the first very faint lightening of the sky heralded the approaching dawn.

The workers picked up the pace, eager to finish the job so that they could go home and snatch a few hours' sleep before the big event.

68

ernando de Lima was astonished. Standing in his doorway was *Padre* João Manuel. It was late, and Fernando had been hoping for some much-needed rest after the day's turmoil. He had just bid good-night to Minister Don Luis de Sauza. What did João Manuel want at this hour?

Even as he mentally cursed the man, he heard himself mumur, "*Bem vindo* (Welcome), *Padre*. If you've come so late, you must have a good reason."

Padre João Manuel came inside, closing the door slowly behind him. "I still don't know if I have a reason for coming."

Fernando glanced at him in sudden suspicion. "Why, then? Have you simply sleepwalked here?"

"On the contrary. I haven't been able to sleep."

"And why is that, *Padre*? Haven't you people at the Holy Office accomplished what you set out to achieve?" The next words stuck painfully in Fernando's throat. "You have the judgment against Don Carlos, and the king has already signed it. So... why the difficulty sleeping?"

João Manuel evaded this question by asking another. "Your Honor, when we met at court this morning, why did you feel the need to insult Paulo de Henrique?"

Fernando chuckled wryly. "It's good to see you so protective of your secretary!"

"That's not exactly the case, *Senhor*."

"So?"

João Manuel was quiet, choosing his words. But when he spoke, it was only to inquire, "May I sit?"

Fernando was embarrassed: In his surprise at seeing his visitor, he had forgotten his manners. "Yes, of course." Inwardly, he thought with rising tension, *Something is going to happen.*

With a sigh, João Manuel sank into a deep armchair. He smiled — a perfunctory smile — and asked, "Doesn't Your Honor know our Paulo by now?"

"I know him." Fernando grimaced. "I might wish I did not."

Absently adjusting the priestly skullcap on his head, João Manuel said, "I agree with that last sentence of yours... fully."

"So?"

"That's just the point. This man that we'd both be happier not to know is preparing some action, apparently, to make us know him even better."

Fernando knew this to be true. The intrusion of the black-clad monks into his house portended nothing good for him. It might very well have been a forewarning that he, too, would find himself a prisoner in the Inquisition dungeon one fine day soon. But how did this touch João Manuel? Was it possible that he, too, was a secret Jew that no one knew about, and was that why Paulo de Henrique was hounding him?

Cautiously, he said, "I'm afraid I don't understand you. How will we get to know him better?"

The priest's silence stretched long, tickling Fernando's curiosity even more. What secret was João Manuel hiding?

João Manuel struggled out of his armchair and began pacing the room, sunk in thought. When he came close to the judge, he stopped and said slowly, "They came to my house last night."

Fernando pretended not to understand. "Interesting."

"It is *not* interesting!" João Manuel snapped. "It is dangerous!"

When Fernando said nothing, the *padre* continued. "He tried to do to me last night that which he tried to do to you this morning. I caught the young masked monk he'd sent. He was carrying — a *mezuzah*!"

He thrust his hand into the folds of his cassock and extracted a small package. Opening it, he cried, "You see? The devil wanted to plant this in my home, so that he might have me arrested later for being a secret Jew!"

Not a muscle twitched in Fernando's face. The story was shocking: It showed de Henrique in an even blacker light than formerly.

Padre João Manuel whispered, "Just as he wanted to do to you!"

It gave Fernando a wry pleasure to see the Inquisition head so afraid. João Manuel had been party to the executions of a good many Jews, and of innocent Christians as well. Now that he found himself in personal danger, he had suddenly become aware of the fact that all was not right in his domain...

"In that case," Fernando said coolly, "perhaps it was a good thing that I insulted him publicly today."

"No! You only strengthened his desire for revenge — and he will accomplish what he sets out to do. He is the most powerful man in Lisbon today. Stronger than I am!"

Fernando folded his arms and gazed at the priest. "And what do you want from me, *Padre*?"

"Nothing. Only to show you the whole picture. To make you understand what is transpiring in our city. To help you see that you made a mistake in arousing the slumbering beast."

João Manuel walked rapidly towards the front door. Fernando's words followed after him: "In that case, isn't it possible that the evidence of Don Carlos' guilt is also just another of de Henrique's plots?"

João Manuel paused at the door, hesitated, then said, "It is possible."

"In other words," Fernando pressed, "you agree that it is possible we'll be burning an innocent man tomorrow?"

João Manuel gave Fernando a long, cold stare. Then, without a word, he turned his back on the room and left the house.

Fernando was not displeased with their talk. It might prove helpful in their last-minute fight for Don Carlos' life. He thought of Roberto Gonzales, Jose de Melo, and the cardinal of Oporto, whom he been awaiting impatiently all evening. Why in the world weren't they here yet?

⥱⥲

Paulo de Henrique reached the Superior Judge's front gate and paused. Just last night he had seen a stranger in this very house — a stranger who had embarked on the dangerous pretense of not being acquainted with the judge. The trusted assistants he'd sent this morning had failed to turn up the stranger, and this failure had caused him to be humiliated. Now the whole city knew that the monks had broken into the judge's house on his, de Henrique's, orders.

Tonight he would investigate the house himself. He must expose the stranger within. All day long, de Henrique's men had kept a watch on the house, waiting for anyone to leave it. No one had left. Therefore, the stranger must still be inside.

De Henrique opened the gate cautiously. Though the hour was advanced, the light in the window told him that everyone in the judge's household were not yet asleep. He was resolved to peek through the window again. If he found the stranger there then, he, personally, would break into the house! He would teach Judge de Lima a lesson in good manners. The judge's insulting manner to him in court that morning was like a burning brand in his heart. He would have his revenge!

He advanced with caution. Fernando de Lima would doubtless take more precautions tonight than on the night before. He knew he was being spied upon and that his secret had been exposed. Had he set guards around the house to intercept intruders? Before approaching the house, de Henrique made sure to leave the gate to the street slightly ajar. It was best to have an escape route ready — just in case.

He stopped short. The front door of de Lima's house had just opened, spilling yellow light into the garden. De Henrique leaped off the path and did his best to squeeze his ample bulk behind a large bush, in the hopes that whoever was leaving the house would not notice him. To his relief, the door closed again and darkness reigned once more.

A figure walked down the path toward the gate. De Henrique huddled behind the bush, nothing moving but his eyes. He narrowed them in an effort to identify the man coming his way. He was wearing a monk's cassock; that much was certain. When the figure was directly opposite him, it was all de Henrique could do to bite back an exclamation. Unbelievable! It was *Padre* João Manuel. João Manuel — leaving de Lima's house!

De Henrique did not budge until João Manuel had passed through the gate and vanished in the darkness of the Lisbon street. Only when the last of his footsteps had faded completely did the secretary leave the safety of the bush. He darted a glance to the right and left, then went out through the gate. There was no point in spying on the house now. From the moment João Manuel had left it, the taper had been extinguished and the window was dark.

"The two of them are plotting against me!" de Henrique seethed. They knew, both of them, that he was their enemy. The good lord had brought him to this spot just in time to witness their collusion. He must see to it that they were arrested and thrown into jail as soon as possible! To arrest them during tomorrow's *auto-da-fé* — now, there was a nice idea. Before they succeeded in snaring him in the trap they were devising...

With a last glance over his shoulder at de Lima's darkened house, de Henrique turned in the direction of his own house. He went rapidly on his way, a small, satanic smile playing on his lips.

"Armando — it's me!"

Armando Batancur felt his tension seep away as he recognized the voice. It belonged to one of the men who had answered his summons earlier in the evening to attend the meeting in the little hut outside the city.

Raphael Gimareines had been keenly affected by the scene in the hut. He felt not only pity, but a deep empathy for Armando. That feeling had prompted him to seek out his friend in this dangerous manner, right here in the Inquisition courtyard. He wanted to try to lift Armando's spirits and to once again explain his own position.

Raphael Gimareines was a man of action. He had hastened to the Inquisition building immediately upon his return to the city. Naturally, he did not attempt to gain entrance through the front gate. He was not a priest and had no credentials that would take him past the guard. Instead, he rode to the part of the surrounding wall farthest from the gate, climbed up on his horse's back, and — under cover of the darkness — clambered from there onto the wall. The courtyard was spread below him, with the building at its center. The place was asleep.

He leaped down into the courtyard. He had once visited Armando's room and hoped to find it again now. Then he suddenly noticed a lone figure strolling, apparently aimlessly, to and fro in the courtyard. Gimareines slipped behind a tree, hefted a small rock, and threw it in the man's direction. He hoped thereby to force the man to turn so that he might see his face. But the man did not turn.

The stroller's continuing silence emboldened Gimareines to advance. He did so with his eyes riveted to the silhouette, which alternately raised its head to the sky or lowered it to face the ground. Something about the figure's build and the way it walked triggered a suspicion in Gimareines' mind. Could this be Armando himself? A crazy idea, he conceded, but one worth investigating. He advanced a few more steps. A closer look made him smile broadly. Yes, it was he!

He placed a hand on Armando's shoulder, causing the other to start violently.

"Armando!" he whispered. "Armando, it's me!"

Armando spun around. "Raphael! What are you doing here? How did you get in?"

"By the quickest and surest route. I climbed over the wall."

"You took a great risk! If you're discovered, we will both be in grave danger."

"If you want, I'll leave now."

Armando did not hurry to answer. Raphael Gimareines was an old friend. He wanted him to stay. But at the same time, Armando was far more aware of the potential danger than his visitor.

"Why have you come?" he asked.

"To be with you a while."

"Why?"

Gimareines shrugged. "I didn't like the way the others left you back there in the hut — alone. I wanted to be with you."

"Thank you. But it's dangerous!"

"I know. I wanted to do it anyway."

Armando peered into his friend's face, his heart filled with a deep gratitude. He whispered, "This may be the last time you see me, Raphael."

"Why?"

"I will not live through the *auto-da-fé*. tomorrow. I have decided to act... and I don't believe I will come out of it alive."

69

R aphael Gimareines gripped Armando's arm. "What do you mean, you 'won't go through the *auto-da-fé*? What do you mean, you've 'decided to act'?"

Armando began walking slowly, and Gimareines fell into step beside him. The light in the guard's booth still burned, its occupant doubtless fast asleep. After many minutes of silence, Armando stopped and said, "I don't know! I don't know exactly what I'll do tomorrow, but it's clear to me that something will happen. This city cannot continue to exist under de Henrique's dictatorship!"

"And *Padre* João Manuel?"

Armando snorted. "*Padre* João Manuel? He's worthless! Even though he tries to act like he's still in charge."

Suddenly, he gripped his friend's shoulder. "Let's go down to the dungeon to see Don Carlos."

"Armando, are you insane? It's dangerous!"

"Let's go," Armando said, implacable in his resolution. "It's important that someone be with him in his final hours. Let's go strengthen his spirit."

Raphael Gimareines breathed deeply, prey to a deadly terror. At the same time, he did not feel capable of refusing his friend.

"What do we do about the guards down there?" he asked anxiously.

"There's only one guard at the entrance. Don't worry, I'll take care of him."

Even before he'd finished speaking, Armando began moving rapidly toward the broad stairs leading into the building. Raphael Gimareines started to follow, but Armando stopped him.

"Wait here. I'll call you when it's safe to come down. When you see me lift the taper three times, that will be the signal that everything is all right." He hurried away, murmuring, "Don Carlos! The last day of your life... And also, apparently, of my own..."

Gimareines saw the darkness swallow Armando. He himself stood motionless. In the silence he could hear his own heartbeats clearly. The situation was bizarre in the extreme. Here he stood, all alone, in the heart of Inquisition territory. What if they found him here? All the guard had to do was decide to take a stroll around the courtyard. As the minutes ticked past, he tried to banish such thoughts. But where was Armando? Why hadn't he returned yet? And for that matter, why had he, Gimareines, come here in the first place?

The wait seemed endless. But finally, it ended. Gimareines saw a flaming taper rise and fall three times. Armando was summoning him.

"How did you get rid of the guard?" he asked breathlessly, when he reached the entrance.

"I just asked him to switch shifts with me. I take over now, and in a few days he's agreed to stand guard instead of me. No problem at all."

The two hurried down the stairs to the dungeon. They were greeted by dank, dark, empty corridors. Armando, who had been down here before, knew which was Don Carlos' cell. He counted the cells he passed by touching the big locks on each door. At number 21, he stopped. Here was Don Carlos.

Jose de Melo was in despair. Roberto Gonzales' state of mind was little better. As for the plump cardinal, he cursed the fate that had led him from his warm home into this doomed adventure. Here he was, stranded on the highroad on this cold night — and he no longer a young man!

Roberto sat heavily on one of the boulders lining the road. His thoughts turned to Rav Menashe in far-off Amsterdam. Before he had set out on his mission to Lisbon, Rav Menashe had pledged that the Jews of his city would pray daily for his success. Had that promise been kept? Or had the prayers, G-d forbid, not been found acceptable in Heaven? Roberto lifted his hands in a supplicating gesture. The gesture was observed by Jose, who was glad that at least one of their sorry group was able to pray at this juncture. He approached the cardinal.

"I'm sorry, *Padre.*"

"Yes," João Batista sighed.

He's angry, Jose thought. It was a frustrating realization. Why couldn't the man realize that he was on a vital mission? Why was he trying to avoid taking responsibility for his imprisoned brother in Lisbon? Jose murmured, "*Atzas Hashem takum.* G-d's plan will endure."

The cardinal only turned his head away.

The coachman piped up: "I know my horses. I don't believe they'll go far. For all we know, they could be waiting a little further up the road right now. With your permission, I'll go search for them."

The cardinal maintained his stony silence. Jose hesitated, then flung his arms wide as if to exclaim, "Who knows if you're right?" Aloud, however, he merely said, "Go."

The coachman disappeared. The minutes dragged heavily after he'd gone. It was dark and cold on the unsheltered road. Then, in the midst of their despair, their ears caught the sound of trotting hooves. Very shortly after that, they were gratified by the sight of the missing horses pulling their lost carriage!

"They didn't go far, my good horses!" the coachman crowed delightedly from his perch. "Please, *Senhores,* climb in and let's be on our way!"

The cardinal sprang to life. He hurried over to the carriage and entered it first. Jose de Melo took a seat beside him, and Roberto climbed in last of all. The cardinal bestowed a smile on Jose, whose reaction was on the chilly side. He was still smarting from the cardinal's behavior on the highroad.

⤳⤶

Armando hissed into the cell's tiny, barred window: "Don Carlos! Don Carlos!"

"Who's there?" Don Carlos demanded from within.

"Shhh... It's me, Armando Batancur — Yitzchak ben Yaakov."

The window was suddenly filled with Don Carlos' face.

"Is it really you?"

"Yes, yes, it's me."

"Why have you come? You know how dangerous it is!"

"I had to come."

"Has something happened?"

Armando pressed his lips together in surprise. Don Carlos asked again, "Something's happened? Tell me!"

"You — you don't know?"

"No. Speak!"

Armando stammered, "Th-they've moved up the *auto-da-fé* t-to... to-morrow... m-morning!"

Silence emanated from the other side of the window. Don Carlos found it hard to breathe suddenly, and the blood pounded painfully in his veins. His eyes sought Armando's. Even through the thick darkness, their eyes did meet: those of the man who, until a few months before, had been one of the most illustrious and powerful in the land, and of the monk, younger than he by a good many years. The only spark of commonality between the two was the fact that they both belonged to the secret Marrano community in the city.

Don Carlos asked quietly, "Why did they advance the date?"

"They're afraid the king might change his mind."

"Why are they afraid? Who's trying to influence him?"

"I don't know... They say it's the prince Alfonso."

"Really?" Don Carlos was surprised. He and the prince were friends, and he knew that Alfonso — thought outwardly careful to maintain good relations with the church — was not a particularly devout Catholic. Still, it seemed strange to hear of him openly opposing the Inquisition...

A new thought struck horror in Don Carlos' heart. Could all this be nothing but a rumor, sowed by Paulo de Henrique in order to taint Prince Alfonso in the eyes of the citizenry? De Henrique had hated the prince for many years.

"Are you sure?" Don Carlos asked urgently. "It doesn't seem possible!"

"I'm not sure, *Senhor*. But the story has it that he is trying to have your sentence changed to life imprisonment."

Don Carlos lowered his eyes. "Then... it is scheduled for tomorrow morning?"

He looked up just in time to see Armando slowly nod his head.

Another emotional silence filled the space between them. Finally, "Thank you," whispered Don Carlos. "Thank you for waking me."

Armando found it impossible to speak. Don Carlos continued, "I want to be awake during these final hours of my life. I want to think over everything I've done in my life. Though I've been thinking about these things ever since my arrest, my hour of judgment is drawing near. My hour of judgment... is near. As you've said... tomorrow morning."

The sound of the prisoner's ragged breath was clearly audible through the cell window.

"In just a few hours..." Don Carlos ended in a whisper.

Tears were coursing down Armando's face. The darkness that surrounded him was a reflection of the darkness in his soul.

Don Carlos' voice floated out to him again. "Be calm, my son. All of us knew that this could happen at any time. I will ascend the stake with a peaceful heart. If it is G-d's will, I will sanctify His Name through my

death. All I ask is that you remember me kindly, and do not allow your-
selves to grow faint of spirit. Be strong, keep our community strong, and
continue to search for Marranos who can join our number."

Armando and Gimareines heard the trembling emotion in the condemned man's voice. It was even more pronounced at his next words.

"Please, my friend and brother, I beg of you to seek out my children,
who have been taken into monasteries. Try to find out where they are,
and even if you cannot help them now, perhaps in later years you will be
able to tell them about their father."

A low moan escaped Don Carlos' lips. Armando said quickly, through
his own thickening tears, "I promise you, *santo senhor* (holy sir) — we will
do everything in our power to find them."

"And please take care of my wife, too..."

"We promise."

Armando raised his hand and thrust it through the bars. His fingers
touched Don Carlos' damp cheeks. Then Don Carlos lifted his own hand
to grasp Armando's. Their clasp was brief but very strong.

"I have one more small favor to ask," Don Carlos said. "Find the cell
where Yitzchak de Castro of Amsterdam lies. He, too, apparently, is slated
to burn tomorrow in the sanctification of G-d's Name."

Armando replied, low voiced, "I don't think that's possible, *Senhor*. It
is dark in these corridors and we don't know where he's located. Apart
from that, we've already been down here a long time. It's too dangerous."

"He needs you! He is young — very young. Only 21."

"Yes, we understand. But to search for him would be a great danger.
We cannot."

Don Carlos sighed deeply. "A pity."

As the two men turned to leave, Don Carlos' voice rent the silence one
last time.

"May you be blessed for the risk you took by coming here."

70

The church bells of Lisbon began tolling even before daybreak. As though on signal, every bell set up its clangorous peal, the echoes rolling sonorously through the still-dark streets and off into the distance.

Sleeping families awoke, lit fires in their homes, and hurriedly readied themselves to join the rest of the populace at the Triero da Paso, the large square near the royal palace. It was a great boon for the soul to witness an *auto-da-fé*. No pious Catholic would willingly forgo the experience.

On this very early Friday morning, the Inquisition building was already astir. Of all the heretics slated for the flames today, Don Carlos was undoubtedly the most famous, but some 120 other prisoners were to receive their just punishments on this day too, punishments ranging from whipping to hanging to burning. There were many preparations to be made.

Monks scurried through corridors as yet untouched by daylight, blazing torches in hand. Armando Batancur, however, still rested in his room. Some time earlier he had bid farewell to Raphael Gimareines, who made his escape over the wall. Armando had returned to his room but had found sleep impossible. He was still in the grip of the powerful emotions released by his brief talk with Don Carlos. The sight of his teacher and leader on the verge of death would not leave him. Though he tossed and turned for hours, the comfort of sleep eluded him.

He heard quiet footsteps in the corridor. As he listened intently, they grew stronger and more numerous. Through the window, the first faint purple streak illuminated the eastern sky. Now he understood. Preparations had began for the *auto-da- fé* processional that would leave the Inquisition building at full daylight.

Armando slipped quickly out of his bed and lit an oil taper. Going over to a wall cupboard, he rummaged inside until he found what he wanted: a dagger. Slowly and deliberately he drew the dagger from its leather sheath and watched the play of the flickering flame on its honed blade. The steel felt cold beneath his fingers. Clutching the dagger to his chest, Armando closed his eyes and murmured a prayer with intense concentration.

≈)≈

Monks in pairs descended to the dungeon. With their heavy metal keys they banged on the cell doors to rouse the prisoners, who until that moment had had no idea that their sentences were to be carried out that day. Even after the doors were unlocked, the keys continued pounding on the iron doors, until every prisoner awoke, startled and trembling.

They encountered the monks' cruel gazes, and were motioned to rise. Weakly, submissively, the prisoners struggled to their feet and stood before their conquerors. The monks tossed each one the *sanbenito* he would wear in the processional. This was a long robe embossed with a black cross. The robes told a story of their own.

A cross that was missing one arm spelled good news for its wearer: That particular prisoner had been reprieved from death. He was required only to be publicly ravuked by representatives of the church. A prisoner who saw a complete cross emblazoned on his robe knew that his repentance had been accepted. He would not be burnt at the stake.

Those who had not repented but had obstinately persisted in clinging to their Jewish faith wore robes depicting devils hurling heretics into the flames of hell.

That day, out of 122 prisoners, only two merited this last robe. Those two were Don Carlos Carneiro and Yitzchak de Castro.

The monks also handed the prisoners' tall hats to be worn in the processional, along with a pair of lit candles to be carried until the end...

≈⊃⊂≈

Armando returned the dagger to its sheath. He dressed hurriedly, concealing the dagger in the folds of his cassock before stepping out into the corridor, where he joined the stream of monks bustling to and fro. For some reason, he had not been issued any official duty that day. He went out into the courtyard.

There he found the first of the prisoners assembled. Some were mounted on horseback while others were thrust into wagon-borne cages. Of Don Carlos there was no sign. Armando decided to march close by the procession all the way to the square. With any luck, he should be able to position himself close to the stake...

At that moment, Paulo de Henrique descended the broad stairs leading from the building. His step was slow and ponderous as ever. His eyes, cool and arrogant, raked the crowd of prisoners. Among the group were quite a few men who had enjoyed positions of power and wealth — wealth which had been confiscated, naturally, for the benefit of the Inquisition. These men returned de Henrique's glance, some with supplication, others with scorn.

"*Padre, por favor* (Father, please)." On impulse, Armando addressed de Henrique.

The secretary turned to him in open astonishment.

"*Padre*," Armando ventured again, "This is a big day for all of us. It is not often that such an important act of faith takes place..."

"And therefore?" de Henrique broke in impatiently.

"Why was I not given any official duty? Why can't I, too, earn merit with the lord, our savior?"

De Henrique pierced him with a penetrating stare, but Armando did not drop his eyes. Inside his cassock he felt the dagger close against his skin. After a moment, de Henrique smiled.

"You are right."

"Then what job shall I do?" Armando asked quickly. It was crucial that he be part of the *auto-da-fé* processional.

"You? You shall accompany me. I'm sure I'll find things for you to do."

"*Muito obrigado* (Thank you very much)!" Armando bowed politely, concealing his excitement with lowered eyes. He could not have hoped for more. Heaven had heeded his prayers.

De Henrique studied the line of prisoners again. "Where is Don Carlos? And where is that youth — what was his name? Ah, yes, de Castro."

"They're coming now, *Padre*," a monk told him. "They were too weak to walk unassisted. Two of our men are helping them."

"Too weak to walk?" De Henrique smiled coldly. "But they were not too weak, it seems, to sin. Bring them here at once!"

≈≈≈

First light broke over the city. The monotonous tolling of church bells still filled the air. Residents of Lisbon and the outlying villages streamed toward the square, which was rapidly filling. Many others thronged the streets leading from the Inquisition to the square. In the two grandstands that had been erected on either side of the square, important personages began taking their places. High government officials were already seated in their designated spots, although the seats reserved for His Majesty Don João IV and his queen were still empty. The king and queen would arrive only after the processional had wound its way through the city to the square.

The stand opposite began to fill with prominent churchmen. Here, the places set aside for *Padre* João Manuel and Paulo de Henrique were as yet unoccupied. Their arrival was expected momentarily.

The milling throng filled the square with noise. Patience was wearing thin as eager necks craned to catch a first glimpse of the heretics. It had been years since the church had treated the people to a spectacle on such a grand scale. Above all, the crowd longed to express its rage and disillusionment with Don Carlos, the greatest traitor of them all.

The long processional began to pass through the Inquisition gate and into the street. At its head, riders on white horses held aloft the Inquisition flag and a giant cross. After them came rows of monks, singing hymns. Those who waited on both sides of the street joined in the singing, genuflecting, kissing their fingertips and waving them heavenward.

The excitement was dramatically accelerated when the first of the prisoners appeared in the street. From the crowd, murmurs of prayer turned into catcalls. Fists were shaken at the guilty men. *"Tiraitores* (traitors)! *Heresos* (heretics)!"* The spectators tried to press closer to the prisoners, but were repelled by platoons of soldiers, assisted by de Henrique's "angels" in black. Their orders were clear. All the prisoners were to arrive intact at the square. That was where the real show would take place.

≈)⊂

Armando rode in a carriage beside de Henrique. Never had his faith in Divine providence been stronger than it was now. After all the plans of action he'd considered against this man, here he was, seated opposite him! Was this a sign that the G-d of Moshe wished him to exact revenge in the name of all the other Marranos — even at the cost of his life?

Apparently, He did. But would that save their beloved Don Carlos?

The carriage rumbled through the Inquisition gate after the long line of prisoners had left it. De Henrique chose a side street that would bring him to the central square before the processional, which he knew would be forced to move slowly through the thick crowd. He wanted to ascend the grandstand ahead of the ceremony, to bask in the admiration of the crowd. João Manuel mustn't arrive even a minute before him.

Armando cast surreptitious glances at the enemy seated opposite. They were alone in the carriage. This was his chance! Armando's right hand moved slowly toward his left hip. His eyes were riveted on de

Henrique who, absorbed in thoughts of his own, seemed to notice nothing of his companion's tension. He was totally unsuspecting. Armando's hand touched the hilt of his dagger.

"Now!" he thought fiercely. "*Now!*"

⁓⌒⁓

As the cardinal's carriage rolled speedily toward Lisbon, Jose de Melo grew more and more agitated. The first intimations of dawn were touching the sky with lilac and rose. It was vital that they reach the city before the parade of prisoners set out for the square. Otherwise, it would be next to impossible to carve a way through the crowd to the dais where the king and the justices sat, and to take action... Now, with darkness still covering the land, Jose had no clear idea where they were located or how far away Lisbon lay.

The cardinal dozed. Roberto sat quietly, abstracted. Sticking his head out the carriage window, Jose shouted up to the coachman, "How far are we from Lisbon?"

"Not too far," the coachman called back. "About another hour."

A sharp pain pierced Jose's chest. Another hour could very well be too late!

71

s the cardinal's carriage drew closer to Lisbon, the going became more difficult. The road that had been virtually deserted all the way from Oporto was rapidly filling up with carts, coaches, and riders on horseback. Everyone, it seemed, was hurrying to Lisbon for the grand, long-awaited spectacle: the *auto-da-fé*.

Jose de Melo ground his teeth in an agony of impatience. Any delay now could prove the death knell to all their plans. The cardinal, dozing fitfully in his corner, swayed along with the carriage. And Roberto's lips never stopped murmuring prayers in Hebrew, prayers he had learned in Amsterdam for the safety and salvation of the Marranos and which had been composed by the rabbinic leaders of the Portuguese community in that city.

Jose's tension mounted as he glimpsed, in the distance, the first scattered houses of Lisbon. They would shortly arrive at the city gates themselves. Jose roused the cardinal, still enraged at the man's apparent apathy. Didn't he care about Don Carlos at all? It would soon be up to the cardinal to act, and Jose wondered how he would function in the face of that seeming indifference. The worry only served to heighten Jose's nervousness.

The cardinal suddenly came fully awake. Jose signaled to Roberto to hand him the letter.

"Here. Take this, and may the G-d of heaven and earth guide you. You know what to do?"

"Yes," answered the cardinal.

"*Padre*," Jose added, "from the moment we enter the city we will have to leave you. It is imperative that we disappear. This holds true for me, and certainly for our guest from Amsterdam."

The cardinal inclined his head, his expression stern and alert. All at once, Jose believed that the cardinal would not let them down.

The carriage stopped at the city entrance. All around them the masses continued to stream toward the central square. Jose and Roberto, still in their priestly garb, descended, nodded a discreet farewell to the cardinal, and saw the coach rumble off. Then the two slipped into the house from which they had emerged a day and a half before, on their way to Oporto.

≈✂≈

Raphael Gimareines arrived at the Inquisition building at dawn. He came on foot.

All night long he had been haunted by the whispered midnight conversation he'd shared with Armando. There was a burning flame within his friend that frightened him. Armando was liable to do something that would place their entire community at even greater risk. He had hinted at murder and suicide, and to Gimareines the words had not rung hollow. In order to avoid arousing suspicion, Gimareines would have to attend today's *auto-da-fé*. He would attend it in Armando's company. He had determined to find his friend and stick close by him until the sad ceremony was over, in the hope of preventing Armando from carrying out whatever reckless action he was contemplating.

Gimareines did not come alone. He had unburdened himself to another friend who had also attended last night's meeting: Jacobo. The two threaded their way through the throng with difficulty, moving always in the direction of the Inquisition building. They made liberal use of their elbows, ignoring the complaints and curses that followed in their wake. Their exertions brought them at last to the gate.

The procession of prisoners was at its height, and the crowd at its noisiest. Suddenly, the noise rose to a roar. Blood-chilling curses rent the air and objects began to fly at the row of condemned men. Though Gimareines and Jacobo stood on tiptoe they could see nothing. Soon enough, however, their ears told them all they wanted to know.

"*Don Carlos o hereso tiraitore!* (Don Carlos, the heretic and traitor)!"

Gimareines' heart beat faster. His leader, so all powerful just a few short months ago, had come to this...

They pushed aside the spectators in their way in order to move closer to the parade. Armando must surely be somewhere close at hand. They must hurry.

Jacobo seized Gimareines' sleeve in sudden urgency. "Look!"

Gimareines lifted his head and saw nothing.

"No! Look there — in the opposite direction! At that carriage, moving slowly."

Raphael Gimareines looked, and blanched. There in an open carriage, watching the parade of prisoners, was Armando. And he was seated beside none other than Paulo de Henrique!

"What do we do now?" Gimareines asked in trepidation.

"I don't know. But whatever we do, the first step is to move closer to that carriage."

~⊃⊂~

"My young friend," de Henrique said suddenly, "you appear a bit tense."

Armando's heart stood still. His hand, gripping the hilt of his dagger, relaxed slightly. He tried with all his might to conquer the storm of emotion that was breaking over him: De Henrique's eyes, sly and half closed, were watching him.

"Yes, I am a little tense, *Padre*. Or — more accurately — excited. I am young, and I've heard so much in the corridors of the Holy Office about the renowned *autos-da-fé* of the past. Today, I have finally merited the privilege of seeing one! Is that not a reason for excitement?"

De Henrique's eyes nearly shut completely in the folds of his face as he smiled his broad smile. The suspiciousness, though, did not leave it. "Yes, certainly, my young friend. It is surely a reason to feel excited. But why the tension? What's troubling you?" He peered at his companion. "By the way, what is your name?"

Armando's hand relinquished the dagger hilt, although, to avert the old fox's suspicion, he did not make haste to remove the hand from his cassock.

"Armando," he said. "Armando Batancur."

"And where are you from?"

"From Eldorado, *Padre*."

"Have you been with us long at the Holy Office?"

"About a year, or a little more."

Armando felt as though he were being interrogated. De Henrique suspected something. Had he seen the secret movement of his hand?

He had his answer a moment later. In a harsh voice, de Henrique snapped, "And why are you hiding your hand inside your cassock?"

The square by the royal palace was packed with humanity. The stand reserved for the clergy held a nearly full complement of Inquisition men as well as a number of Dominican monks. *Padre* João Manuel arrived, basking pleasurably in the crowd's respectful roar of welcome.

He did not notice de Henrique among the churchmen on the dais. Though he was enjoying being the center of admiring attention, João Manuel could never leave behind his apprehension where his wily secretary was concerned. Where was the man now? And what diabolical plots were being hatched in that devilish head of his?

The prisoners' processional had already begun to arrive at the square, but there was still no sign of de Henrique. The king and his entourage were due to arrive at any moment now. Where was that serpent? João Manuel was angry with himself for his continuing fear, but try as he might he could not shake it off.

A blare of trumpets galvanized the mighty crowd. The sound heralded the king's arrival. The grandstand was already filled with his guests: top government officials, foreign ambassadors, and visitors from France and other Catholic regimes who had been invited to watch the spectacle.

All rose. The king's coach, harnessed to six white horses, rolled slowly into the square and moved at the same regal pace toward the royal dais. The king and queen descended and walked toward their seats, attended by a vast number of aides, retainers, and government ministers.

João Manuel noted with interest that Prince Alfonso was missing. All of Lisbon knew of Alfonso's deep and abiding friendship for Don Carlos. He would not come out today to see his friend lose his life on the stake.

72

The directness of de Henrique's question left Armando momentarily at a loss. Involuntarily, almost, he withdrew his hand from his cassock and, by an almost superhuman effort of will, managed to leave it lying in the same position. Paling slightly, he said, "My stomach has been hurting since early this morning. I hope it will pass soon. It's nothing serious, *Padre*."

Armando was relieved to have found this innocuous answer to the Inquisitor's question. He left his hand on his "aching" stomach. De Henrique's gaze was penetrating and still suspicious. Had he believed Armando's story?

"Thank you for inquiring," Armando added. He felt impelled to fill the strained silence with words, any words. He was more afraid of de Henrique's silences than of his worst rantings.

"*Padre*," he blurted desperately, "do you find something suspicious about my hand?"

De Henrique laughed. "No! Why do you think so?" Then his face grew closed and hard. "Although today, one never knows. The city is full of sinners. The 'new Christians' hate me. And do you know why? Because I expose their hypocrisy, their two-faced duplicity!" Again he fell silent, eyes boring into Armando's like two red-hot lances.

Armando felt he could not endure that gaze for long. He tried with all his strength not to let his own eyes fall before it.

"They hate," Armando said, to break the new silence, "but what can they do?"

De Henrique registered amazement. "You are inexperienced. You don't have your finger on the pulse of this city. Why should they not try to have me assassinated — I, who protect the faith against their villainy? Ah, haven't you thought of that possibility? Hasn't it occurred to you that that might happen? It could happen anywhere, even in a carriage carrying just the two of us!"

A genuine pain rose from Armando's stomach directly to this throat. He felt choked. In another second he would break down right here, in front of the man he'd been intent on harming just a moment before. Why had his courage deserted him at this critical juncture? Why could he not satisfy his desire to stab the dark fat heart in front of him, the heart of this evil Christian?

Instead, in a peaceful voice that betrayed nothing of his inner turmoil, Armando said, "No, I never thought of that possibility! It's hard for me to believe that someone would dare harm *you, Padre*. After everything you've done for the faith!"

De Henrique chuckled. "Your words warm my heart. Nevertheless, they do not alter the reality. I must be very careful. That is why I invited you to ride with me. I need a bodyguard to protect me. Today, you are my bodyguard."

For a time de Henrique was quiet. Then, rousing himself as if from a dream, he said, "Tell me, son, do you have any sort of weapon — to protect me from any of Don Carlos' faithful followers who might take it into his head to hurt me? Do you?"

Armando began to tremble uncontrollably. He prayed for this nightmare to end. He had not succeeded in carrying out the mission he'd imposed upon himself: that of murdering his enemy, the man who was responsible for Don Carlos' death. He felt an overpowering urge to escape.

"If you haven't a weapon," de Henrique continued, "I'll give you mine. I have no wish to attend the *auto-da-fé* armed. It would not be suitable for a man of the church."

From the recesses of his cassock, de Henrique drew a shiny new dagger. The blade winked and blinked before Armando's stupefied eyes.

⁓⊃⊂⁓

Don Carlos' eyes were open and his head erect. But he was not watching the crowd that surged along both sides of the processional. He peered constantly ahead, searching among the other condemned prisoners for a glimpse of young Yitzchak de Castro.

From the mob came shouted epithets. Someone flung a rock at his head. Absently he wiped away the blood that trickled through his hair. He had spotted Yitzchak.

Several monks were marching alongside Yitzchak. They lifted a cross in his direction and never stopped talking earnestly at him. It was their last chance to persuade the doomed prisoner to embrace the Christian faith. They did not promise him his life in exchange. Their "compassionate" favor, if he agreed to trade in his religion, would be death by hanging before his body was burned. Don Carlos, noting the way Yitzchak paid the monks no attention at all, felt an inordinate pride in the young Jew, who was standing firm in the face of the great trial that the G-d of Avraham, Yitzchak, and Yaakov had set before him. Don Carlos longed to grip his hand, to strengthen his spirit and murmur words of comfort in his ear before the final ordeal.

A strong blow between his shoulder blades brought him abruptly back to reality. For the first time, he let his glance wander over to the throng of spectators. He saw raised fists, mouths open in shouts of derision, and everywhere, eyes that sparkled with hatred as they watched him.

"*Ana Hashem hoshiah na,*" he whispered in an effort to draw courage into himself. "Please Hashem, save me..."

Suddenly, above the heads of the crowd, he saw a carriage he recognized. It belonged to the Cardinal of Oporto. His friend from the Marrano underground was attempting to weave a way through the raucous horde.

"What is he doing here?" Don Carlos wondered. He stared steadily at the carriage, hoping to meet the cardinal's eye in a glance of farewell, and possibly even to discern, in that glance, what had brought the man to Lisbon. today.

≈)⌢

Raphael Gimareines and Jacobo ran as fast as their legs would carry them after de Henrique's fast-departing carriage. Anxiety for Armando was the spur that lent them wings.

"Faster!" Gimareines panted. Jacobo was lagging slightly behind. "Hurry! Armando is about to do something crazy. I tell you that his life is in danger. Hurry!"

Jacobo put on an additional burst of speed.

To their gratification, the carriage slowed to an easy trot. The distance between it and the pursuers lessened gradually. With a final effort, the two runners gained on the carriage. They seized its sides. In a voice that was nearly breathless from his mad dash, Gimareines cried, "Armando! Armando, what you doing here?"

The coachman pulled up his horses. Gimareines moved closer. "*Padre, desculp muito* (forgive me)! I didn't know that my friend Armando was a guest of *Senhor padre*. I beg your forgiveness."

Gimareines had not missed the dagger in de Henrique's hand.

De Henrique bestowed a pleasant smile on the two young strangers. "Well, well, on a festival day we must forgive such crimes." He beamed benevolently.

Gimareines said nothing, but his eyes searched Armando's face questioningly. De Henrique noticed. "He is my bodyguard today," he explained expansively. "Aren't you proud of him?" He replaced his dagger in its sheath and handed it to Armando.

Raphael Gimareines ventured, "*Padre*, as friends of your personal bodyguard, do you think we can gain entrance to the square?" He paused, then added gamely, "In other words, we are asking if we can ride with Your Grace."

De Henrique favored Gimareines with one of his long, probing looks. Then he said, "Come in. You have received a special privilege today."

The carriage, with four passengers now, continued to lumber toward the Triero da Paso.

≈)⊂

The cardinal's coach struggled to find a way through the milling mass of humanity. João Batista noticed Don Carlos at once, sitting straight and proud on his horse. He didn't think Don Carlos had seen him. He tried to catch the prisoner's eye, to transmit a message of faint hope.

His coachman kept up a continuous harangue at the crowd. "Allow the cardinal to pass! Allow the cardinal to pass! Show some respect for a man of the church!"

His shouts had little effect. Here and there, some conscience-smitten individuals tried to clear a path for the carriage, but each time the swirl of the mob closed the gap. Little by little, however, the carriage managed to fight its way forward. At last the driver succeeded in maneuvering himself into the vicinity of the royal palace, close by the square where the ceremony was to take place.

Some time passed before, with difficulty, he pulled up at the back palace gate. The gate was locked, but guards hurried to open it when they saw the cardinal, an occasional visitor at the palace.

"Stop here!" the cardinal ordered the coachman. He stepped from the carriage and filled his lungs with air in the vast empty courtyard.

"What do we do now?" the coachman asked. From beyond the buildings that ringed the courtyard came the roar of the crowd, sounding like the roll of distant thunder.

"We will walk through the palace itself. At some point we will find an exit that leads onto the square. It's a pity I don't know exactly where they've erected the king's dais. We must reach him."

For all his bulk, the cardinal began to race with surprising agility. The coachman gaped at the sight of a man of the cardinal's years running like a boy; then he dashed after him. They entered the portals of the palace and found themselves facing a long corridor. The place was empty. All the royal servants were gathered at the opposite end of the palace to witness the excitement. The cardinal and his driver had an unobstructed path.

They passed through the king's audience hall, at the end of which they found a broad door. This door opened onto the *auto- da-fé*. It was to be hoped that the king was seated not far away. The cardinal hurried to open it.

Suddenly, he heard footsteps behind him. Before he could turn around, there came a peremptory voice that carried the unmistakable ring of authority:

"*Padre*, Cardinal of Oporto, what are you doing here? And how did you get in?"

The procession of condemned prisoners reached the square. A regiment of the king's soldiers, along with a number of churchmen, had guarded the prisoners all along the length of their route. Don Carlos was the only one who had been slightly injured by the seething mob.

He hardly felt it. His thoughts had wandered far from this place where he was slated to end his life. He tried to keep his mind constantly absorbed in prayer to the G-d of Israel. He had heard in Amsterdam of condemned Marranos, 100 and 200 years before, who had not felt the scorch of the flames that consumed them alive. Their spirits had been inextricably bound up with their Creator. Don Carlos had heard this testimony firsthand from survivors of the flames, who had been subjected to the fire and then saved from death at the very last minute. Once, the dais had collapsed; another time, a heavy downpour had doused the flames. The crowd had interpreted these events as signs from heaven that the prisoners in question were innocent, and had literally forced the Inquisition to release them. These reprieved men, upon their arrival in Amsterdam or Hamburg, had claimed that from the moment they consigned their souls to the sanctification of G-d's Name, they had ceased to feel the heat of the flames. Was it too much to hope that the same thing would happen to him?

As Don Carlos sank deeper and deeper into his thoughts, the hooting of the crowd receded. Only when his horse came to an abrupt halt and he felt himself forcibly removed from it did he awake to the realization that he was standing in the center of the square, the last in the long line of prisoners quietly awaiting their fates...

He lifted his eyes to João Manuel — who quickly lowered his own. At that moment, he saw de Henrique enter the square, to much loud acclaim from the throng. João Manuel gnashed his teeth.

The crowd quieted again. A tense silence spread over the square. Don Carlos knew that the eyes of the masses were fixed on him more than on any other condemned man present. He turned and sought the king, seated in his place of honor on the royal dais. He had served this man faithfully and had acted for many years as his trusted advisor.

The king's eyes, as they met his own, were cold as steel.

73

The Cardinal turned quickly. He was standing face-to-face with Prince Alfonso.

The two men took each other's measure. The cardinal recognized the prince, but the two had never exchanged a word. They stood silent in the vast, deserted audience hall. The cardinal broke the silence first.

"Young man, why aren't you outside, participating in this great festival of faith?" He motioned at the door leading out to the square.

"No, *Padre*, I am not participating in the revelry. However, I see that Your Grace has come posthaste all the way from Oporto to share in de Henrique's celebration."

The cardinal frowned. "You are altogether too open in your statements, Your Highness." He paused, then asked, "Will you show me the way to the royal dais?"

Before the prince could answer, the cardinal added, "And will you accompany me?"

Alfonso straightened, looked straight and stern into the cardinal's eyes, and said, "I will show you the exit from the palace to the square, but I will not be a witness to that awful spectacle."

The cardinal exhibited every sign of astonishment. "What is this? A lack of faith?"

The prince made no answer. The cardinal pressed, "And your father, His Majesty Don João IV, knows about this?"

Alfonso moved closer to the cardinal, who heard his uneven breathing. He began talking rapidly: "Yes, my father knows. Make no mistake, *Padre*: I entertain no doubts about my faith. I agree that we must deal severely with heretics. But the needs of the state are important, too. Don Carlos is an asset to our state! He is an unparalleled military leader. I am taking issue with his arrest and his sentencing to death." He broke off. More softly, he said, "I know I am endangering myself by saying these things. But I am not at all sure that strict justice is being administered in this case."

The cardinal stepped back, startled and amazed. The thought flitted into his mind: "Could this be where salvation will come from?"

In a chiding tone, he said, "I don't understand, my young friend. Is it possible that your wish is to cast doubt on the virtue of the Holy Office?"

"*Padre*, I don't want you to misunderstand me. I believe in the righteousness of the church and of the Holy Office. But I do have my doubts about the purity of *Padre* Paulo de Henrique's motives..."

He took another step closer and whispered in the cardinal's ear: "He hates Don Carlos personally! He couldn't bear the fact that Don Carlos was an intimate and an advisor of the king. He is seeking power, and Don Carlos stood in his way. Do you understand, *Padre*? He was heard saying as far back as a year ago that he would destroy Don Carlos."

Alfonso fell silent, a prey to sudden uncertainty. Had he acted properly in revealing his secret thoughts to this lofty man of the church? If not, the consequences for him were bound to be bitter.

But the cardinal smiled. "I am moved by your honesty, Prince Alfonso. Still, I believe that you've exaggerated in your suspicions against our friend de Henrique. I think he is doing his job faithfully. It's a fact that churches all over the country were newly filled with worshipers once it became known that the Holy Office had been revitalized. That is to de Henrique's credit, isn't it?"

The strong emotion that had loosened Alfonso's tongue did not yet permit him to curb it. He burst out, "That's true, *Padre*. And it is terrible that it's true! You live in Oporto, not in Lisbon. You have no way of knowing just how he has managed to sow fear among the populace. You don't know how many innocent people, loyal Christians, have confessed to being Jewish after awful torture. They were condemned to long years of imprisonment, and sometimes even to death — and who took all their property? The Holy Office! Who has grown fat on this practice? De Henrique! Is this respect for our faith? *Padre*, is this what our savior wants from us?"

The Cardinal decided that the moment he'd been waiting for had arrived. The King's son could help him. After a brief struggle with his voluminous cassock, he extracted the letter he'd received from Jose de Melo and handed it to the prince.

"Read this," he ordered. "Read it slowly and carefully."

Alfonso read the letter, glanced up in astonishment at the cardinal, and then read it again. "But this is wonderful!" he exclaimed wildly. "Come, let us hurry to the king before it's too late!"

The cardinal grabbed his hand to stop him. "Slowly! By moving too quickly to try to save Don Carlos, we may accomplish exactly the opposite. Deliberation, my young friend, is what we need most at this moment."

"But hurry!"

"No, slowly," the cardinal said stubbornly. "De Henrique's men are out in the square in force. They are capable of causing great damage that can't be undone later. A cool head, my friend — a cool head, and not over-excitement."

Alfonso seized the cardinal's sleeve. "Was this the reason you came to Lisbon? Do — do you think as I do, that the Holy Office needs purifying?" There was pleading in the prince's eyes. With all his heart he longed for at least one prominent churchman to support him in his claims.

"Yes," the cardinal whispered. "As soon as I received this letter, I decided to hurry here. I think as you do, and there are a great many others who think as we do. The Holy Office must be cleansed of the corruption and illegality that those in power have brought in. Do not be afraid of me, Alfonso... And now, bear me company to where your father — His Majesty the king — sits. I want him to be the first to read the letter."

Every person in the packed square was focused on the the row of condemned men standing quietly in the center. Some of these hung their heads; others straightened their backs and held themselves as tall as they could. With his height and erect bearing, Don Carlos stood out among the rest.

At a podium close by the prisoners, a Dominican monk began orating in praise of the church and condemnation of heresy. His voice thundered and sank by turns. Many in the crowd crossed themselves and muttered words of prayer. There was a noise like the hissing of waves against rocks. Not far away, a small group of monks still toiled to prepare the stakes upon which two of the prisoners would be burned that day: Yitzchak de Castro and Don Carlos Carneiro.

The Dominican launched into a harrowing description of the horrors of hell that awaited all heretics. The listeners answered fervently, as one: "Amen." They were flying on a wave of religious euphoria, intent on saving their souls.

But dotted throughout the horde were those who had come only for appearance' sake, to avoid arousing their neighbors' suspicion. These were secret Jews — the Marranos. They howled and shouted along with the rest, often even louder than the rest, but inside they wept. They knew that this day marked the closing of an important chapter in the life of their small community in Lisbon. Today, Don Carlos would die for the sanctification of G-d's Name.

The Dominican wound up his oration. A member of the Holy Office, assistant to de Henrique, climbed up to the podium and began reading a list of the convicted men's names and crimes. Those who had confessed to being secret Jews, repented, and promised hence to live as loyal

Catholics were let off with a light punishment. This might take the form of a whipping, exile from their homes for a specified number of years, wearing prison garb every Sunday as they publicly admitted their former sins in church, and the like. After them came the names of those prisoners who had been sentenced to terms of imprisonment of varied duration.

All those whose names had been called stepped up to stand before the podium. They were ordered to bow their heads and answer "Amen" to everything they were told. Then the Dominican returned to shower them with tales of fire and brimstone and lurid descriptions of the hell that awaited these men because of the unspeakable sins of eating matzos on Pesach, circumcising their sons, wearing a white shirt on Shabbos, refraining from eating pork, and fasting on Yom Kippur.

The throng maintained a strict silence throughout, determined not to miss a single word, a single detail, of the performance.

Padre João Manuel and Paulo de Henrique stood side by side throughout the ceremony and did not exchange a word. João Manuel had noticed that his rival had arrived accompanied by three sturdy young men, one dressed in monk's garb and the others in civilian clothing. Who were they? What was de Henrique planning to do here, in front of all this multitude? João Manuel would have been well satisfied had de Henrique been the one to be led to the stake below.

De Henrique himself paid scant attention to the ritual ravuke of the prisoners. His entire being was focused on one man only: Don Carlos. This was the moment he had waited for all these years. From this day on, Lisbon would be his. Not even the king would dare oppose him. How wondrous were the workings of Heaven!

He glanced over his shoulder to make certain Armando Batancur was standing there. As his power grew, so did his fear. It had been a good move to accompany himself with an armed bodyguard. And yet, who knew whether the bodyguard himself was not an enemy? What did he know of this young man, after all? He twisted rapidly to gaze into

Armando's face. The young monk gazed back impassively, then shifted his glance back to the proceedings below.

Though outwardly serene, Armando seethed inside like a volcano. He felt that soon, very soon, he would certainly explode...

De Henrique had scarcely turned back to the square when he stiffened. His sharp eyes had spotted a door opening — the door from the palace, opposite. Prince Alfonso emerged, in the company of a cardinal. De Henrique squinted disbelievingly. It was Cardinal João Batista Tenorio, of Oporto. When had he arrived in Lisbon? And what was he doing on the royal dais, instead of heading for the clergymen's podium where he belonged?

"What is the cardinal of Oporto doing there?" he muttered to *Padre* João Manuel. For the moment, he forgot the dissension that reigned between them.

"He's come, apparently, to join in your celebration." João Manuel spoke ironically, without deigning to bestow so much as a glance on de Henrique.

"*Our* celebration," de Henrique flashed. "Or perhaps you belong together with those Marranos down there."

João Manuel did look at him then, with eyes that darted pure hatred. "Am I to be your next sacrificial victim, dear protector of our faith?"

De Henrique did not answer. In his heart he believed that his chance would come — to oust this fool, the present head of the Inquisition, once and for all.

74

lfonso threaded his way among the spectators to reach his father, the king, with all possible speed.

"*Desculp* (excuse me)," he apologized to the naval minister after inadvertently treading on his toe. With no little annoyance, the honored guests followed Alfonso's reckless progress among them, as he headed toward the central portion of the dais where the royal couple sat. To their astonishment, they watched the esteemed Cardinal of Oporto following breathlessly in the prince's wake.

The naval minister, whose toes still smarted from Alfonso's treatment, turned to the man at his right. "I believe something's happened."

His neighbor replied with a shrug. "Not necessarily. Anything at all is possible with that wild prince."

"Yes, but the man following him is the Cardinal of Oporto."

"You're right. H'm. That's interesting..."

"What do you think it could be?"

"I haven't a clue. If we wait patiently, though, we may find out."

A moment later, the naval minister tugged excitedly at his neighbor's sleeve. "Look at that! The exalted Paulo de Henrique has left his place and is running down toward the stake. Do you see?"

"Yes, I see. Something *is* happening." The man rubbed his cheek thoughtfully. "H'm. This business is beginning to be very interesting..."

⁂

Alfonso approached his father and bowed formally. King Don João IV had superb control over his own emotions. He glanced at his son out of the corners of his eyes. His first inclination was to ignore the prince's obvious desire to speak with him. Then he noticed that Alfonso was not alone. Like others before him, the king wondered, "What is the cardinal of Oporto doing here?"

"Sire," Alfonso began without waiting for permission to speak, "Something terrible has happened."

The king made no answer except to chew his lip. His son's outburst, before the interested gaze of all his guests, mortified and enraged him. But Alfonso paid no heed to his father's reaction. He hurried on eagerly, "Your Majesty, I need you to listen — lest your reign be stained with the blood of the innocent!"

The prince had deliberately spoken in a raised voice; he wanted the others to hear. Those seated nearby listened avidly. They also noted the king's mounting fury.

Alfonso raised his voice still more. "Father, a terrible travesty of justice has been perpetrated. The responsibility rests with us. Our family, the royal family, will not be able to lift its crowned heads before the populace if the outcome of this misfortune rests on our shoulders."

With a rapid movement of his hand, he thrust the letter at his father.

⁂

Paulo de Henrique ran.

He scrambled down from the elevated podium where the upper echelons of the clergy were placed, rudely jostling anyone who stood in his way. Armando Batancur, his "bodyguard," ran after him. At his heels galloped Raphael Gimareines, who feared for his friend's behavior, followed by Jacobo.

De Henrique carved a path to the center of the square. The monks, busy tying Yitzchak de Castro to the stake that jutted up from the pyre of branches, stopped to gape. First the unusual activity on the royal dais, and now this strange behavior on the part of the Holy Office secretary, told them that something was definitely afoot.

After a moment, however, they returned to the task at hand. One monk held a large cross directly to Yitzchak's face.

"You are yet among the living, young heretic," he intoned. "You can still save your soul from eternal perdition."

Yitzchak's eyes were screwed shut. He was trying with all his might to preserve these last moments of his life for himself and his G-d, the G-d of Avraham, Yitzchak, and Yaakov. The monk's babbling was confusing him. The tight binding around his arms and legs hurt. Already he could feel the blood stopping to circulate in his legs.

Still the monk persisted. He lifted the cross higher, stepping so close to Yitzchak that the cross almost touched his face. "Acknowledge our savior. Acknowledge him, young man!"

Yitzchak was overcome with repugnance. Trussed for the fire, his head was the only part of his body that could move. This he butted at the cross with such force — and so unexpectedly — that he nearly succeeded in knocking it from the monk's grasp. The monk had to struggle to maintain his hold on the heavy cross. Watching him — though his head ached from the force of the blow — Yitzchak smiled slightly. It was the smile of a victim who has managed to distress the enemy, even in only a tiny measure.

The monks stood around the pyre, ready to light it. But they were halted in confusion by the stentorian tones of Paulo de Henrique, who came running up to them.

"Stop at once!" he shouted. "Release this man immediately and quickly — quickly, I say! — tie up Don Carlos. Hurry, hurry!"

"B-but *Padre*," one of the monks stammered, "Don Carlos was chosen to be burned last — to let the people go home with a 'good taste' in their mouths..." They were loath to undo all their work in preparing Yitzchak de Castro for the flames.

"*Do as you are ordered!*" de Henrique thundered frantically.

The monks exchanged quick glances. They knew the secretary of the Holy Office well enough to realize that when he was enraged about something, it was best to jump to obey his orders without the slightest delay or opposition. Slowly they began moving aside the outer branches of the bonfire that surrounded Yitzchak's legs, and began untying the knots that bound him.

"Faster!" de Henrique screamed. "Look over there, at the king!"

The monks lifted their heads to the tall dais, where the king was reading some sort of document. Near him stood his son, the prince, and some clergyman whom they found it impossible to identify from the distance. They did see, however, that those seated around the king were conferring together in excited whispers.

De Henrique did not know the exact nature of what was happening up on the royal dais, but a profound fear told him that it had to do with him. Some unexpected occurrence had arisen, connected somehow to himself. It was enough to see hated Prince Alfonso up there to realize that his efforts were being undermined.

An even more powerful apprehension swept over him, leaving him cold and limp. Had some fresh plot been prepared to save Don Carlos? He was well aware that Alfonso had been assiduously working toward that end. Had a new loophole in the law been uncovered? And what was the Cardinal of Oporto doing up there?

Bereft of answers, he was determined first of all to hasten Don Carlos' execution with all possible speed. To burn him at once, without all the usual pomp and ceremony. To dispense this one time with the traditional priestly exhortation to the condemned man before his death. If only he could see Don Carlos burned, all of Alfonso's machinations would be for naught. Once Don Carlos' body had gone up in flames, the prince would be faced with a reality he no longer had any power to change.

De Henrique's order — and, more to the point, his manner in issuing it — galvanized the monks into action. While several busied themselves with removing Yitzchak de Castro from the stake, others hurried off to fetch Don Carlos.

Don Carlos was awake and alert to every nuance around him. He saw the unusual activity on the royal dais, and took note also of de Henrique's frenzy. What did it all mean? Could it possibly have anything to do with him? Dare he grasp at a straw of hope, here, at the very edge of death?

He had no way of knowing. But the sight of his friend the Cardinal of Oporto, leader of the Marranos in northern Portugal, aroused — almost against his will — a glimmer of hope in his breast. He adjured himself not to waste these last precious moments in vain dreams. He must set an example for the entire secret Jewish community of Lisbon. The other Marranos must remember him with pride. He must show himself faithful to his G-d and his Torah to the bitter end.

Don Carlos was raised to the stake. Monks bound his legs securely, then his arms. The one with the heavy cross tried to bring it close to the condemned man, but de Henrique, to the monk's stupefaction, brushed him impatiently aside. He was consumed with a burning impatience. Every second counted now. Don Carlos must be burned before the king had the chance to issue any sort of order to the contrary.

He cast a hasty glance at the royal dais. He saw the king pass the document he'd been reading to the Superior Judge, Fernando de Lima. Fernando read it. Suddenly, the treasury minister, Don Luis de Sauza, rose from his place and went to sit beside de Lima. He, too, perused the mysterious paper. De Henrique's heart began to slam painfully inside him as he saw the minister remove another document from his briefcase and compare it with the one in his hand.

A faintness crept over de Henrique. "That's the note!" he thought wildly. "What's happening?" Something completely unexpected, that much was certain. And he was convinced now beyond a doubt that it was connected to Don Carlos.

Involuntarily, his eyes went to the clergymen's stand. *Padre* João Manuel stood motionless as a statue. "What's the matter with him?" de Henrique wondered in a frenzy. "Doesn't he see what's going on?" If he did not, he seemed to be the only one. A hush had fallen over the entire throng as they observed the strange proceedings. "Is he a part of the plot as well?"

Never before had de Henrique experienced this degree of insecurity. He felt baffled and bewildered as he faced Don Carlos on the stake.

Armando stood directly behind the secretary. Every fiber of his being quivered with tension and an overmastering desire for revenge. His eyes went from Don Carlos to the pile of wood arranged below him, ready to burst into flames. Had Don Carlos even noticed his presence?

More than anything in the world, Armando longed to thrust two daggers into de Henrique's black heart: his own, and the one that de Henrique himself had given him to carry in his role as "chief bodyguard." But this did not seem to be the right moment. For one thing, there were people milling about the center of the square who might conceivably prevent him from carrying out his aim. And for another, he found it impossible to perform the act under the eyes of the watching multitude. It was too late to save Don Carlos, and he must not bring disaster down on the heads of his own people in Lisbon.

"What to do?" he prayed silently. "Oh G-d, have mercy on Your people, so faithful and so downtrodden!"

The monks had done their work well. Tightening a final knot, they stepped away from Don Carlos. "*Padre*, we are finished."

Another monk, superior to the others, asked, "Shall we read the sentence to the condemned man now, and the list of his sins?"

"No," de Henrique answered shortly. "There's no time."

The monks were petrified. They had never known such a disruption of the orderly ritual. The church and the Inquisition had instituted that ritual — and here was the secretary of the Holy Office, himself, telling them to disregard it!

"What do we do now?" the monk asked humbly.

De Henrique didn't hear. His attention was riveted on the king, from whom he found it impossible to tear his eyes away. He saw Judge de Lima hand the King the note from Don Carlos' file, the note he'd just received from de Sauza. The king compared the two, as de Lima stood beside him, talking earnestly. De Henrique sensed the danger growing nearer.

Suddenly, the king rose to his feet. At once the rest of the eminent group on the royal dais did the same. The silence of the crowd deepened. No one moved or even breathed, the better to hear what their sovereign had to say. Those seated at the greatest distance from the dais hoped fervently that others, more fortunately situated, would relay the news to them without delay.

The king passed the two documents to his son, Prince Alfonso. The prince stepped to the front of the dais, regarded the multitude silently for a moment, then began to speak in a loud voice that was nearly a shout.

"In the name of the King of Portugal, His Majesty Don João IV, and after consulting with the leaders of the kingdom and with the Superior Judge, charged with upholding justice in our state, the king has decided to suspend judgment on Admiral Don Carlos Carneiro pending further investigation."

A murmur, like the rising of a wave, rippled through the square. The prince continued:

"The illustrious Cardinal of Oporto, *Padre* João Batista Tenorio, a man dedicated to the church and the true faith as well as to the royal house, has brought a letter written by the hand of Pedro Alvares, the sole witness in the case against Don Carlos. Alvarez, as you know, disappeared before the start of trial. This new letter, of whose authenticity there can be no doubt, completely changes the picture regarding Don Carlos' guilt."

A small fracas began in the center of the square. De Henrique had run up to the monk who was holding the burning torch, wrested it from him, and was attempting to light the bonfire himself!

Armando Batancur sprinted up to him and seized his wrist in a powerful grip. "*Padre*, not now!" he said urgently. "This is a direct ravellion against the king! Don't worry, *Padre*, you will see retribution fall on your enemies yet. You are the keeper of the faith. But *not now!*"

De Henrique tried to shake him off, and the two began to struggle. With one thick fist, the secretary planted a mighty punch on Armando's face. Dizzy and disoriented, Armando felt as though he were about to drop. But stubbornly he fought off the weakness, never relinquishing his iron grip on de Henrique's wrist.

Other monks ran up — some to offer assistance to Armando, others to help de Henrique. The center of the square began to fill with churning, shouting figures. A contingent of the king's guard began riding along the perimeter of the square, though they did not yet enter it. The sight of those grim riders had a certain calming effect on the grappling figures. Armando was still clamped with amazing force to de Henrique's wrist, leaving the burning brand to dangle impotently from the secretary's hand.

On the dais, Prince Alfonso began to shout.

"This is what is written in the letter the Cardinal has brought:

> *I beg your forgiveness for having vanished from Lisbon before the time to testify against Admiral Don Carlos Carneiro. That is the reason, in fact, for my disappearance: I did not wish to testify falsely in court.*
>
> *I am the man responsible for his arrest. I am the one who left a note for the secretary of the Holy Office, Paulo de Henrique, to find in his door. I disappeared because I was afraid that the secretary would take his revenge if I did not testify as he wished. As a pious Christian, my conscience began to prick me. It is with deep shame that I admit that, in a moment of weakness, I allowed Paulo de Henrique to persuade me to falsify a note accusing Don Carlos Carneiro of being a secret Jew.*
>
> *From this, my place of concealment, I heravy assert that I never saw Don Carlos enter the home of the heretic rabbi of Amsterdam. In all the time I spent as the admiral's trusted aide, I never saw anything to hint that Don Carlos might be, Heaven forbid, a secret Jew. It is my devout hope that the lord will forgive me for succumbing to the Holy Office secretary in a moment of weakness. His enduring hatred for Don Carlos drove him to find a way to bring him down, and he used me to provide false testimony for that purpose.*

Alfonso paused. From the square rose an agonized bellow: "Lies! The enemies of our faith are spreading lies and plots against the Inquisition's just judgment!"

Armando, his two friends who had joined him, and several other monks surrounded the screaming de Henrique, as though afraid he might explode before their eyes. The prince continued to shout:

"Superior Judge Fernando de Lima, and other eminent men seated here, have compared the handwriting on the two documents. It has been ascertained that the same hand wrote both. It is the hand of Pedro Alvares, longtime aide to Admiral Don Carlos Carneiro. He has denied the accusation that he was forced into making. And he has laid the blame for this appalling travesty on the shoulders of *Padre* Paulo de Henrique."

"That," Alfonso cried above the rising murmur of the crowd, "is the text of the letter. It was carried here in person by the esteemed Cardinal of Oporto. In the name of truth and justice, the cardinal saw the need to bring the letter here to Lisbon and to hand it personally to the king. And thanks to the compassionate mercy of Heaven, he has arrived just in time to prevent the royal house of Portugal from perpetrating an act of horror which could never be erased!"

The crowd erupted. Monks ran anxiously to the line of prisoners to keep them quiet. Above the din came a final roar from Prince Alfonso: "In the name of His Majesty, King of Portugal, remove Don Carlos Carneiro from the stake and return him to prison until his case can be judged anew."

The crowd surged and muttered, disappointed at being denied their long-promised spectacle. Their voices rose and swelled like the roll of mighty thunderclouds. De Henrique, a gleam of madness in his eyes, screamed, "Light the fire! The heretic Alfonso has turned the king against us! Alfonso is an agent of the Marranos! The true faith will vanquish all! *Light the fire!*"

The monks stood uncertain and confused around the stake. As for Don Carlos, he felt more at peace than at any time since his arrest months before. His nephew, Pedro Alvares, had written that letter in an attempt to save his life. It was a sign — a hopeful sign. Maybe Pedro would finally draw closer to his own roots, to his Jewish heritage. The thought brought Don Carlos infinite joy.

Meanwhile, the mob had grown distinctly unruly, spilling over into the square itself. Armed guardsmen began fanning out to every corner in an effort to maintain control. Several of them neared the stake.

De Henrique's shriek pierced the tumult. *"Light the fire!"*

A fanatic young monk grabbed the burning torch from de Henrique's hand and thrust it at the pyre of wood. The fire rapidly caught on the dry timber. Don Carlos began to feel the heat on his legs.

Then other monks, fearful of the king, ran to douse the flames. The surrounding mob grew noisier, more disorderly. Fistfights erupted between supporters of the king and of de Henrique. Someone unbound Don Carlos from the stake. At that moment, de Henrique — who had in a burst of superhuman strength managed to pull free of Armando's steely grip — dashed at him.

A pair of monks hurried Don Carlos away, and de Henrique ran headlong after them with Armando hard on his heels. Two of the king's guardsmen began galloping toward the scene of the fracas. De Henrique reached his enemy and forcibly pulled Don Carlos around to face him.

Weakened from torture and his ordeal on the stake, Don Carlos nevertheless gazed at de Henrique with cold, calm eyes. De Henrique was purple with rage. His hand groped at the folds of his cassock, searching for the dagger he knew he'd brought with him. Where was it? Where had it disappeared to?

Then he remembered. Turning, he searched for Armando, who came running up at that moment.

"The dagger, please," de Henrique panted. "Quick, return my dagger!"

Armando divined de Henrique's intention. He scanned the faces of the monks holding Don Carlos, and saw nothing in them to reassure him that they would protect the prisoner. He ran up closer to de Henrique, pulling out the dagger as he came.

"Here is your dagger!"

With a single rapid thrust, he sent the blade straight into de Henrique's heart.

De Henrique's eyes opened wide, staring at Armando in astonishment. Then his eyelids flickered and closed. He stood on his feet for another instant, then slowly sank in a heap on the ground.

The crowd that had gathered around them did not at first absorb what had happened. Armando himself stood stock still in shock. Raphael

Gimareines and Jacobo, who had followed him throughout, reacted first. They grasped Armando by both arms and hustled him away as quickly as they could. It was not difficult to lose themselves in the tumultuous throng. They had hardly gone when two guardsmen rode up to the scene. One of them leaped off his horse and bent over de Henrique. He looked up and solemnly intoned, "The *padre* Paulo de Henrique has returned his soul to its Maker!"

Shrieks erupted from the onlookers' lips. Hats were removed and hundreds crossed themselves. Some people dropped to their knees and prayed. The guardsman bent closer over the body and pulled out the bloodstained dagger. As if in confirmation of his earlier pronouncement, he looked up and declaimed loudly, "The *padre* is dead!"

From the crowd came further screams. "It's not possible!"

The guardsman held the dagger aloft for all to see. Clearly etched in gold on the hilt were the letters PdH — De Henrique's initials.

"It is his own dagger. He has done this to himself."

The storm strengthened. A few thought of venting their emotion on Don Carlos, but were prevented by a quick-thinking guardsman who scooped Don Carlos up onto his horse and galloped through the crowd toward the royal dais.

It was difficult for Don Carlos to stand on his feet. Two royal guardsmen supported him as he stood before the dais. Prince Alfonso descended, grasped his friend's shoulders and embraced him. When Don Carlos looked past the prince to the king, he was met with a cool, neutral gaze. He saw Fernando de Lima whispering to the king. Presently the Superior Judge stepped forward and announced:

"In the name of our sovereign, His Majesty Don João IV, the decision has been made to exile Don Carlos from Portugal." He held up a hand to forestall a reaction, then continued smoothly, "It is impossible to ascertain beyond any doubt whether or not Don Carlos has been a loyal Christian. From his confession during the Holy Office's interrogation, it appears that not all the suspicions against him are completely groundless. However, since the case against him rests solely on false testimony, extracted in such a way as to cast a shadow on the royal house, the king had granted clemency to Don Carlos. In place of death, he is sentenced to exile."

The faces of the surrounding crowd reflected their disappointment. Don Carlos bowed to the king. "I am forever indebted to His Majesty. It pains me to know that I will no longer be able to serve the land I love.

"However, be that as it may, I have a single request: May my wife and children be included in the decree of clemency?"

There was a brief pause. Then the king nodded once, in the affirmative.

⤙⤚

The flag of Holland waved from the *Vandervalda's* mast. The gangway that had brought the passengers aboard had already been removed. Among the passengers that lined the deck, one drew the eye more than any other. It was Don Carlos. Beside him at the railing stood his wife Beatriz, weeping tears of joy. Their three children, newly released from a monastery outside Lisbon, raced and played on the deck. Not far from them, gazing out to sea, was Roberto Gonzales.

Roberto never made his identity known to Don Carlos. All through the journey home he did not tell Don Carlos that his nephew, Pedro Alvares, was studying Torah in Amsterdam. He also did not reveal the fact that he had been the one who had brought Pedro's letter to Lisbon — the letter that had saved the admiral's life. As the ship prepared to sail, Roberto's lips framed a heartfelt prayer to the Creator of the world, Who had given him the inestimable privilege of rescuing Don Carlos from the flames.

Very few people came to see them off. Don Carlos waved to Prince Alfonso who, apart from the Marranos, was the only friend he had left in Portugal.

The ship weighed anchor. The shore slipped away as the ship plowed into the vast ocean toward Amsterdam, city of freedom. Don Carlos breathed deeply of the sea air — the air of liberty. He looked into the faces of his wife and his children, and in their eyes he glimpsed the bright light of hope.

AFTERWORD

Don Carlos and his family arrived safely in Amsterdam, where they were accorded a royal welcome. His meeting with his nephew, Pedro Alvares, was highly emotional. After some time spent recuperating from the effects of his months in prison, Don Carlos devoted many years solely to the study of Torah.

The news arrived from Brazil that Raphael Chaim had landed safely, along with Luis and his friends. Raphael Chaim dedicated himself to teaching the Marranos of Brazil the Jewish laws and customs.

Yitzchak de Castro was sent back to the dungeon until, a number of months later, he was taken to be executed in the flames of the *auto-da-fé*. When word reached Amsterdam, the community was plunged into a period of deep mourning. Sephardic *kinos* (elegies) were composed in memory of Yitzchak's passing, a tragedy which was felt throughout the Jewish world. Rabbi Menashe ben Israel recorded the entire episode in his book, *Mikveh Yisrael*.